The Celestial Jukebox

PUBLICATION OF THIS BOOK WAS MADE
POSSIBLE IN PART BY GENEROUS GIFTS FROM

Wiley and Clare Ellis

and anonymous donors

The Celestial Jukebox

a novel

Cynthia Shearer

The University of Georgia Press
Athens & London

Paperback edition published in 2006 by
The University of Georgia Press
Athens, Georgia 30602
by arrangement with Shoemaker and Hoard
© 2005 by Cynthia Shearer

Book design by Mark McGarry / Texas Type & Book Works
Set in Trump Mediaeval

Printed and bound by McNaughton & Gunn
The paper in this book meets the guidelines for permanence and
durability of the Committee on Production Guidelines for
Book Longevity of the Council on Library Resources.

Printed in the United States of America
06 07 08 09 10 P 5 4 3 2 1

Library of Congress Cataloging-in-Publication Data

Shearer, Cynthia.
The celestial jukebox : a novel / Cynthia Shearer.—Pbk. ed.
        p.   cm.
ISBN-13: 978-0-8203-2838-6 (pbk. : alk. paper)
ISBN-10: 0-8203-2838-3 (pbk. : alk. paper)
1. Africans—Mississippi—Fiction. 2. Delta (Miss. : Region)—Fiction.
3. Race relations—Fiction. 4. Popular music—Fiction.
5. Teenage boys—Fiction. 6. Mississippi—Fiction.
7. Immigrants—Fiction. 8. Jukeboxes—Fiction.
9. Guitar—Fiction. 10. Musical fiction. I. Title.
PS3569.H39145C45 2006
813'.54—dc22   2005031566

British Library Cataloging-in-Publication Data available

Portions of this novel appeared in slightly altered form in the *Oxford American* and
the *American Literary Review*. The author wishes to express her gratitude to the
National Endowment for the Arts for its generous support.

The author and publisher gratefully acknowledge permission to reproduce excerpts
of the following copyrighted material: "I Hate Song" by Woody Guthrie, © 1965
(renewed) by Woody Guthrie Publications, Inc. All rights reserved. Used by permission. "Big Science" by Laurie Anderson, © 1982 by Difficult Music, reprinted with
the permission of the author. "Fujiyama Mama" by Wanda Jackson, © by Hammerhead Music/Microhits. "Mama, You Been on My Mind," © 1964, 1967 by Bob
Dylan, reprinted by Warner Chappell. "Are You Ready for the Great Atomic
Power" and "Satan Is Real" by the Louvin Brothers © by Ira and Charley Louvin.
"Decoration Day" by John Lee Hooker, © by John Lee Hooker. "Franklin D. Roosevelt, a Poor Man's Friend," by Willie Eason, © by Willie Eason, reprinted by Tradition Music Co./Mango Tone Music, BMI. Every effort has been made to secure
permissions. We regret any inadvertent omission.

I hate a song that makes you think that you're not any good.
I hate a song that makes you think you are just born to lose,
bound to lose, no good to nobody, no good for nothing,
because you are either too old or too young or too fat or
too thin or too ugly or too this or too that. Songs that
run you down or songs that poke fun at you on account
of your bad luck or your hard traveling.
I am out to fight those songs
to my very last breath of air and my last drop of blood.

           —WOODY GUTHRIE

Today, like any other day, we wake up empty and frightened.
Don't open the door to the study and begin reading.
Take down a musical instrument...
There are hundreds of ways to kneel and kiss the ground.

           —RUMI

Motifs of music and religion

Contents

The Celestial Jukebox

Introit

Once upon a time in that part of Mississippi where every town's name reads like a memory of some better place, a girl with a honey-colored braid down her back stood by the side of the road and stared at a hand-painted sign. PROPHECY GARDEN OF KING LOUIS NARCISSE, it said. She had come from Madagascar, through Dublin and Dundee, then Como, then Little Texas, to Hollywood, Mississippi. She knew she was in the right place when she read the sign, red and gold paint laid on in generous strokes to cover an advertisement for an extinct oil company.

—*Would you be needing some help?* said a voice behind her. She turned and looked into a face she knew. It was a black girl not much older than she but dressed as a woman. It made the girl a bit faint, remembering.

—*Litany, it's me*, said the girl with the braid. —*Do you remember me?*

—*Gootness*, Litany said softly, in the vaguely custodial voice she had always used with the girl and other white children. —*What you doing way over here?*

—*I'm going to New York.*

—*Baby. Have you eat today?*

—*No*, the girl answered.

—*Well, before you go to New York, you got to come in here*

with me and eat you a little something. King Louis say the greatest sin is to let somebody else go hungry.

Litany took off her church gloves, snapped them shut inside her patent leather purse, and took the girl with her. Home was down a lane of red roses, where the fence was a holy host of spangled signposts. White tomato stakes, threaded with wire and twine, sharp points aimed at the sky to snare any spirits of evil intent. At the front gate, a swaybacked bottle-tree, shuddering under the weight of the bottles. The girl touched one, and several clinked in answer. The sound made her homesick for Litany's mother.

Later in the little clean kitchen, Litany bustled around with the expertise of a much older woman, turning up the fire under pots that she had put on the stove early that morning. The girl stared at the roses etched into the heavy silver of the fork. It had been her grandmother's fork, one of sixteen that had lain in a felt-lined box. She took a few bites, chewing slowly, tasting also the salt of her tears. Had there been a time when someone loved her, or just a time when she had believed it? She glanced up to see Litany looking at her with pity. When they had been children, Litany had sometimes looked at her with awe. She was white. She had been to Paris.

—*Baby, I know trouble when I see it.*

The room was dim and bare, except for an iron bedstead, a man's clothes hanging on a nail, and a magazine picture of the emperor of Ethiopia Haile Selassie taped to the wall. Litany closed the blinds to make the room even darker, and brought her a neatly folded rag with yellow primroses and dogtooth violets stamped on it, the kind of cloth that could be found in small boxes of laundry soap flakes.

The chenille bedspread was covered with a peacock fanning

its tail, and she traced with her finger an imaginary road between its tufts of red, blue, purple, and green. She had done this some years before when she chanced to nap on the bed in the house Litany had grown up in. The girl lay back on the bed and held the cold wet cloth to her head, and her mind cleared. She waited for sleep with the hope of a penitent. When she remembered how to feel safe, she slept.

On her better days, the girl moved through the small house like a sleepwalker, touching objects without really seeing them. In the front room on a sewing machine table was a collection of records in a wire rack, *The Rev. Louis Narcisse and the Celestial Tones, The Rev. Louis Narcisse and the Mt. Zion Spiritual Choir, King Louis Narcisse and His Wings of Faith Choir.* On the wall hung a magazine clipping of King Louis himself in his white eyelet robes and gold mitre, his hands folded in prayer. Sometimes when Litany was at work cleaning houses of rich white ladies in Memphis, the white girl would play the records, listening to hear where Litany had been when she ran away to Oakland, California, to sing in King Louis's choir.

The girl listened to the gospel records and tried to imagine Litany being one in a retinue of white robes, marching and singing with the bishops, princes, and missionaries dressed in black tuxedoes. She could see it, the retinues of the chosen, the King's fingers fat with jewels, touching the votive candles on the altar. King Louis was sanctified. Litany was sanctified.

The girl, in her worst moments, was seasick as a green sailor.

One morning she walked into the kitchen wearing a borrowed Woolworth nightgown, looking for the pot of strong tea that Litany brewed in the mornings. Instead, she smelled coffee, and she closed her eyes at the assault of it. When she opened them, it was to see Prophet Royal Pegues's eyes looking back at her, remembering when they'd been children together. Then his pecan-colored eyes went cold and accusative: she was *white*.

This was once upon that time in Mississippi when a black man could find himself hanging from a tree if a white woman with a quickening belly chanced to be under his roof. There were those who would kill him first and ask whose baby it was later.

Prophet left the house only hours after he'd got there. When the girl heard that he was sleeping at the cotton gin, she got together her meager belongings and walked out to the road. She waited, but no car stopped for her. After three hours, Litany came out, already wiping her hands in some invisible fold of her skirts. —*Cold rain set in, he be back. Come on back in the house and eat you a little something. I'm too tired to fight you about this, baby doll.*

The cold rains set in, and he came back.

He would strip out of his work clothes on the back porch, and it was understood that the white girl was to stay inside until this was done. When he had left his blue overalls folded on a chair and changed into khaki pants much like the white man he worked for also wore, he would put on his red velvet cap and his gold spectacles and be transformed, or so the girl thought. He was still a young man, but the glasses made him seem older. When dinner was ready, Litany would say her Christian grace and Prophet would say his Muslim one. Afterwards, Prophet would retire to the one soft chair in the house and, by the light of a kerosene lantern, read from his red leather-bound Koran or the *Chicago Defender*. The girl would bring in the firewood in gratitude for the food and clean the kitchen in penance for being white. If the light was good, she would piece the star quilt for her coming baby.

One night she caught Prophet watching her as she smoothed the quilt top across her ripened belly, as if to see if it would fit the baby. He looked down into his holy book, frowning. She caught him watching her from the window one dusk, when she was picking all the green tomatoes off the vines. He had not spoken a word to her in the months she'd stayed with them, but somehow his wish had been conveyed to her that the tomatoes be picked and pickled lest they go to waste in the freeze that would occur that night, as per the *Farmer's Almanac*.

The news traveled from farm to farm, then beyond: *white girl, black man*.

Carloads of drunk white fraternity boys from Ole Miss would drive by on Saturday nights to get a look, and throw their beer bottles over the fence made of twigs whittled to points, and into the Prophecy Garden of King Louis Narcisse. At least twice an old white preacher pulled up in front of the little house and parked his evangelical vehicle, a black hearse outfitted with four black speakers pointing in the four directions like blighted amaryllis bulbs.

After watching the white girl work in the black man's garden for a while, the preacher would switch on his microphone, clamp his bony fingers around it, and harangue her from the roadside. —*For the wages of sin is death,* AMEN, *and the mark of the Beast will be upon your race-mix child,* AMEN.

The first time the white girl felt the baby kick inside her was on such a morning, hoeing weeds in a patch of winter greens, carefully the way Litany had showed her. Then there was the glint of sunlight on the black hearse, the white man's face contorted with rage. She'd seen the same man hawking his Cuban Queen watermelons from the back of the black hearse in Clarksdale. On that morning Prophet walked past the preacher when he came home from work, passing the white girl without looking up. Later that night the girl heard his heated murmurs to Litany on the other side of the wall.

Prophet touched her before he ever spoke to her.

She was weeding in the garden, and he was walking home from work, and he heard the car full of Ole Miss boys coming before she did. He stepped around into the sunlight to put himself between her and the flying beer bottles, so that they hit his back and not her belly. He put his hand out to steady her, to keep from knocking her down with his sudden movements, and held her shoulders briefly.

The boys called out obscenities, but neither the white girl nor Prophet heard them. Maybe it was the light in the Prophecy Garden of King Louis Narcisse, or the benevolent watchfulness of Litany at the kitchen window, or the eye of God itself. The fear passed when the Ole Miss boys passed. Prophet looked at the white girl, and his eyes held both kindness and sorrow. He vanished into the stalks of corn with a rustle, like Solomon into someplace vaster than voices.

She brought him water once when he was in the field. She took down the old white gourd calabash that had been Litany's mother's from its peg on the kitchen wall. I AM POURED OUT LIKE WATER, it said in green letters around its red painted rim. She knew from the look on his face that she'd done something wrong. It had to do with the gourd. White people were not supposed to touch it. He looked back up at her, and she took a deep breath, stared him down, held it out. So he drank, his eyes meeting hers over it. Then she raised the gourd to her own

mouth and finished the water he'd left, and wiped her mouth
with the back of her hand. She was testing him, and he knew it.
His face softened with concern, and he said to her, —*They get
you for that, you know. Drinking after colored.*

She began to love him then.

—*I would be black if I could,* she said.

He began to love her then.

She came to know every rustle of his leaving in the mornings
and in the evenings the sound of his boots on the loose stack of
cinderblocks that served for back steps. He set the world aright
just by stepping into the yard. She could stand anywhere in the
garden and feel the full strength of his silences. It was something to do with the little red Koran. The white boy's baby
inside her could kick her sideways, but the black man's steady
silence seemed to sanctify her.

She heard him singing in the garden one morning:

> *Who's that a-writing? John the Revelator*
> *Who's that a-writing? John the Revelator*
> *Who's that a-writing? John the Revelator*
> *A book of the seven seals.*

She moved on with her rake, piling leaves around the base of
the gardenia bush in the garden of King Louis Narcisse. Her
middle was still small enough that she could slip into the seat
of the GROTTO OF ALL FACE, an old johnboat upended and shin-
gled entirely with bottle caps. She sat, the October sun warm
on her face, and waited with a patience that could pass for
prayer. The baby relaxed inside her, hearing the music, and the
undertow of sleep took them both, mother and child.

A few days later, at noon, the white girl was scattering some feed for the chickens in the front yard when a long black Chrysler pulled up and backed into place as if a quick getaway might be necessary. The white woman who got out of the car was middle-aged and fat, dressed in fabrics that subsequent generations would use only to upholster sofas. She had a clipboard in her hand. She called the girl's name, said she was looking for her.

The visit lasted twenty minutes. The woman talked of how it would be necessary to see doctors and get the proper care for the baby. Her words filled the shack like a soothing chant, *what's best for the baby, what's best for the baby*. She presented the girl with some health tonic and papers to sign. While the woman chattered about how pleasant the hospital in Memphis would be, the girl shoved up the sleeves of Prophet's old military surplus sweater she was wearing, and she signed. The girl was too tired to think about what it all could mean. The baby kicked, and she thought of the room waiting for them at a Memphis hospital, with perhaps a window overlooking the river, which she would point out to the baby when she held it up high to look out at the wide, wide world.

After that, they would go to art school, she and the baby.

The first Saturday in November was a cold one. Litany and Prophet spent the day in the garden, harvesting whatever could be pickled quickly. The girl could no longer bend over to pick greens, but she could still reach the faucets at the sink to wash the sand from them. Litany had procured a small piece of salt meat to go in them, and the smell itself was nourishing to the girl, who sat at the kitchen table stirring the cornbread batter. It was going to be a good meal. The jars of tomato pickles were arranged neatly on the windowsill. It was a new kind of pleasure, to see the different shapes and colors of the jars, and to know that they had cost nothing beyond the original price of the mayonnaise or jelly they had held.

The house was full of that kind of quiet economy. Suppertime came, so Litany turned the kerosene light out, and they ate in the dark. The girl closed her eyes and tasted the iron in the greens her own hands had helped to grow and pick, and she thought, *So this is what living is. It is an agreement not to let yourself die.*

The girl sat down in a kitchen chair, suddenly exhausted and sleepy. Her back hurt. The baby seemed angry about its confinement.

The house began to feel like an oven to the girl, so she went outside, into the Prophecy Garden of King Louis Narcisse. The wind had begun to blow a little, and she followed a sawdust path through whirring windmills made of an old refrigerator she'd seen Prophet take apart once. She wound through twisting shadows cast by stark silhouettes of stovepipe animals until she found what she was looking for, an old church pew that had been painted red and encrusted with paste jewels from dimestore necklaces. THRONE OF THE CHOSEN, the jewels spelled. She sat down slowly, so as not to rile the baby, then lay down on her side. Drifting into sleep, she thought that after she had the baby she could perhaps dance.

She was dreaming, someone was beating her with boards, Ole Miss boys were throwing them at her from a passing car. To keep the boards from hitting the baby, she woke. No one was beating her, the baby was fighting its way out of her, tearing her open. The pain in the low part of her belly caused her back to stiffen, and she cried out in a low moan. She tried to sit up, but she was too tired. She remembered that she had no clothes for the baby, just the star quilt that was not quite finished. When she could, she walked back into the house to lie down in her bed.

—*Litany*, the girl whispered, calmly, and then the pain overtook her. —*Help me!*

—*It's just your time, that's all*, said Litany.

The girl lay crumpled in the backseat of the car, which belonged to a black preacher at Litany's church. She could hear the sound of sumac and chinaberry limbs slapping at the windows of the car as it rumbled over the twin ruts that doubled as a cattle path to a certain granny woman's house. The granny woman gave her warm tea that stank of weeds, and she did not hear Litany and the preacher when they left her there. The granny woman was tending her herbs outside when she heard the girl cry out the familiar name of a dead midwife, Litany's mother.

—*Ariadne! Ariadne!*

The granny woman lit one candle and taught the girl to stare into the center of the flame. The knife the granny woman slid under the bedsprings did not cut the pain. The incantations she muttered did not clear the confusions. The wet towel she tied to the end of the bedstead for the girl to hold like the reins of a horse—it did not provide direction. The baby was born a boy, and the first time the girl saw him was the only time she saw him. He was wrapped in a soft old damask tablecloth that had been her own *grandmère*'s.

While the girl was asleep, the white woman in the long black Chrysler came, and the granny woman knew better than to argue with her. It was the time in Mississippi when a white woman could call the law on a black granny who delivered a baby without a white doctor in surgical gloves present to collect his money for it. So the granny handed the gold damask bundle to the white lady, who extracted the baby and gave the tablecloth back. The baby was soon on its way to the Palmer Home in Memphis, where it was sold for three thousand dol-

lars, cash on the barrelhead, to a barren white couple who lived
on Lake Shore Drive in Chicago.

When the white girl came out of her sleep, the granny gave
her tea that stank of different weeds, and the girl asked for her
baby. The granny offered her sweet potato pie, and the girl
asked again for her baby. The granny looked out the window
and said nothing. The girl began to sob. When she could walk
again, she asked to leave. The granny advised against it, but the
girl was gone by morning.

When Litany and the good women of her church finally found
the girl four days later, she was sitting on the wide windowsill of
the big fanlight that overlooked the river, high in the old Abide
house. She was wrapped in the gold damask tablecloth that had
been her *grandmère*'s, her hair tangled with dried sweat and
tears. Her blue eyes seemed too bright, as if her very mind were
burning itself up behind them. She had a very high fever and
could not seem to hear them or answer their questions.

The high room reeked of oil paint. The walls were covered
with paintings, animals fleeing a burning ark, a black Jesus
chopping up his cross rather than bearing it, and babies with
angel's wings and missing faces. There were verses that seemed
like scripture but weren't, scribbled so hastily they looked
wind-borne.

RETINUES OF THE CHOSEN: I WOULD BE BLACK IF I COULD.

When the paint had run out, she had used chalk pastels. She
had drawn whole rosaries of dark women, stretching like a
wave across cotton fields. A Star of Bethlehem that exploded
into colors no one in those parts had ever seen before. Monkeys

perched like lookouts on parapets, the sun was a bloated enemy.

> BY THE WATERS OF BABYLAND
> WHERE I SAT DOWN
> AND HERE I WEPT
> REMEMBERING BLACKJACK ZION.

At the center of an orange candle flame were a hundred hellish faces, drawn with such detail that the church ladies leaned in close as if to find themselves there. But the faces were all white. The words snaked around the room with a force that made Litany and the ladies respect the white girl at the same time that they were grateful not to be visited by the same spirit that had passed through her.

Not long after, the girl spent some time in the Western State Mental Institution in Bolivar, Tennessee. Nothing is known about those years of her life.

When she was twenty-two, a bus put her off in the middle of the highway before the Celestial Grocery in Madagascar. She went straight back to the old Abide house and studied her work from years before for several hours, as if to find instructions to herself there. She added a few more words.

> COME CLOSER
> ANYONE EVER USED AND ABANDONED
> BESIDE THIS RIVER.
> HOW IS IT YOU LEARNED TO LOATHE THIS LIFE?
> THERE IS FOOD FOR THAT FAMISHMENT HERE.

She collected some old books and carried them down to the boathouse, where she would live for the rest of her life.

The first winter she burned books to stay warm. By the second winter, and every other winter for the rest of his life, she had a cord of firewood almost as tall as her boathouse, personally cut and delivered by Prophet Royal Pegues, even after his hair was white and he had been to London to visit the queen, to play for her at the Royal Albert Hall.

Even after the girl became an old woman, she didn't go back to the old Abide house much, except on moonless nights when the words on the walls could be counted upon not to roar out at her with the intensity of caged animals. On such occasions she thieved old books from herself out of her grandfather's old library, carrying them, one at a time, back to the boathouse over a period of years.

An Inquiry Into the Moral Nature of Man
Encyclopedia of Animal Husbandry
The Sorrows of Young Werther

She ripped pages out, and folded them carefully or scissored them into elaborate silhouettes, and clipped them onto clotheslines and twine she'd cobwebbed between trees. With time, they swelled and faded in the sun and rain. The gold embossed leather covers she stacked in a corner for later use.

In all the years after that, she could be seen tending her roses, laying a labyrinth of oyster-shell paths inside a homemade picket fence made of chinaberry branches she'd honed to razor sharpness with her oyster knife. Angus Chien, the proprietor of the Chinese grocery, thought he could walk unobserved one Christmas Eve to leave a basket of ham, bread, and chocolate at the boathouse, but she was sitting in the fanlight window up at the old Abide house and saw him from high above. Six months later she left the same basket at his door, full of blowsy roses.

And Dean Fondren, a farmer, felt obliged to call on her when
he purchased from a Memphis holding company the tract of land
on which the old Abide house, her grandfather's, still stood like
a marooned riverboat. On that afternoon, she had seemed not to
hear him as he explained that she was welcome to recover whatever she wanted from the house before he, well, before it was
time to take it down. But as he was leaving, there had been some
altercation of blue jays in the trees, and she had looked up,
instantly. She could hear, he noted, when it suited her.

Dean Fondren developed the habit of plowing around the
Abide house the same way he plowed around the cinderblock
church and small cemetery that accompanied it, and around
the arpeggio of sharecropper shacks that had once belonged to
the big house. Sometimes he found baskets of roses on the seat
of his pickup, and once, a little birdhouse made of Coca-Cola
caps. The roof was made entirely of a book, *Encyclopedia of
Animal Husbandry.*

And a young black boy named Aubrey Ellerbee had an
encounter with her one rainy night when he ran away from
home to escape a beating from his mother. He had run across
Dean Fondren's fields to crawl through a broken window at the
True Light Temple of the Beautiful Name, which had been abandoned by then. He was wet and shivering, and rolled himself
into the cotton curtains that covered the little alcove where
christenings occurred. He heard a sigh behind him, *spirits,* and
gasped with fear. He saw a small woman with wild gray hair sitting in the back pew, wearing a hat as if she were there to wor-
ship, and she raised her hand gently as if to reassure him she
meant him no harm. Her eyes were like blue jewels in the dark.
He fell asleep with the odd idea that the woman, though white
and though disconnected from everything around her, was protecting him. She was gone by morning. There was a paper bag

beside him, holding a ham sandwich and a Hershey bar, and some men's clothes that were too old and too large. He devoured the food and had no idea that she was watching him from the boathouse as he walked out to the highway to hitch a ride, shirtsleeves flapping like a scarecrow's as he tried to thumb rides to Memphis, which he had heard was a better place.

Six Mabone

When the skinny Mauritanian boy came off the plane at Memphis, he was wearing his lucky running suit of ice-blue parachute cloth, which happened to be his only suit. His shoes bore the name of a great American basketball player, or so he'd been told by the Quakers who'd given them to him before he left Africa. He hesitated just a few feet past the plane's door. He could smell lingering perfumes and smoke, the dreams and errands of a thousand others. A river of bodies bumped him from behind, eddied around him, whorled off in a long stream. He was not tall, but he stooped in the accordionlike exit tunnel, as if he were stepping off a spaceship into an invisible headwind, *America.*

A pretty woman with skin brown as his own beckoned to him to hurry, and he stumbled forward. Her smile was dazzling in its insincerity, as if she were trapped inside a television. Her eyelids were painted with amazing opalescent green grease. The boy's pulse unfurled in his ears with the soft fury of rose petals. So the first emotion he felt on American soil was an exquisite embarrassment.

Two days of traveling and Boubacar could not stop staring. Women outside Africa were every shape possible, every degree of naked. It was an assault on his eyes. Some wore the blue jeans pants that showed exactly how they were shaped beneath. Their mouths were painted reds and corals and sapphire pinks. The men in Mauritania would be required to curse them or to confine them indoors for the protection of their immortal souls.

In America, men did not even look up from their newspapers.

There would be no one to meet his plane, to call out his name, *Boubacar.* His uncles would be working, at the casino in Mississippi. There was no time for the luxury of an airport greeting. His uncles might return to find themselves replaced by some other newcomer equally adept at carving carrot-roses, or spiriting baggage off big American buses, or smiling without rancor at old infidel women with no manners. A worker had taken time off for his wife to give birth, so his uncles had said, and found himself replaced that very day by another Mauritanian, someone from his same street back in Nouatchkott. In his pocket was a picture postcard to help Boubacar find the casino. It was shaped like a giant green shamrock, a plant of auspicious meanings to the Americans. Also on the card was the name and address of their trailer park, and the name of the Quakers who had brought him to America. Below that, the name of a Memphis man to contact if there was trouble, CHARLES PAZAR, U.S. IMMIGRATION JUDGE.

America was a prism of voices, from televisions bunched like grapes near the ceilings. Hardly anyone in the airport watched these televisions. Boubacar stared as if he were receiving instructions from the white-haired generals nodding into cameras, describing tall missiles with their hands. A fat lady clapped her hands in joy because she had won some waxed string with which to clean her teeth, a *lifetime supply.* Children bit into candies that gushed imaginary playmates that danced about their heads. Blue water swirled in a toilet bowl. Beautiful women stared into the camera and explained the merits of paper with which to clean one's backside. The boy stood intently. It was paper of extraordinary softness and vitamin E for the well-being of the backside. —*Vitamin E,* he repeated softly.

Everyone was *bizan* in America, his mother had explained. Even the ones who used to be slaves. Their homes were copies of the castles of the kings of France and England. —*They have special rooms only for shitting,* she'd told him, —*and not one single room in their houses for prayers. Not even a corner! Not even a mat! And the water you would use to bathe in, they use to wash it all away with a flush. And further: they pay money to strangers who allow them to ride bicycles nailed to the floor!*

He must not be weak in America, his grandmother and his mother had warned. Weakness had befallen a boy from his neighborhood who had not heeded the warnings of his mother. That boy had simply vanished, into the godless streets of Memphis. Back in the alleys of Nouatchkott that boy's name was now passed from child to child like a scorched thimble.

Boubacar looked around for signs and indications.

The man in the customs uniform said something to him about his bag that he did not understand.

—*Open, bag, son,* the boy heard. He opened it quickly. Everything he owned was in it, his two threadbare shirts and his collection of cassette tapes containing the entire musical history of Africa. The customs inspector, a tall and elegant black man, lifted up an old shirt to get a better look at the tapes. *Salif Keito. Stella Chiweshe and the Earthquake, Chief Doctor Sikiru Ayinde Barrister and His Fuji Commanders.* The man's eyes flared for a moment with something the boy could not interpret, and then the word *passport.* The boy felt true fear.

His father had died many years before in such a casual moment. A passport, a soldier, a crossing into Senegal.

Boubacar produced his passport, opened it, and offered it

with trembling hands to the customs agent, who studied it, then him.

The passport had cost a lot of money and would be a source of distress to his uncles, his mother had warned him, because she had not understood to bribe the official into altering the date of his birth. In America, it was of great advantage to be eighteen. Boubacar was, in fact, fifteen, and it said so on his passport.

The customs agent took his bag and slid it onto a cart, and an attendant began to wheel it away. Boubacar stood very still, the fear leaving a sharp taste in his mouth.

—*Good God*, the black soldier said slowly. —*You from Africa. You speak English?*

—*I am speaking small English sometime*, the boy said slowly, with trace elements of French.

—*That's what my teachers used to say about me*, the soldier laughed. —*Come on and I'll show you where to get your bag back.*

They went down long wide corridors that seemed to house whole streets of people selling doughnuts or dinners or newspapers, balloons, Elvis t-shirts. He studied a t-shirt closely, and was amazed at the price, thirty dollars. It made him dizzy to think of such money. He hesitated at the escalator, and watched the soldier get on it, and then saw the top of his head disappearing as others impatiently stepped onto it. Boubacar closed his eyes and got on, staring first at his toes and their nearness to peril, then at the top of the soldier's head, following it. The escalator spat them all out at the same point, and the soldier was waiting for him there. The soldier shouted to a man, a white stranger across the whirling carousel of bags, —*Hey man, grab that big one there.*

The white stranger lunged for Boubacar's bag, and the boy's heart stopped. He would never see his cassette tape collection again. What if they were a conspiracy of thieves?

But the stranger affably handed Boubacar's bag over the heads of others to the soldier, and disappeared. The soldier found his own huge black duffel bag, and Boubacar watched him covertly as he stepped through the double electric doors, out into the afternoon air. Fat silver planes sheared off into flattened gray sky. Boubacar saw fluorescent light glowing under gray concrete ramps where taxis idled. Holding his bag tightly to his chest, the boy went through the doors and began to make his way towards the snarl of concrete where cars shunted onto and off ramps.

Boubacar shifted his bag over his shoulder and started across the rows of creeping cars.

—Wait, the soldier called after him, and clapped his hands. —Where you headed?

—Mississippi, the boy said.

The soldier stared at him sharply and shifted his duffel on his shoulder. —You come all the way here just to go there? Wherebouts in Mississippi?

He produced the casino postcard with his uncles' address on it and handed it over to the soldier, who studied it a few seconds before handing it back.

—How your people come to be in that place? It ain't even a place no more, just kind of pass it on the way to the casino. Used to be a good little barbecue place there, run by a Chinese.

Boubacar shrugged, looked out the window. Perhaps there would be a truck with other travelers on the back of it.

—I got a woman waiting for me over on McLemore, but it won't be the first time I told her a lie. You want to go have some of that barbecue with me? Let me call this gal on my cell. Wait—you Islam? They got chicken.

—Islam, the boy heard, and nodded, and put his hand on his own chest. He was staring at the cell phone, aspiring to own one.

—*Lord have mercy,* the black soldier said. —*Welcome to America, brother.*

It was the spring of 2001.

Boubacar followed the soldier into the sea of cars, and America was suddenly a hundred hectares of automobiles. Dirty pickup trucks, little red coupes, silver bullet-shaped sedans. *Toyota,* he read. *Jeep.* He knew these words. He gasped with pleasure when the soldier stopped in front of a 1965 Chevrolet Impala with antique license plates. It was a color the boy's mother called *aubergine,* big as a barge. It had an abundance of taillights. Boubacar looked at the soldier, his eyes luminous with respect. While the soldier put their bags in the trunk, Boubacar stood with his hands on the hood of the Impala, his eyes closed, humming. The song was "Six Mabone," the old Lulu Masilela hymn to American cars.

An American white boy with hair as pink as candy paused to listen, nodded his head in appreciation, and made a sign with his thumb up. Boubacar stared with appreciation at the white boy with the pink hair. Others stared at the humming boy, then at the boy with the pink hair, and moved on. Boubacar appeared to be bestowing some kind of benediction on the car, blessing it for its long life and its many venerable headlights. He made small involuntary noises of pleasure as he strapped himself into the passenger seat. He held himself upright as if he were inside an egg that might break. The boy's face was swathed in a smile as he looked at the soldier and made the thumbs-up sign. *Chevrolet!*

America was tattoo parlors and taquerias, pawnshops with black prison bars on their windows, and strip clubs with neon women's legs scissoring in the afternoon air.

America was whole horizons filled with copies of the castles of the kings of France and England, cheek by jowl, with barely enough room between them for their cars to pass.

The soldier cleared his throat. —*What your people do? Back at home? You not from Somalia are you? I been to Mogadishu before.*

—*Home, Somalia, Mogadishu*, the boy heard. He stared ahead, not knowing where to begin. He had been instructed to stay strictly away from Somalians in America. They had bad tempers, and they liked drugs and guns more than they liked people, his grandmother had said.

—*Mauritania*, he said simply, pointing to himself.

There was no word for it, *harutine*, in English. It was far too complicated to explain to a stranger. His mother had warned him not to try to explain to strangers. In Mauritania, people had gone to jail for trying to explain it to French television crews. They had put money in the hands of his grandmother, paying her to lower her veil and look into their cameras, there.

—*Look into the eyes of the Western world*, the French man had said. —*Let them see the face of slavery.*

A white Quaker man from Harvard, which was in Massachusetts, which was in America, had put cash into his mother's hands to purchase Boubacar's freedom and finance his trip to Mississippi. Television cameras from America had filmed the white man from Harvard buying him to set him free, signing the papers. Boubacar had seen the cash as it disappeared into his mother's clothing. When the white man from Harvard had left for Morocco taking the French television cameramen, his mother had used the money to purchase a little Sudanese refugee girl to fetch the water every day. The remainder of the money had gone for food and medicines for his grandmother. It was a good transaction, and he was headed to America.

Bizan "Master" (handwritten annotation)

—*You will be* bizan *in America,* his mother had said fiercely, giving him a rough kiss good-bye. —*All are* bizan *in America.*

America was endlessly flat, a horizon of billboards clipping past the car. *Treflan...Mississippi Chemical...Lucky Leaf Casino.* The boy stared at the image of a giant beautiful woman smiling in a French maid's costume, *Spend the night with me.*

They passed a series of other signs, and the soldier read them aloud in increments as the car whipped past them. *Where Will You Spend Eternity? Prepare to Meet Thy God. Repent.*

—*What is this meaning?* Boubacar asked the soldier, pointing to the signs.

—*Like when you sorry for the bad thing you did, like it say in the Bible.*

The boy nodded, thinking the government had put it there. —*Repent,* he repeated. It seemed a worthy ordinance of the municipal sort.

—*They tell you anything about Mississippi?*

The boy shook his head. —*Casino money is very good in my village. Very much.*

—*It was some troubles here, long time ago,* the soldier said. —*Used to could see peoples hitchhiking, hopping freight trains, anything to get out of those cotton fields. Time to pick cotton, white man stop the black man walking on the road, minding his own bidness, put him in the police car, put him out to work on the county farm. Jailhouse first, then they decide the reason. Cotton all picked, you free to go on down the road. So a lot of 'em go. Chicago, Detroit, Milwaukee, Oakland. Never come back except maybe for the Fourth of July, Decoration Day, driving they big Lincoln or some little bitty Jaguar, to put the flowers on they mama grave.*

freedom ~ devotion of the violands 'yards (handwritten marginal annotation)

The words escaped into the air before the boy's mind could snare the images.

Abraham Lincoln, the boy nodded. But *Jaguar?*

—You see that big wall of dirt over there?

The boy looked and nodded.

—That's the levee. That's what hold the river back, keep it from flooding everybody out. Got the bodies of black men in it. White men took 'em out there and helt the gun on them while they dug it and built the levee. Black man fall, shovel the dirt over him where he fall. Some of them bodies had bullets in 'em when they fell. That was a long time ago. The soldier glanced over at him suddenly, then looked back at the road.

—See, everybody else all the time trying to get the fuck out, and here you go, trying to get the fuck in.

—Get the fuck in, the boy agreed, nodding. *Fuck?* What was *fuck?*

The soldier winced. *—I need to teach you some more English,* the man said. *—So you don't sound like you straight off the boat.*

—Straight off the boat, the boy echoed. *—I will be having money in America.*

The soldier glanced at him, speechless, then eyed the road. *—Delta is a good place to learn music, but ain't no money there. You want money, they ain't got it in Mississippi.*

The venerable eggplant-colored car hurtled forward, deeper into America.

The boy stared out the window.

America was a flat, wet desert, infinite fields, the black water of a long lake curving like a scythe around a band of trees. There were few human beings in sight, just a farmer on the tractor in the long field. A dog followed the tractor. Birds whirled above both tractor and dog like a mandala of black ink spots.

—*What you looking at there used to be the Mississippi River. Long time ago the river moved itself over. That lake there is what got left behind.*

Boubacar watched the man's face for signs and indications.

—*I'm not shittin' you, man. River just change its mind and move sometime. But that lake there has got the same gar and catfish to match the ones in the river.*

The boy climbed out of the big car carefully, as if the land might be liquid. He closed the car door with equal care, *Chevrolet,* lest he harm it. He looked around him.

—*Madagascar, Mississippi,* said the soldier. —*Just like it say on your piece of paper there.*

America, it seemed, was old wooden buildings leaning precariously on stilts, like old cranes wading in the black water, facing the highway with an air of fatigue. America was an empty parking lot in front of a store with a porch and a tin roof. A fading painted Coca-Cola sign announced, CELESTIAL GROCERY. A jivey red neon pig leapt perpetually out of the same blue neon barrel. An enormous old tree was shedding pink blossoms all over its porch and the bare earth in front of it. The store was like an angular gnarl affixed to the base of the tree.

A skinny Chinese man in a dirty red apron was sweeping the porch of the store. About his ankles, a gaggle of three calico cats seemed unconcerned about his moving broom. The fallen pink petals seemed to float to the Chinese man's broom. On the porch rails beside him, a pair of black binoculars rested.

The air smelled sweet. Blossoms continued to fall around the Chinese man's shoulders onto the porch. Cats murmured and moved warily out of the path of the visitors, but they didn't mind the broom.

Boubacar stared at a particular calico bent over an enormous serving of tinned meat on a chipped saucer with moss roses and violets ringed around gold edges. Boubacar bent gently to pet the cat, as if to congratulate it on its good fortune. The cat had been offered more meat in one meal than Boubacar's family would see in a given day in Mauritania, and in an elegant dish.

Boubacar studied a small round red-and-white sign on a stand:

EAT

OR WE BOTH STARVE.

The soldier looked around, one foot on the bottom step. —*You got any of that good barbecue?*

—*Pit man died here a while back,* the Chinese man said. —*Ain't had no goot barbecue since then.* The Chinese man's words had rolled out of his mouth like sleepy fat birds, a southern drawl that did not match his Chinese face.

The soldier blinked and grinned. —*This boy here come all the way from Africa,* the soldier said. —*Got family here somewheres.*

The boy held out his hand to the Chinese man, and said in his French-inflected English, —*I am . . . straight off the boat.*

The Chinese man's mouth twitched cryptically as he accepted the boy's hand and allowed him to pump it up and down, priming him for conversation. —*Got quite a few from Africa here,* he said. —*Most of 'em stay over there in those trailers.*

He pointed out the plate glass window overlooking a porch. Behind a small abandoned gas station was a tired constellation of trailers, cramped in a parquet pattern too close together beside the field that seemed to go on forever.

They had noted the arrangement: the crop was of more importance than the people.

Behind the gas station, the three rusting silver Airstream trailers seemed larger than life. They'd been identical once. Now they were distinguishable by dent and ding and habitation. One now had old soft drink cans and auto parts sorted neatly into piles in front of it, and on its outer walls were large black whorls of spray-painted symbols, slightly Arabic. They registered to the eye like a reply to the red whorls on the gas station. The second trailer had stacks of wooden pallets leaning against it, and children's toys strewn about its steps. Another was neat as a pin, with ground already spaded up for a garden inside a makeshift fence. That would be his uncle Teslem's kitchen garden, Boubacar knew. He looked around for signs of Uncle Salem: that would be his satellite dish affixed to a top corner of the trailer.

—*I don't know about this, my man,* the soldier said. —*Look like some kind of gang war goin' on here. Lemme check your piece of paper again. Yessir. This the right place.*

The door was locked, and no one answered his knocks.

They were working, of course. He would wait.

The soldier was ready to depart. He was rattling the keys to the six-mabone car, walking around it looking at the tires. His frown telegraphed itself onto Boubacar's face.

—*Well, I be goddamn,* the soldier said, looking around as if he were looking for something. —*Look like I have lost me a hubcap. That sucker cost me a hundret and twenty-five dollars.*

—*Twenty-five dollars,* Boubacar heard, and began to fish in his pockets for money. He was trying to understand what the man had said. He wasn't sure yet which bills signified what, so he fanned them all out in his palms and held them out to the soldier. He was trying to translate what it was the man had said. —*I. Be. Got. Damn.* Did he mean to damn God or did he mean God had damned him?

—*Naw, man, put your money away.*

The soldier took out his wallet and thumbed through bills like a phone book. He took out a twenty-dollar bill. —*This is a gift from me to you,* he said. —*Here's the deal. You want to get in the game with the music here, you go in that Chinese place over there, and you play the jukebox with this money. Use to be a juke in there that was older than Jesus, nearlybout.* He put the bill in the boy's hand, and curled his fingers around it, then clapped a hand on his shoulder.

As the soldier walked back to his parked car, the boy wondered if he would ever see him again. —*I do not forget you!* he called out.

The soldier waved and wheeled the big car around. Its tail-lights flared briefly, *six mabone,* and then it was gone.

The boy walked in a wide circle inside the courtyard. Toward the high grassy levee holding back the big river sat a big abandoned white house with a tattered Mylar banner hanging from its balcony, NATION OF ISLAM. In Mauritania such a house would have been a marvel, an honor to inhabit, and care would have been taken with its paint. It would hold many families in his country. In America, it stood empty.

Next door, a rickety boathouse stood on its piers over the water, and stark, strange animals made from bright stovepipe stood about it. A sign arched over an oyster-shell path from the road to the boathouse, ANARCHY GARDEN OF THE MEZZALUNA MILLENNIUM. Tiny dolls dangled like little white corpses from it. The small trees around the boathouse were cobwebbed with gold lights strung in a disorderly way. Silver disks made from pie pans reflected the sun, and shards of colored glass dangled from strings and clinked dully together. On the bare branches of a dead tree, bottles of many colors were upended. The boy knew instantly what he was seeing: the bottles would detain whatever spirits meant harm to the household. He theorized that the neighbors could be from Senegal, and this reassured him. No village should be without its *sorcière*.

The boy sat wearily, then lay down in an old lawn glider under a tree. He put his satchel of cassette tapes under his head in order for the entire musical history of Africa to give him beneficial dreams. He could see the stars through the tatters in the glider's striped canopy. He began to doze, his eyelids fluttering softly. His soul spooled back to him the sounds of his day, its arrivals and departures etched into the air in the soft world-weary Babel of airport-announcer voices. He listened closely to his dreams, but could not quite seem to translate them. Then came the voices of the women in his mother's household, patting their calabashes and dishpans with the palms of their hands, singing *Jag-u-ar, Jag-u-ar*, with respect for a certain kind of French fighting plane whose skins had been salvaged years before to make cook-pots and dishpans.

Someone's white grandmother wandered through his dream, wearing a striped pony blanket and a black bowler hat. Her eyes burned blue. In her hands, the silver hubcap from the six-mabone car, like a holy vessel or a serving dish. *La sorcière*, Boubacar noted to himself in drowsy clarity. He crossed into the realms of deep sleep, too tired to fear that she might thieve his soul.

Schottische

For as long as the living could remember, the Celestial Grocery
stood beside the highway at Madagascar, a bowlegged sentinel
overhanging the black water of the oxbow. A tarpaper shack on
stilts, it was the kind of country store most casino tourists sped
past without looking up. Angus Chien, the proprietor, usually sat
on the porch of the Celestial at dawn and again at dusk, smoking
quietly alone, staring out over the surrounding fields. Drivers
passing at certain hours on Highway 61 saw a gaunt Chinese
man in a stiff white shirt, sleeves rolled up to his elbows, smoking his upside-down Marlboro like an elegant European. His hair
was gunmetal gray and matched his pants and shoes.

Habit kept his left hand folded like a stiff paper crane,
tucked neatly under his right elbow, surveying the scene with
his legs crossed, one foot swinging. Most times he took his
binoculars down from the nail where they hung on the wall and
set them on the porch, just in case. Most times he made a cur-
sory check to see if all his neighbors were accounted for, a
small handful out in the middle of nowhere who had learned to
look out for each other.

The hot peppers and zinnias growing in big Luzianne coffee
cans on the front porch caused discomfort to a certain kind of
traveler who wanted every new place to resemble as closely as

possible the place he'd just left behind. The Celestial was the last of a constellation of Chinese-run country stores that used to exist in almost every river town between Memphis and New Orleans.

To find the original painted sign for the Celestial, you had to know where to look. An ancient pressed-tin Coca-Cola sign leaned against the porch under the empress tree, its red circle faded to mauve by years of sun and rain. A Chinese symbol was hand-painted in black over the circle. Angus Chien would explain to anyone who asked that the Chinese symbol was a good thing, that it conveyed his wish for long life to all who entered.

On the evening that the Mauritanian boy had arrived, Angus sat outside and read for the eighth time a certified letter he had received that morning. Some outfit calling itself *Futuristics*, with a riverfront address in Memphis. Every time Angus read it, it said the same thing. Somebody wanted to buy his land right out from under his feet, as if his life were somehow over.

Angus slammed the letter shut yet again and put it back in his shirt pocket, where it had been all day. He took a deep, nourishing drag from his cigarette. He had thought his parcel of land too tiny to be of any interest to anyone. It could only be of interest to someone with a grandiose plan. He stared over at the low buzz of green light that was the casino in the distance. He looked at the wide fields that surrounded the store and even the highway. He tried to remember who owned what.

If you walked a hundred yards one way, you were on Dean Fondren's property.

A hundred yards the other way, you were on Aubrey Ellerbee's.

Dean Fondren was white; Aubrey Ellerbee was black.

Straddling their land was the True Light Temple of the Beautiful Name, a defunct little cinderblock church.

If you walked around the church from the store, you were standing in the cemetery among dead soldiers and slaves and Angus Chien's own two loved ones, his father and his wife, as well as a stone that already had his own name on it, a special two-for-one deal he'd lucked into when his wife died. It was an elemental strangeness of his life. He had been at peace with it for many years. Angus could look out half the windows in the store he lived and worked in and see the patch of earth that would one day cover his bones, and the stone with his name on it. It was not his true Chinese name, but the one the missionaries had given him. This was another elemental strangeness, that the tombstones all bore the names that missionaries had given his father, his wife, and himself, without noticing that they never really became Christians. The names had proved to be as useful as their traveling papers in America, and so they had used them.

An eighteen-wheeler passed, slowing momentarily, *Hanjin*, and the driver blew the horn, a deep gratifying honk that nudged Angus Chien's sternum. He knew the driver, a man who always bought B. C. Headache powders and generic cigarettes. Angus stood up, threw his cigarette off into the dirt, and brushed off the seat of his pants before he went inside.

The Celestial Grocery was the unacknowledged heart of the little dying town, the kind of place to get live fish bait at five in the morning or eggs over easy near midnight if you could catch Angus still up. Inside, plaid flannel shirts from Taiwan were shelved next to sardines from Finland and pantyhose from North Carolina. Cheap cotton-candy-textured baby dresses from the Philippines hung on a rusty rack alongside camouflage t-shirts from Alabama meant for deer hunters. Shotgun shells and tractor sparkplugs, Elvis and Ole Miss t-shirts, baby formula and diapers, herbicides and hemorrhoid ointments, horse liniment, bridles, hoop cheeses, plastic rosaries, tired shopworn apples, and yellowing dog-eared heads of cabbage. Customers, whether they lingered or were just passing through, always left smelling like ambient tobacco and hamburger grease. Costs were always tallied on a red lacquer abacus that had come all the way from China in 1938.

The jukebox was a Rock-ola that had come all the way from St. Louis the following year. It had not been serviced since the riots in Memphis the night Martin Luther King died, when the Memphis Novelty Company was looted and its lease records burned. Its playlist was the musical equivalent of the ant in the amber glass at Pompeii: customers could choose almost anything they wanted, as long as it had been released before April of 1968. Johnny Cash, Otis Redding, Carl Perkins, Percy Sledge, Slim Harpo, Wilson Pickett. Regular customers knew not to spend their own money on the jukebox, but to reach up into the Dixie cup on top of it and borrow a red-painted coin from Angus. Choosing a song did not mean that you'd actually get to hear it, hence the free money. The jukebox had never been quite right since the company that owned it had converted it from 78s to 45s. Sometimes it played the flip side of what you asked for. Sometimes it played the same song over and over for months, and Angus had to keep it unplugged. Sometimes it played nothing.

The Celestial did not look like much on the outside, just a subsistence-level business affixed to an empress tree that wept pink blossoms in the spring and valentine-shaped leaves in the fall. In Angus's hands, it had put his son through the Wharton School of Business. Now this son worked for a large food distributor with an Italian name in Memphis, and drove a fast little car made in Japan, and did not ever seem to have the time to visit Angus. He called him on a cell phone sometimes when he was stuck in traffic, to ask his advice on matters of the stock markets in New York and Hong Kong. Only once did he ask about Tokyo. If you asked Angus what he knew about the Nikkei, he'd hang up the phone in disgust.

Angus was hurrying to get the CLOSED sign flipped forward on the front door when he heard a truck pulling into the parking lot. He turned the lights out. It was after ten, he thought crossly. Just as he peered out the plate glass window in front, there was Aubrey Ellerbee, cocking his hat back on his head, grinning, peering back at him.

Angus was startled, and bunched up the calendar when he stepped back. Aubrey wiped his feet before he came in.

—*Whoa, Aubrey, you like to give me a heart attack.*

—*Just need me some smokes, is all.*

—*I thought you was them gangsters come to rob me,* Angus said, unlatching the door.

—*'Gangbangers' is what they call them now, I believe,* Aubrey said as he stepped inside.

Angus shrugged and ambled back over to run his finger along the cello-wrapped packages, as a librarian might search for a particular title. *Camels,* he remembered. Aubrey smoked Camels.

—*Who we got over there in that trailer?* asked Aubrey.

—*Disciples? El Rukns? I can't keep my gangsters straight in my mind. These the ones got that shiny jacket with the crown jewels on the back and all.*

Angus shook his head and walked to the window. He saw the lights at the old trailer. It seemed like such a senseless waste. A Memphis company that rented the property out to transient criminals when the workers who toiled in the fields had to sleep wherever they fell. —*Them people need to get on back to wherever they come from. Probably been run out of Memphis, I imagine. Now you take them Africans. Africans is good people. You got any Africans working for you?*

—Can't get 'em, Aubrey said. —*They all want to wear them tuxedoes over at the casino. Listen, I need to axe you a favor, Angus.*

—*Axe me.*

—*It's a lady come down here from Memphis the other day, in one them little government cars.*

—*Yep. We talked a little bit. She wanted to know where they stay at night. Told her to talk to you.*

—Well, Aubrey said, —*I need to axe you to not do that no more.*

—*Tax man after you?*

—No, *isn't no trouble,* Aubrey said, and scratched at the back of his neck, displacing his hat. —*I just need for you to not do that, is all. If she needs to know about the people work for me, she has to talk to the man that brought 'em here. Name is Tomás Tulia, up at Friar's Point. He handles all their living arrangements and such like. I don't know nothing about 'em, except that they show up in the mornings and they leave in the evenings. If they ain't legal, it ain't my doings. If where they stayin' ain't up to code, it ain't my problem.*

Angus saw Aubrey cock his cap back even further, the way he did when he was dancing away from the truth. —*Africans still in that other trailer? Africans is good workers, but you don't catch them in the fields or on the side of the highway, no sir. They over in the Lucky Leaf for the air-conditioning.*

—*Toting that luggage for them yahoos that get off the buses. Well, they are good customers, Africans. Pay cash.* Angus looked straight into the other man's eyes. He did not smile.

This was a polite reference to the fact that Aubrey was in arrears with his store tab.

—*Be nice to be able to pay everything with cash,* Aubrey said. —*Sometimes you got it, sometimes you ain't. These Hondurans is going to break me.*

Angus's tongue felt fat with what he could not bring himself to say. It wasn't the Hondurans that would break Aubrey, it was the casino, or the loneliness that drove him to spend his nights over there. The ensuing silence discomfited Aubrey, as if he could hear Angus's thoughts, and so he shoved words into the empty air.

—*I reckon you seen where they broke ground for that Dixie Barrel.*

—*The what?*

—*Dixie Barrel, up the road a ways. One of them Arkansas chains. Big doings, twelve gas pumps, souvenir shop. They working three shifts of Mexicans to get it open by the end of the month. I'm surprised you can't hear the racket all the way over here. I can hear the backhoes and dozers going all night long.*

—*Souvenirs of what?* Angus asked.

—*They is people in this world that will pay three dollars for one cotton boll wrapped in a little baggie,* Aubrey laughed. —*How about a chocolate-covered soybean?*

Angus was silent a moment. —*Twelve pumps? Ain't nobody around here need no twelve tanks of gas all at the same time.*

—*I'm sorry, Angus. I thought you knew. I should have kept my mouth shut.*

—*No, I'm glad you told me. I like to know what's out there. You get one of them letters from that outfit in Memphis?* Angus asked, pulling the letter out of his shirt pocket. —*Talking about buying everybody out.*

Aubrey had a strange look on his face, as if he thought he'd had the only letter.

—*Gambling company. You aiming to sell out and go, Angus?*

—*I ain't goin' nowhere*, Angus said. —*I be here till it's time to haul me to my spot out there.*

—*Shit*, Aubrey said affectionately. —*You'll still be here with that broom on the porch when my ass been cold in the ground for ten years. Hell, I'm already gambling everything I got, every day. I gamble that the rain will come. I gamble that the sun will shine. I could lose it all*, kapow, *just like that. I guess you heard they gonna put me in that Standard and Poor now. Kinda funny how I work all them years buss my ass to not be poor, which is standard around here, just to end up in some book say 'standard' and say 'poor.'*

Their voices softened as they ran through the customary recitative of local births and funerals and surgeries. It was an old and mutual comfort that occurred many a time late at night in the Celestial, drifting off into calm discussion about such matters as the value of a dollar bill or the merits of a particular sparkplug.

After Aubrey left, Angus began to sweep the floor in long, irritated arcs, dragging his big broom over the knotty pine floors worn thin by a hundred years of shoes shuffling in and out. Angus stooped and peered at a dark spot: a dead bee. He felt a twinge in his back and stood up sharply. He went to get the broom, and as he reached for it, he was looking at an old fly-specked yellowed newspaper clipping stapled into the soft pine of the wall. To an outsider, the clipping was a dark block, indecipherable. Aubrey's photo was under all that yellowed age.

The clipping was put up there by Angus in 1973, when Aubrey was fifteen. He was the first black boy in the Future Farmers of America in Mississippi to win Grand Reserve Champion at the fair in Memphis. In the photo, he wore his blue FFA jacket, and stood with Dean Fondren, holding the bridle on a sweet-faced Hereford steer with a forehead wide and flat as an anvil.

Angus had the whole history of Madagascar on those walls, the wedding and birth announcements, obits, and local engagements. As the years had passed, the walls were covered with accounts of riverboat wrecks and local sons lost in the wars, those declared and those that weren't. There were black schoolboys in Abe Lincoln stovepipe hats, and most recently, a clipping from the *Wall Street Journal* about Asian carp that had escaped from catfish farms, known to leap into the boats of bewildered fishermen in the back bayous off the Mississippi. But Aubrey's had been only the second black face to be tacked up on the Celestial's wall. The first had been a newspaper clipping of Howlin' Wolf, lying on his side onstage in Chicago, playing his saxophone. It was scotch-taped in the center of a constellation of white debutantes and beauty queens who'd once coursed across the local horizon for a few summers like soft, pleasant meteors, dancing to his music in smoky back-roads clubs before they married into old money and early obscurity.

Bending to his broom again, Angus thought he heard music, then looked up to silence. Looking down he noticed more dark spots, and bent closer. Altogether, five dead honeybees. He'd heard that bees have their own undertakers who fly the fallen ones out of the hive and drop them in midair. He swept them gently into the dustpan, the same dinged red tin one with black roosters on it that he had used when he was a child sweeping these same floors for his father. For some reason he suddenly could remember the first time he'd seen it as a boy, shiny and fiercely red and seeming supremely Chinese. On its back was stamped *Made in U.S.A.*, the first words he had learned to read in English.

He looked up at a crack near the ceiling where the bees came and went. He decided not to understand what he was suspecting about the bees. He'd worry about it another day. It was the empress tree that made the bees single out his little store, year after year. They had made it through another winter just like he had. He'd not begrudge them their spring and their summer. What the state health inspectors didn't know wouldn't hurt them. He carried the dustpan of bees outside onto the porch and emptied it over the rail onto the roots of the empress tree. The dead bees were hardly visible on the ground, the same brown color as the dirt the empress tree had nourished itself with to make the pink flowers that had fed the bees and turned them brown.

—*Feed you back to the tree that fed you*, he said aloud, startling himself. So it had come to this: funeralizing over dead bees, with nobody to overhear and laugh with him about it. His laugh snagged in his chest, sounding like aluminum foil when it tears.

Then he heard again the thrum of good music, the kind that didn't come boiling nastily out of a car window. He had definitely heard music. Low guitar, low laughter. Then he saw movement beneath the two old blackjack oaks near the True Light Temple of the Beautiful Name.

He strained to see what he could. Still holding the broom, he got the binoculars off the porch rail. A scuffed white Econoline van, cascades of Tejano music escaping from its open back door. He could hear voices veiled by the trees that lined the little creek bed. He saw the tiny flare of a cigarette passed from hand to hand. Why did they smoke in a circle, and only one cigarette? Did they not know he had bales of cigarettes for sale in his store? They were gathered in a small group around the door of the church.

Apart from the group, a small dark figure danced in the field alone, spinning and turning slowly. As Angus focused the binoculars, the figure became a small woman, arms raised. Her skirt was full and black, with flowers embroidered on it. It swished around her shins as she stepped carefully amid the newly plowed furrows. She was barefoot. You didn't see that much anymore, barefooted women.

She thought no one at all could see her.

She danced alone but held her head canted back a bit, as if in ceremonial tenderness towards some imaginary loving partner who was not there. It was the western dance called schottische. Angus had seen the lessons for it on television, cowboys with deadpan faces twirling women with petticoats flashing. But when the dancer in the field moved, she had a look on her face Angus had not seen in many years. It was a look meant to be private, full of the kind of light that only one man gets to see in a certain moment, usually in a bed.

This bothered Angus, and he lowered the binoculars a moment, respectfully, and took another drag off his cigarette. Then he raised them again. She was older than he had thought, but she moved like a young woman. When the music ended, she curtseyed to the empty air. She vanished into the trees, and Angus was left alone with the broom in one hand and the binoculars in the other. He felt aggrieved and out of sorts, his habit when he was given the gift of sudden unsolicited understanding.

Inside his store Angus put the broom and binoculars in the same places they'd occupied for almost twenty years, and he leaned against the counter while he dialed a long-distance number in New York slowly and carefully, reading it off a wall covered with pencilings in Chinese and other phone numbers and figures. Angus's voice took on a different timbre when he spoke Chinese, dropping into a deeper range. Because of his Delta accent, the party on the other end of the line sometimes had to ask him to repeat himself. It was his cousin, a jeweler, who always eventually insisted on English, which seemed to be the only common language he could find with the Delta Chinese.

—*Say again?*

—*Dixie Barrel. Arkansas outfit.*

—*Is good. Time for split, maybe next month, next year. How much you want?*

—*Same as usual.*

After they had inquired as to each other's loved ones, Angus put the phone receiver back in its cradle and then subtracted some numbers from a column that snaked around photos of Johnny Cash and Wanda Jackson, using a chewed yellow Number Two pencil tied to a nail on the wall with a piece of brown jute. He then penciled in the same amount in a column of figures that had somehow over the years begun to curl around a Clarksdale *Register* photo of a sweet potato that resembled Winston Churchill somewhat. He began to unbutton his shirt as he walked into his quarters in the back of the store, leaving the pencil swaying on its string like a clock pendulum.

National Steel

Boubacar felt along the wall with his hands until he found the light switch, and turned it on. *Off, on. Off, on.* A miracle. Where did it come from? He ran the faucets in the bathroom, and flushed the toilet twice, watching the pristine water swirl and disappear down the porcelain drain. Where did it go?

So much water, abundant as air.

The uncles had let him sleep for the better part of two days, and then he had heard a car and was awake, confused, until he remembered where he was. *Mississippi. America.*

There had been something else, a noise he had heard in his sleep but couldn't remember. Children shouting? A woman crying? He took mental stock of his possessions. His satchel was under the bed for safekeeping. His father's cassette tapes were safe. His portable player was back in Mauritania. And his lucky suit, it was neatly folded on the back of an old wood-slatted folding chair. He studied the message painted on the chair: *Ibrahim Bros. Funeral Home, Clarksdale, Mississippi.*

Boubacar turned on the small television, a *miracle*, and America emptied itself into the room. America possessed a machine for cleaning the floor so powerful it had the force of a hundred hurricanes. A pretty but starving woman in a blue ball gown spun a large colored roulette wheel, and dispensed money, and a fat chef served roast duck with *foie gras*. Men drank beer so that women would come to them. Obese girls waited in suspense to be told who had fathered their children. An entire symphony orchestra of a major European city played music to encourage the purchase of the paper the Americans wiped their backsides with.

Men with iron hooks driven through their bare flesh hung suspended like marionettes, spinning. The boy stared, confused, thinking this was a service offered for sale. A beautiful woman demonstrated how to tint your eyes another color with little plastic lenses. —*And they're disposable,* she said, with a toss of her head.

On the shopping channel women sold jewelry and rugs, their hands stroking the goods in a way that any child would envy. On another channel, black women in spangly dresses bobbled their breasts and waved their hands around and sang, —*Where dem dollars at? Where dem dollars at?* A few minutes later, young white musicians smashed guitars on telephone poles and sneered into the camera. Were guitars being sold for such purposes? He couldn't tell. The guitars sounded like terrible dying animals when they were smashed.

—*And they're disposable,* Boubacar said softly, imitating the lens-seller's voice perfectly. His head hurt from watching the Americans on television.

In the kitchen, he turned the lights off and on before settling himself at the table with a bag of Oreos. Someone was pounding on the metal door. He peered out the window but could see no one. He went to the door and opened it cautiously, peering through an inch of space.

—*Hey man,* said an American voice. —*You callin' somebody with them lights? You in trouble over here? We was wondering do you need some help.*

—*No,* said the boy, his voice high and shaking. —*No problem. The light is very good. America is very good.*

—*Rashad just told me to check it out. We didn't think*

nobody was over here. Then when the lights start goin' on and off, we get a little worried. You do the lights like that, somebody might be calling in the law to come help you, see what I'm saying?

The man was looking past Boubacar into the room behind, his eyes panning the room. In his hand he held a small silver cell phone, as if he were a soldier of great purpose.

—*Later, man,* he said to the boy, and walked back towards the steady lights of the other trailer.

—*Later, man,* Boubacar practiced his English once he shut the door. —*Later.*

He opened the refrigerator and drank milk from a plastic jug. It would be hours before anyone was home. He was famished but bewildered by the little kitchen with its appliances and cupboards. The cupboards contained cans and boxes indecipherable to him. He opened a box with a picture of yellow corn and a chicken on it, but it contained only dry brown flakes that did not taste like chicken or corn. The flakes turned to a gummy paste when he put them in his mouth, so he drank more milk from the jug. He was eating like an American, like an astronaut. Someone in his village who had been to university in Florida had told him that once the Americans began their space travel, they all began to eat like astronauts.

He was not sure what food belonged to whom, and did not wish to offend his uncles. On a piece of brown bread he put something that was the color of butter but was not butter, and drank more of the milk. It would be necessary to replace what he had taken from his uncles. He would go to the store. He looked out the kitchen window and saw that the lights were still on at the Celestial.

In the little store, the Chinese man barely looked up as Boubacar came in. He continued to wipe the worn Formica tabletops, his arms sweeping in practiced loops. The napkin holders and salt shakers clinked as he slid them first left, then right. Boubacar inspected some pink pickled eggs in a large jar on the counter. The Chinese man came over, wiping his hands on a red apron. A pretty dark-skinned girl with a red bandanna wrapped around her head was washing dishes in a deep sink of crudely welded sheet metal. She turned around and smiled at him. She had a gold tooth. His eyes fluttered shut, and he turned away in confusion.

Then he saw the jukebox. It was the most beautiful thing he had seen in all his fifteen years. It was old, made of wood and chrome and glass and colored lights. His lips tried to form the word he was reading. *Rock,* then something else. The front was like French cathedrals he'd seen in his mother's photos; the top had jade-green epaulets of Bakelite scrolled and carved in the Chinese way. He perused the labels, and could read some of them. He could see the neat rows of 45s inside the glass dome, the little plastic tone arm shaped like a clef note.

Rock-ola. It was the most beautiful thing he had seen in America, displacing the Chevrolet in his mind. He had to play it. The dark-skinned girl was still watching him.

He fingered the change in his pockets, held out the entire amount to the Chinese man, waited for instructions. The Chinese man separated two quarters from the dimes and nickels and pennies, as if they were abacus beads. The boy slid them in the slot. The coins clinked into some hidden inner box. The Rock-ola came alive, its forward lights batting like the eyelashes of an old coquette.

Boubacar smiled. His hands fluttered, not knowing what to choose. He pressed buttons at random. A guitar twanged, and he was thrilled: *Are you ready for the great atomic power?* He put his hands on the machine in a proprietary way. It was his money playing the song, so the machine was his for a few minutes. The boy was mesmerized, his mind fumbling over the words like a blind person being handed too many unfamiliar objects at once: *atomic, saviour, fire, rain.*

He noticed that the dark-skinned girl had wrinkled her nose, but her eyes were still smiling at him. The jukebox blinked blue, green, amber, then changed records.

—*I like the American music very large*, he said.

The girl shrugged. —*Where do you stay?*

—*I am straight off the boat*, he said.

The girl broke into peals of laughter.

—*My name is Ayesha Pegues*, she said. Boubacar's eyes widened at the name, his own mother's. It seemed like a message of sorts.

—*I am Boubacar.*

They spoke a bit. She seemed to know about his uncles. Something passed across her face, a shadow, a question—he wasn't sure. Her nails were painted the rich pink of pomegranate seeds, and there was a gold chain at her throat. She was pretty enough to confuse him, more than the women in the television, but the nakedness of her face caused him to look away sometimes. It seemed the polite thing to do. If such a girl were his, he'd make her cover her naked face in public. She had already turned from him; she was looking at the front of the store.

Three figures stood there, young black men each wearing black baseball caps, backwards. Each hat had an elegant "D" on the front. They added up to more together than they would have alone. One of them was the same man who'd knocked on the door when Boubacar was testing the lights. The Chinese man narrowed his eyes a bit watching them, as the girl followed them out to the parking lot. The Chinese man shook his head, and busied himself with a sheaf of receipts.

Boubacar studied with intense interest the labels of the Rosedale peach and tomato cans. He had just selected a can of sardines to take to his uncles when the door opened again, and Ayesha came back in. She seemed upset, and when she looked back over her shoulder, Boubacar saw that she was afraid.

Sharp words passed between her and the Chinese man, some matter of disagreement. The Chinese man was telling her to leave. He was pointing to the door. He turned his back on the girl, and began to bother himself with the dirty stove. The girl took a purse from a hook on the wall, and stood defiantly until the Chinese man counted out the money that was her pay and slid it across the wooden countertop to her.

—*Your daddy was here, he'd break you of your bad company*, the Chinese man called after her. But she was already gone, her steps like soft drumbeats out on the wooden porch. Boubacar studied the coils of rope and the sacks of catfish feed and the rubber fisherman boots, black with crimson linings and upturned toes.

Boubacar pointed to the eggs and held up two fingers. The Chinese man fished them out with grimy steel tongs, placed them in a small Styrofoam box, and pinched its edges closed. Boubacar chose bananas and chocolate. He studied carefully a can shaped like a rocketship with a picture of a wedge of orange cheese on it. He put the can down, then chose a Blue Horse school tablet and pencils.

—*Get you some Saltines there, and I'll show you how that works*, the Chinese man said, and motioned to the mysterious rocket-ship can. Boubacar handed the can across the counter and watched the man snap the orange cap off and turn it upside down. He resisted the urge to take a step backwards and stood while the man spread a curlicue of orange onto the cracker. It was unlike any orange the boy had ever seen. —*Try that*, the man said, already fixing a curlicue for himself.

Boubacar waited until the man was putting a cracker in his own mouth, then he touched his tongue politely to the cracker. Cheese, it was. Astronaut cheese. Very salty and good.

He had his gift twenty-dollar bill ready when the Chinese man totaled up the cost. He would use the change for the jukebox. He sat down at a table and opened his paper bag of food. The Chinese man began to scrape at the old stove with a bricklayer's trowel to get the day's grease off.

—*How old are you? You got a green card? You want a job?* The Chinese man called over his shoulder.

—*Fifteen*, Boubacar said. —*What is green card?*

Angus studied him. —*Can't no cash pass between us until you get your green card, but I can give you food and such like. I'll be needing help at night*, Angus said to him, wiping his hands on his apron. —*If that suits you.*

—*That green card*, the boy echoed, and he was already stepping over to the jukebox.

—*Wait*, the Chinese man called out. —*Don't keep putting your own money in that thing. It don't always give you what you axe for. Get you some quarters out of the Dixie cup up there. Play D-17. Play that one. See what you get.*

Boubacar reached in the cup, smiling. America: so rich, money was lying around like water in paper cups. Each quarter was painted red or pink, and he recognized the pink: pomegranate, the same as the fingertips of the girl with the gold tooth, whose job he had just taken somehow.

It didn't matter, he told himself. She was a girl, she should be at home, not out among strangers after dark. What man would marry such a girl who had mingled so freely with strangers?

He pressed the buttons, waited. Guitars with strings that sounded like big rubber bands filled the air. A young woman's voice was rough and shrill at the same time.

I've been to Nagasaki
Hiroshima, too
The same I did to them, baby,
I can do to you.

The Chinese man grinned. —*That's rockabilly. You know rockabilly? Wanda Jackson. Nineteen and fifty... I forget. That's her pitcher on the wall over there.*

The Chinese man's crabbed finger gestured toward a fly-specked photo on the wall, a bosomy young woman in a tight bodice. Beautiful breasts were beneath that bodice. The boy strained to hear the words of the song. He couldn't quite match the beautiful face and breasts to the angry voice.

Well, you can say I'm crazy
So deaf and dumb
But I can cause destruction
Just like the atom bum.

The Chinese man's name, he learned, was Angus Chien. By closing time, which was ten o'clock, Boubacar had learned how to sprinkle the pungent sweeping compound on the floor and whisk it clean, and how to get the stove ready for the next morning. When he was done with the tasks he'd been given, the boy looked up to see Angus watching him, his fingers pressed together like the steeple of an infidel's church. He awaited more instruction, glanced around the store.

—*You come of a evening, you help me get ready for the next day. Play the jukebox all you want.*

Boubacar thought of the girl, Ayesha, but he did not think she would hold it against him that he now had her job. Females understood the way things must be. The man must have the job. Women fetch water, he thought, remembering watching his little sister balance two buckets coming from the common well on his street.

But in America there was plenty of water to go around for all. Water was as inconsequential as air. What did women do?

—*Later, man,* he said to Angus, giving the thumbs-up sign, and walked out into the night, bearing his small sack of groceries and some Nutty Buddy ice-cream cones that Angus had insisted he take home.

The fat calico had finished its meat and was washing its face. The sun was going down over the river, which the boy could sense but not see, and the sunlight reflected off the cheap brass lamps and metal drum kits in the window of the junk shop next door. BLACKJACK ZION RESCUE MISSION, said the sign. OPEN MONDAYS.

The boy paused in front of its window, peering past its black iron bars at the merchandise within. Magnificent shiny wigs, stiletto-heeled boots, paste jewelry piled like treasures of impostor pharoahs. A small smoke-colored cat dozed peaceably curled inside the hollow bass drum of a flashy red drum kit. Musical instruments hung suspended from the ceiling, dangling like sausages. A silver disco ball reflected the light of the red neon pig hundreds of times at once. On the wall above the drum kit hung an odd guitar made of silver steel, with elegant chrysanthemums etched into its side.

It was like a cinema spaceship with strings.

It was like a dream someone had had of the future, once upon a time.

It was the most beautiful thing he had seen in all America, more than the jukebox, more than the Chevrolet.

Boubacar raised a hand and pressed his fingertips against the glass that separated him from the guitar. He studied its every detail, and counted the chrysanthemums. *National Steel*

Guitar, he read, but he could not make out the price. Steel cones were built into the side of the guitar, shaped like loudspeakers. He leaned so close to the glass his forehead struck it. The silver guitar mesmerized him, filling him with something that felt like prayers, like possibility. The guitar was old and venerable, and he knew somehow that it was not one of the disposable ones.

He would never smash the silver guitar, if Allah blessed him enough to own it.

To smash an instrument was to destroy the spirits it harbored.

He would never part with it, if ever he happened to own it.

—*Later, man,* he said softly, his fingertips still on the glass. He was reluctant to leave it, as if it might disappear. He had to go. The Nutty Buddies would melt.

America is easy, Boubacar reasoned, walking away. You get off the plane, you are *bizan.* You ride in the six-mabone car, they give you a job. In paper cups they have free money painted red like the toes of fancy women. Crossing the dead orchard, he held up an arm and whirled in circles like a Sufi, and some words from the jukebox suddenly organized themselves in his mind: *Are you ready for the great atomic power?* In his loneliness the boy imagined that the stark trees of the dead orchard watched over him, old ancestors refraining from comment.

Provenance

Some time before it arrived at the Blackjack Zion Rescue Mission, the National Steel guitar had been resting in its case on a street curb in midtown Memphis, next to its somewhat rightful owner, a white boy named Chance Semmes who was sitting in front of the Hi-Tone Club. The boy and two friends were surveying the evening's possibilities for getting into the club without being of legal age. All three had dark hair gelled into spiny spikes, and each was dressed entirely in black, right down to the steel-toed boots they called shitkickers.

He was fifteen and did not particularly enjoy ownership of the guitar, which had been his great-grandfather's. He hated the unwieldy heaviness of the guitar, and used it more as a retro fashion accessory than an instrument. It was always useful for attracting a certain kind of girl. Someday, during the finale of some rock concert starring himself, at the close of some song he would compose himself, he planned to raise the National Steel over his head and smash it downward, full body slam in World Wrestling Association style, bringing his black-booted foot down on it again and again. He had imagined many times the orgasm of dissonance it would create.

On the last evening the guitar was in Chance's possession, he had taken it out of its case and was duplicating some chords to a Slipknot song when a vintage bottle-green Comet with New Jersey license plates pulled into the parking lot beside the Hi-Tone. The car was its own profundity, campy tailfins aglow.

A black girl with blue eyes leaned out. She wore a fringed scarf around her slender neck, loosely coiled in a way that hinted of bohemian life. She was beautiful enough to stun the three boys speechless.

—*Can you tell us where we can hear some blues?*

She was black, her eyes were blue. Beside her in the car was a pallid young white man with an uninspired goatee. He seemed to be in a chemically altered state. A blue heeler with vacant eyes was sitting up expectantly in the backseat. Chance had the presence of mind to walk over to the car and lean in, the guitar dangling beside him.

—*What kind of blues? Tourist blues are down on Beale Street.*

—*Real blues,* the girl interrupted.

—*The Harlem Swing Club. Just over the line in Mississippi. I can take you there,* he said, surprising even himself. He'd never been there but had heard about it in the Hi-Tone.

—*Most excellent is thy name,* droned the guy with the goatee, in the kind of nasal pomposity that indicates a certain degree of being stoned.

The boy put the guitar back in its case and put the case in the backseat of the green Comet between himself and the dog, which kept glancing over at him and growling faintly. The dog kept its growl deep in his chest, as if he knew it was wrong.

—*Shut up, Cobain,*

—*His name is Cobain?*

—*Yeah.*

—*Cool.*

At the first REPENT sign tacked to a tree, the girl had slowed the car down.

—*You'll want to be careful on this road,* the pallid goatee said to the girl. —*Pretty little black wench like yourself.*

—*This is the highway Bessie Smith had her wreck on,* Chance offered.

—*Excellent, most excellent.* The goatee pulled out a cell phone and flipped it open. He moved his fingers over the buttons like someone doing the decades on a rosary, then spoke into it. —*You'll never guess where I am. I'm on the road that fucking Bessie Smith died on.*

—We, the girl corrected him. —*We're on the road Bessie Smith died on.*

Chance didn't correct either of them, suddenly unwilling to explain about the hospital in Clarksdale not taking her in, about the Riverside Hotel. He didn't want them to think he was some emo blues geek. The boy was well versed in blues but stopped playing it on the same afternoon his mother praised him for it. And he wouldn't be caught dead at the crossroads in Clarksdale where Robert Johnson met up with the devil. That was for pale New Yorkers, to step out of their cars and look around as if they'd landed on a remote moon of Pluto.

He told them about Prophet Pegues, about the Chicago record contracts that robbed him, about the bank Prophet robbed and his years in Joliet, about the Nation of Islam. He told them about the Dutch and the Japanese who flew in to Memphis and took cabs to hear the Prophet play. Then told them about the old man's refusal to make records ever again.

—*Well, we'll just see about that,* the goatee murmured. —*We'll just see.*

—*He's a producer,* the girl said proudly.

Chance felt an uneasy mingling of envy, interest, and dismay.

Navigating by hearsay at the Hi-Tone, Chance knew they had arrived when there were cars lined up on the highway. The license plates were from counties all over, *Tippah, Adams,*

Coahoma, Sharkey, Issaquena. The doors slammed on the green Comet after the girl parked it on the shoulder a good mile from the Harlem Swing Club. They walked in silence down the highway to the club. Dark figures milled about outside, silhouetted by the flashing-arrow sign.

—*Just keep looking straight ahead and walk in,* the boy repeated what he remembered hearing someone say once at the Hi-Tone. —*It makes them nervous if you actually see the crack deals, especially if you're not buying.*

The old alligator guitar case attracted some stares when the boy carried it inside.

The pool table was obscured somewhat by the bent backs of black men in thin shirts, intent on the quiet click of the balls kissing sharply before they rocketed into side pockets. A woman was sitting at a little aluminum boat table that served as the admission gate to the club, and she took their money and slapped an "X" on their hands with a Sharpie. She hardly saw the white boy with the guitar case, but she took in every detail of the black girl's elegance, her gossamer scarf wound in interminable circles around her long neck. She noticed the boy's guitar case then, and her eyebrows arched skeptically.

—*I came to jam with the Prophet, if I may,* the boy with the case explained, and the woman closed her eyes in annoyance.

—*Well, you too late. Less you want to play in that graveyard out there,* she said, her eyes revealing no emotion of any use. An amplifier squealed and growled in a corner, and there was a soft curse into a microphone.

—*Oh,* the goatee said in ravaged breath. —*If that's the case—*

The woman looked at him with supreme boredom. —*No refunds.*

—*This music will be fine,* the girl said.

—*Ain't nobody play in here except my sons. You bring your*

dog in, he got to pay, too. But you best put your git-top back in your car. We are not responsible for no accident or theff.

So Chance walked the gauntlet of bemused stares from the crack dealers and their customers to put the case back in the car. Twenty or so others saw him lay it in the backseat of the old Comet. Back inside, the sons of Prophet Pegues had begun to cover their father's old songs thickly and inaccurately, the way apprentices might approach the laying of brick.

Two men in overalls danced with each other, jelly glasses of the last of Prophet's white lightning in their hands. White frat boys from Ole Miss stood rooted to the floor with their pretty dates from the coast, except for one in an SAE shirt who danced alone like a circus bear chained to the floor.

—*Excellent, man,* said the goatee, nodding, and seeming to address them from a great distance. —*Most excellent.*

The coastal girls somehow disturbed the simple ecology of the place, their expensively manicured nails reaching for the tawny bottles of Chivas they'd brought with them, lined up on the table like a barrier reef between themselves and the black people. The black people drank the last of Prophet Pegues's rotgut, clear as lighter fluid, out of Bama jelly glasses, or coffee mugs that said things like *Coldwater Taxidermy* or *Bank of Holly Springs.* When the blue-eyed girl brought him over a cup—*Grambling State Athletic Department*—Chance's eyes had flared.

—*How am I breaking the law? Let me count the ways,* he said appreciatively.

In the meantime, a black boy of about ten or eleven was tuning an electric guitar in the chicken-wire cage. A girl of thirteen or so was frying catfish on the other side of the pool tables.

By the time Chance was feeling the effects of the rotgut, he was dancing between two women in matching gold lamé sports coats, each woman big enough to crush him. A sharecropper in railroad overalls polkaed over and tipped his hat, and the boy shook his hand and bowed. By the time Chance got around to dancing with the black girl with the blue eyes, she had already taken off her elegant scarf and wound it around the goatee's neck for safekeeping. The goatee didn't dance; he assessed the players in the chicken-wire cage, his head nodding efficiently like a metronome.

By that time the crackheads outside were circling the green Comet, admiring its frog-eye headlights and its campy tailfins. One of them thumped his hand on the hood: —*You hear that? Man, they don't make 'em that solit no more.*

All leaned in to admire the upholstery, and there they saw the old guitar case.

Antique cars were easy. Only a wire coat hanger was required.

By the time someone located a coat hanger, Chance was walking in the field behind the Harlem Swing Club, headed for the cemetery with the girl and the goatee in tow. His Grambling State mug was still half full, but his head was hollow and incandescent enough to light their way in the dark. The goatee was following a few paces behind with his cell phone, murmuring into it, trying to get a witness. The blue heeler whimpered a little, but was afraid enough of the immense open space that he sniffed the ground carefully, as if it would be necessary to remember his way back. They made a processional of silhouettes that the crackheads could clearly see.

In the same moment the boy was sinking to his knees in the dry weeds near a new grave with a small tin nameplate staked at the head of it, one of the crackheads, also a son of Prophet Pegues, was lifting the National Steel guitar out of the backseat of the green Comet. So great was his respect for the old car and the beautiful girl who had driven it there, the crackhead locked the door when he closed it, and polished the chrome a bit with the sleeve of his jacket.

By the time the National Steel was locked inside the trunk of the crackheads' taxi-painted Chevrolet Caprice, Chance was recumbent on Solomon Chien's tombstone, sipping at the moonshine with grim determination. It occurred to him that he might never see home again. The stars wheeled in the sky, and the tombstone under his back felt warm. He was unable any longer to offer resistance to the great universe above, and he raised his mug of rotgut in salute to the stars.

The girl was walking in a wide arc around the field, her arms up, as if to take it all in.

The goatee had raised a witness on the phone, and waved his arm as he spoke, looking around him, the very model of a modern minor mogul. —*Prophet Pegues*, he said. —*No tombstone. Why do they always fucking die without the money to have tombstones?*

—*Because assholes like you take all their money*, Chance giggled from galaxies away.

The girl held her skirts up delicately with one hand and her cigarette lighter aloft with the other, reading the names on the stones aloud, —*Solomon Chien, Rose Chien. These people are Chinese!*

—*There are Chinese graves here*, the goatee duly relayed into his phone to his witness.

She stopped before a fierce homemade grave, Portland cement with scriptural statements carved on its surface. She waved the lit cigarette lighter over the grave in a wide arc. Pressed into the cement surface were bits of china and colored shards of old bottles. The china looked like rotogravure in the darkness. She knelt in the grass and stared closely at the china. Haviland moss roses. It matched the chocolate pot on the sideboard in her parents' house in Princeton. Centered in the shards of china and bits of bottle was a glass-covered cameo of a woman in the prime of her life with her hair marcelled into waves, and a high lace collar. The girl read the inscription aloud.

ARIADNE JONES
1875–1943

Chance studied the night sky. Red dots coursed across the region formerly known as heaven. The red dots were probably enormous metal jets full of people, the pilots navigating by the instructions of distant strangers they'd never see. He imagined that he could see vapor trails of each plane, concentric, redundant webs of light. The satellites were out, companionably interleaving what must surely be a multitude of human voices with the contrails. The boy was very drunk, and it all seemed very profound.

—*Look*, he said. —*Look at that.*

The girl had taken out her own cell phone. She and the goatee had their backs to each other, each conversing to distant witnesses.

—*Mom?* the girl said, her voice sounding captive in her throat. —*What was the name of the town where your grandmother lived?*

—*We have got hold of the most amazing hooch*, the goatee said to his distant witness. —*Here in a fucking cemetery in fucking Mississippi. I may never leave here, man.*

—*Listen.* The girl held her phone out so her mother could hear. —*This is Mississippi.* The wall of frog music and locusts roared into the phone and up to the satellite.

—*Oh, baby*, a woman's tinny voice came from across the continent, bouncing off the river of stars above and into Chance's ears. —*Why you want to be back in that place?*

—*It was meant to be*, Chance explained to the multitudes whose voices he could see above, holding his Grambling State

mug carefully aloft. His other hand seemed to caress the weary
brow of the night.

Back at the Harlem Swing Club, the crackhead's hands shook a
bit as he fumbled with the clasp to the old case, then he laid it
open like a neatly filleted fish on the hood of a black Escalade
to whose owner he owed a few thousand dollars.

—The car, man. Don't scratch the car.

There the old guitar lay, pocked and dinged. Its nickel plating was worn away in certain spots, wherever hands and fingertips lingered so long before. Rashad had no respect for musical
instruments, but he had a deep and abiding respect for debts
owed to himself. He motioned for the crackhead to open the
guitar case, imagining fat rolls of cash within. Underneath the
guitar, yellowing sheet music was strewn, and other random
papers that looked like a rebuke to Rashad, whose ability to
read was on the underside of average.

The crackhead said, —Get three thousand for this on eBay.
Maybe four.

Rashad rifled around in the sheet music while his fingers
traced along the velvet, checking, checking, looking for secret
compartments, the money. When he found none, he handed a
piece of sheet music to the man in a jeweled jacket next to him,
who read it as if it were malodorous:

YOU CAN PLAY THE HAWAIIAN GUITAR

JUST LIKE THE HAWAIIANS

ONLY 4 EASY MOTIONS

WE FURNISH EVERYTHING

SEND FOR DETAILS TODAY.

Rashad fondled his chin hair and studied the face of the crack-head.

—*Don't make me have to kill you, nigger.*

It was meant to be, Chance thought the next afternoon, stumbling downstairs to his solicitous mother, holding his heavy head, remembering that the guitar was gone. He would have to delay telling his mother, but he felt strangely free. He already had visions of the next instrument he would own. He called a friend, and by nightfall was picking out the tablature of a Silverchair song he liked, on the borrowed red Fender Stratocaster he liked. He felt a certain amount of reassurance in the fact that there were thousands of guitars like it in the world, and thousands had learned to play them well. Some had learned to play powerfully.

People had heard that Silverchair song and killed themselves.

Now that was *power,* the boy mused.

When the crackhead brought the National Steel guitar into the Blackjack Zion Rescue Mission, the nun knew him, not because he was a crackhead, but because she had been present at his birth at the nuns' clinic in Tutwiler, nineteen years before. She always remembered, whenever she saw him. There had been some back-and-forth between the sisters about the birth certificate. She herself had been the only one to know how to spell *Haile Selassie Pegues.*

—*Was this your father's guitar?*

The young man shrugged and did not raise his eyes.

—*I can go twenty-five on this. No more.* She counted out the bills. Paying too much only made room for more trouble.

She had him hang the guitar in the window next to a dobro, with the faux alligator case open.

The sheet music was found by the side of the road by Bebe Marie Abide, who was out scavenging for whatever the evening's celebrants left behind. Her face had softened at the sight of the pages strewn like abandoned valentines, fly-specked and damp with dew. She had gently pried the wet pages apart with an oyster knife she always carried for safety from predators.

Standing in her Mexican pony blanket and black bowler hat, she studied the sheet music by the side of the road, and could easily have been mistaken for someone reading a map.

> I'll weave a lei of stars for you
> To wear on nights like this
> Each time you wear my lei of stars
> I'll greet you with a kiss

Voices in her mind arose, then fell, fanned into flame by other voices. Connections announced themselves: a ringing in her ears and the taste of metal on her tongue. Years peeled away like burning skin. Her mother's paintings burning in a bathtub. The image of herself, the painting of her as a little girl, burning in the zinc bathtub. Paris, 1938. The trees like black lace against the winter sky, the Hawaiian music on the jukebox in the American club, the waiter who said, —You like that Sol Hoopii, huh?

She bundled all the pages together and took them home to her boathouse. Holding in her mouth a chocolate football to fend off the gunmetal taste, she weighted the pages with old books to flatten them. Using the trusty oyster knife, she cut them to fit perfectly inside the walls of a bottle-cap birdhouse she had made from green Heineken beer caps picked up in the alleys of Memphis. For a roof, she clamped on the cover of an ancient leather book, *The Sorrows of Young Werther,* and wired it firmly down.

By the time that particular bottle-cap birdhouse with the Hawaiian sheet-music walls had been sold in Memphis, the National Steel guitar was hanging high above its opened faux alligator case and a red drum kit pawned by a crystal-meth aficionado from Coldwater. On the first day the guitar was there, the calico cat from the Celestial Grocery sniffed daintily at the velvet lining of the alligator case below, contemplating its origins. Then she climbed daintily into it and rested her rotund, pregnant belly, looking around in quiet relief, *here.*

By the time her kittens were born in it, they were shaded by an ivory *peau de soie* wedding dress pawned by a Colorado girl who backed out of a Delta wedding at the last minute. The nuns had hung it like a canopy to give the cat some privacy and some shade from the morning sun.

By the time Boubacar the Mauritanian boy arrived in America and saw the National Steel on the wall, the kittens were old enough to climb out of the case. They often played around a gold plaster-of-Paris bust of Elvis sporting several layers of costume jewelry necklaces of the sort Baptist ladies with blue hair used to wear to church when Eisenhower was president, as well as a couple of medallions that said *King of Comus.* The Elvis bust was the sort you had to be very drunk and persistent to win at traveling carnivals. A deckhand from the dredger *Stackolee* had lost a week's wages winning it. His woman had brought it in and left with enough Enfamil to feed her baby for two days. While the kittens romped and swatted the Mardi Gras trinkets and beads on the bust, the Mauritanian boy looked up at the guitar and thought, *mine.*

Golden Cities, Golden Towns

—*Why don't you use your own guitar anymore?*

—*What?* the boy named Chance shouted to his mother, over the traffic outside. —*What did you say?* He paused with his ear unstoppered, the little black foam disk of his headset poised for reinsertion.

—*I said, why don't you use the guitar we gave you? Grandy's old silver National.*

—*I'm using Darby's Fender right now*, he shouted, looking suddenly away from his mother. —*What I really need is a Fender Strat. When you get paid?* He turned his attention to the small game device in his hands.

It was rush hour in Memphis, down by the riverside. An eighteen-wheeler blocked her view on the right, presented her with the message *Hanjin*. A man in a red pickup truck with a cab full of migrant workers was trying to muscle his way around the truck, forcing her left when she needed to merge right. On the radio, a breathless preacher harangued the airwaves, in trailer-park English, about the coming apocalypse.

She could see ahead and above to the tight fistula of traffic she would have to nudge their Volvo station wagon into to get the boy where he needed to go. His guitar teacher had moved his studio to a walk-up over the Perez Cigar Company downtown, which added ten miles onto the drive, plus the double-helix of six-lane traffic. Raine had just enough time to look at the driver before the red pickup truck moved another few inches, threatening to ram her. TOMÁS TULIA, GENERAL CON-TRACTOR. The driver's eyes met hers, and they carried no emotion. It was nothing personal, you just couldn't look into someone's eyes out there; you might drift two inches to the left or right and inadvertently kill someone.

She glanced back at the road, then at her boy. His hair was sculpted into an explosion of small spikes, like a spiny undersea anemone that needs to intimidate its predators. Somewhere beneath that carapace of grooming products and electronic bings was the boy she loved fiercely.

—*Where will you be when the hand of God takes you up?* said the radio preacher. —*You cannot know the day. You cannot know the hour. But God knows. He has set the alarm. And you keep hittin' that snooze button.*

The *Hanjin* truck seemed to be listing towards Raine's car as the ramp rose up before them and curved. Raine gripped the wheel and leveled her eyes straight ahead. You couldn't slow down, or you could die. You couldn't have a flat tire, or you could die, just in a matter of seconds. If anyone stopped to help you, that person could die, too. She had her son in the car, both of them a hair's breadth from sudden death, and her palms were sweating.

Raine's boy was mouthing words with his eyes closed, as if it were the anthem to some alternate nation, —*I don't care about anything but me.*

They were almost to the midpoint of the double-helix, which usually felt wide open and calm in the same frightening way that the eyes of tornadoes feel open and calm. The *Hanjin* truck accelerated only enough to lumber over directly in front of her, causing her to tap her brake softly, once, as of telegraphing a plea to the car behind her, *please.* She fought the urge to close her eyes. The center of the double-helix always felt like a vanishing point, like she was being erased, a mere dust-mote among other swirling specks. She blinked against the urge to close her eyes.

They could meet their deaths right then and there, with only the screams of strangers for instruction. The holy-roller preacher for her, some rock-and-roll druggie for him.

Gripping the wheel tightly with her left hand, she reached out and pushed the *seek* button. *American woman, stay away from me,* snarled the radio. The boy stared out the window, out where some better life surely lay, elsewhere.

Chains of eighteen-wheelers proceeded at breakneck speeds hundreds of feet above her in the air. She felt assaulted with information. Vehicles floated onto the freeway, anchored by nothing. Somewhere far below was her husband's office window, but she could not turn to look.

As she guided the car into the curve of the exit ramp, she felt faint, as if she were entering a dark tunnel. Why did she want to close her eyes? What was there to keep them all from simply floating off into space? It certainly seemed possible at those speeds. Gripping the wheel, she passed within five feet of a tanker—FLAMMABLE CONTENTS—traveling at eighty miles per hour. She slowed to accommodate a horse trailer from Broken Arrow, Oklahoma. Big brown eyes looked back at her through metal slats, hurtling through space at seventy-seven miles per hour.

Tyson Foods, Hunt, Dixie Barrel, the big trucks dwarfed her Volvo.

She was now only a hundred feet above the actual earth, the ground, the earth, where the guitar lesson was to take place. It was necessary to drive three blocks in the opposite direction and then to turn back. She slowed down, her spine congealed.

In a flash of irritation, she punched a button, any button.

—*Every man for himself,* Laurie Anderson sang. —*Yo de lay hee hoo. Golden cities, golden towns.*

—*Listen to this,* Raine said. —*You'll like this. I used to listen to this in college.* Her son grimaced at the indignity of being forced to listen to any music by anyone old enough to be his mother. Older women were irrelevant in his universe, except when they wrote checks.

Raine wanted to lay into the boy about how she felt shame and embarrassment when he went out into the world wearing, as he did every day, what appeared to be a toupee made of spiny sea urchins. And the shoes, the *shitkickers,* she mourned. They were vaguely reminiscent of grainy old photos of secret police in totalitarian states.

It was all about camouflage and protection, she reminded herself. She stayed silent for the rest of the drive. The boy had not noticed her problem with the ramps, and she was grateful. There were certain advantages to being invisible.

The sun glinted off the Pyramid, and then it was downhill all the way.

It was insane, what being *sane* required.

Raine parked near Court Square, so Chance could walk alone up the street, past panhandlers and pimps and purveyors of certain controlled substances. She went into the Yellow Rose Café to wait the hour out. She took an empty table by the window.

—*Just coffee, please,* she said to the young waitress, who seemed relieved at the simplicity of it. Raine pulled a sheaf of student papers out of her book bag, fifth-grade social studies quizzes, and put on the gold-rimmed eyeglasses she wore on a black cord around her neck. *Indentured servants were old they didn't have any teeth,* she read. That was offered by the son of a cotton broker who sat in a shaft of sunlight every morning in her first-period class, beautiful and vacant in a Renaissance kind of way. She folded the paper shut, put it at the bottom of the pile. She took off the glasses and let them drop where they dangled below her breasts.

She kneaded her left temple with a forefinger, to loosen the stubborn little knot of pulse there. When *did* she get paid again?

Fine needles of rain were beginning to fall. It had been years, really, since she'd been to this part of town. Across Court Square, young junkies on the benches still leaned into each other with the tenderness of old lovers. Lovers still languished in the drug afforded by early love, oblivious to the old addicts. The junkies still nodded to themselves in profound and private benediction. An aging white hippie sang listless, proficient blues with a tarnished voice, her guitar case open for donations.

The Kress building stood out like a terra-cotta birthday cake trimmed in blue, yellow, and green piping. On the sidewalk in front of its doors, a small figure sported a Mexican pony blanket and a baseball cap atop a black bowler. Raine had seen the woman before around town, selling roses and bottle-cap birdhouses from an ancient card table. This day, she also seemed to have possession of a Walgreens shopping cart. The cart had a sign:

ROSES CASH AND CARRY.
BIRDHOUSE CUSTOM MADE.

The little woman stood with feet solidly apart, as if an earthquake were imminent. She unfolded a black plastic garbage bag with great care and slipped it over herself for a raincoat. She had cut a hole for her face. She wore the garbage bag with panache, as if it were a superhero's cape.

Raine opened another student paper, ran her finger down the crease, and began to read. *Denture servants was free, but not free to go. Like we have Lupe, and she can't leave, but she is not a slave. Slavery is bad. Lupe is good to me and always has my snack ready after school. She went to see her children last summer.*

Raine put the paper on the bottom of the stack. She stared out the window.

Raine's husband's office was four blocks away, but she never went there. Over the years she had learned not to surprise him there. She might be interrupting an important *policy* meeting with the flavor of the week, one of the endless procession of women with the same names, *Candy Randy Sandy*. They were usually blonde, and somewhere roughly half his age, afflicted with the same inevitable intoxication with the *self* that was to twenty-year-olds what acne was to teenagers.

Raine stared out the window at the little old woman selling roses. She supposed the woman simply folded up the whole little operation at sundown and went . . . *where?* It seemed a stunning luxury to Raine, for a moment, the way the woman had nowhere to go, no home, nothing to anchor her.

Most of the Court Square pedestrians avoided looking at the old woman. A young red-haired woman in a stunning silk suit tripped along gamely in her spiky high heels, while the men she was with did not even break stride to accommodate her. She stopped and bought a birdhouse, examining each one very carefully before choosing. They were made of metal soda bottle caps wired together, Raine saw as the woman walked closer.

The men had walked on without her, as if her mission were

not important enough to warrant their attention. They came into the Yellow Rose, taking the table next to her, still talking. Raine looked away.

—*It's the kind of thing you dream about,* the young man said. —*Once in a lifetime.*

The other man was like one of a thousand in Memphis, a kind of soft-spoken blue-eyed blond man who spends a great deal of money to look exactly like the others: unnoticeable.

—*How so?*

—*All that land is dirt cheap. Nobody knows about the proposal yet. So the window of opportunity is very narrow here.*

—*Is it a done deal? The bridge?*

—*Bill hasn't passed in Jackson yet, and that will be under wraps for a while, till all the land can be consolidated into one parcel.*

—*How long?*

—*I'm working on it. Delta people are slow to change.*

—*This could be really, really big.*

—*No shit, Sherlock.*

—*The Gaming Commission?*

—*No biggie. The casinos want it, so they want it.*

The young woman looked up then and saw Raine staring at her intently, and her eyes rasped across Raine's middle-aged body and face, coming to rest on the gold glasses dangling from the black cord and dropping to her flat sensible shoes. The younger woman's eyelids narrowed triumphantly: *I will never let myself become you.*

Raine let her eyes meet the younger woman's, and she smiled sweetly as if to deflect her contempt. Raine had believed, once, that she'd never wear glasses on a string the way old ladies did. Here she was, the glasses dangling on the string.

They paid their check and left, deep in conversation. Raine looked at her watch. Twenty minutes to go.

She saw then the papers still tucked under the place mat on

the table they had occupied. Raine reached over and slid the papers out in the same motion she was extracting bills from her purse. The waitress was enchanted by the tiny television behind the counter: a pregnant woman hurling a chair at one of the three men who could possibly have fathered her child.

—*Thanks,* Raine said, laying the money down on the counter. She walked out with the man's papers in her hand. She had thirty minutes before her son returned from his lesson.

She hurried to cross Court Square, oblivious to the panhandlers. She couldn't see the red-haired woman anywhere. Maybe she could just mail the papers back to the address on the letterhead. It was not good letterhead, she noted, but the cheap and sleazy kind.

She glanced down at the letterhead. *Futuristics.* They were papers concerning possible land purchases in Mississippi. Her eyes came unfocused at all the legal language. She walked as fast as she could. She thought she could see the couple a block away. She didn't agree with their mission, but it seemed the right and helpful thing to do, to return their papers to them.

Why was she intent on helping them out? she wondered idly, slowing her pace a bit. Why was she always moving in the opposite direction from the one she believed in? She stopped. She looked around. Over by the Kress building was a trash receptacle brimming with refuse. She walked over and stuffed the papers into it carefully.

—*Birdhouses, custom made,* the little figure in the garbage bag called out dispassionately, like a carnival barker. —*For all your birdlike needs.*

A man in a uniform was shaking his head and pointing down the way, to the river, *move along now.*

The little figure in the garbage bag came into focus, the more Raine watched.

Her hair was wispy and wild, like the dimestore decoration that used to be called angel hair. Her baseball cap said *Yoko-*

hama Carp. Beneath it, her eyes burned blue and electric with inquiry. She was standing in a shaft of afternoon light that made her squint.

—*Is there a problem?* Raine asked. She was a teacher; she was accustomed to taking charge of confusion in public. The man was not a policeman, but some kind of hospitality volunteer for the city. His chest was cluttered with badges and ribbons, testaments to municipal meaninglessness.

—*She don't have a license. I'm sorry, it's the rules. If she go on down there on Front where the tourists go, nobody say anything.*

The old woman's shoulders seemed to sag beneath the black garbage bag, and she looked away from them when she spoke. —*There has been some mistake. My father was Henri Matisse, you know.* Her voice had a rasp, an edge that commanded attention.

In the silence that followed, Raine could hear the screech of the trolley and the drone of a plane overhead. The hospitality man grinned foolishly and shook his head, as if to spur on his next thoughts. He had a walkie-talkie holstered on his belt, and the weight of its importance brought a certain John Wayne swagger to his movements.

—*She best be movin' on now*, the hospitality man said.

—*I can hear everything you think*, the old woman said confidentially. —*Down at the bank, they're bettin' against me. Bettin' against me with telephone dimes. They think my citizenship in the gulag of good women is only honorary.*

The uniformed volunteer peeled the walkie-talkie out of its holster and began to punch numbers. He spoke officious things into it, to distant people.

—*Here, I've got thirty dollars*, Raine said to the woman in thin, breathless sentences, while she rummaged in her purse. —*What will that buy me?*

The woman's eyes burned bluer for a few seconds. She waved her hand elegantly over her goods. She selected three bunches of roses soaking in a faded plastic Baskin-Robbins ice cream tub. They were the color of parchment, tinged with coral.

—*Fire and Ice, mighty nice,* the old woman said, smiling at her without looking at her.

The woman wrapped the roses carefully in newspaper, making small noises of pleasure down in her throat. She handed them to Raine, gently as handling a newborn. —*But wait,* she said, in perfect mimicry of a television announcer. —*There's more. I can tell by your shoes, you used to be somebody.* She lifted up a small birdhouse, and said confidentially, with a kindness that seemed real, —*A little fresh fruit from the orchard of abandoned dreams.*

—*Oh, gosh,* Raine said, oddly and irrelevantly happy. The birdhouse walls were green Heineken caps wired together. It was lined with old sheet music. Its roof was a scuffed leather book, opened and attached with baling wire to the bottle caps. Raine studied the faded gilt title on the spine. *The Sorrows of Young Werther.*

lost love

—*I can't believe you actually paid money for that,* her son said, coming across Court Square to the bench where she sat waiting for him with the birdhouse in her lap. He stared at it, his eyes full of impeachment. The boy had recently acquired the notion that all family income was to be applied to his rock star ambitions.

—*How did your lesson go?* Raine asked.

—*Okay, I guess,* he shrugged. His hands bongoed on the dashboard. He mentioned a video game, a mere $159.99. He *needed* it. He would somehow acquire lesser stature among peers if he did not possess it.

Raine took the long way home, turning the car south onto the first street that had no bridges, no high ramps, no roller-coaster ride. So the first few minutes of the ride took them in the opposite direction of the one they needed to travel.

That done, she turned the car toward home and then hesitated at the last bridge between them and the street they lived on, the curving viaduct on Poplar. She could see, on the other side of the bridge, rows of expensive, dignified houses, one of which belonged to her family.

It's not even a real bridge, she told herself, *just a fat place over the road.* Her heart seemed to sweat in its socket, her hands throbbed on the wheel. Shooting pains flickered across her temples. It was getting worse, her driving problem. The ramp thing was turning into a bridge thing. It seemed to happen whenever she had to drive a car up off the surface of the earth into a high place.

Raine's son was still staring out the window, lip-syncing angry songs about experiences he could not possibly have had. She could read his lips. *Fuck, bitch, ho, homey.* No matter how often she heard the words, it was like being jabbed in the heart each time. Why was he so enchanted with such ugly music?

She was at the bridge; her nerves felt under assault.

What was the name for it, how you had to keep doing something even though your better mind knew it was crazy? Raine took a deep breath and drove across the bridge, a ball of fear in her chest like a hot, swallowed scream. Her foot came off the accelerator, touched the brake, then lifted, and they crossed into the tree-lined conduit home.

Home was Magazine Street, a republic of votive televisions, in any one of the many warrens of the upper-middle classes. It was a neighborhood of strangers, knit together by the shouts of its children playing outside at dusk, and the wispy smell of its perfect dinners cooking. You could peep through its Palladian windows and see the descendants of Big Cotton and the descendants of slaves now living side by side in separate but equal luxury homes. All houses conformed to a similar covenant, as if a certain standard of cheerfulness had been agreed upon in advance. Zinnias appeared punctually in the window boxes in summer, pansies and kale in the cool months. It was all about reassurance, that neighborhood.

After the big daddies of Magazine Street had come home from the jobs they often despised, after they suffered their twenty minutes of contact with their children at the dinner table, they retired to their big chairs in front of their big televisions. There they would sit for entire evenings, pushing buttons on their remote controls, in a manner reminiscent of the space captains of their own childhoods, steering the great vessels they were doomed to inhabit, through the anxious straits and infinite steppes of various hostile galaxies. Outside, in brass letter-boxes intended to evoke simpler centuries, envelopes were at the ready for the postman. It was all about insulation, about keeping squalor and crime out of that neighborhood, crisp mortgage checks often going out in the same mail with other checks made payable to corporations that piped the gunfire and squalor of ghettoes right back in, via cables laid under the Tifton turfgrass. So when a mother such as Raine arrived inside the back door, dressed in her crisp khaki slacks and pink pinstriped shirt, the first words to greet her might well be, *Freeze, muthafucka, or I'll blow your fucking brains out.*

In the Orchard
of Abandoned Dreams

As the copper saucepans gleamed on their racks at night, the mothers of Magazine Street donned their trendy tortoiseshell glasses suspended from black strings around their necks, licked their thumbs, and turned the pages of their magazines, drugged by dulcet imperatives: *Use this handy organizer to appear ten years younger and freshen up that timeworn house.*

Raine Semmes was an obedient habitué of the Magazine Street trance.

Pink is the new beige. Lemongrass is the new rosemary. Parsley is the new groundcover. Freshen up that tired foyer with flowers that express the true new you.

Raine was not born with ornamental beauty, so she had always dreamed the obedient, serviceable dream. Clean sheets on the beds of her children, good china cups and saucers, a decently run household, *order.* She put the pumpkins on the porch when it was time. She put the bulbs in the ground when it was time. She painted the walls a new color when it was time. Financiers in distant cities could borrow millions, banking on the dependability of Raine and numberless other mothers like her, depending on them to respond in certain ways to gentle signals applied with the carefully researched rhythms of a tidal pull.

It was a serious matter, the keeping of the house. The slightest neglect could cause a loss in the value of the property, and everything they had was tied up in that house. Home décor could not be too radical, lest you offend the future owners when you were ready to sell.

Houses were the new banks. Everything the families had was tied up in them.

Raine kept her kitchen radio set on a golden oldies station. Sometimes she sang along when she was alone. She liked to remember the songs, where she'd been when she'd heard them, who she'd been with, who she'd *been*.

> *Close the door, shut the shade.*
> *You don't have to be afraid.*
> *I'll be your baby tonight.*

So much time had passed. She'd been a child in blue jeans and Birkenstocks then. Now she was a woman in Birkenstocks who wore her glasses on a string around her neck.

Her hands began to shake, and she pressed them against the taps of the faucet to steady them, as if the kitchen were a ship riding a sudden swell.

Chance came into the kitchen, and on his way to the refrigerator, flipped the radio to a station he liked, music that always sounded to Raine like a closet full of angry coat hangers, or car crashes in slow motion.

—*Hey. I was listening to that,* she said.

—*Just a minute. Just this one song.*

—*Put it back where I had it.*

Sullenly the boy turned the dial back. He poured himself a glass of milk and left. He left a pool of spilled milk on the counter, as if menial elves would come forth later to mop up. By that time the Doobie Brothers were singing about China Grove.

—*It's all old crap*, the boy said angrily from the stairs.

The first time Raine had heard "China Grove," she'd been rolled into a blanket under the stars with Matthew, out in some farmer's field, beside a little pond. Now there was a mall on that farmer's field, acres of asphalt.

Now she and Matthew had a son who could suck all the oxygen out of a room just by entering it.

He was angry about not getting the new video game, she realized. At last count, there were seven big-ticket items he *needed*, enough to exhaust three months of her teacher's salary.

She stared guiltily at the bottle-cap birdhouse on the kitchen windowsill. She rubbed her fingers across the velvety smoothness of the worn leather book spine transmuted to birdhouse roof. *The Sorrows of Young Werther.* She remembered it with rue from college. How did it go? The young man who offs himself after a girl doesn't want him? Was that the one? She laughed out loud. At least it was good for something.

—*From the orchard of abandoned dreams*, the Rose Lady had said. It was canted at an angle so she could see inside when the porch light shone through. She leaned in to read what was scrawled on the sheet music inside.

The clothes dryer buzzed, Raine's cue to keep moving. After folding the boy's clean underwear, Raine took it upstairs to his room and paused a moment, her eyes panning the room. The faux-alligator guitar case was not in its place behind his door. It was not anywhere in the room. The boy tapped at his computer keyboard, his back to her.

—*Choose an identity*, the game droned.

With this game, it was possible to assume the persona of a hoodlum who could bludgeon street-corner prostitutes to death. She stared at the screen over his shoulder. Identical spurts of electronic blood exploded from a female figure's head every time the simulated male figure kicked her between the legs.

She had bought the boy the game, not understanding what it was.

All the boys on Magazine Street had this game. Some of the dads played it with their boys. The mothers mentioned it sometimes among themselves, quietly when the males were not around, then dropped the subject, which was a way of pretending it didn't matter.

No one wanted to be a complainer or an ingrate.

Virtual screams came from the boy's computer. He didn't realize Raine was in the room. He smiled like a satiated porn star.

Raine shoved his clothes into a too-full drawer and fled the room.

Pink was the new beige, houses the new banks, and violence the new pornography.

A wall away, Raine's daughter, Callie, was gluing magazine pictures of tropical frogs into a scrapbook. The expression on the little girl's face was grim and determined: she was saving the world by gluing the pictures of the frogs into the scrapbook for her teacher at school, carefully.

—*That's great, baby,* Raine said softly, and put her arm around the girl.

Folding her daughter's rosebud-trimmed panties and training bras, then rolling her socks into delicate bundles, her mind kept seeing the digital image of the woman's form, the blood spurting, the electronic kicks. She tried to remember the phrase she'd studied once in college. Something about when you are required to keep believing or doing the opposite thing to what is logical or right. *Distance?* Was that it?

She couldn't remember the name for it, but she could

remember that it was considered dangerous if practiced on a mass scale.

What was it?

Whatever it was, it was the new religion.

She was already dressed in what her children referred to as the Lucille Ball pajamas, baggy pink candy-striped silk trousers and shirt. She brought a vase of roses into the bedroom and put them on the table beside her bed. She wanted to be able to smell them in the dark. She read in a magazine that you could influence your dreams by choosing the scents you were exposed to while you slept.

Her husband was packing for his trip. He glanced at the roses with a frown and disappeared into his closet. It was the money. She had spent money frivolously. Flowers were for special days, wooings for young girls, atonements to wives.

—*Which should I take?* Matthew asked, holding two ties up to his chest, as if he had awarded her a kind of importance that was merely ceremonial, as if he'd included her in his travel plans, as if she would not spend the next week trying to compensate the children for his absence.

Why don't you ask Candy Randy Sandy?

Had she said that? No. She had just thought it.

—*Take the silver diamond pattern one. It matches all four shirts.*

—*Actually, I think I'll take the gray one.*

Where was he going? She had meant to listen at dinner, but her thought of bridges and guitars and the birdhouse had crowded it all out. She noticed several of his shirts in a pile on the closet floor, entangled in hangers, and she bent to straighten them. The shirts would have to be ironed again. He didn't have enough room for his shirts. She had two racks of stiletto heels she never wore anymore. Those could go.

—I can tell by your shoes, the Rose Lady had said. *—You used to be someone.* Raine was bundling all the discarded shirts up to take them to the laundry room, when he finished and turned out the light, as if no one of any importance were in the room, no one at all. She could hear him going down the stairs. She was left kneeling in the dark, clutching shirts, with the odd sensation that she used to be someone. Back in the time when Matthew would sometimes look at her as if he saw her.

Upstairs, the virtual streetwalker died and died and died. In the master bedroom, the German tanks rolled into Poland, exhorted by the Führer. No one was watching. Down in the family room the camera zoomed in to the breasts of a young girl flopping up and down as she screamed and ate live larvae, hungry for the camera. No one was watching.

Downstairs in the kitchen Raine picked the birdhouse up off the windowsill again and tipped it up to study all its facets. It reminded her of a simpler time. Its back wall was lined with the cover of a Blue Horse school tablet. Another wall was lined with yellowed sheet music, *a lei of stars for you.* Over that was a tiny red version of the same runic scrawl that had been on the Rose Lady's shopping cart:

> COME CLOSER ANYONE
> EVER ABANDONED BESIDE THIS RIVER
> HOW IS IT YOU WERE TAUGHT
> TO DESPISE YOUR LIFE?
> THERE IS FOOD FOR THAT FAMISHMENT HERE.

Raine felt the hair tingle at the base of her neck, and she put the birdhouse down. It seemed to have grown hot in her hands. She leaned against the counter, her heart beating. She looked inside again, as if she were receiving secret forbidden instructions.

IN THE ORCHARD OF ABANDONED DREAMS
I AM POURED OUT LIKE WATER
IN THE CITIES OF THE CAESARS
I POUR MYSELF OUT LIKE WATER
LIKE LAUGHTER OVER FROZEN RIVERS.

Staring into the birdhouse, Raine had the odd feeling of being elsewhere, up high, in the dark, capable of seeing vast distances, hundreds of miles in all directions.

Near the back wall of the garage, Raine rolled up her silk pajama sleeves and studied the stacks of neat cardboard packing cartons that had become a kind of storage system for the family. Garages held the secrets of the households, all the cartons of stuff no longer acceptable inside half-million-dollar houses. Somewhere in there was an old anthropology notebook with the word she'd needed all day. But she needed to find the guitar.

It had been her grandfather's, an old National Steel with steel resonator cones, and Art Deco chrysanthemums engraved into its sides. She'd been told it was a collector's item, very valuable. It had always been in the attic when she was growing up. She'd claimed it when she went off to college.

Inside its faux-alligator case was an old ad her grandfather had clipped from a 1937 movie magazine:

YOU CAN PLAY THE HAWAIIAN GUITAR
JUST LIKE THE HAWAIIANS * ONLY 4 EASY MOTIONS
BECAUSE OUR NATIVE HAWAIIAN INSTRUCTORS
WILL SHOW YOU HOW!
WE FURNISH EVERYTHING * SEND FOR DETAILS TODAY.

She loved her grandfather's old guitar and sheet music. It was happy music, mostly, songs like "Hawaiian Rose." Pinned to the velvet of the lid was a yellowing postcard photo of Sol Hoopii at eighteen, smiling, his hair slicked back, three years after he stowed away on the Matson line to get to America. It had been a craze, Hawaiian guitar. There was even a vintage instruction booklet, with photos of plump modish Minnesota matrons smiling for the camera, silver Nationals laid across their laps like steel babies to be burped. She wanted to see these old things again.

Raine had had the guitar cleaned and tuned to give to Chance for his tenth birthday.

She opened each carton, and the guitar was in none of them. It wasn't there. And what had they done with all the old Bob Dylan records? And the anthropology notebook?

I can tell by your shoes, you used to be somebody.

Ensconced in the big bed in her Lucille Ball pajamas, Raine read more magazines. Her faucets, she realized, were out-of-date. So were the lavatories. It was all raised basins now. Everything was Etruscan, even though two years before, she'd installed hand-painted sinks after the fashion of *Provence.* She tossed the magazines on the floor, disgruntled. It never stopped.

Some years before, Raine had won the door prize at some meaningless teachers' luncheon, a blank book, covered in blue raw silk. On the first page the previous year, she had copied out the names of the full moons from the almanac. *Cherry Moon, Strawberry Moon, Full Hunger Moon.* The rest of the pages were blank, and had been for years. That color was no longer popular. She had acquired the habit of staring at the blank pages for long moments, her mind racing with unspoken, unspeakable truths. The tip of the cloisonné pen was in her mouth. There were certain secrets to be harbored from the young at all costs.

Asleep a few hours later, she had a gauzy rose-scented dream. A man she didn't know well was seated across a restaurant table from her. She could not make out his face. The sun was going down over an ocean, tinting the dream the color of coral. A full moon shone through cracks in the walls, which were made of green bottle caps. The man could really see her, and he liked what he saw. The napkins were Hawaiian sheet music folded into fans. Raine and the man talked in low murmurs, corroborating each other's stories before it was time to return to wherever each had to go:

—*I used to think that . . .*
—*Remember when we all thought that . . .*
—*That was back when I still believed.*

She woke with her hands cramped around the sheets like startled starfish. Her heart pounded as if there had been some terrible accident somewhere. No accident had occurred. It was just a random dream. Nothing had changed. The stars had not even stirred. The moon was still full, still the same old silver bauble in its dark socket. The dream was still real, pleasant enough that she wanted back into it.

What had she been about to confess?

That she had once thought marriage would be like shelter.

That she had thought it would be like living inside some old soft Bob Dylan song.

She got up and sat in the window seat, listening to the rhythms of her husband's breathing. His bags were packed for his next trip. The house was quiet, orderly. Her children were asleep. But her heart seemed to be beating sideways, the same way it did on high freeway ramps and suspension bridges. Everything felt dangerous, but you had to ignore the danger and keep going, or die.

What was the name for it, the pretending that everything was normal?

Dissonance, Raine remembered with mutinous, bell-like clarity. *Cognitive dissonance.*

Eat, or We Both Starve

Every time Angus Chien heard an unfamiliar rustle at the door to the Celestial, he looked up expecting to see the dancer in the field, perhaps come to buy something from him. On the day he had decided he'd never see her again, he heard steps on the porch and looked up hopefully, but it was only the mailman bearing the day's portion of coupons and come-ons. This day brought a creamy envelope resembling a wedding invitation. *Mr. Angus Chien, Esquire.* He tore it open carefully and removed a glossy brochure with raised gold embossing: happy, tanned oldsters in tennis togs, mint julep glasses aloft in a toast.

Here's to you. You've earned it: Arcadia.

There was a tightness in his chest when Angus looked at it. It troubled him just as much as the letter that wanted to buy his land and store. He scratched his head in irritation and threw both envelope and brochure promptly into the trash, as if they were radioactive. *Assisted Living.* Some people were always yapping at your heels, ready to take over before it was their time.

It gave him a heartache and a backache at the same time, that brochure and its lies. *Serenity of the golden years.* As if there weren't doctors on the premises ready to relieve you of every dime you'd ever earned. He studied the diagram of the floor plan. Remote sensors tracked the resident's movements and beamed a record of it to some central switchboard where clean-cut hipsters were at the ready with their clipboards. A machine in the bathroom dispensed pills. *Moisture sensors signal certain needs in clothing changes.* A happy hipster nurse helped an old man board a shuttle with a vague casino logo on its side. Angus blinked like he did when he was in sunlight that was too bright.

Now they'd finally gone and done it. They'd taken away the necessity of gamblers ever going home again.

It was an outrage.

It was genius.

During the day Angus stubbornly dumped other refuse in on the brochure. For an entire day, the senior citizens in tennis togs toasted the ceiling through potato peels and lemon rinds.

At the end of the day, Angus sacked up the garbage and took it to the big green Dumpster behind his store. The sack seemed heavier than usual, the brochure accounting for the extra weight. He hoisted the bag over the edge of the Dumpster. Then he had a sudden regret. What was the name of that company? He stood on some discarded railroad cross ties and reached for the bag he'd just tossed. He tore a hole in the bag and gingerly pulled the corner of the brochure out, brushing the coffee grounds off it.

Futuristics. That was the name.

He heard a noise, a rustle and a muffled clank. For an instant, the image of the dancer in the field flickered in his mind. He worried that she was in the Dumpster, looking for food, and that their first meeting would be in such circumstances as to make him look like an impoverished fool, scrabbling about in garbage. He quickly jumped back down to the ground and brushed the coffee grounds off his hands. But the noise he'd heard turned out to be only Bebe Marie Abide, who sometimes scoured the Celestial's garbage for bottle caps or other treasures to use in her birdhouses.

She was crouched in the narrow place behind the Dumpster as if no one could see her. It was a little covenant she and Angus had: if they met at the Dumpster, each pretended the other wasn't there. Angus had learned to cull certain choice items for her, to set them aside, such as the little wooden crates the olive oil came in, the aluminum cans the lard came in. She had been especially pleased the time he got rid of the velvet clip-on hair bows from 1969. Soon they showed up in her artwork. Angus saved all bottle caps from the Celestial, and from time to time set a paper bag or coffee can of them down on the ground so she'd not have to dirty her hands.

Back inside the store, he phoned his cousin in New York.

—*Been looking at a outfit out of Memphis call itself Futuristics. Run something look like a old folks home hooked up to a hospital on one side and a casina on the other. How much it go for?*

—*This is very good. Number One . . . Go no way but up.*

—*Well, I'll be having some of that then.*

—*First thing in the morning.*

Later Angus said aloud to his cats, shaking an open tin of Finland sardines onto their chipped Haviland moss-rose saucer.

—*Yaw the one got the Assisted Living plan, look like.*

A day later, Angus was just about to sweep the porch when he again sensed someone outside. He paused inside his screen door, his nose barely brushing it.

The dancer from the field was standing in front of the Rescue Mission next door. He was pretty sure of it. His ear could pick out her voice above the others of her entourage. They were standing there admiring the old National Steel guitar. One of the young men played air guitar and sang something sad. Another imitated the first in a gruff falsetto, then growled something in low ridicule. They were waiting for Angus to open the store, so he threw the door open ceremoniously, pretending to notice them for the first time. Then he ducked back inside and snatched his red apron off, just in time to be busy stacking green bottles of Okee-Dokee Hot Sauce when they came through the door.

They nodded curtly at him and fanned out into the aisles. They had with them a scuffed cheap Styrofoam ice chest, *Vacationeer* embossed on its cracked lid. Their refrigerator, he guessed, and made a note to himself to give them a couple of bags of ice for free. From all appearances, they were living out of that Econoline van of theirs.

—*How yaw doin' this morning.*

Angus had never been the type to hover, and generally, Hispanics didn't steal. They were too afraid of contact with the American law, so he didn't worry about that. It was the rich Ole Miss kids you had to watch.

The Hondurans shopped as a pack, four men and the woman. It was early morning, and the men all looked sleepy. They spoke softly to each other. The dancer looked around the store skeptically, and her eyes came to rest on Angus. She raked her eyes mercilessly up and down his gaunt, lanky frame.

Angus braced himself against the force of it, then swayed a bit under the strength of her stare. He decided to stare back.

Her face was lovely in a weather-beaten way. She wore her wrinkles like soft confessions: she'd got them from smiling, and from squinting into the sun. She had been quite beautiful once, he could see. She carried herself as if she still were. What was left of her beauty was mostly a kind of hauteur. She wore tight men's jeans and work boots, and a pink sweatshirt encrusted with rhinestone jewels that said *Selena 4-Ever*. Her earrings were baroque gold hoops, too big to be real gold.

Giving him the benefit of the view of her shapely behind, she walked over to finger a strand of star anise that hung on a string beside the calendar from a Chinese wholesaler in New Orleans. Then she turned and looked wordlessly into Angus Chien's face again.

—*Let me know if I can help yaw*, he said. He wondered if she could understand a word he was saying.

As she stepped sinuously about the store inspecting his wares, Angus learned her name, *Consuela*, when one of the others called to her. *Mamacita,* others called her. She studied the cleaning supplies. She selected almost all the meat Angus had in his case, sniffing it all with bored suspicion before she agreed to purchase any. She bought the bacon uncut. Her sons brought big bags of flour, rice, and meal over to the abacus.

Consuela took her time looking around, scanning the tattered clippings on the walls, her face revealing nothing as she took it all in, the faded photos of the barge wrecks on the river, the launching of the dredger *Stackolee*, the locally grown eggplants and Cotton Carnival Queens. She looked hard at the picture of Aubrey Ellerbee and his Grand Reserve Champion steer.

—*Mira*, she called to the other. —*Es el hombre en su juventud.*

So these were Aubrey's famous illegals, Angus understood. This was what the government lady from Memphis was not supposed to see. He took a painted quarter from the Dixie cup atop the jukebox and slid it in the coin slot. He found what he was looking for, then punched the numbers and held his breath.

He kicked it.

He slapped the top of it.

He stepped back and stared.

The Rock-ola's lights flashed, and music filled the room.

> *Adios, paisanos queridos*
> *Ya nos van a deportar.*

Angus let his breath out. The Banuelos Brothers, one of the oldest songs on it, left over from some summer past when there were more Mexican faces in the fields than black ones. Nobody had played it in years. All Angus knew was that it had to do with deportation, and that the Hispanics had always loved it.

Consuela approached the old jukebox as if it were venerable livestock, and ran her finger across its name, *Rock-ola.* Her nails were painted blood red. She tapped at its Bakelite epaulets to see if they were real. She peeped into the cup of painted quarters. She turned to Angus with a social smile, nothing more. Angus smiled back.

She moved from shelf to shelf, alternately inspecting his wares and his thin defenseless frame. She assessed him with the same appraisal she'd used for the stacks of bagged cornmeal, as if both were merely *suitable*, no more. Angus shifted from one foot to the other, his skin chapped by the stare.

A Chinese woman, he thought in his discomfiture, would have had the modesty to lower her eyes and wait for him to inspect *her.*

Consuela pulled a quarter out of the Dixie cup and slid it suggestively into the coin slot. His heart froze. The coin clanked into place. He smiled. He already knew what she would play, the only other song in Spanish on there, a torch song by Lydia Mendoza.

The jukebox cooperated.

Her brood of young people stopped and listened. The song was old, and they'd never heard it before. She went to look at the Filipino baby dresses. She ran a practiced finger along the seams of a yellow lace dress with a green velvet ribbon sash, and an absurdly small matching green velvet purse safety-pinned to its side. Angus hoped she wouldn't look too close. The dress had hung there for three years, and the safety pin had rusted into the side of the dress. He could remember the day he'd hung it there as if it happened ten minutes ago. Ten minutes ago, he could not remember.

Angus felt then that the Celestial had congealed around him, slowing him down over the years. He'd spent most of his living hours in the same thousand-square-foot shack. He began to move quickly about the store, straightening shelves with the same precision he remembered having as a young man.

He felt deflated when the Hondurans were checking out. He felt odd, taking their money. He listened to their voices fade as they left the porch. He heard the Econoline's doors slam and its engine start up. He stepped to the window and watched it leave, saw it bump across a rutted turnrow back to the church. It seemed odd to him that the men were not already in the fields working. Most of the Hispanics started their day about five. He wondered what it was they did. Maybe he was wrong and they didn't work for Aubrey. Maybe they worked nights at the Dixie Barrel construction, only they didn't have that look that they'd been put to hard, ill use.

That same evening, Angus trained his binoculars on the True Light Temple. He could see Consuela setting up a little screen of floral shawls and Visqueen over the back of the Econoline van, propping it up with cut sweet-gum saplings.

Consuela had a little traveling garden, greens and herbs in stubby earthen pots. She broke off bits of herb as she cooked on a little brass charcoal stove. Angus felt guilty about his big Garland stove going unused in there at the moment. Steam rose from her pot, and Angus inhaled deeply. He could only smell his same old store, sunlight on wood, shingles.

He could not remember the last time he'd eaten food cooked by the hand of a woman. He thought it might be three years before, when he had the flu. Dean Fondren's wife had made him some soup. This was another essential strangeness of his life: he was surrounded by others, yet he often felt solitary as some unnamed creature at the bottom of the sea.

He could not remember the last time he'd had a decent tamale.

Angus watched with odd hunger as the Hondurans crouched in a crescent around the pot to eat, dipping their tortillas. Consuela waited. Angus took a deep breath, trying to smell her cooking. Focusing the binoculars, he studied the quiet satisfaction on their faces. They didn't talk. They ate as if they had no particular quarrel with the world.

When they had finished, Consuela ate alone, scraping the bottom of the pot with pieces of tortilla. Her fingers were rough and beautiful carrying the food to her mouth. Angus was mesmerized with respect. She was no stranger to hard work. Something about the way she could make do with so very little. She was a survivor, much like himself.

When Consuela came into the Celestial the next day to get cigarettes, Virginia Slims, Angus calculated her sales tax with a slow flourish on his red abacus. Her lips were painted a deep red, and her eyes were smiling at him. He was more alive when she was around, he realized with dismay.

She paused to inspect the cotton-candy Filipino baby dresses, sliding them along the rack. She had the entitled air of a rich woman but the common sense of a poor one. It was an arresting combination, in Angus's mind. When her back was turned to him, Angus found himself staring at her sturdy, solid hips and the small of her back, and the way her hair curled at the nape of her neck. As she turned back around, she caught him staring, and he noted that that pleased her, before he snatched his eyes away.

Angus meant to ask would there be anything else, please, but his mouth was as wayward as the jukebox sometimes.

—*Can you cook American? he asked. —Scrambelt egg? Hamburguesa? We ain't had a good tamale in this place since Reagan was president. You got a green card?*

Consuela smiled uncertainly, fingering the old gold hoops in her tiny ears.

—*Day shift*, Angus said, louder. —*Need me a day cook.*

The youngest of the men whispered to her. His brow was knit with some half-formed worry. Maybe he was the one who could speak English. They whispered together as if he weren't there.

—*Tell her*, Angus said to the young man, —*tell her I can get her out of them hot fields. Hundert dollars a week.*

Consuela raked him with the stare again, appraising him not only as a boss-man, but as a *man*. Angus felt his spine go straighter.

—*Tell him*, Consuela said in almost-perfect English, —*I don't work in the fields.* Not taking her eyes off Angus, she said, —*Ask him who will feed my boys if I cook for him?*

Angus blushed then, in pleased shame. Her English was as good as his own, except with a little touch of Texas. This, too, was intriguing and charming to Angus. —*You all welcome to take your meals here.*

Consuela nodded crisply, as if to seal the deal, and then she looked askance at the big Garland stove. The whorls of grease on it were as substantial and established as Florentine frescoes. Without another word, she came around the counter and shoved her red plastic purse under the counter and washed her hands in the deep sink, and looked at Angus for further instructions.

It was a full two hours before he understood what he'd done. Not only had he hired an illegal, he had offered to feed her four sons.

The farmers who drank their coffee under the blue marlin

seemed somber at the change. They all took their caps off and hung them on the antlers of the chandelier, the sudden exposure of their balding heads making them meek as church-mice. They couldn't complain about the coffee: it was excellent. They glanced at Consuela when she wasn't looking, and then shot nervous looks Angus's way.

He ignored them. He asked her to fry him two eggs and some bacon for his lunch, and she did it perfectly. She arranged it all like a face on a plate, the eggs like wide-open eyes, and the bacon strips smiling back at him.

—*Give you heart trouble,* she said with a stern look that thrilled him somewhat.

—*Es verdad. Already got heart trouble,* he answered, and she was pleased at his Spanish. It was no lie, his heart was in trouble, beating too fast for a few moments with five kinds of happiness.

That night, as Angus waited patiently in the dark for his night's portion of sleep to come to him, he heard Consuela's voice float across the dark fields.

> *Adios paisanos queridos.*
> *Ya nos van a deportar.*

After all the years of hearing it, he finally understood it, and the knowledge left his heart feeling charred. He studied in his mind all the things somebody should warn the Honduran lady about. He himself had mastered the secret: if you agree to be lonely the way the needle in the haystack is lonely, you can vanish into America, you can get sufficiently *away* from whatever drove you from home. Angus lay in the dark, cold pearls of sweat popping out on his brow.

Nanking, 1938. He could barely remember it. White stone steps, grooved with the footsteps of his ancestors. Big pots of red flowers in Foshan pots, innocent hours in the sun lining up his tin English soldiers, under the watchful stares of stone lions. Soap bubbles with his little sister, swordfights with his father's long-stemmed pipes. His little sister's porcelain English doll shattered on those steps, the day he was running with his fingers like crushed twigs in his father's strong hand.

Home? A child's soap bubble that had popped long ago. He could not even remember his sister's true Chinese name, only the one the missionaries had given her, *Alice.*

The rest of what he'd seen was retrievable only by random access, such as the night he'd been watching television and saw the carved stone bodies on Hindu temples in India, curled around each other in a tangle of ecstasy, but he'd been struck with the resemblance: how the burning mutilated bodies of a hundred women could crumple like flowers and curl into each other, as if, *what?*

As if life and death were the same force. As if each could be mistaken for the other.

He'd always thought it best to stay silent on the subject.

Angus sat up, patted around in the dark on his bedside table for his cigarettes, sat on the edge of his bed, and listened to the wind brush the empress tree against the old store. The branches creaked against the tin roof in a syncopated rhythm that was almost music as he listened, watching the shadows from the yellow porch light rock gently to and fro, as if he were afloat in a small boat on a black sea.

The first spring he and his father were finally safe in Mississippi, his father had explained to him that the empress tree grew from a seed that had fallen out of packing excelsior that spilled from crates that came from China. The next year when the empress tree first flowered, its blossoms were the same pink as the little English voile dress his sister had worn to the missionary church. Seeing that, Angus pointed to the pink blossoms and cried out, —*Alice!*

It was the first and last time Angus ever saw his father weep.

The empress tree grew fast, and Angus and Solomon Chien always accorded it the same respect they'd give to any newborn or ancestor, any refugee from the world's weather. Every spring when the pink blossoms arrived, the same word always formed in Angus's mind like a fragile bubble, *Alice.*

Green Comet

When he couldn't sleep at night Dean Fondren lay on his side and watched out his bedroom window for Angus Chien's porch light at the Celestial. When the porch light came on in the dark, Angus was up and making the first pot of coffee, which meant it was about five or so. Though Dean was not a regular over there, the little yellow light was a welcome sight during the weeks his wife was away, a reference point for the nearest other soul. It helped Dean locate himself in the vast black nights.

He didn't sleep well without Alexis, who was downriver with their daughter and new grandson. He rolled and tumbled the whole night through. It was the time of year when he didn't sleep well. He had borrowed, some weeks before, an amount of money that was incomprehensible to him, in order to get his crops in the ground.

The grandfather clock in the foyer parsed the night hours in deep, reassuring bongs, then settled into steady ticking. The rhythm resurrected an old childhood memory, of driving in an old International pickup truck with his father, seeing a chain gang beside the highway. They were clothed in black and white stripes, chanting, their pickaxes going into the ground with the precision of watch movement.

GET up in the MORning so GOT damn SOON —
CAIN'T see NOthing but STARS and MOON.

Dean's mind kept plowing the same furrows of worry. He was uneasy about his daughter's new life. She had a new baby boy, and she had chosen to live at the literal end of the earth with its father, a park ranger, just a boy himself. They lived down in the bird-foot part of the Delta, past New Orleans where the Mississippi River fanned out into the Gulf.

It was the last place you could consider yourself on dry land.

Every farm toxin that entered the river from Minnesota on down put out to sea there. Who in his right mind would want to live there?

His son-in-law the bird-counter, apparently. And what's more, he was holding Dean's daughter hostage to his bird-counting down there. And now his new grandson too.

It was not the first time in his life Dean had borrowed more money than he could comprehend. And it was not the first time in his life everything he'd ever worked for was wagered on a certain six weeks in which it might rain too much or not enough. It was an old knowledge in his bones now: he could lose the land beneath his feet sixteen ways from Sunday, depending on several floating variables of rain, sun, and the federal government. He had learned to live with that knowledge, the way one learns to live with an old wound. He was old enough to know better, but daybreak, in recent years, rendered him fragile and wary as a new lamb.

If Alexis had been home, he could have curled himself around the certainty of her soft, sleeping form and kissed her awake. He had pulled himself back from perdition on more than a few dark nights of the soul, just by traveling that six or so inches to her side of the bed. But her side of the bed still had his newspapers and farming journals piled on it. She'd never been gone so long from him before. So when he finally saw the light come on at the Celestial, he was grateful. He got up and dressed in the dark.

Dean's border collie rode over to the Celestial with him, pacing in the bed of the pickup truck, as if she thought anyone's breakfast besides her own was a waste of good daylight. She was accustomed to going straight to the fields, and she fussed at him a little when he parked the truck in front of the store.

—*Just a little while,* Dean said to her, —*and then we'll go do some work.*

She waited on the porch with another dog that had been one of her own puppies, watching the fields for signs of life, making fussy whimpers at the blackbirds already gleaning whatever they could from the dirt. Dean went inside to order himself some breakfast, an indulgence owing to Alexis being gone. He took his hat off as he went in and laid it up on the defunct cigarette machine. The regulars over there needed the place too much, he thought. They each had their own place staked out on the deer-antler chandelier that dominated the center of the room, and they always hung their hats there, on the same point they'd been hanging them for years. That way, if anybody stood up suddenly, he wouldn't put his eye out. Latecomers had to hang their hats on the tail of the stuffed blue marlin that hung on a plywood plaque on the wall behind the long table.

The Telephone Pioneers, they called themselves, and they played the same betting game over and over every morning, an elaborate ritual understood mostly by themselves that involved insulting each other and moving unlit matches around. They always seemed to be betting on something trivial, like whose heart was the hardest. It was a vicious monotony Dean did not participate in.

Angus had a new cook, a Honduran woman who seemed overwhelmed with their requests, so Dean waited for the right moment to ask for his breakfast, and poured himself a cup of coffee. He took a turn around the room with the coffeepot, filling any empty cup, ducking to avoid hitting his head on the deer-antler chandelier.

Already the Telephone Pioneers were off to the races:

—*Feller in here the other day said every pesticide known to man could connect up someday.*

—*So what was he selling? Burial plots?*

—*Weren't selling anything. Said if you could do the math, it's all connected. Saudi Arabia, South America, everywhere.*

The big yellow Cockrell Banana truck pulled up outside, causing Angus to curse softly. The man never failed to show up right when things were too busy. —*Consuela,* he said, —*let me show you how this goes. Take just a few minutes. Dean here can get his own breakfast.*

Dean smiled crookedly and reached into the egg bin and selected two of the biggest brown ones, and broke them onto the hot grill. He checked the bacon Angus had going under a bricklayer's press. Over the sizzling, he listened with one ear to the conversation, watching their sunburnt hands slide across the table pushing the matches.

—*It was this other feller in here the other day. Said down there in Brazil they's a place where there ain't no limits, feller can kill five thousand birds in a day if he wants. If you can pay your ticket down there, brother, you can shoot all you want. Go home happy.*

Dean looked up suddenly from Angus's stove, in time to see he was being watched. He turned away from it, the dull gleam of something in the cloudy eyes of an ancient farmer who'd been old when Dean was a child. Maybe the gleam was greed, or the memory of lust, but it made Dean's heart feel like a cold fist for moment. He flipped his eggs, and put his bacon on a plate. He sat alone at a table by the window, understanding that the Telephone Pioneers had somehow pulled him onto their radar for a while. Maybe he was not the only one who'd been counting the days Alexis had been gone.

—*You got you some new help staying on your place, Dean?*

Dean had never liked the man who asked, a wiry little red-haired catfish farmer and card-carrying Klansman, a Baptist with all the expertise in gossip of an old useless woman.

—*Nobody I know of, why?* Dean replied pleasantly.

—*It's a old green Comet parked over there by the well. Been there all night, look like.*

Dean sighed, and looked out the window. There it was, nosed in between Ariadne's old homeplace and a chinaberry tree, like a badly hidden Easter egg. He knew what he was going to find: young people.

—*Probably just some stray young'un with a guitar, I imagine,* Dean said, and ate his breakfast in silence.

While he finished his breakfast, he rehearsed his little speech he would have to make later: *Son, you can't stay here, and I'm sorry.* Maybe it would be one of those bespectacled New York types looking for a good song to steal from an old black man with no lawyer to defend him. Or maybe it would be the other type, the young boys going nowhere fast, who showed up with little more than the guitars on their backs, looking for money or meaning or magic. The pawnshop the nuns ran was full of the abandoned dreams of those boys. Even so, to Dean it seemed the airwaves were full of such young men, their tributes to their temporary loves being played over and over and over. Some of those boys crossed over into middle age wearing too much makeup and Spandex tights and hairdos not unlike

the whores of their epoch, screaming obscenities for their supper, long after they were old enough to know better.

When he was done, Dean got his hat off the obsolete cigarette
machine and slid a five-dollar bill under the red lacquer abacus
beside the cash register. He left, their words still eddying
around him. Belle and her grown puppy stood up expectantly
when he came out the door. A black Escalade had pulled up and
parked next to his truck. Dark men in black leather sequinned
jackets piled out of it.

Dean tipped his hat ever so slightly as he passed them and
made eye contact with the one that seemed to be the head of
the pack. The man had cold, steel-colored eyes, and he looked
back at Dean with a glance of hatred so commonplace that
Dean could bear it without the slightest wince. It was nothing
personal: the man hated him because he had white skin. Dean
understood.

Gangbangers. He'd heard that name for them on television.
They had appeared in Madagascar with the punctuality of mag-
gots after carrion, once the casino came.

With Belle whimpering in protest in the back of the truck,
he waited until they came back out and shoehorned themselves
all back into their car and drove away. He kept a shotgun in the
cab of his truck, and he and Angus and Aubrey had learned to
look out for each other over the years. Madagascar had never
been big enough to hire a policeman.

The gangbangers, who had no visible means of support,
rented an Airstream trailer to live in, and seemed never to live
in it. The Hondurans, who were the hardest workers Dean had
ever seen, harder even than the Africans, had nowhere. So they
lived anywhere they could fall at night. Some were bivouacked
in the old empty church. He'd heard rumors of work camps so

far back from the river roads that nobody knew what went on there, and nobody had the nerve to ask.

The green Comet was still parked at Ariadne's old shack.

He went to get the tractor. He told himself that if the car was still there at sundown, he would go over there.

He stared at the house, the church, the old artesian well. Nobody needed to be drinking that particular water.

The well still ran clear water, but Dean wouldn't drink it. It was channeled into a stubby standpipe surrounded by Portland cement, with bits of broken colored glass pressed into it to spell ROOSEVELT FRANKLIN DELANO. It was somewhat of a shrine to certain visitors since it had been the sole source of water during a particular civil rights march. Martin Luther King, it was said, had had water from that well.

The Memphis tourism folks had come up with some swindle that involved cheap flights from Amsterdam to let Europeans stare at Mississippi. The previous year, a busload of German tourists had stopped once and snapped their cameras at him when he was on his tractor. Then he had seen them gulping handfuls of water from the well, rubbing it on their arms as if it were holy water. One of them, a young female in bib overalls with wet green hair and a brass ring through her nose, ran breathlessly over to him and said, —*Show us please where you kept the slafe! Where did you keep your slafe?*

He stared at the girl, took a deep breath and said, —*In the same place you keep your Nazi lampshades.*

The girl had raised her camera then, and snapped, catching him with his arm raised as if warding off a blow. He vowed to break the camera of the next tourist who tried that.

—*I chest love the Souse,* she bubbled. —*Ze cotton, ze big daddee. So grotesque.*

The field Dean needed to plow was a sea of yellow weeds blooming already. He plowed them under with each pass of his tractor and opened rich brown earth. White egrets collected around the new furrows, keeping their distance according to some etiquette of their own. Dean was working against the weather report, the rains rumored to be moving up from the Gulf across Louisiana. He wanted to get the land ready for the rain.

The red-winged blackbirds perched on the power lines and watched. They had the proper sense of scale, he thought. They didn't blame him for the evil done to others before he'd even been born. To them he belonged in that picture just as much as the sun and the weeds and the furrows. He submitted to the rhythms of the tractor and its turns, and lost himself in thought. He glanced up once at the green Comet parked at Ariadne's shack and wondered what son from the suburbs was over there trying to find a truer version of his life by singing the songs of old black sharecroppers. It was hilarious, he thought, whipping the tractor around sharply in the turnrow. White boys who'd never gone hungry a day in their lives, hollering about the pain of it all.

For money!

He could probably make more money on the radio, hollering about the pain of farming, than by actual farming. There probably was more money to be made in Hollywood movies about the failure of farming than in actual farming. You could earn a living faster in America by hollering about your troubles for one audience or another, rather than doing anything about it.

This was the new way, he thought angrily, pulling the tractor around again so sharply that Belle yelped and got out of the way. She decided to go sit in the little cemetery that he was plowing around, inside the failing iron fence for safety.

—*Look at you*, he called to the dog, and she wagged her tail.

—*Look at me*, he said out loud, his voice lost in the noise of the engine. —*I'm down to talking to the dog now. Even the dog don't want anything to do with me.*

To anyone passing by, it would have appeared that Dean Fondren was talking to himself, but he was talking to Alexis.

After they had come home from signing the bank loan, Alexis and he had sat stunned in her car in the driveway, staring out at the fields. It always put the fear of God in them, that trip to the bank. It almost took the fight out of them that time.

—*Well, madam, I have enjoyed your company this morning, but I better move on to what I have to do*, Dean said gently, leaning over to kiss her cheek.

—*I never thought I would die here*, Alexis had said absently, staring out as if she weren't aware that he'd kissed her. She lifted her arm and waved it in an arc enclosing the field. —*Where we will spend eternity, I guess.*

—*Well, did you have some other place in mind?* Dean had said after a while, in exasperation. —*I mean, that's the one thing I can name in this world right now that nobody has figured out some way to charge us money for—our burying place.*

Alexis had cried a little then, and Dean felt tender and irritated with her at the same time. He knew it had something to do with the letter he kept in the glove compartment of the truck. A Memphis business with vague intent wanted to buy his land. *Futuristics.*

—*I've never seen a grandmother cry before*, he tried to tease her.

—*You watch me*, she said.

And when it was time to come home from seeing the new baby, she'd decided to stay there, at the literal end of the earth, irritated with him for how he'd talked to his son-in-law.

—I don't know why you would want to live at the literal end of the earth, Dean had said, when he learned that the boy and his daughter planned to just take the baby home from the hospital in New Orleans, get in a park service pirogue, and ferry themselves home to their cabin that overlooked where the Mississippi spilled into the sea. Dean had wanted to yell at the boy about how unfair it was to hold your loved ones hostage to your work like that but couldn't bring himself to say it in front of Alexis. She could probably tell a thing or two about being hostage to a man's work. Any farmer's wife could.

—*Earth is round*, the boy had shrugged. —*There is no end.*

So Dean walked later with the boy an hour, intending to suggest that he devise some kind of game plan for his life, now that he'd chosen his life's hostages. As they walked, the boy had suddenly put his hand on Dean's arm to silence him.

—*Listen. They're here.*

—*Who?*

—*Migratory American songbirds.*

The marsh was alive with them, Dean could see, beginning with a gray-green cord across the horizon that seemed to thrum and vibrate. The boy began the recitative of their names, —*Warblers, vireos, thrushes, grosbeaks, tanagers, flycatchers.*

Dean stared and blinked.

—*This is the first dry land they see after they leave the tropics*, the boy said. —*They fly all night across the water to get here.*

—*But that's hundreds of miles*, Dean said.

—*They do it*, the boy assured him. —*Every year at the same time.*

Then the boy had knelt on one knee and worked some figures with a stick in some silted mud. —*The Gulf eats forty square miles of shore a year.*

—*Meaning,* answered Dean, —*they have farther to fly every year.*

—*There ya have it,* the boy had said. His face had been full of something the old people in those parts would have called *zeal.* In any other human being, Dean would have respected it deeply. But as it was his own daughter's husband, he felt genuine fear.

In that instant, Dean devised a plan. He would get the boy interested in farming. He'd show him you could put in three hundred acres of soybeans and bird-watch at the same time. And he could count all the birds his heart desired.

He could already imagine Alexis's objections: why would he want anyone else to be enslaved to the same piece of land he'd been a slave to most of his life?

Everybody has to be a slave to something, he thought.

He took the letter out of his pocket and threw it out into the air. *Futuristics.* He plowed to the end of the row, turned, and plowed his way back to the letter. He had to turn the wheel ever so slightly to the right to catch the letter in the last disk of the harrow. He'd used the same precision to halve snakes before. When he looked behind him, he couldn't see the letter anymore, only Belle, plodding thoughtfully along behind him, no questions asked, as she expected to do the rest of her life. Dean felt satisfied. He'd returned that piece of paper to its point of origin, *earth,* burying it before it could bury him.

The Wastrel

Boubacar loved the nights when the rain came down in big silver sheets, pounding the tin roof of the Celestial. On such nights, there was nothing to do but unpack the cardboard boxes left that day. On such nights, America was an honorable ache between the shoulder blades, after hours of building pyramids, *Campbell's, Chef-Boyardee, Hormel, Betty Crocker, Pillsbury,* while the jukebox played old songs of the Americans' ancestors.

Take these chains from my heart.

I . . . fall . . . to pieces.

She loves you more than me, big river.

America was the smell of cigarette smoke, *Marlboro-Camel-Newport,* glued to your skin by ambient cooking oil, *Mazola-Crisco-Shur-Fine.* Boubacar practiced his customer relations as he dusted shelves in the Celestial Grocery. *I'm sorry, we are out of that brand. Yes, we carry that brand, but it's on back order. No, we do not stock that brand.*

One evening when there were more cats in the Celestial than customers, Angus explained American business to the Mauritanian boy. If you could own a product's name, you could be rich. *Mahatma* could not call its rice *Uncle Ben's.* Nor could they call it *Minute Rice.* If you named your rice something that was already taken, the law would make you pay money and change the name. Or you might go to a judge and the judge would decide the matter.

This phenomenon was called *brand name*. It was not to be confused with *brand new*, which was not the same.

The lesson halted when the door opened, and *la sorcière*, the woman who lived among the stovepipe animals and pie-pan fetishes, came in the door wearing her black garbage bag raincoat.

—*Evenin', Miss Abide*, Angus said. —*Wet enough for you?*

The woman bobbed her head in confusion and looked around the store. She seemed disoriented, or just hungry to the point of distraction. From beneath her raincoat she produced a small flat parcel wrapped in a brown paper bag and twine. She held it out to Angus, and Boubacar watched warily.

La sorcière. Some you could trust, some not. He'd never seen a white one.

—*What you got for me this evenin'?* Angus was saying, entirely comfortable. He smiled kindly at her as he pulled out a pocketknife and cut the twine. —*Well, you got it wrapped good for such a rainy night like this.* He gently opened the paper, and there lay a small sign of sorts, bright yellow paint over an old auto license plate, with blue lettering: WHERE WILL YOU SPEND ETERNITY? Green trellis vines with rose blossoms were painted to look like they were growing among the words. Boubacar stared at it, unable to understand if it was a good sign or a bad sign.

—*Well, now. That is something I been needing*, Angus said. —*Where can we put it so them that needs to see it can see it?*

The woman watched in pleased silence as Angus untacked some old flyers for gospel choirs that no longer traveled to those parts. He hung the sign on a nail, and tipped it delicately with a long finger until it hung straight.

After she had made her selections and left, Boubacar asked Angus what the sign said.

—It says 'Where will you spend eternity?' Tawmbout where will you be after you die. Now you take me, I have already put in my reservation out yonder.

The boy pondered the question for another hour or so. It was an odd word, *eternity.*

He thought of how Angus always gave her chocolate footballs, and how he was not much concerned if she paid him with money or not.

Angus did that from respect, the boy realized, not fear.

Walking home through the dead orchard, the boy felt like he had fallen into riches. He had *Bumblebee Tuna* and *Hunt's Tomato Paste.* He had macaroni and cheese in boxes and cans with pop-tops. He had biscuits in tubes. He had cereal puffs and crisps and flakes and chips. It would be a good night. It was payday.

It was his habit, when he was freshly scrubbed after work, to munch dry corn flakes straight from the box in front of the little red television, while his food, *Totino's* or *Chun-King* or *Swanson,* came to a speedy bubble in the microwave Teslem had bought in the Clarksdale Wal-Mart. When the little oven beeped, the food was ready. Then he would sit with the television and eat, schooling himself in the ways of the Americans.

The boy's English was improving, and he was losing his French accent, opting for the nowhere accent of television.

When he wished to, he could sound like an emissary from anywhere. As was his custom in the center of the dead orchard on the walk home, he practiced his English with his sacks of groceries.

Take advantage of the incredible savings this week only.
And with the added cash rebate.
It's not just a lifestyle, it's a life.

America was the hot shower waiting at home for him, a sheik's share of hot water, *all you can eat,* with *Zest Lava Dove*

Irish Spring, and the bottles of television shampoo in jewel hues, *Suave, Pantene Pro-V, Johnson's Baby.* He had one of each.

As he came around the corner of the abandoned gas station, he saw the men from Memphis leaning on their cars, smoking and talking. Standing in an uneasy way, hemmed in a bit by them, was the woman in the black garbage-bag raincoat. She kept touching her black bowler hat as if to secure it in case there was trouble. She took a few steps towards the tangle of kudzu and hubcaps that was the side gate to her yard, and one of the men moved to block her way.

—*See, we don't mind you going through the garbage, long as you don't tell nobody what you see there, maybe. Maybe you can help us out sometime, like drop off some merchandise for us, earn a little extra cash.*

The old woman ignored them, tapped her ears and shook her head. She was pretending she was deaf, Boubacar realized. His grandmother had taught him to walk in a wide circle of respect away from those who commune with the spirit world. He was standing between her and where she needed to vanish into, so he bowed deeply, then moved aside. She nodded at him, her eyes like blue flares, and she vanished into the kudzu, rustling as she went, and there was low laughter from the men against the cars. By then she was making her way toward her rickety boathouse, moving with the same practiced wiliness he'd seen in the starving street cats of Nouatchkott.

Boubacar bobbed his head quickly as he walked past them. There was the one who had told him to stop playing with the lights, who was called Li'l Smiley, and there was the one called Rashad, and another he didn't know. Their low mumbles seemed to brush the back of his head with rudeness as they stared at him. Then Rashad's voice swung out like a grappling hook.

—*Hey, man. You want to make some money?*

Boubacar turned to see if they were speaking to him. He

was at a loss for what to say, but there had been that word, *money*. Slowly he walked over to the car. He shifted his grocery bag of products from one arm to the other so he could shake hands. He'd seen American men do this a lot, shake hands. But the handshake this man offered was upside down, with crooked fingers.

He noticed the dazzling car then, like a city taxi, the colors. Magenta, gold, purple. *Chevrolet Caprice.*

—*I need me somebody to deliver a package for me,* Rashad was saying. —*You work at the casino? You go to school?*

—*Naw, man,* Li'l Smiley said. —*He got Ayesha's job. In the evenings.*

—*At the Chinese store?*

Boubacar looked curiously at the two of them, and he smiled in spite of himself. He was pleased to be recognized by them. Normally they looked right past him as if he did not exist. He could smell their soaps and shampoos, and the clean-laundered smell of their clothes. *April-fresh softness.*

—*Here's the deal. A buddy of mine needs a package when he stop through tomorrow, and I can't be there. But you will be here anyway, right? So what you do is, just give him his package. I pay you for your trouble. You know what I'm sayin'? It's very confidential.*

—*Confidential,* the boy echoed.

Another man guffawed softly, and threw down a cigarette decisively, as if the matter had just been settled.

America was himself, right now, standing out under the stars talking with black men who drove expensive and interesting cars. But something was not good about these men. They looked at him as if they shared a private joke about him.

—*Before you go to work tomorrow, you stop off here and I'll give you the package,* the man said.

Boubacar stared blankly. He had the same feeling around

them that he had around the Somalians he'd met: that he, Boubacar, was nothing to them, that they could kill him with no more effort than they would use to kill a mosquito. He could not pretend to be deaf, but he could pretend not to understand English. That was the solution.

—*And a happy evening to you also*, he said, beaming, backing away. —*Good evening.*

Boubacar let himself in the door of the trailer, balancing the bags in his arms. He set the bags down on the table and began to make his choices. A package of pink coconut-topped Sno-Balls? Rosedale tomatoes or peaches? Star-Kist tuna and Snickers bars? He tore open a candy bar and peeled the paper back like a banana, then bit slowly and thoughtfully into it.

He heard a noise behind him, and turned, candy bar in hand.

From the chair beside the window an older Arab man with almond-colored eyes was staring at him. Boubacar slowed his chewing, swallowed.

—*You have your mother's eyes*, the Arab said in French, nodding his head once in greeting, bowing to the boy without rising from his chair. He was wearing white robes and a red skullcap, the Koran open on his lap.

It was the Wastrel, the Sufi master whose father had owned the boy's father's family. The boy had seen him only once before in his life.

The man now looked back at the boy, patiently, his cigarette poised in midair on its way to his mouth, which was in no particular hurry to clutter the air with words. Some said the boy's father had died protecting the Wastrel.

—*Yes*, the boy said, and he bowed slightly. His grandmother had taught him to fear Sufis: they could see into your head, into your secret thoughts. Boubacar noticed then that the television was on but the sound was off. It was a news channel, with words crawling along the bottom of the screen, up the side of the screen, and pictures flashing quickly. The Wastrel took a deep drag off his cigarette while America raged silently behind him: a crocodile snapping, a race car exploding against a wall then blossoming into petals of red-orange fire, a Boy Scout troop in a soapbox derby, a man holding a test tube up to a light.

—*Well, here we are.* The Wastrel's voice was warm and gravelly.

—*Yes.*

—*And how is your mother?* the Wastrel said.

—*She is well. She sends you her warmest regards.*

—*Do not think for one minute that I believe you,* the Wastrel said. —*But a lie is a great kindness now and then.*

The boy nodded in shame, and his throat burned. He felt impaled on the man's gaze, trapped by his words.

—*If not for your mother's beautiful legs, we'd have had to walk everywhere in Paris. She wore short dresses, and stood in the streets of Paris and danced, to make the taxis stop.*

Boubacar smiled in a troubled way. He knew that his father had traveled to Paris with the Wastrel, because the Wastrel's father had owned his grandfather. The boy's father had supported them both in Paris by playing in a club in Montmartre. His mother had never told him that she had gone to Paris also. He could not imagine his mother in a short dress, not in a million lifetimes.

—*Believe it, it is true. The world has not always been as it is now. Women did not always cover themselves so.*

Boubacar looked puzzled. There was nothing he could remember.

—*The last time I saw you, I made your mother so angry that we have not spoken in many years.*

—*Why was she angry?*

— *I asked her to marry me.*

The boy laughed in spite of himself, remembering the difficulties of life with his mother. Then suddenly a memory came
to him. —*You took me to the market and bought me almonds.*
His eyes went involuntarily to the Wastrel's hand, remembering what it had felt like to clasp onto only one finger of it.

—*Yes.*

They stared at each other, each wondering what the other
remembered.

Then the Wastrel's words came like a flood, as if he'd waited
a long time to say them. —*Your mother needed money and she
could not be persuaded to come to Senegal with me. An old
man tried to purchase you and your mother from me for a good
and useful sum. This was the beginning of all the confusions.
You could hear the government men on the radio saying there
will be no more selling even when Arabs were buying Africans
in the streets. People were still paying good sums for children.
One boy sold his brother! So I asked her to marry me.*

—*But you owned us. Already.*

The Sufi waited.

—*No man ever owned your mother except your father. If
you are blessed, you will understand this when you are older.*

—*I am fifteen,* the boy said defensively.

—*I see that,* the Sufi said patiently. —*Do you know your
father's songs?*

Boubacar shook his head. —*I was too little,* he said. —*I
remember him singing, but not the songs. My mother would
cry if I asked her to sing to me after he was gone.*

—*Your uncles say you love music as much as he did.*

Boubacar felt a wave of homesickness.

He had been a human jukebox in Nouatchkott, cycling the
streets with his father's little library of cassettes in a French
wicker picnic basket, and a silver Sony boom box strapped to

tall steel rods welded to the bicycle by a relative of his grand-mother's, the way it was done in Dakar. This was after the great drought pushed so many from the failing farms to the barren tent city of Nouatchkott. Many had huddled there at the continent's edge, *bizan* and *harutine* and tattered chickens alike, poised for flight.

For the nominal fee of about one penny, Boubacar would play a song for pedestrians or lovers or tourists, Ali Farka Toure, Thomas Mapfumo, Baaba Maal, Papa Wemba, Maryam Mursal. And a John Lee Hooker tape in perfect condition, found in the Dumpster behind a hotel where American hang-gliders had stayed.

The money always went to his mother.

—*I am liking American music, the Johnny Cash, the B. B. King,* Boubacar said, realizing that he was saying something appalling even as the words left his lips. The boy's smile faltered and faded out.

—*Would your mother approve?*

The boy looked down in shame.

—*It is a boy's duty to listen to his mother.*

The boy said nothing.

—*It is likewise a man's duty to forget a lot of what his mother says.*

The boy looked up and saw the Sufi smiling. For the moment, he thought it wise only to speak of music. —*What is Adam Bum?*

The Wastrel turned and smiled thoughtfully. —*Perhaps you mean 'atom bomb'?*

—*It is American song on the Chinese jukebox.*

—*Ah, Atomic Bomb.*

He paused, and watched the boy for signs of understanding. —*L'Américain was first to teach himself how to destroy the world so many times he has lost count.* He pointed to the television. —*To L'Américain, everything is commodity. Even his misery. His misery is his music. He sell shares of it in the stock market. 'Futures,' he calls it, like his pork bellies. Time-Warner, Columbia, RCA, Sony. These are Jewish businesses. For a price, everyone can sing along to the same misery. 'Ooh, baby, baby, I am dying, I am drowning in the sea of myself.'*

Boubacar's smile faded from his face. He had never seen a Jew. His mother and grandmother had told him Jews were Allah's people by a different name, and they were people, good and bad, just like anyone else, but harm could come to those who suggested that in public.

—*You will stay away from the American music,* the Wastrel told the boy. —*You will pick up your father's songs and carry them. This will be your work.* He said this in exactly the tone of voice that the masters in Mauritania used to address the slaves they owned.

—*I do not play any instrument,* the boy said.

—*If you want to play kora, we will find someone here to whom Allah speaks kora.*

The boy thought guiltily of the silver guitar in the pawnshop window, every etched chrysanthemum shimmering. He thought of all the songs on the Celestial jukebox that he had not heard yet.

—*Maybe it will be oud you learn to play,* the Wastrel said. —*But I am thinking it is kora. The cook in my father's house was from Senegal, and he was the one who put the kora in your father's hands. In two days he was speaking kora fluently. Allah decides such matters, not ourselves.*

Boubacar stayed silent, his mind ablaze with thought. He decided to say nothing about his job.

The Wastrel motioned to the boy with his finger, *just one*

second, and produced with the stealth of a magician a cello-wrapped package of the sort the boy had seen in the little Chinese store, factory food of the infidels. Garish pink Sno-Balls, rolled in coconut. The Wastrel was proposing that he eat one. When the boy took the first sweet rubbery bite, the Wastrel clapped his hands once, *now*, as if the rest of the boy's life were now commencing.

Incantation to Control Another

The first time he saw Consuela coming across the fields before daybreak, a spell came over Angus. He felt larger than life had previously allowed, as if he were suddenly starring in a movie he was watching. The sight of Consuela caught him off guard as he paused in his sleeping clothes with his hand on the switch to the porch light. It was time to turn it on, but he hesitated, watching her approach, like a bright flower blooming right up out of the field. Slowly she came, dressed in yesterday's clothes and carrying her clean ones for that day in a scuffed Tommy Hilfiger shopping bag. He unlocked the door for her and stood bravely while her eyes scraped over his rumpled sweatpants and threadbare Fruit of the Loom t-shirt. Then he stood behind the counter fiddling with the abacus for safety.

—*You up mighty early*, he said.

—*Momento*, she said, and vanished into the lavatory with her bag. She was in there a long time, long enough for Angus to go back into his quarters behind the store and change into his own day clothes. By the time she came back out, smelling of the strong soap in the push-button dispenser on the wall, Angus was grinding the coffee. He looked up and saw her in a dime-store dress with flamboyant hibiscus blossoms splashed this way and that. Her hair was freshly washed, and she had put on spotless white Keds, the slip-on kind nobody wore much any-more. Her lipstick was very precise. She shoved her shopping bag under the counter, ready for the day.

Angus stole glances at her often, and the day did not seem like such the same circular errand it always was. Between the breakfast rush and the lunch rush, he tried to make small talk with her.

—*So how long you been in Mississippi?*

—*A while*, she said, and he could see the question troubled her.

—*You like it here?*

She shrugged, chopping jalapenos. —*Have business here.*

—*Your boys work construction? The highway or the Dixie Barrel?*

She shrugged again, and scraped the chopped peppers into a pot of chili. —*We move around to different places.*

At dusk, her people showed up for their evening meal, and all sat at the big table under the blue marlin. They were very quiet, as if their Spanish might be offensive to their new bene-factor. They watched Angus with wary eyes while they took tortillas and stewed meat from the big plates Consuela passed around. Angus moved about the store like a young man, filling their tea glasses.

Angus studied them. The young Hondurans ate the way American young men used to eat. They took their hats off, crossed themselves and muttered prayers under their breath before they took one bite. They bent to their food humbly, almost religiously, elbows on the table. They moved bread across their plates like implements. They cleaned their plates and thanked him shyly as they left.

Consuela stayed to clean up. That accomplished, Angus watched her leave, carrying a large plastic jar of clean water from the store, all the way across the field, balancing it on her head. It made him remember, with a sweet pain, the way the serving-class women carried water in Nanking. He could still see them clearly, a lifetime ago, quiet women moving with elegant precision through the streets, carrying big earthen jars as regally as if they were the crowns of empresses. They had seemed like moving flowers, too.

She is not ashamed, he thought, watching Consuela. He found it dizzying to think much about the distances it was possible to travel in the human world.

In the lavatory he found three tiny black bobby pins left behind, and he tucked them into his shirt pocket, intending to return them to her. He examined them closely, imagining her making the small gesture he'd seen his wife, Rose, do many years before, some way of opening a bobby pin with the teeth before sliding it into her hair.

It became a ritual he followed, waiting at the window to see her cross the fields in the morning, and watching her carry water home at dusk. On the fourth night, Angus scrubbed his own tin shower stall with a Brillo pad until it didn't look forty years old anymore, with the intention of offering it to Consuela. He opened a bar of pink Dove soap from the store and set it on a saucer on the small sink. His towels were ancient, artifacts of some extinct detergent that hadn't been manufactured in more years than he could remember. He cast about in his mind for the right way to offer her the use of the shower. He didn't want to give the wrong impression. He could already hear the teasing of the Telephone Pioneers about it, but he didn't care.

He watched her go into the lavatory with her shopping bag, unable to speak, unable to do more than grind the coffee or hide behind the abacus where it was safe.

Within weeks, little patches of green shoots were growing on either side of the steps of the Celestial's porch—tansy, and yarrow, and odd-leafed things coming up in his pepper-plant pots. He eyed them cautiously. Some high school kids had planted marijuana seeds in his peppers one time. He had not known what they were until the Clarksdale sheriff's deputy pulled up a few of them and came inside to tease him about them. It had taken months for the Telephone Pioneers to get off that subject in the mornings.

Then he saw Consuela conferring one morning with the man from Memphis who supplied him with certain notions like thread, buttons, and school tablets. This was the same man who brought skillets and the baby dresses from the Philippines. Not long after that, she cleared over some of the buffalo plaid shirts to make room for a new line of merchandise.

There were then yellow bright aerosol cans, *Money House Blessing*, in purple English on one side, Spanish on the other.

There were little tissue-wrapped bundles of incense, and tall candles in long glass tubes: *Spark of Suspicion, Fire of Love, Inflammatory Confusion, Weed of Misfortune, Beneficial Dream*.

There were fat little red heart-shaped bottles of oil no bigger than his thumb, *Glow of Attraction, Fiery Wall of Protection, Dove's Blood, Crucible of Courage, Amulet for Big Heart Confusion*.

There were little black satin bibelots and green booklets, like the *Papa Jim Magical Herb Book* from San Antonio, complete with recipes. He opened one and read it slowly.

To conquer another, take a High John the Conqueror Root and anoint it with John the Conqueror Oil. On a piece of parchment paper, write the name of the person you wish to control and soak the paper in the controlling oil.

There were stapled plastic bags of gnarled roots that looked like the testicles of extinct animals. There were little feather and chicken-bone fetishes to hang from rearview mirrors. There was scented parchment paper and special pens with which to inscribe the appropriate curses and blessings. There were squat, empty cork-stoppered glass vials and flagons in the shapes of diamonds, spades, hearts, and clubs, waiting to be filled with the materials of mysterious and questionable intent.

Hoodoo goods.

Angus fingered a Ziploc bag that held what appeared to be dried orange chicken feet curled into ominous little fists, and he felt carried back to some other time, before there were Latinos, before there were Chinese, when there was only one pack of common ancestors.

When he noticed the invoice for the hoodoo goods a few days later—angelica, bergamot, black candle tobacco, grains of paradise—he set his jaw.

He was out about three hundred dollars, wholesale.

The spell was broken. He no longer felt larger than life. He felt small and vulnerable, even defeated.

Angus had had to fire workers before, and it had always taken a lot out of him, and left him feeling sour for months. He thought of the little yellow baby dress from the Philippines that Consuela liked and decided to give that to her when he fired her. If she was so sure her grandchild was going to be a girl, she probably knew what she was talking about.

But that same day, he noticed that a van load of Mexicans who were working on the Dixie Barrel construction all came in to eat, and most of them bought something from the hoodoo section before they left. One of them even bought a baby dress, hauling it up before the abacus carefully by the sleeve so as not to get dirt on it. So he didn't say anything to Consuela about firing her. He thought of all the business he'd lose if she went away.

The pattern continued for days. Angus saw groups of workers he'd never seen before, all Hispanic. During the noon hour, the place was full for the first time in years. *Mamacita, Mamacita*, they called her. Every table was ringed with white-shirted backs bent over plates of Consuela's food. It was, for a an hour or so every day, the way it once was before everybody local lit out for the factories in Memphis, and he knew the satisfaction of giving hot food to hungry people so they could push away from the table and go work hard. He gave up his ceremonial figuring on the abacus and did the figures in his head. There wasn't time for the abacus. He had not had such business since the night of the King riots in Memphis.

These are good people, he thought, inexplicably, watching them.

Sweeping the porch one evening, while Consuela smoked a cigarette on the steps, he spotted some paper trash caught under one of her herb bushes. He stepped around her carefully and leaned over to pick it up. It was a bright orange flyer, with photos of workers in the fields cut and pasted and then photocopied. *Trabajadores*, it said in handwritten letters. *Vámonos.* Something about a meeting and the time and the place. The place was the True Light Temple of the Beautiful Name. Did she intend to start holding church there?

—*Is nothing*, Consuela said, snatching the paper from him and wadding it up in her pocket. But her eyes darted back to look at Angus again, and he knew then that it was something.

He found another one that evening, folded up in the trashcan in the men's room. He uncreased it and studied it. —*Get you some tape out the drawer and put it in the window about your meetings*, Angus said. —*Nobody can see it in your pocket.* He got some tape from the drawer and put it in the front window, bottom corner, next to a flyer for a Brunswick-stew benefit for a spina bifida baby in Rosedale. He noticed

later in the day that Consuela had taken it down, then forgot
about it.

—I hear you in the labor union business now, Dean Fondren
said softly that same evening when he stopped in to get some
dog food.

Angus wiped his hands on his apron and stared levelly at
Dean. *—Come again?*

*—They sayin' you helpin' the Hondurans put a union
together.*

—A what?

—A labor union. Dean was speaking so quietly that Angus
could hardly hear him.

In that isolated part of Mississippi the phrase is used quietly,
in the same manner one would raise the possibility of a deadly
contagious disease.

—They who?

*—Some old boy at Moon Lake told it to me like I was sup-
posed to do something about it. Said they are having meetings
in your store. The Hondurans.*

Trabajadores, Angus remembered. *Vámonos.*

—Is a lie, Angus said. *—If they meet, they meet in the
church, I guess. Ain't no law against it, is it?*

*—Not that anybody around here has ever stood on cere-
mony where the law is concerned,* Dean said. The two men
stared at each other, and Angus sighed.

*—Well, I just thought I'd pass that tidbit along to you so
you can mind your hindsides, is all.*

—You talk to Aubrey about this? They his people.

*—Well, not really. Same fella furnishes the workers to him
that brought them to that Dixie Barrel going in up the road. So
Aubrey doesn't have much to do with it.*

—*He works them, don't he?* Angus said brusquely. —*He writes the checks, don't he?*

Then Angus remembered his own arrangement with Consuela. Cash only, and all the hot food her boys could eat.

Was it legal? What was the law? He had no idea.

Angus took special pains combing his gunmetal gray hair the next morning, steeling himself for the questions he had to ask Consuela. He put on a clean shirt. He left his apron off. You couldn't fire somebody wearing an identical apron to the one she would have on. He sat on the steps of the Celestial smoking, watching for her. She was running late, he noticed. He tried out different ways of talking to her. *I ain't aimin' to be in the hoodoo business . . . You heard about Ku Klux Klan? These same old boys who love your tamales will use the Klan to drive out anybody talks about labor union. They done it before, they'll do it again.*

After a while, he saw her coming, carrying her bag with her work clothes in it. She sat down beside him and bummed a cigarette from him, which thrilled him silently. They sat together in the thin light of daybreak. She cast an anxious eye towards the van and the church, wanting her sons to get up on time.

What did they do, exactly? Angus had no idea.

Then she stared down at her clean white Keds, and he watched the sun rise. She seemed troubled. Angus felt tenderness, seeing that. He had always wanted to broach the subject of the sleeping arrangements over there, like who slept where, but she had this way of making him feel like it was none of his business. She had her dignity. She leaned over to pull a weed up out of her herbs growing in Angus's dirt.

Herbs, weeds. Both looked the same to Angus. He took a deep breath and got ready to plunge into the subject that was heavy on his heart, the expenses he had incurred according to the hoodoo invoice. His tongue took off in its own direction, however.

—*I have always carried a buckeye in my pocket,* he said shyly and formally, not unlike a young boy, and not unlike the courtiers in the old dynasties. After fishing deep in his pants pocket, he pulled out a burnished brown buckeye and held it out in his work-worn palm. —*It was give to me by a old conjure woman by the name of Ariadne the night my wife died and left me with a new baby boy to raise. Old woman figured I needed me some protection, I guess. And I did. Boy, them was some times.*

Consuela looked at him, and took the brown buckeye from him and rubbed it between her thumb and finger, regarding it with the same respect she would accord to rare currency. She closed her fingers around it, as if to capture Angus's heat in her hand. He trembled a bit, understanding that the buckeye was going to feel very warm to her hand, having been nestled all day near the most private parts of himself. Nobody had shared that particular kind of heat from him in many years, and he felt like an oyster pried open by her presence. She looked back at the empty fields.

—*Buckeye is good protection,* Consuela said, cradling it in her palm. —*But I make you something better.* Then she slid the buckeye down the front of her dress, tucking it into the cleft of her breasts. Angus's face burned then, and he stared sharply off at nothing with a crooked grin.

An empty fertilizer bag blew across the parking lot like a tumbleweed in a cowboy movie. The sight of it made Angus feel solid, permanent. He wanted to say something rash about faith and belief, about the moments of amazement and awe he sometimes had, such as when he sat smoking at dusk and realized he had never missed a meal in his life, not even in the worst of times.

—*Might be some trouble coming to me or to you, but I hope not.*

Consuela stood up and looked at him, waiting.

—*Somebody is going around saying you are here to start a labor union. You know anything about that? That could be trouble around here.*

—*Is Hector. Is his job. He gets money from the people in Florida. Immokalee pickers.*

—*That Tulia know about this?*

—*I talk to him tonight.* Consuela shrugged, taking a slow, suggestive drag from the cigarette, which was actually one of Aubrey's Camels that he hadn't come in to buy yet. —*He ask me to go the dance with him tonight at the casino. Freddy Fender.*

Angus lifted his chin sharply, as if she'd clocked him. Freddy Fender at the casino. Angus had seen the posters.

She took a long drag from the cigarette and threw it down at their feet. He reached over with his foot and ground it out for her. He felt bleak sorrow creep into his marrow, like a poison, a hex. He knew with certainty that Consuela was not telling him all she knew.

At closing time that day, Angus noticed a shiny red pickup truck parked outside the Celestial. The engine was running, and the windshield reflected the sunset so fiercely that he could not see the face of the driver. The truck had fat haunches and a spacious crew cab. You could sleep two in the backseat of a truck like that. It was bigger than Angus's bed. He didn't want to think about it.

Consuela seemed to hurry and tarry at the same time. She wiped the tables slowly, and she hurried into the lavatory. When she came out, Angus winced a bit at the loud report of her boots on the old wooden floor. The boots were red, with

purple piping and quail-feather inserts. They were Texas boots.
Her feet in those boots had an authority that had nothing what-
soever to do with him.

Consuela had doubled the amount of makeup on her face,
and she'd pinned up her hair with a red-jeweled chili pepper
clip. She put her little white Keds under the counter for safekeeping until the next day. She stood waiting beside the cash
drawer for Angus to pay her, making the usual ceremony of
counting out the crispest and best twenties just for her. Angus
thought suddenly of the casino, a fat, money-sucking larval
colony on the landscape across the field, and he grew sullen. On
impulse he said, —*I got to wait to Monday to pay you. I'm
short this week. Had to pay for all that hoodoo merchandise.*

Consuela's face showed no response, but her eyes searched
his, looking for the answer.

—*I pay you Monday,* he reiterated, but she had turned away.

A handsome dark-skinned Hispanic man of about fifty stood
in the door, dressed in a white shirt and a bolo tie, ready to take
her to the Lucky Leaf. He was studying the various flyers taped
to the window. A gospel sing, a potluck dinner, free tetanus
shots. He pointedly did not come in. Consuela smiled in a troubled way at him as she left, and flipped the OPEN sign to
CLOSED. Angus was left lost in the wake of her perfume, musky
cloves and cinnamon. He saw her little white Keds, toe to toe
beneath the counter, and he felt the sharp gift of grief arrive in
his chest.

She had no need of him.

She would be out dancing in those boots that night, and
Freddy Fender would be standing up there hollering about his
wasted days and wasted nights. Angus himself would be spending another Saturday night rooted like a tree to his TV chair. He
didn't even know how to dance.

Why not? The question was fat in his chest, like heartburn.

He had lived his life like a king in his countinghouse, one foot nailed to the floor, pivoting between the abacus and the phone that connected him to the stock market. Others meanwhile had been seeking out places to dance, holding women close in roadhouses up and down the highways, listening to songs about wasted days and wasted nights.

Angus knew all about wasted days and nights. He had spent too many of each in the store alone, while the jukebox blared for him alone.

That night Angus drank a six-pack of beer and fell softly into black-velvet slumber. He dreamed Consuela's white-dove shoes were shining in the dark like incandescent birds as she danced in the store. He dreamed he was her partner, and he knew all the steps of the schottische, all the moves. Their arms were intertwined, *grapevine, grapevine.* In his dream, she adored him.

High John the Conqueror Root

Consuela was late for work the next morning, which did not surprise Angus. He sat as long as he could on the porch at dawn, then flicked his cigarette off into the weeds and went inside. The Telephone Pioneers groused because the coffee was too bitter. They complained over their rubbery eggs, —*Where's Consuela at?*

During the ten-thirty lull in business, Angus turned from staring out the window, and there was the little nun come to open the Blackjack Zion Rescue Mission. He needed to speak to her, to see why they were only open one day week. He gave her enough time to get the door open and get settled in, and he said to a customer, —*I'm going to slip next door a minute. Got coffee in the pot there if you want it.*

The little nun was bringing in a case of Enfamil when he walked in. The nuns ran the county baby milk program out of the Rescue Mission, dispensing it to anyone who could show the right papers, as best as Angus understood it. That was the thing that gave him his tax break. Without that, it would not have been worth any business-minded person's time to keep the place open. He stared around. Some of that stuff, he swore, had been around town when he was a young man.

Suddenly, he didn't have the heart to mention the tax business with the nun. He didn't want to cause any local babies to lose out on their free milk, or for their mothers to have to drive to Clarksdale to get it. He felt the urge to buy something, anything, to give the nun some money to take back with her for her day's work.

He stared a long time at the National Steel guitar with the chrysanthemums etched in its side. —*How much you asking for that guitar there?* he said. She named the figure and he paid her twice that from a roll of bills in his pants pocket. Some of the customers stared when he walked in with it, but they didn't say anything.

He hid it at the back of the store, under his bed, not sure what his intent was. It felt like mysterious insurance, to hold something Consuela and her people had admired. It was true he couldn't dance, but maybe if he gave it to her, that might be a good thing. *A good thing for what?* he wondered.

When he came out of the back, Consuela was with her back to him, sliding her feet into the little white Keds. She had slipped in without a sound.

—*Well good morning,* he said cheerfully, startling himself, and the Telephone Pioneers. He was relieved that she even came back, after he'd held on to her money. She murmured something to him he didn't understand, turning her face from him, hopping on one foot to get the second shoe on. He stepped around again to face her. It was a little dance, his stepping to the side, her turning to avoid showing him her face.

—*Wait a minute,* he laughed. —*This ain't no dance.* She turned to face him then, and it was an old woman's face. Her hair had barely been combed, and she wore no makeup. There was a purple-black crescent underneath her eye. It had been many years since Angus had comforted a crying woman, and the confused voice that came out of him sounded to his own ears like the voice he'd used with his children, but he pulled

Consuela to him then, and put his arms around her. —*Every-thing be all right.* His heart felt strong and full of things he wanted to say, and he wanted to hold her tight.

She made a small noise and held herself carefully, favoring her ribs, and he realized that she was bruised and hurt. He thought of all the twenties still in the cash drawer, *her* twenties, and felt genuine shame.

—*Mamacita,* he said, and began to rock her from side to side. He liked the sound of his voice saying it, so he said it again, —*Mamacita.*

He was amazed at how you never forget, no matter how many nights you've wasted, how to offer the oldest form of shelter, which is your own arms. He could feel his own buckeye, still between her breasts, pressing like a hard knot against him now.

—*Guess my old buckeye didn't do you no good then. You going to tell me how I can help you? You going to tell me what I need to do to help you in this world?*

She began to cry then, but collected herself, and pulled away from him and adjusted her clothing and her dignity. She poured herself a cup of coffee, something he'd never seen her drink. He stood fast, waiting for his answer. She seemed to speak reluctantly, as if a logjam of complicated thoughts were running up against her limited English.

—*I am American citizen,* she said. —*Naturalize in Houston, Texas.*

Angus swallowed and flinched, already feeling the weight of whatever she was going to tell him.

—*I come to here to get my sister's girl. My sister pay to send her to me, so she can work and, send money back, and she don't ever come, not for ten months. And my sister don't hear nothing for ten months. She tell me the coyote got the paper to my sister's house for the money.*

—*They who? What money?*

—*I think is Tomás Tulia. The coyote who takes her from Brownsville tells me Tulia's people took her to Memphis, Tennessee. I go to Memphis, Tennessee, and my boys come in one night and tell me she might be in Delta. So we go down to Hernando. She is there, she is have a baby soon. We got her, but they keep the papers about my sister's house. Hector goes to get the papers, and he don't come back.*

—*Tulia had her?* Angus asked. —*And she's your niece, not your daughter?*

—*I think was Tulia. Some men were selling her every night. If she try to go, they say she owe money, she got to pay off the money to get the paper to the house back.*

—*How much money we talking about here?* Angus asked.

—*Two thousand dollars American.*

—*Tulia what drives that big-ass red truck? And you went to the dance with him?*

—*I went to ask about Hector. Hector is gone four weeks.*

Angus stared, his mind clouded with guilt. He'd thought she was after Tulia for a different thing. —*So he beat you,* Angus said. —*To scare you.*

—*Was not him. Was after he drop me off to go home. They jump me. Don't take my money or nothing, just jump me.*

Angus stared outside. So the deed had happened while he was not too far away. It was a painful thought.

—*But I think was Tulia's men,* she said.

—*And what did he say to you about Hector? When you axed him?*

—*Said he didn't know Hector, but he would look into it.*

—*You think this is because of the meetings, or because of what Hector knew about the girl?*

—*Everybody know about the girls,* Consuela said angrily. —*They got many girls. Nobody cares about them.*

Angus put in a phone call to Aubrey's office, a rehabbed

Quonset hut across the road. Angus could see him pick the phone up. They were looking at each other over the top of Consuela's head, speaking on their phones.

—*Say hey, Aubrey?*

—*Yes sir.*

—*Got a problem with your buddy Tulia.*

—*He ain't my buddy. He just gets me the workers.*

—*Well, one of my help showed up to work all beat up today. Look like he might have had something to do with it.*

—*Just leave it alone, Angus. It's their business and they'll settle it amongst themselves. They'll move on, and we can all get back to work, and they'll quit with all this talk.*

—*What talk?*

—*This union talk.*

—*Sound to me like you know more than you telling me, Aubrey. That Tulia is a bad bird, Aubrey. Bad doings. He's buying and selling his own kind.*

—*As opposed to buying and selling them that ain't your kind?*

—*It's a law against buying and selling whatever kind,* Angus said.

A cavernous silence came from Aubrey's end, then a long sigh. —*The law always been kinda flexible out here, and you know it,* he trailed off and then sighed. —*Just let it lay, Angus, let it lay. You get the government lady coming down here and next thing you know—*

—*Yep. They might be taking you out of that Standard and Poor book.*

—*Angus, the whole country would go under if we all paid real wages.*

—*Aubrey, you know what was the first American food I ever put in my mouth?*

—*No, Angus. Tell me what was the first American food you ever put in your mouth.*

—*It was a tamale, and it was hot. It was give to me by an old colored fellow on the street in Vicksburg. Gave my daddy one, too. I guess he knew we was straight off the boat and didn't have a pot to piss in or cook in. And didn't matter to him that we couldn't even speak enough English to say 'pot' yet, but he had it in his mind to help us.*

—*Your point being?*

—*I don't rightly know,* Angus said testily, staring out the window to Aubrey across the street. He could see Aubrey playing with the phone cord and examining his nails. —*Look, I didn't ask to come here, and your people sure as hell didn't ask to come here, but nevertheless we all here now.* Angus shifted the phone receiver from one hand to the other. —*Is it any toilet in that church, Aubrey? Any running water? They got laws now about that stuff, don't they?*

—*I got nothing to do with it. I don't even know who owns that property. Well, she works for you. Why don't you provide her with a place to stay?*

Angus put down the phone with a click, feeling trumped. Consuela had come back in. She had covered her bruises with some makeup and some hauteur.

They worked for three hours in silence.

—*I got something for you,* Angus said finally, and disappeared back into his apartment to retrieve the old National Steel. She turned around just in time to see him standing there with the hulking dark guitar case, like a gangster toting a gun.

A ravaged shadow played across her face, as if she thought Angus had just complicated her life too much. He wanted to speak to her about the first time he'd seen her, dancing alone in the field, but he lacked the nerve to bring it up.

—*What is this?* she asked softly. She had a troubled look on her face as if it presented some new obligation to her, another mouth to feed.

—When you get Hector back, we could use some music in here sometime, maybe make more people come by. Hector said you had to sell your guitar in Texas.

She opened the case and ran her finger along the strings, even the broken one.

—This guitar is very good for some people. Is not so good for others. She was smiling in a kind way, but not an enthusiastic way. Angus closed his eyes a minute, in a puzzlement of pain, and felt as if a horse had kicked him. He'd wanted to bring a little magic into her life. He suddenly felt foolish. He should have put running water in the old church instead. She'd probably have hugged him for that. Then she nodded sharply once, as if to some offstage conductor, and then the hauteur overtook her.

—Gracias, she said softly, about the guitar, and after a polite moment, she put it in its case and propped the case by the door.

Absurdity was in the air then. He'd told her he didn't have the money to pay her, but he'd spent more than that amount on a guitar she neither wanted nor needed. She could not eat the guitar, nor wear it, nor feed it to her people she was being responsible for, when a lesser woman would just be piled up on welfare watching soap operas all day.

Later it seemed to him that the tamales were more piquant and hot than usual, and he felt a small moment of fear. After she'd left, carrying water on her head and the Hilfiger shopping bag on her arm, he noticed that in the little cigar box where Consuela put her IOUs for things she got at the store, there was a ticket for John the Conqueror root. She had bought some of the hoodoo merchandise for herself, and he could feel twinges in his own heart.

He wondered if she aimed to use it on Tomás Tulia, or on himself.

Where Will We Spend Eternity?

Each morning Dean Fondren took up his plowing right where he'd left off, as if he were resuming his place in a book. The earth opened itself to the same page as it had for as long as he could remember. White egrets appeared and followed in the wake of his plow to collect their breakfast. He was as reliable a force in their lives as the sun or moon. He wondered how and what they would eat if he were not there to turn the earth up for them.

They do fine, he reminded himself. The egrets were the descendants of descendants of the ones who'd followed him the first spring his father had taught him to plow, when he was not quite nine, and his feet could barely reach the clutch.

The marsh in the bottom was business as usual, and a blue heron stared regally at him from a discreet distance, eyes like isinglass beads. The sky showed neither rumor of rain nor his son-in-law's songbirds. The green Comet was backed into the trees again. The sun was not quite up, and he could see the flicker of a candle inside. Dean hadn't seen anyone go in or out. He wished Alexis were home, because she would help them work out some solution. Getting out of his truck at Ariadne's, he felt a pang of annoyance with Alexis for not being there when he needed her. She usually was the one to run the kids out of there, and they never got angry.

The porch boards creaked when he approached the door. Though he owned the old shack now, he rapped with his knuckles on the door frame. The rusted-out screen had been cleaned up a bit. Behind that, the old door frame made of mismatched lumber seemed to undulate with painted serpents, winged slave ships, caravans of elephants and tigers. Still legible in faded paint on the door:

TIME IS DRAWING NIGH
WHERE WILL WE SPEND ETERNITY?

There was motion in the house, steps. Then there was stillness. He rapped again and called out, —*Anybody home?*

The door creaked open, and he saw a soft brown-skinned face, a blue eye fringed with charcoal lashes. It was a girl, a young woman, and she was frightened.

Of *him*, he realized with sorrow.

—*Hello?* he said. As an afterthought he quickly took off his hat and held it in his hands, like a nervous suitor.

—*Hello*, the girl said, warily. She had one hand behind her back, as if she were holding something heavy.

—*I've come. . . . This land is posted, see. It's private property. This is my land. I live over there.*

The door opened wider, and she stepped back, but she did not invite him in. She had long black hair that fell in soft waves. She was wearing some absurd costume, like some commoner's idea of a French boudoir maid, right down to the fishnet stockings. He'd seen that costume on a billboard on the highway, announcing the new casino: SPEND THE NIGHT WITH ME. There were a few little pitiful things of hers on the windowsill behind her, a hairbrush and a bottle of lotion. A fat half-burned candle with flowers pressed into it.

Ariadne's old pictures overtook him then, coiling around the ceiling. The whole ancient catastrophe was recorded on Ariadne's walls: thousands of dark thumbprints were smudged over and over, dark bodies, back to back and belly to belly, seeming to float from the holds of old wooden ships, to ascend to the right hand of a dark-skinned god. Snakes cowered in obeisance to angels, and devils fled from righteous children. An open book with wings hovered over a burdened earth, and the scales of justice were broken. In the open book were words laboriously copied with the uncertain calligraphy of an illiterate, words that had struck fear in him as a child:

YOU UNBELIEVERS

YOUR WORK IS A MIRAGE

WHICH YOU IN YOUR THIRST

SUPPOSE TO BE WATER,

UNTIL YOU COME TO IT AND FIND IT IS NOTHING.

He was relieved to see the girl had the sense not to tamper with the art on the walls.

The girl stepped out on the porch then as if the house were hers, not his. She looked out over the field. The yellow blossoms were almost all plowed under. —*You're ruining my view*, she said playfully, and her voice was a rich surprise, all East Coast boarding school. —*This is the part where you tell me I have to leave, am I right? What happens if I don't? Do you have me put in jail? Are you the Big Daddy around here?*

The air was suddenly alive with all the things Dean couldn't say. Maybe this girl would like nothing more than to go back to where she came from with a story about a white Mississippi farmer. So many arrived with only the ideas they'd got from television. It made him tired to think about it.

But she was smiling at him, and he looked down quickly and saw the red shoes then. Red high-heeled suede sandals, the kind Alexis had worn once.

—*You're safer here with the snakes than in jail*, he said.
—*You here by yourself?*

The girl nodded, winding her long hair into a coiled knot at the nape of her neck. Through the door he saw what looked like a homemade mandolin near the stone fireplace. Ariadne's old conjure words seemed to couple and move like a train, with the careful script:

FALLEN FALLEN

IS BABYLON THE GREAT

AND ALL NATIONS

HAVE DRUNK THE WINE

OF HER IMPURE PASSION

—*You work over at the casino?* Dean asked, jingling his pocket change.
—*Temporarily,* she said, succinctly. —*I'm doing field research.*

This caused Dean to exhale slowly, shaking his head. Did she have some boy at least to stay with her and make some pretense of protecting her?
—*What's your name?*
—*Peregrine Smith-Jones,* she said.
—*Well, Peregrine, I reckon I am telling you that you can't stay here,* he said as gently as he could. He saw her chin set slightly, as his own daughter's had when she didn't get her way. —*Whereabouts you from? Where's your people? Do they know you're out here by yourself?*

The girl said after a few seconds, —*My parents teach at Princeton. I came here looking for my great-grandmother's house. Her name was Ariadne Jones. I'm writing my senior thesis about her.*
—*This is it,* Dean said. —*She took good care of this place in*

her prime. But you don't need to be sleeping out here. The biggest copperheads in the county nest here.

—*I could pay you,* the girl offered, and this annoyed Dean. This was the trouble with the whole country. Too many people thought that anything is negotiable if you just pay, or extort, a high enough price.

—*You couldn't pay me enough, young lady,* he snapped. —*Not enough to have you here in this place by yourself, nobody to be responsible for you.*

—*One more night,* she dickered with him, a spoiled girl using the same voice she probably used with her own father. —*Just until I finish. My research.*

—*Research,* he echoed flatly.

She showed him an old whitened Café du Monde coffee can filled with aluminum circles, and each circle was numbered. He stared. He had not seen that can since he was a child. She shook the can, and in the quiet of the evening it sounded like a snake rattle. She looked into his face like a child beseeching him. —*I won't bother anything. I won't bother you, either. I just want to be here. Look, I found this. These little things have numbers on them. Every number is different.*

He could tell her plenty, but he chose not to. He wished for Alexis then, because she would know how to handle the girl. —*I tell you what. You can stay here another night, but I want to set some conditions.*

She nodded and her earrings dangled then, good silver and pearls, not cheap at all. And her eyes were not cheap. She was an average decent girl, he decided. She seemed to have manners. He could only pray that she was sensible.

—*No fires, no candles,* he said. —*And the water in that well out yonder is no good. You're not to drink any of it. Now come out here with me and let me get you some things to keep with you.*

The red shoes caused her to walk with light staccato steps across the porch. She paused uncertainly at the edge of the field, but Dean strode on with purpose and climbed up into the cab of his tractor. He rummaged behind the seat and produced a large black flashlight and a squat black lantern. He also took a plastic jug of drinking water he kept there. She was unbuckling the red shoes then, and when she leaned over, one hand went up to cover her breasts, to keep them from spilling.

He felt a kind of shame then, not at himself, but at how the adult tribe revisited its same old vices on each new crop of the young. Here was a girl who wanted to be something, and the only act the world would pay her for at the moment was to dress like a whore.

Who could blame the young for always wanting to secede and start their own fatuous nation?

A mottled dog, a blue heeler, came around the corner of the house then, a low tentative growl in its throat, as if the dog were not quite sure of its meaning.

—*Cobain*, the girl said, holding out her hand, and the dog came to her, ignoring Dean.

—*Not much of a watchdog you got here*, Dean said. —*He let me get right up to your door.*

—*He's not mine; I'm just babysitting him.*

—*No fires, no candles*, he repeated. —*And you don't want to use that well out there. It's contaminated.*

The girl accepted his offering gratefully and with grace, cradling the black lantern on her hip like a child. Dean felt impaled by her eyes, the way they took him in. He wished that he'd been wearing a better shirt, a real one from Clarksdale, instead of an old flannel one from the Celestial Grocery shelves. What had she called that dog? *Cocaine? Nubane?* Something to do with drugs, if he recalled correctly.

When Dean got home, he parked the tractor under a big black-jack oak and then watered the horses. He took off his work boots and left them by the back door. He stood in his sock feet before the opened refrigerator and drank cold milk straight from the jug, something Alexis did not allow. He rummaged and found something to make a sandwich with. He remembered Belle then, slumped balefully on the back porch, head between her paws. Usually Alexis fed her, and he had forgotten. He shook the sack of dog chow, and she stood at attention while he poured some into her bowl and got more water for her. He stood on the back porch with the dog, eating his sandwich wrapped in a paper towel, with the opened milk jug on the rail beside him. Belle crunched her food companionably. Dean reminded himself to joke with Alexis the next time she called, to tell her he was reduced to eating with the dog for company.

This was the first time Alexis had not been at home during spring plowing. That in itself felt like the end of something. Normally she would sit across the table from him and devise some way to remind him delicately that he also needed to plow the little corner of the yard reserved for her flowers and vegetables. —*These are the last of the field peas,* she might say, or —*Let's try those new pink tomatoes this year.*

That was Alexis's way, to do things quietly, in a soft-spoken way and without harming anyone's feelings. It was one of the things he loved most about her, a certain economy with her emotions, though her feelings ran very deep. It had caused him to misread her sometimes, but in her quiet way she always gave him time to figure things out. Sometimes it took a long while.

—*Where we will spend eternity,* she had said that day in the car.

Maybe she was trying to outrun it.

Dean looked at the old wicker gardening trug that had been his own mother's and thought of the times he'd teased Alexis for using a basket with holes in it. Her little spade and clippers were in it, some rumpled clean-laundered gloves. Normally this time of year those garden gloves would be damp with dew and dirt. They were folded where she'd left them after first frost the year before.

On a nail beside the kitchen window, Alexis kept a pair of field glasses, *sharp focus from twenty feet to infinity*, so the box they came in said, and this was how she kept up with him when he was working. The land was so flat she could find him almost anywhere with them. Dean pulled them down and raised them to get a better look at Ariadne's old shack. He wondered what the college girl ate, if she was a vegetarian. She had the door open. The girl herself came into his sights after some searching. She was wearing blue jeans and a pink sweatshirt. She had a notebook perched on her knees, sitting on the front step. He tried to read the shirt. *Boston? Brown? Bowdoin?*

Out on Highway 61, the cars slid up and down like abacus beads. A big black Escalade passed on the highway, and it slowed down at the distant sight of the girl's lights. Music boomed across the night from its open windows. Men hung out the windows and shouted unintelligible things, the wind carrying only the rudeness across the field. The girl looked up, then bravely back down at her notebook, pointedly ignoring the men in the car. But Dean had noticed the tremor of fear play across the girl's face. For the first time he realized that it was as difficult for her to be there alone as it was for him to let her stay there alone.

Dean brought the glasses down suddenly, as if he'd suddenly seen into the nakedness of her heart. She meant no harm. Harm was a human language she had not yet learned to speak. That was precisely why harm could come her way.

Dr. Bongo's Palm Oil

One condition the Harvard Quakers had set for Boubacar was that he attend American school. One morning when the yellow school bus bound for Clarksdale squealed to a halt in front of the Celestial, Boubacar almost missed it. He was standing before the window of the Blackjack Zion Rescue Mission, mourning quietly. A wide space gaped empty on the brown pegboard where the old National Steel guitar had hung. It was the most beautiful object he'd seen in all America, and it had vanished. The faux-alligator case was likewise gone. The fat smoke-colored cat now draped itself like a sleepy sandbag over an old Peavy amp instead.

The boy felt the fever of a dream leaving him. There was nothing yet to go in its place, and he felt cold.

He looked back at the window, at the chartreuse tuxedo with the black ruffled shirt. A poster was taped inside the window, with five men in similar suits leaning affably together: *The Mighty Sons of Destiny.* He looked at the date: *Sunday night.* He looked at the place: *True Light Temple of the Beautiful Name.*

Boubacar stepped up onto the bus, feeling hollow in his heart about the guitar. The schoolgirls always fell entirely silent watching him, their eyes biting him. He stumbled in the narrow aisle between the seats. In his country, a young man of his years would not be subject to such scrutiny. Girls would be in their own proper school, not on this big yellow bus, judging him. There would not be such a magnificent bus for mere children. The bus would belong to a civil leader or sheik, at least.

Someone made a low threatening sound at the back of the bus.

Boubacar's face felt hot, and he backed up and sat down on the front seat in confusion, beside a kindergartner perched on the edge of the seat, her small hands gripping the metal rail with the certainty of sparrow's feet.

—*Hey, man,* the bus driver growled, —*front seats is for little people. Git on back there with the big people.*

He moved back a few seats, setting off a wave of titters muffled by hands over mouths. He found about four inches of vacant seat on which he could rest one thin haunch, bracing himself with a foot against the driver's sudden jerking stops. He sat beside a boy with a pick in his hair who seemed mildly amused and annoyed at his presence.

The back of his head seemed to be burning. He turned around suddenly to look.

Twenty or so pairs of adolescent eyes were studying him.

There were murmurs among the girls, then nervous laughter. *Let them look,* he thought angrily.

America was just another realm of misunderstandings.

He turned back around and rode with his chin jutting out, a slight readjustment of the angle of his jaw, which made him feel more sure of himself in the world. School was simply something the laws said he had to do. He would find another guitar entirely. Perhaps a little red one shaped like a stingray, like the ones the American boys smashed on the television.

The American students in Clarksdale whispered about him when he passed them in the hallways, and he caught their drift in bits and snatches, *African dude*. American students lounged so freely in their desks, their expensive sneakers squeaking on the linoleum floor that was mopped every night, as if the place were a hospital. They were rich, these American poor. They had pockets full of coins and chewing gum, and small Japanese gadgets that simulated the wars they'd won and the ones they had not fought yet.

Boubacar had brought Teslem's small ghetto-blaster to school the first morning, with the intent to make a little money before school by playing the African songs for his future schoolmates, a nickel a song. They had walked past him in annoyance, and some had laughed and pointed. He would never try to play the tapes at school again. It was a painful understanding: in America, every man was already his own jukebox, with wires connecting his head to the rest of the world, through little flat silver machines that played discs.

Clarksdale High was hallways crammed full of black teenagers dressed like famous athletes and rock stars.

A girl he didn't know took him by the arm. —*You can't wear the same thing every day. This is America.*

America was the burning imprint of a girl's hand on your arm. America was feeling your one lucky suit of parachute cloth shrinking on your skin, burning you.

America was a tinny, watery Sousa march through a tired trumpet in sixth period, and Boubacar attempting to answer it with cascading ripples on a xylophone, to collapse the melody into itself and play it fast, several times, so it could be repeated more often, after the fashion of a Cape Verde band he liked.

And America was the white Baptist band director putting his hands over his ears, then over Boubacar's hands on the big kettledrum.

—*No no, no no. Sousa is not ta-TAta-ta-TAtta-ta-tat. Sousa is TA-TA-tata-TA-TA-tata.*

That evening, the Wastrel explained: American school music was like the music of old American and British wars. Proof: they dressed their musicians like soldiers with big hats and epaulets and caused them to march around like an army on its way to a war.

—*L'Américain, he likes his wars,* he said, scouring his plate with the last of the Wonder Bread. —*I have a package for you.*

Boubacar thought immediately of Rashad and the other Disciples and the packages they wanted him to carry for them. It could not be a good thing, if they began to bring them here. But the small item the Wastrel held out to him was simply a cassette tape in a bag. *Tower Records,* the bag said. The boy smiled like the shy child he still was, and began to beam. Gifts in his life had been few.

—*Eh,* the Wastrel said, —*it's Boubacar Traore. Do you know his music?*

The boy stared quizzically at the Wastrel.

—*I didn't think so. Well, then. Let us hear it.*

He took it from the boy and slid it into the boom box on top of the refrigerator. The kitchen was fragrant with meat and onions cooking in spices. Boubacar could smell cinnamon and cardamom and bay, and some kind of pungent pepper. The Wastrel had made the rice the way the Wolof people ate it, as only he knew how to make it, with too many kinds of meat, too many spices, so that it was wonderful. A small canister of Dr. Bongo's Palm Oil was also on the table. The Wastrel used the oil for the drum-skin.

The Wastrel had his gold spectacles on and was reading the fine print on the cassette liner to see if he knew any of the musicians personally. —*You were named after Boubacar Traore, you know. Your father and I named you the night you were born, when Boubacar Traore had been forgotten by the world. He was a tailor in Mali, making suits for fat Englishmen. So we gave you his name. I am certain your mother never told you that.*

—*No,* the boy said. There was, apparently, a lot of his own life lost inside the memories of others.

He shoved the Dr. Bongo's Palm Oil aside on the table. Then he spooned big heaps of his meat and rice onto the disposable plates that said *Dixie,* which was where they were living, roughly, *Dixie.* They ate the hot food with expired Wonder Bread Boubacar brought from the Celestial.

—*The only real wonder here,* said the Wastrel, balling his bread into little pills, —*is that L'Américain considers this to be bread.*

When the Dr. Bongo's Palm Oil was on the kitchen table, a music lesson was coming. The lessons were usually prompted by some error the Wastrel had perceived in the boy's ways. The first happened on the night the Wastrel had walked into the Celestial Grocery and found him leaning against the glass of the old jukebox, listening to a Muddy Waters song, *Lucille.*

Boubacar could feel the Wastrel's disdain radiate throughout the store like electricity. He left without saying a word.

Later at home the Wastrel put out his cigarette when the boy came in and looked at him intently. The boy put a sack of groceries on the table and began to pour himself a glass of milk.

—*So you are studying the music of Jews now?*

The boy looked up, wiping his mouth with the back of his hand.

—*Muddy Waters was a black man,* the boy said. —*I have seen his photo. He looked a lot like Tariq Haifez, the Moroccan who used to come to Nouatchkott to buy the scrap metal—*

—*It was a Jew who controlled his music,* said the Wastrel,

waving a hand, as if that would close the subject. —*You can ask your MTV if you don't believe me. A Jew in Chicago.*

The boy had then asked Angus Chien.

—*Well, I never really thought about it much. But yes, Chess Records was two brothers and they were Jews. A lot of white men traveled around in these parts looking for talent. Like old Speir, down in Jackson. As for him being a Jew or not, I don't know. Never really thought about it.*

Another lesson had occurred when the Wastrel found the boy mesmerized by MTV, by black-raincoated young men screaming their sorrow in the rain.

—*Such sorrow is well rehearsed,* the Wastrel said. —*The Jews know a commodity when they see it.*

The boy said nothing, remembering Angus's words, but he turned off the television.

So the music lessons were part punishment, part gift, part roadmap to the forbidden in ways the Wastrel did not intend.

When the dishes had been rinsed clean, the Wastrel turned off the Traore music and brought out his Wolof drum and sat with it between his knees in the kitchen. He played a tentative rhythm that seemed to ask questions of the air, and then ripple into three streams at once. Then he stopped abruptly. He tuned the drum by tightening the leather strings that held the goatskin in place. He held his head to the side, in case the skins snapped. Men had been killed by the skins of such drums, or so Boubacar had been told by his grandmother when he had asked for one once.

—*This was your father's first real song,* he said, taking a deep, nourishing drag from his cigarette between applications of oil to the skin he had just tautened across the drum. —*You have heard this one?*

Boubacar shook his head.

—*It is called 'What the Sand Says.' The first time I ever heard him play it, I could hear your mother weeping in the next room. We played this in a club in Paris one time, and I tell you even the stone lions outside the doors were weeping.*

The boy nodded with a bowed head. He remembered a saying of his grandmother's: *The Sufi thinks Allah speaks to him first, everyone else later.*

The Wastrel closed his eyes and hummed the melody to help himself remember the words. He whispered things softly, as if confiding in the drum, shaking his head, and then Boubacar saw the song begin to possess him like a visiting spirit. By the time the words began to leave his mouth, he had already forgotten the boy was there.

Long ago, Allah turned his back on the ancestors. He took away the rain.

Why? the ancestors inquired of Allah's back, which was the blowing sand.

Allah answered over his shoulder, you have angered me in a way that is not trivial.

How? the ancestors had entreated the back of Allah, the blowing sand.

Allah answered over his shoulder, you cut the citrum trees that would have shaded your children's children.

Trees in the desert, can you believe it? It once was so.

But that was our ancestors, the people cried. They needed the wood.

Your trees were dead treasure in the cities of the Caesars, the blowing sand said.

And your trees were tables at which you were not invited to dine.

And your trees were ladles from which you were forbidden to drink, bowls that would not feed you.

Where did the rains go? the people inquired of the blowing sand.

The rains went to Senegal, said the blowing sand, where there are many trees.

When you no longer had trees to sell, you sold each other.

Which is why, in the cities of the Caesars, there are slaves.

Where did the lost songs go? The happy song the cutters used to sing in the forests.

I took the song because you were not worthy.

Teach us the song again, the people begged.

Listen, said Allah. Listen closely.

And the people heard: blowing sand, blowing sand.

When the song ended, Boubacar's head jerked forward as if he had been leaning on the song for support. He felt strangely empty. He could not remember his father, or the song. His heart was full of a vague hunger, for the world that existed only in the memories of others.

—*You understand that your father's song was forbidden, and why?* The Wastrel cupped his hands together to rest them.

The boy nodded.

—*Do you understand why he continued to sing it?*

Yes, yes, the boy nodded.

—*And do you understand why forbidden songs must be sung?*

Again the boy nodded, *yes.*

—*You will learn this song,* the Wastrel said, with a thump to the big Wolof drum.

The boy didn't answer. He thought of the National Steel guitar, and fell silent. He was suddenly tired. He wanted the lesson to be over. He wanted to be alone, listening to American radio, perhaps. He felt like an old man already. The song had turned him old.

He looked across at the long shimmer of the casino over on the edge of the flat world.

He wanted a bicycle.

He wanted a boom box.

He wanted to circle endlessly in the parking lot, being a human jukebox for coins. No, he wanted to be lost in his father's song again. The world was an ample open place when that song was being sung.

He wanted to play the song.

—*I will tell you something else you do not know*, the Wastrel said. —*I wanted to take you for my own son. I asked her twice to marry me: once before she met your father, and once after he was killed. The answer was still the same.*

The boy looked at him, then away. The remote complications of the elders made him uncomfortable. He could not imagine his mother marrying. To do so would require happiness, smiles. He wanted, suddenly, to extricate himself from the whole history, to take only their songs and leave the rest.

He wanted to become an American.

The National Steel guitar shimmered in his memory like a mirage.

The Wastrel was drumming with his large hands on the table, lost in the sweet madness that overtook him sometimes. He could balance the drumming with the talking, pulling Boubacar backward and forward in time. It was the beginning of another music lesson, a kind of catechism the boy would put the

Wastrel through, one the boy came to love very much. The boy shoved the jar of Dr. Bongo's Palm Oil to him, to urge him to reach for his drum.

—*What about Cape Verde?*

—*Cape Verde is the portal through which Portuguese music flowed into Africa. They could not stop it.*

—*And Zimbabwe?*

—*Zimbabwe flowed into Ghana, there in the mbira. Mapfumo did that. They wanted to stop him, too.*

—*Senegal.*

—*Senegal bleeds into Mauritania in the kora. Kora was the knife that cut into your grandmother's old Moorish songs. Senegal is the future. This is why it is dangerous. All good music is dangerous. This was the river,* the Wastrel explained. —*All the great ones had entered it. Thomas Mapfumo, Salif Keito, Ali Farka Toure.*

One was in the river, or not.

One had to choose.

His father had chosen, and his father had died.

—*Take, for example, the great Bani of Dakar,* the Wastrel said, and began to sing a familiar song, and Boubacar began to sing it with him:

You may have gold
Or you may have silver,
But you may not love yourself
That is the way of God.
You did nothing to deserve it.

—*But Bani did not choose,* Boubacar said. —*They told him he would do it. So he was a slave.*

—*It is the highest calling,* the Wastrel said, shrugging. —*To be the slave that frees the others. Bani was the collector of the songs, the stories. He kept them safe, he kept them alive.*

At the Clarksdale school, the white teacher's geography test was on crisp white paper. Some of the words Boubacar could read, some not. *Cape Verde,* he could read but he couldn't label it on the map, so he drummed Cape Verde with two pencils.

—*Quiet, please,* the teacher said. —*I don't want to tell you again.*

So he drew the lineage of Cape Verde drummers, a tree of drummers' names in the margins of the test, which he failed.

Because of his sometime English, he was put into classes with younger children who spoke in fat-tongued happy confusion. It was a shame so great he could not tell his uncles or the Wastrel, and certainly not his mother, who wished for him to apply himself with diligence to his studies in America, whether she approved of America or not. In his new classes, he began to function as a kind of caretaker or orderly, which earned him high praise from the teachers. He found a closet full of maracas, ukuleles, baby bongos, and xylophones, some of which had never been taken from their original wrappings. He taught the retarded children to play them, rather than hurt each other, when their real teacher was outside smoking cigarettes.

—*American school is easy,* he joked to the Wastrel. —*All you have to do is fail their tests and they let you be the teacher.*

—*You must finish school,* the Wastrel said. —*We have to send the proof of it to the Quakers. You cannot get the green card until you finish school.*

School was pointless. The yellow bus he continued to ride to Clarksdale most mornings. After that, when the bus emptied its passengers in front of the high school, he walked empty-handed down the sidewalk and past the entrance of the school, his eyes on the little dusty city of Clarksdale. On the first day he found himself in the middle of the town, reading a small sign framed and nailed to the door of a church.

> *Friend,*
> *There is a welcome*
> *In this Church for thee.*
> *Come in and rest, and*
> *Think and kneel and*
> *Pray.*

He went inside and sat, watching the light change in the stained glass windows, doves and lilies and other emblems of importance to the Christians. He dozed off on a pew, and was awakened by grim Christian chords pealing from gold pipes in the ceiling. A tiny, ancient white woman with a wayward corona of henna hair was slapping her tiny hands on the keys of the organ. Her small well-shod feet moved strenuously as if she were in the throes of strangulation.

To hear the music of the white Christians in Mississippi was to understand why they always thought they were being punished. It was a punishment to listen to such sorrowful music. In the painting behind the woman playing the sad music, a white man with a brown beard and a white loincloth twisted in agony on a crucifix, his face full of light in the midst of suffering, like the faces of rock-and-roll stars, *L'Américain*.

He could not wait to share with the Wastrel this insight!

But to do so would entail explaining how he had acquired the insight.

He would tell the Wastrel nothing.

He had learned something: he had finished with school.

Gasoline Sutra

Magazine Street reverberated with amplified squeals, as if cats were mating in a distant canyon. The boys in the neighborhood had formed a band. The futures trader agreed to park his Saab curbside so they could practice in his garage. The neighborhood dogs sometimes growled at the noise. The boys frailed at their guitars, singing words they had composed in spiral notebooks in study hall at school that very day, mostly about girls they wanted to love or kill.

Sometimes a particular girl from the next street over joined them, attracting stares when her parents dropped her off at the curb with her squat little Pignose amp. She had a short flamboyant wedge of hair, the color of bougainvillea.

The garage was on the other side of the fence from Raine's herb garden, so close that if she lingered she could feel the bass chord through her shoe soles. In the quiet moments she eavesdropped on their conversations, watering can in hand.

—*Swinefart? Warthog? Pighog.*

They needed a name for themselves. The girl with the bougainvillea hair envisioned something else. She pulled a few deep chords out of her bass guitar and countered. —*Heart—thwart? Hungry Heart? Fetal Heartbeat? Heart Sutra?*

—*Sutra? That's like, a good thing, right? No chick things.*

—*Swineheart*, Chance offered. He preferred something with *death* in the title. It made him feel older and less virginal.
—*Deathwart. Deathfart. Pigdeath. Deathpig.*

—*Deathpig, definitely*, Darby agreed. —*That's it. No, wait. Deathpork.*

—*Deathpork*, the drummer said.

—*No fucking way*, the girl with the bougainvillea hair said.

They laid into a song collectively like an old truck stripping all its gears, the drums skiffling along listlessly. Over that, the boys chanted one line over and over, in a perfect imitation of synthesizers: —*I asked for water and you gave me gasoline.* Again and again the girl's voice overtook theirs, and the effect was eerie, almost Appalachian, with the female complaint rising above the males, —*I asked for water and you gave me gasoline.* The girl with the bougainvillea hair had a voice that resonated like a crystal tuning fork above the simulated anger of the boys.

—*Look*, snapped the son of the futures trader, grinding to a halt. —*Don't sing it like such a victim. Sing it like you're mad as hell and you're not going to take it anymore.*

—*Blend*, said the son of the futures trader to the girl. —*You want to blend with us.*

—*I need a cigarette*, the girl said, and slid her guitar strap around until it hung upside down on her back. She stepped outside.

The boys swaggered, grimaced, and sneered. They experimented with every possible inflection on the same sentence, *I asked for water and you gave me gasoline.* They did it the way the professionals did, pacing like caged animals, humping the empty air. They did not notice that the girl was truly gone until quite some minutes later. They waited a few minutes and shared the remains of a joint, thinking she was fetching the cans of Red Bull in the refrigerator. That was part of her job, the background vocals and the little amp. They had worked up quite a sweat. The drummer got nervous.

—*She's gone, man. Maybe she quit.*

—*So what. Fuck her, if she can't take a joke.*

—*I think it's worth considering here that that's her Pignose you're plugged into there.*

—*She was just the eye-candy, asshole. Major extraneous. Plenty more where she came from.*

—*Deathwort.*

—*Pigfart? Swineheart.*

—*Swineheart is taken.*

—*Swineheart is taken. Those rap guys from Mendenhall. What about 'Deathpork'?*

—*Deathpork. Definitely.*

—*Okay, let it go. Let's do the gasoline song until we nail it.*

—*'Gasoline Sutra.'*

—*Excellent.*

On Wednesday, on the way to the guitar lesson, there was the same slightly nasty ritual between Raine and her son about the radio. She had set it on a golden oldies station she liked when she picked him up at school, and as soon as he got in the car and slammed the door, he reached for the dial.

—*Wait, I'm listening to that,* Raine said. —*Lay, lady lay,* Bob Dylan crooned. —*Lay across my big brass bed.*

The boy slid down in his seat, sullen. —*That stuff is so . . . not helpful,* he said.

—*Why wait any longer for the world to begin? You can have your cake and eat it, too,* Bob Dylan sang, and Raine sang along with him, but trailed off to silence when she saw the expression on the boy's face. She tried to make light of it. —*Hey, you know what? If it weren't for that song . . .* she trailed off again, remembering the college apartment in Midtown, the bay window, the high bed, the afternoon light as it was reflected by the old National Steel guitar onto the boy's father's body, Matthew's boy body.

—*What?*

—*Nothing.*

Without listening for her answer, he found what he was looking for, wails and screams, guitars that sounded like insects rasping their legs together to attract mates. He began to sing along to the song he preferred over hers, something about how there was no mercy left in the world, *no mercy, no mercy.* He stared out the window, slipping into the safe skin of his inner life. It insulated him from all the pleasantries he found so unpleasant.

Raine looked out the window just then, to see a man who looked almost exactly like, *no,* who *was* her husband, passing with a young woman in a tight short skirt, tripping alongside him like a Pomeranian in high heels, fresh out of obedience school. Could it be? It was definitely Matthew. He was talking to the woman, smiling, and Raine almost hit the brakes, then sped up before the boy could see. She turned into a parking lot at the corner, it was too late.

—*There's Dad,* he said, already opening his door to get out. Matthew and the girl were halfway across Court Square by then, so he called out, —*Dad! Dad!*

Matthew stopped and turned around, and the girl did a quarter-turn, like a model on a runway. Then the three of them stood watching Raine walk to them slowly.

—*Hi,* Raine said to Matthew. Her voice was thin and high, annoying even herself. —*I was just in there waiting for Chance to finish his lesson,* she stammered. She waited to be introduced.

—*Oh, you didn't tell me you have a son!* The girl cried to Matthew, as if she'd been suddenly included in the most intimate details of his life. As for Raine, the girl ignored her, according her no more significance than a washer or dryer or other ubiquitous household appliance in a home improvement ad.

—*I have a meeting,* Matthew said, looking at his watch, as if he'd not heard the girl. He was wearing a pained expression and a shirt Raine had ironed at six that morning before she went to work.

It had been crucial to his day, somehow, that particular shirt.

—*Wednesdays are guitar, remember?* Raine said, her voice cracking. She waited, as she might at a cocktail party, to be introduced. The girl looked at her watch. Raine didn't catch her name, *Candy Randy Sandy,* they had all run together over the years.

Invariably, each girl always thought she was the first, the only, the *one true one.*

When she was in her twenties, Raine would be angered to meet the girl.

When she was in her thirties, she felt a perverse pleasant vindication upon meeting the girl, understanding the pain in the girl's future that she could not see yet.

Now that she was in her forties, she felt concern for the girl whenever she met her, imagining the decade or so of bad karma that Matthew was going to release into the world when he told her good-bye and retreated to the safe confines of home.

—*Well, have a good . . . meeting. We're off to guitar.*

Halfway down the block Raine turned and watched her husband walking away, saw the young woman lean into him, drinking in every word. They were crossing Court Square again, on the same brick pavement Raine had walked on, years and years ago, on their first date.

Same sidewalk, same oak trees, and that other thing she'd lost somewhere along the way, the faith, the blind belief that she could be his *one true one.*

Her son waited politely while she wrote the check for the month's lessons, and stared away sharply in annoyance when she fanned the check in the air to dry the ink. That move used to make him chortle with laughter when he was small, she remembered.

—*I'm taking the bus home,* the boy said, suddenly, his hand still on the door handle. —*But I need money.*

The boy did not realize the basic absurdity of his own position: he had to ask her for the money to snub her with. She couldn't answer, and her heart hurt. She felt the same odd tug of severance she'd felt when he'd taken his first wobbly steps away from her. Fifteen was long past time to be taking a bus on his own. She put a wad of crumpled bills in his hand.

She went inside the Yellow Rose and had a cup of stale bitter coffee. The waitress leaned over and poured fresh coffee into her cup, and it seemed a kindness of great magnitude. She was staring out the window.

—*See somebody you know out there, honey?*

—*No,* Raine murmured. —*Somebody I used to, a long time ago.*

On their first date Matthew had taken her to see *A Clockwork Orange,* a matinee on a Saturday afternoon. They'd come out of the theater a few blocks from Court Square, a few streets over from where he had just snubbed her. They both were squinting in the thin sunlight and walked near-deserted streets towards the river bridge. Matthew had been explaining what he wanted to do with his life, something about rivers and bridges and chaos theory, and Raine had been listening, while the images of the film still burned on her retinas.

A woman had been bludgeoned to death with an *objet d'art* shaped vaguely like a penis. Everyone in the audience had laughed. She felt like she was in the presence of a foreign tribe then. Raine was going to write that down in her notebook when she got back to her apartment. It wasn't savages in Sumatra exactly, but it was *something*.

—*Hello little girl,* Matthew had said softly, circling around her like a shark, imitating the actor in the film. —*You know you should be more careful when you go out. I mean, somebody could just come up to you and . . . kiss you just like that.*

He was strong and gentle at the same time, and she could feel his lips breaking into a smile before they left hers.

—*Besides,* he said, —*you just let me pick your pocket.* He waved a hair barrette at her, and she tried to snatch it back.

Later at her apartment, after the wine and the soft Bob Dylan songs he'd brought over to play for her, they were lying naked together like spent puppies, and she'd whispered to him, —*How did you know to do that?*

—*Do what?*

She thought of the exquisitely gentle things he'd just done with her. —*It's like you are trying to make me forget the bad stuff in the movie.*

He had shrugged then, crossing over into the place in her mind that had always been reserved for heroes.

Leaving the Yellow Rose, Raine took the first turn that presented itself, not knowing where she was going. She found the station she usually listened to, the one that played only the music that she had heard when she was young and confident and in love.

Close the door, shut the shade. You don't have to be afraid.
Just call me angel of the morning, angel.
My life has been a tapestry of rich and royal hue.

But it was unbearable. It all seemed like a great conspiracy

now, those three-minute songs that somehow sealed everybody's fates. She had been sent out into the world armed mostly
with a head full of soft songs, thinking marriage would be like
inhabiting the soft Bob Dylan song about the big brass bed.

And she had always *meant* to be the angel of the morning,
only to find herself years later as the eternal house servant, personally culpable for each speck of dirt or despair, her pockets
picked clean by the whole enterprise, without even the means
to buy a bus ticket out of town.

She'd asked for water. The world had given gasoline.

She set the radio on *seek*, and drove an hour out of her way
to get home, avoiding the double cloverleaf intersection. She
picked up her husband's pants at the dry cleaners on the way
home and paid his bill. Her eyes were open but she saw nothing
as she drove carefully past the Dinah Shore song about taking a
sentimental journey, past the Caribbean child blowing *La Mar-
seillaise* on a banana leaf, past the jingle for the super-sized
funeral home that insinuated she didn't love her children
unless she purchased a particular cemetery plot for herself well
in advance of its need, and preferably at that very moment, to
get the 10 percent discount, available for a limited time only.

Catfish Blues

Raine was parked at the curb on an old tree-lined street in Midtown in Memphis, talk radio on low. She was staring at the old Victorian house she'd once lived in during college.

—*Hello, you're on the air.*

—*See, it's like this. Everybody wants to be a rock star.*

She'd had the upstairs apartment on the left, the one with the odd window. How many years ago? A mullioned bay window it was, set into the cupola of the house like a faceted jewel that caught the sun at certain times of day. She hadn't known that word, *mullioned*, then.

The first time she'd made love to Matthew, those little beveled panes had cast prisms of light that made their naked bodies seem golden for the duration of the sunset. She could remember in great detail the Dylan songs that echoed down the stairwell and out into the street: *Lay, lady lay. Lay across my big brass bed.*

On this day being there felt like returning to the scene of a crime.

A boy with a green mohawk haircut and black shitkicker shoes came sauntering down the steps from the neighboring apartment. He was not much older than Chance. The boy sneered at her, as if she were from some enemy camp: the tribe of Mom. She put the car in reverse too quickly and lurched away, as if caught in some kind of criminality. —*Hello, you're on the air*, said the talk show host.

She fled farther towards the river.

Raine didn't see the low bridge until it was too late to turn away, but suddenly there it was, wide and curving. She clenched the wheel and cursed, braced herself as if collision were imminent. Then on the bridge, crossing the Wolf River. She felt light-headed, as if there were nothing beneath her, nothing beneath the car, as if she were simply having a nightmare. Once on solid ground again, she wanted to hit the brakes, but there was traffic behind her. She pulled over into a parking lot on the shoulder, and put her forehead against her fists atop the steering wheel. Cold wet pearls of sweat ran down between her breasts.

A man in a Brooks Brothers suit walking past glanced over at Raine. She turned her face away, pretending to be dialing the radio. He was carrying a briefcase in one hand, his necktie in the other. Her skin prickled with cold sweat. The man stopped, turned back to look at her. He walked back, and came to the window beside her.

—*Are you okay?*

She nodded, having heard him perfectly through the glass window.

—*Do you need help?* he asked, shouting more than was necessary through the glass. He was probably harmless, but she was afraid of him just the same.

—*You sure you're okay?* he asked, and shifted his briefcase to his other hand. —*Well then. As you were.* He walked on, swinging the necktie idly, humming some vaguely familiar song.

He had crossed the same bridge she had, on his way home from work.

She was amazed that there were men like this, who thought of home before dark.

She followed the road and found herself in a park that ran alongside the river. She pulled the car into a parking slot, and gripped the wheel with sweaty hands. She would walk, she decided. She would give herself the luxury of a walk alone in a place she'd never been. The water of the river was up to the midriffs of the trees, and the currents were swift. Whole trees floated by, shunted by sheer force towards the Mississippi. Old people sat in umbrella'd quietude, some tending two or three fishing poles at a time. Fishermen called out encouragement to each other. Most had tall buckets beside their chairs, murky shapes twisting inside them visible through the white translucent plastic. One little white woman in a lawn chair was holding a simple cane pole curving towards the weight of something under the muddy churning water. Raine walked closer.

It was the Rose Lady, wearing the same baseball cap: *Yokohama Carp.*

Behind her, a Seesel's shopping cart was loaded with a few unsold birdhouses and the empty milk jugs the roses had been in. *She's having a good day,* Raine thought. *She's sold all her roses and she's got a big fish on her line.*

An old black man in overalls called out something to her, instructions or encouragement, but his words were whipped away by the wind. The cane pole began to bend like a boiling noodle, and she riveted her feet into a more solid position. Her eyes were locked on the water in grim determination. Raine and the man in the overalls took separate paths towards her.

From the opposite direction a man appeared, the man in the Brooks Brothers suit, stuffing his tie in his pocket. He was taking off his coat, rolling up his sleeves, moving to the little figure at the mercy of the bent pole. All three converged at the same time where the small figure was struggling with her cane pole. All eyes were set on the quicksilver place in the water where her cork had disappeared.

—*Pole liable snap off,* the old black man allowed.

—*Maybe not,* the man in the suit said, looking around for something. —*Hold this,* he said to Raine, handing her his coat. She took it by the collar and folded it once and held it to her chest.

—*Got a dip net in her cart there,* the black man offered helpfully, and the man in the suit picked it up, twirling it.

The Rose Lady planted her feet solidly, and made small noises of pleasure and dismay.

—*Just hold him steady and work him a little closer, and we'll get him for you, okay? You don't want to give him too much play,* the suit man said. He was dressed like a stockbroker, but his voice betrayed an acquaintance with country ways.

The black man laughed and turned his cap around backwards in readiness.

—*Hold this,* the suit man said, and handed Raine the dipnet. He unlaced his shoes, black wingtips. He peeled his socks off. He rolled his pants legs up to his knees. His long shins were thin and white, with dark whorls of hair. Raine handed back the net.

—*Here we go,* the suit man was saying, wading out. The black man in overalls hovered at the edge, leaning towards the water in moral support.

The Rose Lady was making a low humming sound, and she began to rock on the balls of her feet a bit. The backs of her hands were veined and rough, like the guesswork on old maps. Raine stood biting her lip, still holding the man's coat.

—*Here we really go this time,* the suit man said, addressing his remarks to something under the water. He was oblivious to the brown water lapping at his rolled cuffs, and Raine closed her eyes at the strange illicit pleasure of it, the ruination of a perfectly good suit. He reached out gingerly to grab the line and took all the pressure off the flimsy cane pole, which the Rose Lady continued to grip with both hands. The force of the struggling fish pulled the muscles in the man's forearm taut.

—*Somebody fixin' to have a fish dinner tonight,* the black man said, and turned his hat a quarter-turn.

The man in the Brooks Brothers suit swept the dip net into the water softly and brought it up. —*Here you go, old fella,* he said to the fish, with the gentleness of an apology. —*You should have stayed up there in St. Louis with the missus in the Winnebago, buddy.* They saw its enormous belly first, the color of mud-stained pearl, and its sides were heaving with effort to escape. It suddenly jackknifed in the net, splattering the suit man's white shirt, but he seemed not to notice.

The old catfish was as long as the suit man's arm, and twice as thick. Its eyes were fierce buttons, surveying them, his enemies. They were quiet then, respectful of how long he had spent surviving to his present size.

—*Oh, holy glorious,* said the Rose Lady after a moment.

—*There now,* the suit man said gently, lowering the dip net into the bucket to give the fish a rest. He reached over and rummaged in the little tackle box beside the chair, somehow knowing that there would be a pair of pliers there. —*There now.*

—*I thank you,* the Rose Lady said, finally. —*I thank you kindly.*

—*You were going to lose your pole,* the suit man said, looking around to see where he'd flung his shoes.

The Rose Lady pulled back the tarp covering her shopping cart and displayed her wares, the book-and-bottle-cap birdhouses. —*Be my guest,* she said ceremoniously to the man who'd saved her fish. He chose a low squat one with a tawny leather roof edged in gilt: *A Moral Inquiry into the Nature of Man.*

—*Would you, please,* the man said, handing Raine the birdhouse.

—You hold it right there, the black man said. *—I got a little camera.*

Raine was half-listening to them talk, and murmuring admiration for the fish to the Rose Lady, who stood with her hands clasped, peering into the bucket. She wondered how the woman would get it all home, or even if she had a home to get it to. She looked up and the black man was motioning her into the photo. They stood on either side of the Rose Lady, who held up the now sluggish fish, her arm shaking with the effort. Raine stood with the man's coat still folded against her chest, and the birdhouse at her side. At the last second, the man reached across to put his arm around them both, and Raine felt his fingertips brush the center of her back at the base of her neck.

A stranger's fingers across her skin at the base of her neck: every nerve Raine owned was suddenly ready for occupancy.

The black man in the blue overalls snapped the photo, with the Wolf River behind them at twenty feet above its normal level.

—Now what did I do with my coat? The suit man looked around, picking up his briefcase.

—Your wife got it there, the black man said, marrying them with a glance.

The suit man smiled mischievously. *—Honey, what's for dinner?* He began to walk towards some balconied apartments.

Raine followed him, holding out his coat and his birdhouse. The black man had seen her in her mom purdah, the khaki slacks and the pink pinstriped shirt that she wore entirely too much, mostly because it was a dependable sort of camouflage. Why shouldn't Matthew's girlfriend have looked right past her? She was dressed like the mom appliance in the household the girl had grown up in. Maybe she looked like Mom to Matthew, too.

The suit man led her through a maze of sidewalks and stone

fountains and figures, past little expensive trees, upstairs to his own door. The doors were situated so that no one's door faced anyone else's. A brindle cat murmured to them and bumped the suit man's bare calves with her head while he unlocked the door. Raine hesitated on the small balcony, and he turned with a questioning look. She held out his coat and birdhouse, though she would have liked to study the inside of the birdhouse. He smiled, reading her doubts on her face.

—*You can come in*, he said. —*I'm harmless.*

Behind him, Raine saw several jukeboxes in various states of deshabille and repair. —*That's a lot of jukeboxes*, she said, stepping across the threshold. —*Do you sell them?*

—*Collect them*, he said, dropping to the lower registers of a stage whisper. —*Don't breathe a word to the neighbors*, he added, taking the birdhouse from her and setting it on the floor. —*They'd be scandalized. They'd report me to the city.*

—*Do they work?* Raine asked, looking around at the jukeboxes. She could count seven in that room alone.

—*Some do*, he said. —*Some will someday.*

She followed him obediently, past the ones that looked like spaceships or robots, reading the playlists while he talked about the makes and models. He did something at the back of a jukebox with a screwdriver, and soft aqua lights flashed on its front, SEEBURG, and she saw an old 45 drop into play. She leaned over staring into the bubble of the glass. *Jimi Hendrix, 'Catfish Blues.'*

> *Well, I wish I was a catfish*
> *Swimmin' in the deep blue sea,*
> *I'd have all you pretty women*
> *Fishing after me, yeah, fishing after me.*

—*Actually, the Muddy Waters version is much better*, the man said. He busied himself unrolling the cuffs of his pants, and she looked away. It seemed too much an intimacy with a stranger to watch. He punched buttons as he passed one jukebox, and it began to play: *I got no special rider here, no one to feel my pain.*

—*What does that mean?*

—*'Special rider'? It means 'girlfriend,'* he called back over his shoulder. —*The illicit kind.* He looked at her intently, and she looked away, at a different jukebox.

—*Would you like a drink?*

—*No, thanks, I need to get home.*

—*You're married*, he said, stating it flatly like a change in the weather.

—*Yes*, she said.

—*Happens to the best of us*, he shrugged, and she laughed out loud.

—*How long have you had that problem with bridges?* he asked softly, and his words seemed to burn her as he spoke. —*I saw you when you came off and I thought*—

Raine raised her hand as if to ward off any more words, and she set the birdhouse down on the floor and laid his folded coat over it.

—*Sorry*, he said. —*Sorry I brought it up.*

She waved his words away, good-bye, and backed out the door, saying things of no consequence. When she believed she was out of his sight she ran down the stairs, her hand groping in her pocket for her car keys.

The Rose Lady was trudging across the bridge with her bucket and her umbrella in her shopping cart, heading out into her homelessness. Raine felt oddly satisfied, as if she'd been on a momentary vacation, to have been lost in the maze of someone else's world for a while. Driving, she felt like she was fumbling for the port of entry back into her own. She crossed the Wolf River bridge too fast, and wondered what the jukebox man would say about it.

She passed a bus stop, and there was her son, with his guitar slung over his back, trying to look like a troubled troubadour. She waved, telegraphing concern. He suddenly needed to study his shoes intently, as if he hadn't seen her.

He'd seen her. Surely he had. It was the kind of big milestone one never recorded in the baby book: the first time your child passes you on the street as if you are some stranger.

She must have driven the double-helix six-lane hell, she realized, without even seeing it. She had obviously crossed it, because she was on Union Avenue, headed home. —*See*, she said to the absent jukebox man, which is how she had come to think of him.

She wondered what his name was.

She wondered if he had wondered what her name was.

She wondered what risk management was, actually.

The jukebox man was not harmless.

Satan Is Real

Dean Fondren studied the black plastic flats of bedding plants on the porch of the Celestial Grocery. There were peppers and eggplants and squash, even pumpkin. How many tomato plants would be enough? Normally Alexis would have already started their kitchen garden from seeds, but this year she was gone. He set three of each vegetable into a cardboard tray, put it in his truck bed, then went inside to pay Angus.

What would he do with the vegetables when they came in? Surely Alexis would be home by then. Regulars at the Celestial had stopped asking about her, and a quiet fell over the place whenever he walked in. The odd situation of his being alone seemed to fit some preconception they had of his odd ways. It occurred to him that he could grow old and die in Madagascar, and the only people who would have known him would be his wife and Angus. Maybe.

—*Got three of everything,* he said, pulling out his wallet. The Honduran woman stepped aside deferentially to let Angus handle the cash. Angus dumped Dean's change into a mayonnaise jar with a photo of somebody's sick baby taped onto it, without even offering it to him.

Dean felt foolish suddenly, paying twenty dollars for plants that Alexis could have grown from seed for pennies. It seemed like the end of something.

And it seemed the end of something else when he himself was on his knees at dusk, kneeling in the little plot of earth that he usually harrowed up for Alexis, admitting to himself that those who canned and preserved at home anymore were probably spending more money than they were saving.

His fingers felt fat when they tamped the dirt around the plants. Alexis's fingers were elegant and slender. He watered the plants gently with the leaky garden hose, racked the hose, and went in for the night. When he couldn't sleep, he walked out onto the porch and surveyed the little garden. Was it woman's work he had done? Who had helped her all those years that she had put up the vegetables? Who could blame her for not being there now? She had come home just long enough to get some more clothes, and then she went back to the new grandbaby.

Before he went to bed Dean stared into the doorway of her little workroom off the kitchen where she kept her sewing machine and her canning things. The jars were all washed and shelved, as if she meant to make use of them. It was reassuring somehow to see them. He'd rather have a bread and butter pickle from her shelves than all the fancy jars in the stadium-sized supermarkets of Memphis.

Getting dressed the next morning, Dean heard Belle barking at something in the yard, and his first thought was *Alexis.*

But it was not Alexis, he saw, looking out the bathroom window as he shaved. It was instead the blue heeler dog he'd seen with the Smith-Jones girl, dog-nosing in the vegetables he'd just planted, rubbing its snout happily in the fresh hummocks of dirt that held the spindly, fragile plants. Dean threw down his razor and ran out of the house.

—*Shoo*, he said. —*Get on from here.*

The dog stood in its tracks and stared stupidly at him. Its markings were ugly, as if someone had flung the leavings of sharpened pencils on him. Belle stood beside him, telltale smears of dirt on her nose, too.

—*You, Belle. You know better than that*, he scolded her, and she tucked her tail and retired under the porch behind the trellis, her private spot for being ashamed.

—*And you, Mister Cocaine, or Nubane, whatever your name is. I said* git *from here.*

Dean lunged at the blue heeler, and it ran across the field and headed straight for Ariadne's house, which could only mean the girl was still over there, unless she'd abandoned the dog.

Dean stared at the old Comet still nudged into the bushes and devised a new plan. He pulled out a kitchen drawer, and just as he suspected, Alexis had left her car phone there. He normally didn't believe in such absurdities as a phone in the car, but he bought it so she'd feel safe, so she'd feel like she could find help if she needed it. To get that phone for her, he'd had to deal with a satellite-dish-dealing fool in Greenville who'd clapped him on the back like he had received communion in the Holy Church of Useless Expenditures.

Dean took out the phone and put a piece of white freezer tape on the end of it, and wrote his house phone number on it. He picked up the extra flashlight in that drawer, slid his bare feet into some loafers, and went out the door. Belle waited expectantly, and he told her to get in the truck. Daylight was burning.

In the grocery, the Mauritanian boy was wedged between the wall and the jukebox. Dean could see his back, and his thin hand as it reached up into the cup of painted quarters. A truck

driver from Marvell, Arkansas, was cooking his own hamburgers, munching from a bag of potato chips. He waved the grill
spatula at Dean, saying hello.

—*Haven't seen you in a while*, Dean said.

—*Just here to check on Mr. Ellerbee. They told me to stop
off and see if I could catch him, see why he's behind on his
order.*

Dean understood the code. Something was wrong at
Aubrey's.

—*Well, I'll tell him you came by*, Dean said. —*He'll be
rolling in here sometime soon.*

—*Yep*, Angus agreed, looking Dean in the eye. —*Aubrey be
around here soon.*

—*What are you doing back there?* Dean asked the boy, and
peered around behind. The boy's English was not good, but he
said something about fixing the music.

The truck driver advised the boy in a loud voice, as if to be
from Africa was also to be hard of hearing, —*Here in America
we got a thing called the* seek *function. What you need to do
is, put you in a reddio with a* seek *function.*

Dean noticed that the floor behind the jukebox was covered
in greasy dust, the cords snarled with dustballs. He got a broom
from beside the refrigerator and had the boy sweep the dust out
and put it in the trashcan under the counter. He was amazed
Angus hadn't burnt his own business down years ago.

The boy stepped back, and with the light of expectation in
his dark face, dropped a red-painted quarter in. Within seconds,
the store was filled once again with the nasal strains of the Louvin Brothers.

All hope fell from the boy's face, and the truck driver cursed
and laughed. —*Is not the Slim Harpo*, the boy said, grimacing.

Dean found the batteries he needed to give the girl for the
flashlight. He wondered how long they had been hanging there,
and if they still worked. He reached for his wallet, and threw

some bills down on the counter. —*The rest can go to that sick baby, I reckon. Angus, these batteries is older than my flashlight.*

—*Walk you to your truck, Dean,* Angus said, and Dean knew something big was coming. Angus could impart major news with no more fanfare than the rustle of leaves. After they'd passed down the steps, Angus opened the truck door for Dean, and then patted it when he closed it behind him. Dean looked back at him expectantly.

—*Aubrey's got himself in a situation.*

—*What do you mean?*

—*I think that casina there has took his best tractor. Can they do that?*

Dean looked sharply across the field at the casino, a sort of low-slung commotion over by the horizon.

—*I reckon they can, if he put it up for money to gamble with. Depending on what condition he was in when he signed. If he signed anything.*

— *If they can take his tractor, they can take his land, don't you imagine?*

Dean closed his eyes and kneaded the bridge of his nose. —*He don't get his cotton and beans in the ground soon, the bank will have his land before the crooks do.*

When Dean pulled his truck up near the porch of Ariadne's house, he left the engine running while he put the batteries in the flashlight. Then he swung out of the truck and told Belle to stay. He looked at the old house.

—*Peregrine?* He called out softly. —*It's just me.* He realized she didn't know his name. —*It's Dean Fondren,* he called out. —*I just came to see about you.*

There was no answer, so he stepped inside. The rustle of the brown paper bag he was holding seemed loud as gunshots. She wasn't there. Her jeans and pink sweatshirt were on the floor. *Bowdoin*, the shirt said.

There were small photographs pinned to the bare boards of the walls: the shack, the artesian well, Angus's store, the Harlem Swing Club. On the floor was a small CD player, and the homemade mandolin, and some notebooks. His eyes came to rest on one of the notebooks. *Fieldwork of Peregrine Smith-Jones.*

There were sketches of Ariadne's house, the carved animals around the door, and the carvings over the stone fireplace. There was a sketch of his long field, like a brilliant yellow sea; there was his John Deere, with him on it. She had every detail, his hat, the arc of egrets, and the dog a black smudge following in the new furrows. She had put the redwings on the power lines, little black commas. He lifted the page, peeked at the next.

There was a small diagram or chart that seemed at first to be the tracks of herons, then it came into focus. The words startled him; he recognized the names, *Sid Hemphill, Napoleon Strickland, Othar Turner.* It was as if she'd eavesdropped on his childhood somehow. His first memory of Clarksdale was of Sid Hemphill playing his cane fife in the train station. That was 1942 and Hemphill was an old man then, but not too old to materialize out of the hill country and play for the troop trains shunting the soldiers down to New Orleans. The memory of that music made the hairs bristle on the back of Dean's neck. It was like no other music on earth. It was music for those heading off to die.

On another page, words seemed to float up out of the margins of the notebook and roar out of the walls at him:

HOW MANY MILES TO BABYLAND?
THREE SCORE MILES AND TEN
CAN WE GET THERE BY CANDLELIGHT?
YES, AND BACK AGAIN.

He knew then that the girl had been in the old Abide house. He left the cell phone and flashlight on top of her notebook,

and went back to the truck and wrote her a note on a horse-feed
receipt. Belle whimpered and wagged her tail while he used the
hood of the truck for a flat surface: *Call if you need help.* He
went back in and left the note with the phone, then stepped
softly out of the shack, as if he'd been intruding. He got back in
the truck and drove towards the Lucky Leaf Casino.

The casino always seemed to Dean like some vaguely pornographic piece of cardboard left behind on the horizon to fool
tasteless Americans who couldn't afford the *real* Europe. Up
close it was even more pornographic, a Roman palazzo grafted
onto the front side of Versailles, painted a Disney-fied puke-
green. His heart felt violated as he looked at it. It occupied
what once had been Israel Abide's main cotton field, which had
been so large it had taken six cotton pickers at the time to work
it. Now most of that field was covered in asphalt. Cars and
trucks from Arkansas, Louisiana, and Mississippi were wedged
as close to the entrance as possible. Dean found a parking place
and sat clenching the wheel of his truck. He kneaded the bridge
of his nose and pondered the main entrance.

Liveried valets from Africa and Arkansas loitered in purple
coats with golden epaulets under a splendid fringed purple
awning. The Africans spoke English with French accents, murmuring in exaggerated politeness to squinting senior citizens
debarking from buses that could double as ambulances. Mississippi had not seen such tasteless excess since before the Civil
War. Everybody knew the sad outcome of *that*. It was a bad
sign, when people seemed to have more money at their disposal
than common sense.

Dean had never been inside any casino. He wasn't sure
where to start. He took off his hat and walked slowly with it

clamped over his heart, as if for protection. He noticed the noise first, the hypnotic drone, an electronic beckoning, like thousands of dreamy false coins falling, a way of wooing fools.

The lights were dim in some places, bright in others. Women in French boudoir maid costumes whisked past him, holding trays of drinks aloft, brushing so close he could hear their nylons rustling. It was an enormous aboveground cavern, he decided, a big bunker with no windows. *So they'll lose track of time*, he thought. There were thousands of people in there.

Who *were* these people? Fools imported from God knows where for the sole, express purpose of separating them from their life savings.

He witnessed black sharecroppers in overalls feeding coins into slot machines, *Pot o' Gold, Luck o' the Irish, Dealer's Choice.*

He witnessed white-haired women from the Midwest, seamstresses and retired nurses perhaps, in industrial-strength capri pants and sneakers, grinning as fake coins fell out into their gnarled hands. They chortled with delight to each other, —*Marge! You gotta try this one!* through mouths constricted like tight, lipstick-encrusted anuses.

He witnessed a wizened little blue man attached to a portable oxygen tank on wheels, standing in line to change his money into casino scrip. Clear plastic tubes ran from the man's nose to the tank. In a previous life, the man had been pink-skinned, but now he was blue.

Dean witnessed young farm girls, plump as pullets, cozied up to beery aging cardsharks. He saw seasoned old hookers from Memphis dandled on the knees of Ole Miss fraternity boys. He saw newlyweds squandering the fortunes of their unborn.

He watched as two plump pairs of Mennonites bellied up to the all-you-can-eat salad bar. The husbands had their hair politely slicked back. The women spoke quietly to each other, in their homemade floral dresses cinched at the waists, their little black caps pinned tightly to their coils of hair.

Mennonites in a casino, Dean thought in despair. *This is the end.*

He wandered the aisles of the slot machines, the blackjack tables, looking for Aubrey, looking at the cheap pilastered accoutrements of legalized theft, at the mindless murals of the old moss-draped *trompe l'oeil* plantations on the walls, while uniformed overseers stood stationed like sentinels at discreet intervals.

Burn it down, he thought rationally, arson pulsing in his brain like a prayer.

Dean wandered speechless, understanding that fire could be a holy thing.

Dean saw the cheap fancy woman from behind first, and then he saw Aubrey sitting on a barstool watching the baccarat tables. She was leaning over him, wearing a short skirt about twenty years too young for her prunelike knees, and leopard-skin high-heeled shoes of the sort called *mules*. The makeup on her face seemed to echo the trompe l'oeil on the walls, and the dim lights took about fifteen years off her face. Aubrey was wobbly on his barstool, and Dean saw that she was helping to buttress him against his own inclination to slump to the floor. Dean watched a minute, studying how to proceed.

—*Hey, buddy*, Dean said softly. —*I'm the posse they sent out to take you home.*

—*Not yet*, Aubrey said, shrugging the woman's hands off his shoulders. —*Just gettin' goin' good here. Where's that gal with my drink?*

—*Aubrey, have you eaten today?*

—*We fixin' to eat, sure. We got us a room last night, and they sent some food up.*

Dean shifted his weight back on his heels. Aubrey could

have walked home, it was that close. Maybe he hadn't wanted to sleep with the white woman in his dead wife's bed. Maybe he'd wanted the cheap thrill of some tawdry cigarette-stinking public room. He had to figure out some way to get him away from the woman, who seemed all too helpful about separating him from his money. Aubrey seemed to have no particular respect or regard for the woman, which was unlike him.

—*Come walk outside with me for a minute*, Dean said, and put his hand under Aubrey's elbow. —*Let's go get us some air.* Something about the way Dean cupped his hand under the elbow, like the mere courtesy one would extend to a woman— it infuriated Aubrey, who stood up and pulled his arm away.

—*Leave me be, Dean*, he said. —*I'm right where I need to be.*

—*Awright, then. Suit yourself. Just give me the key to the big New Holland, and I'll get somebody started on the long field.*

—*Ain't got no key*, Aubrey said sullenly, like a child caught in a falsehood.

The cheap fancy woman had a worried look on her face, and she seemed to busy herself with something of no consequence just a few feet away. She pulled a compact out of her purse and inspected her lipstick, and in that instant Dean loathed her, and wanted to shout at her to go back to whatever backward stinking alley she hailed from.

A heavy hand rested itself on Dean's back. An oily voice behind him said, —*Sir, is there a problem here?*

Dean turned and saw the man who had spoken, a white man, his black hair clipped close to his head, in the manner of a dandified television wrestler. His chest was a massive expanse of elegant pinstripes, silk shirt, and a minuscule fresh red rosebud pinned to the lapel. He wore a gold earring and some kind of name badge, but Dean didn't have time to read it. The man had hold of Dean's wrist by then and applied pressure so gentle it seemed friendly, but the man was prepared to increase the pressure if the spirit moved him.

—*This man needs to go home and see to his farm*, Dean said angrily, raising his voice as if he were announcing the fact to even the little midwestern widows across the crowded room. —*He's got a crop to get into the ground.*

The casino manager dropped Dean's arm like a hot potato, but the smile stayed affixed to his face. —*It's a free country, sir,* the manager said.

—*No man is free in this place,* Dean said, shaking with rage. —*Not even you. Sir.*

Dean had tripped some kind of invisible wire of alarm in the place. Others in fine suits sporting rosebuds arrived, muscled overseers standing on what once had been all cotton fields. They wanted him gone from there. They made their presence known, and stood silently while the manager pulled something out of his pocket. He held out pseudo-money, something resembling old plantation scrip. Dean batted his hand away with his hat, then put his hat on his head.

—*Come back when you can stay longer, sir,* the man said in an impersonal business-college voice. —*You have a good one now.*

Dean walked out, past the restaurants hawking six-dollar hot dogs, and stepped out into the sunlight and bus exhaust fumes. An enormous woman in a red gingham windbreaker and tan capri pants breezed past, reeking of magnolias. He could hear her thighs chafing together, *whisk, whisk.*

Dean could not remember where he'd parked his truck. It should be easy to find, he thought, because it was probably the oldest thing out there. The light poles were numbered, so people could remember where they'd put their cars, but Dean hadn't noticed them going in, and now he had no idea where his truck was. He came around a row of cars, and noticed the huge fountain then, rippling with water. Concrete cherubs cavorted, while concrete angels with the bodies of whores watched over them.

Then he saw the cotton-pickers and combines, arranged in a circle around the fountain. Each one had a *For Sale* sign on it. He wondered for a confused moment why the gaming company would be going into the farm implement business, and then the answer rose in his heart and sickened him. This was a cemetery for farmers' dreams. His eyes came to rest on one particular tractor, and his hands began to shake. *New Holland.* It was Aubrey's all right, he was sure of it. He'd driven Aubrey to Clarksdale to pick it up.

He walked closer, put his hand on it, then leaned over and rested his forehead sadly against its big metal fender as he might have against the flank of an amiable old draft horse.

—*There's a kind of justice in this, don't you think?* a girl's voice said, and Dean cut his eyes over towards the voice. He saw red velvet sandals. He looked up. It was Peregrine Smith-Jones, dressed in her French maid's costume. She carried a camera, an expensive, professional-looking one with a telephoto lens like a proboscis.

—*I don't see where anybody's misfortune is justice*, Dean said quietly.

—*I mean, the big daddies could finally lose their plantations, right?* She talked in a flirty way that annoyed him as much as her words.

—*Well, this one here belonged to a Big Daddy who has black skin. You can put that in your notes for Brown or Boston or Bowdoin, all right? Tell 'em there's something bad wrong going on down here. And my best friend is in there now a-losin' the shirt off his black back, most likely.*

The girl's mouth slackened, and she looked back at the cotton-picker. Dean raged on, unable to stop.

—*You ever see them old ignorant men at carnivals, givin' them fake baseballs to kids that will never understand why they can't knock the milk bottles down? You are no better'n that.* He saw that he had really stunned the girl, but he could not stop himself from saying more. —*I reckon it's your job to get those people in there drunk enough to lose everything they ever worked for. Don't let me keep you from your business, ma'am. You know there's more'n one way to be a slave to white men.*

She strode away, and he thought he'd made her cry. *Well, good,* he thought savagely. There was hope for the world when the young could still be shamed. He spotted his truck then, over her shoulder, and pretended he'd been headed that way all along. He stalked down the sidewalk under the fringed awning, straight towards it. Brassy horns bleated somewhere beneath the chemically green turf. *Hidy, Hidy, Hidy, Ho,* sang Cab Calloway. *Minnie the Moocher,* burbling up from secret pipes in the ground. It sounded like sly ridicule. Music for old people to squander their children's inheritances by.

I Am the True Vine

The story of how Aubrey Ellerbee came to be listed in Standard and Poor was best known by Angus Chien and Dean Fondren, since they had tampered with his fate when Aubrey was still a child.

One day long before, Dean was coming out of the Celestial when he saw a long black hearse pass on the highway and then turn out into the middle of his field to the cemetery. He thought he'd seen a flag on a coffin inside. It was 1971, the same year some college kids were burning American flags all across the country. He saw the hearse stop and inch its way into the ruts that served as a road across the wide field. Now he could see that there was indeed a flag draped on the coffin inside. He could see the mitered corners through the hearse's rear window.

But nobody's been digging, Dean thought. By then Angus had come out to stand with him.

—*Who is that?* Angus said, raising his binoculars.

—*I have no idea*, Dean said, watching the driver of the hearse, a black man from Clarksdale, pacing around in the cemetery. The coffin was a long exclamation point of red, white, and blue against the colorless landscape.

—*It's been a mix-take*, the black man said as Dean walked

up. —*Telegram just say to take receipt of the body and bring it here. Ain't nobody here. Don't say who the next of kin is on this.*

—*Who've you got here?*

—*This would be,* the driver said, looking at a clipboard with what appeared to be an invoice on it, —*P.F.C. Raymond Ellerbee of the U.S. Army.*

Dean walked back to the Celestial, where Angus was sitting smoking on the porch steps. Angus raised his eyebrows as Dean walked up.

—*Helen Ellerbee's boy, the one they called Ray-ray.*

The two were quiet a moment. —*I didn't even know he was in the service,* Dean said. —*Did you?*

—*They got their own world,* Angus said. —*They don't tell us their business. You know that.*

To the other farmers drinking coffee inside, Dean said, —*It's a man from Ibrahim Brothers out there with a soldier to bury, and no grave to put it in.* He poured himself a cup of coffee slowly before he turned around to face them.

—*Ain't no man. Just some old boy from Clarksdale,* someone murmured.

—*I ain't diggin' no nigger grave,* somebody else said.

—*Let that boy drivin' that hearse do it,* another said.

Dean stirred his coffee and felt the muscles in his jaw clench. Wordlessly, Angus had brought him a new square shovel right off the hardwood wall. —*You rather have the spade, come on back and get it. This one will corner up your edges real nice.*

Dean poured a second cup of coffee into another to-go cup, and carried the two cups out into the field with the shovel tucked under his arm. He handed the coffee to the hearse driver. When they had finished the coffee, they began to dig. He could feel the eyes of the other farmers burning into his back from across the field. He had carried a cup of coffee to a black man. It was treason.

Dean was a young man then, and welcomed most kinds of physical labor. Not long into the digging, he saw a young black boy coming across the field with a shovel. Dean nodded a greeting to the boy. Wordlessly the boy jumped into the long pit and began to help. He was only about ten or eleven, but he was strong and attacked the earth with a kind of vengeance. He said not a word the whole time he was digging, but once Dean saw him wiping tears away. The black man from Ibrahim Brothers saw the boy's tears and began to sing.

> *I am the true vine, I am the true vine.*
> *I am the true vine—my father is the husbandman.*

The boy synchronized the movements of his shovel to the older man's and began to sing with him. Dean had never heard the song before, and the best he could do was match the rhythm of his shovel to theirs. It was like stumbling upon some old thing much older than they were, to work to a common rhythm. When they were done, the boy seemed stronger than when he'd arrived. The hearse driver was arranging green felt over the mound of raw earth and Dean was helping him to unfold some chairs, when they saw the boy was gone, walking across the field with the shovel over his shoulder.

That was the first time Dean ever laid eyes on Aubrey Ellerbee.

The second time Dean laid eyes on him was some hours later, when Aubrey was standing in a cheap seersucker summer suit in the middle of winter, wearing big borrowed shoes, no socks on, trying to salute his father's grave through his tears. He was the oldest of six children, some still clinging to their mother. The mother stared into Dean's eyes with a kind of defiant hatred. He was the only white face at the graveside.

—*Ma'am*, Dean said softly when he shook her hand. —*If I can help you in any way.*

She was shaking with rage, and he didn't begrudge her that. It was a white man's war. Somebody white had to pay. His was the only white face before her. He was elected. He bent to shake the boy's hand, and when he did, the boy sobbed aloud, and threw his thin arms around Dean's waist. Dean could feel the boy's stout little back through the thin threads of the seersucker sports coat, somebody's cast-off Easter suit from years long gone.

—*Get offa him!* the mother shouted at the boy and slapped him across the temple. Dean had seen the same old gesture a hundred times in his life, when a black mother slaps a black child for being too human around whites.

—*Your daddy was a good man*, Dean said, hugging the boy so tight anyone standing near could hear the very breath being squeezed out of him. —*Your daddy gave his life for America.* Years would pass before Dean would see the misguidedness of his remark. Ray-ray had not given his life for America. Ray-ray had put himself in front of bullets shot by folks he had no personal quarrel with, because it was the only way at the moment that America would give him the money to put food on his family's table.

Across the field near the Celestial, on what seemed like the rim of another separate earth, a row of pickup trucks was parked facing the cemetery, and there were white farmers holding guns. For one bleak moment Dean misread them. He thought maybe they meant something fitting, like a twenty-one-gun salute, and then he knew. They were there to hold the future at bay, at gunpoint.

That night Dean lay in the dark as Alexis held him, trying to tell her about the song the boy sang with the hearse driver. Dean felt he'd been given an extraordinary gift, to have spent his afternoon that way, down in a hole with two black people, digging. He didn't know any other white person who'd ever been given such a gift. Alexis was the only person he could tell it to. They lived surrounded by people who would have been so frightened of that gift they'd have punished Dean for seeing it that way. They'd poison his well or his horses, or harm his wife or child.

The third time Dean saw Aubrey Ellerbee—not long afterwards—he spotted him walking along Highway 61, about a hundred yards past the city limit sign that said MADAGASCAR. At first Dean thought it was a scarecrow headed north, shirt-sleeves flapping. The figure moved resolutely towards some better place, probably Memphis, wearing old clothes that had once belonged to somebody bigger. It was mid-morning, and Dean did what most fathers do at the sight of a child out of school during school hours. Dean stopped his truck on the side of the road to see about him.

—*Son?*

—*Yes, sir.*

—*Your mama know where you at?*

Aubrey said nothing and held his bundle tighter. —*Nawsir.*

—*Don't you reckon she'll be worried about you? How come you not at the schoolhouse?*

Dean kept his hands on the steering wheel and sighed, already weary with the knowledge that if he intervened in the boy's life, it would mean more than giving him a ride back home. In those years, a black boy would have made no other choice but to obey an older white man. But Dean wanted the boy to choose to go back.

—Have you eat yet today?

The boy shrugged uncomfortably. He was the sort of child made suspicious by anything that resembled normal kindness. Dean could read the boy like a book: he had not known much kindness.

—Well, come on back to the house with me a minute and we'll get you some food for the road.

Dean brought a plate of food out from his own kitchen and stood with his arms folded while the boy ate sitting on the tailgate of the truck. When Dean saw how the boy gulped at the food, lungs heaving, Dean went back inside and brought out a glass of cold milk and a piece of sweet potato pie.

—Son, how come you not in school today? Dean said, looking at his watch. The boy's eyes rose to meet his, flown open like shutters. It was that word, *son.* Aubrey had wiped his mouth with the back of his hand and said nothing. *—You go to the new school or the old one?*

Integration was optional that first year, and the "colored" school was a dilapidated white frame building near the railroad depot, on a scrap of land too low to plant cotton on. The best that could be said for it was that it had windows and a floor. In the winters, when it was full of children, the wind whistled through the place like a fife, and the train passing through rattled the windows.

—Well, Dean said softly. *—Don't you reckon you ought to give it a go? School ain't even been let in a week yet. I think your daddy would want you to be in that school, if he were here to tell you.*

The boy's eyes had welled with tears then, and he looked out over the fields in misery.

—School, now that's your business, I guess.

Aubrey nodded, and swallowed a bite of pie like it was solid rock. Dean busied himself unloading some salt blocks and feed

sacks from the co-op. When he looked up, the boy was stagger-
ing under the weight of a hundred-pound feed sack slung over
his shoulder, heading to the barn with it. It was the boy's way
of paying for his food. Dean's mind was already racing with the
possibilities.

—*I could use me a sidekick around this place*, he said to
Aubrey, stopping just short of rubbing the top of his head with
his knuckles.

The boy's mother lived at the end of a row of shotgun houses
down a rutted dirt lane. She came to the door in a floral dime-
store wrapper, trailing the fluttering and giggles of small children behind her. When she understood that Dean was there
because of the boy, she boxed the boy's ears with a balled-up
fist, no questions asked.

—*No!* Dean shouted, and an eerie silence followed all down
the lane. —*I just came to see if he can do some work with me,
is all.*

The mother made a comment as to what she would do to
the boy if he didn't do good work, and Dean waved the words
away with his hat, impatiently swatting away a hundred years
of history. —*He'll do just fine,* Dean said.

The next morning, when Dean went out to start work, there
was Aubrey, asleep high up under the eaves of the barn on top
of some hay bales. For the next several years, Dean would never
ask why he often needed to sleep there. He did build a little
shelf for him and put a folded blanket and pillow on it.

Word got out, by Christmastime. When the sixth graders at
the private academy drew names to exchange gifts, Dean's
daughter received, anonymously, one black baby doll. She
brought it home proudly. That night Alexis hovered protec-
tively near her, brushing her hair, singing songs, shielding the
girl from the joke she hadn't got.

Dean, on the other hand, was ashen with rage that night,

and walked out into the frosty pasture with his hands clenched into fists deep in his pants pockets. He walked all the way to the creek bottom, circled the cemetery where Ray Ellerbee was buried, and then disappeared into the stand of trees to cut a feathery young cedar. He dragged it across the field to the house. He mounted the tree in a store-bought stand, and Alexis covered its base with a quilt of blue and white stars. They strung lights around it in generous scallops, and pulled out old blown glass ornaments of chapels and angels and fruits.

Dean bought two bicycles at the Western Auto in Clarksdale. One for his daughter and one for Ray-ray Ellerbee's son. He arranged for the two different deliveries. He sat up late alone that night. The retribution, he knew, would come in picayune ways.

First came silence. The others turned away from them, even in church, as if they harbored contagion. They even began to shun the child. Dean's daughter was somehow not informed about the night the white children would go caroling together. Dean could not believe it when he heard their voices carrying across the fields without her. He could not believe that grown men and women could conspire to punish an innocent child. Alexis answered the distant voices by singing in the kitchen, rattling her rolling pin and cookie sheets. In no time, she had the girl laughing, waving buttery stars and angels, believing that she was decorating them for the less fortunate of the world.

Later that night they awakened to the sounds of gunshots and trucks passing. His neighbors were taking target practice at his mailbox.

The silences in the Celestial Grocery were heavy enough that Dean stopped going inside for coffee in the mornings. Angus Chien stocked a good supply of black baby dolls and no white ones, in cellophane-wrapped boxes with red and green bows. It seems the other little girls envied Dean's daughter's black baby doll, and more than one white farmer had crept in late to buy his daughter a black one. All Dean ever knew was that on Christmas morning the church seemed full of radiant little white girls clutching new black baby dolls, sitting with their stone-faced parents.

Not a word ever passed between Dean Fondren and Angus Chien on this subject. Angus chose to spend his Christmas morning that year sitting on his porch in a new blue sweater sent to him by his son, smoking peaceably. His store was not open, *per se,* but could be if needed. Eggs, yes, but no gasoline. If the *bok guey* were going to burn Dean Fondren's house down, it would not be with gasoline Angus Chien had sold them.

And when Miss Bebe Marie came in to get her one brown egg, she had something wrapped in a bundle she wanted to show Angus. She pulled back the fringe on a black shawl so old its red roses had turned brown, and there he saw an old, old black doll, an effigy of the great dancer Josephine Baker, with tiny yellow chalk bananas for earrings. Then she lowered the fringe to cover it, and passed back out into the evening.

This was how Angus developed the habit of watching the fields with his binoculars at dusk and dawn.

By spring, Dean had taught Aubrey Ellerbee to drive the truck and the tractor. Other boys his age were still on their knees pushing toy race cars in the dirt. Dean could see that the boy was a born farmer. It felt at times like playing a big fish, giving the boy enough line to run on before he set his hook.

He put other things up on the boy's shelf in the barn, a gyroscope, a Red Cross manual, some comic books, the beginnings of a stamp collection. All this while he was paying him ten dollars a week.

—*How much it cost to get a farm my own self?* Aubrey asked once.

—*Depends. You have to stay in school.*

The hook set. The boy completed a year of school with almost perfect attendance, and Dean titled over a half-acre for the boy to grow vegetables for his family. He explained the piece of paper to him: it meant that his mother could not sell it, nor could her boyfriends sell it. The land was Aubrey's to keep until he was an old man.

Word got out that the little swatch of vegetables growing near the old church was the black boy's scrap of land. One night while Dean and Alexis were at the white church with their daughter, someone laid waste to Aubrey's little crop. There were tire marks all through the ruins of it, stopping just short of Dean's soybeans. Dean was not sure how to read the threat. Had he violated them because he'd helped a black boy, or had he violated them because he'd opted for soybeans rather than cotton? He knew them well enough to know that what passed for farmer politics often disguised a pragmatic underbelly having to do with profits. Dean responded by taking Aubrey with him to the Celestial Grocery the next morning. He bought Aubrey his first cup of coffee, heavily doctored with milk and sugar. Dean saw the boy's knuckles tighten around the cup when the other farmers came in.

—*Just be yourself, and eventually you'll be among friends here*, Dean said.

Angus came over quietly with the coffeepot, and brought Aubrey a cinnamon roll, and fussed over him a bit. There was a greasy silence at the long table under the blue marlin. Angus ignored them and vanished into the back of the store.

—*Hey, Hop Sing*, one of the farmers called out in a low voice. —*We need more of that stuff you call coffee.*

Angus walked out from behind the bamboo printed shower curtain that divided his apartment from the store. He was carrying a shotgun, which he stood in the corner behind the abacus, just in case.

The men were quiet, except one who asked in a stagey voice, —*You refusing us service?*

—*Be no need of that Angus,* Dean said quietly. —*We all among friends here. This boy here is named Aubrey Ellerbee, and he's a natural-born farmer. That's his daddy buried in my field out there. His daddy probably was shot down over there in Vietnam some afternoon when you boys was in here shootin' the shit.*

No one offered to shake the boy's hand.

—*I reckon you all got sons and I ain't,* Dean continued, —*so it's easy for you sit there and think your work will go on when you are no longer on this earth. And if you think you can hold your sons here to help you, well go right ahead and tell this boy he can't farm. And when your boys are up in them air-conditioned factories in Memphis, me and Aubrey here, we aim to keep farming no matter what you do. We'll help you when you need help, and we'll ignore you when you need ignoring.*

They turned then to see whose side Angus Chien would take, and they saw the shotgun up on the countertop, and his hand on its stock. The barrel was pointed vaguely in their direction.

—*Now Angus, they'll be no need of that,* someone said, and Dean himself got the coffeepot and filled their cups. It was 1974, and they had been shamed into entering the future.

By the time the future arrived, Aubrey Ellerbee's acreage had eclipsed Dean's.

The sons of the white farmers had left for Memphis desk jobs.

Aubrey started his own crop-dusting company, with a lithe little yellow plane that could land crisp as a wasp. He had a fleet of tractors, combines, and cotton-pickers. He was a man of means, meaning he lay down every night owing over a million dollars.

After his wife died in her forties, leaving him without children, he gradually came unmoored in his little world. He would shower after work and wander over to the casinos, where the pretty waitresses always acted like they were glad to see him, and they soon learned his name. Each night he lay down to sleep having wagered every dime he owned on the next day, on the wayward variables of rainfall, the fluctuations of government subsidies, plus the migratory flights of Hondurans. It was one such night that he first went to the casino. It was four in the morning and he was feeling crushed by his own weightlessness, so he got in his truck and drove over. A pretty girl brought him a drink. He watched the blackjack tables so long that a manager came and spoke to him in low tones about the necessity of joining in or moving on, in order to keep the participating clients comfortable.

Clients. The word had made him feel more substantial, and he had reached for his wallet. Pretty soon he had some debts he hadn't counted on. On the same day that Consuela Ramirez went to work for Angus Chien, Aubrey had just driven over a New Holland tractor to sign over to the Nevada gaming company that owned the Lucky Leaf Casino. He'd have a whole summer to get it back.

That was several hundred thousand dollars ago. When he got too nervous about it all at night, when the debts cuddled too close for comfort, he'd get up out of bed and get on the Internet and search for himself, look himself up on the NASDAQ as if to reassure himself he'd not yet been buried alive.

Money House Blessing

Nothing pleased Angus Chien more than the sight of nature thumbing its nose at him, going about its secret business. One morning he looked out the store window to see a shimmering pale green mass in the coils of green wisteria that could never quite conquer the old empress tree. Acadian flycatchers, like goldfinches tinted green, stopping off on the way back home to Canada. In the sunlight, they looked like they'd been buttered. They could have perched anywhere along several hundred miles of the Mississippi River flyway, and they had chosen his empress tree while it was still pink with flowers. He was honored and humbled at the same time. He held his breath in order not to disturb them, and motioned for Consuela to come to the window.

Wiping her hands on her red apron, she came. Seeing them, she pressed her fingers to the glass. —*Hola, amigos.* She turned a smile to Angus and said, —*We got these in my country.*

They stood together at the window in silence watching. If either had so much as taken a deep breath, they would have touched. Angus was suddenly afraid to breathe. He imagined raising his hand to touch her hair, but it stayed on the windowsill next to hers. There was no one else in the store. There was no one else in his heart, Angus realized, but this woman who made him feel safe and still. She smelled wonderful to him, cinnamon and soap and cumin.

The birds hopped from branch to branch, impatient, in anticipation of something unseen.

Then, as if some silent summons had passed through their little hollow bones, they were gone. Consuela turned back to whatever chore she'd been doing, rattling some steel pots in the deep sink, and the sound was a great comfort to Angus. There was something about the sound of a woman banging pots in a kitchen that made his feet feel more securely planted on the earth, as if he suddenly had more of a right to stand on the same wood floor he had owned for forty years. And yet he seemed to float through his day. One small woman now protected him from everything he'd never realized he needed protection from.

In the weeks following Consuela's bad evening with Tulia, they had grown closer, though they spoke less and less. She often seemed sad and tired, and Angus would try to cheer her up by playing the jukebox for her. He was working up to asking her to dance, he realized, some evening when there would be no one else in the store but themselves.

The flycatchers came to the empress tree punctually for four days, perched on the bare blossomy limbs. They made the whole tree tremble. For three mornings he called Consuela over to the window, and she came, drying her hands on a towel, and he understood that she was doing it just to humor him, in the way women will humor men, and this pleased him. It became a shared little ritual of their mornings, before the other customers came in. He felt in those moments slightly tipsy from too much sudden life, from sharing something with her and no one else. Then, as if by some hidden code he couldn't hear, on the fourth morning, the pale green birds got some signal to vanish, almost as soon as they had perched. He watched them go, tracking them with his binoculars. He understood somehow that they would not return, not that season.

At noon, when the air in the Celestial was full of quiet Spanish conversations, Angus looked out the front window and saw the big red truck pulling in. Tomás Tulia, riding high on the hog in his luxury liner of a truck that the workers jokingly referred to as *La Reina Maria*, the Queen Mary. What was worse, Aubrey Ellerbee was seated on the passenger side. Angus was outraged. It was bad enough that Aubrey would ride with the man, but they meant to come in his store. He put the binoculars down and positioned himself with his hands on the abacus, as if it would steady him.

Consuela saw them when they came in, and turned her back, busying herself with chopping some green herbs. Angus made it a point to stand in front of her, between her and Tulia.

As soon as they entered, all conversation in Spanish ceased, and the eyes of all the workers were suddenly trained down at their plates. Tulia made the air in the place ominous, seeming to threaten the other men just in the way he carried himself. Even his muscles were too much under his control, too over-defined, like he lifted weights.

Tulia said something to the workers in Spanish, and Aubrey inspected his fingernails. This is how Angus knew that whatever Tulia was telling them, it was wrong. Whatever it was, the men didn't like it, but they were being polite. Some glanced up at the old Pabst Blue Ribbon clock on the wall.

—*You got some business to transact with me, Mr. Tulia?*

The man smiled, and looked at his watch, as if to dismiss Angus.

—*You in my store, ain't you? You got business here or not?*

Aubrey put a hand up as if to warn Angus away from whatever errand he was about.

Angus heard Consuela make a small, sad noise, then she vanished behind the shower curtain at the back of the store. This brought a smirk from Tulia, who was still silent. Most of the workers had cleared out by then, some just tossing the money on the counter and not waiting for their change. —*I know what you're up to here,* Angus forged on. —*You doin' the same thing to these people that was done to my people and to Aubrey's a long time ago, and I'll thank you not to do it in my store. You was telling those men they got to buy their food only from you, cause you the boss. You come in here again, I call the sheriff, tell him everything I know.*

The room was silent as the noon crowd watched Tomás Tulia for his response. Tulia's glare slowly cooled to something indecipherable, a polite silence that made Angus feel mocked. As Tulia's silence lengthened, he began to smile in a confident way. Angus had an odd thought: *they put him in Rotary Club.* Nobody'd ever asked Angus if he wanted to be in the Rotary Club.

Tomás Tulia nodded curtly, and left the store.

Angus suddenly had business to tend to at the far side of the store, something sudden and invisible that involved rearranging cans of chili. Aubrey did not understand at first that he was being ignored, so he called out, —*Well, Angus, I need to get me some cigarettes, I guess.* He tapped his fingers on the counter.

Still Angus would not acknowledge his presence.

—*Say hey. Angus.*

Angus turned his back to Aubrey then, and dusted shelves. The Telephone Pioneers ceased their low-octane banter.

—*You refusing me service, look like,* Aubrey said, a small scrape of sorrow in his throat. The years fell away. He was an unwelcome black boy once again, as he had been many years before.

—*Look like,* Angus agreed vehemently without turning around. He noticed with dismay that it was the hoodoo goods he was dusting so seriously. He hoped Aubrey had not noticed that.

—*Aw, Angus, give him his smokes,* somebody said.

Angus came over then and picked up the coffee can with the toilet money in it. —*Man if you ain't got the do-re-mi for a forty-dollar sink and some PVC pipe for them people that's working for you out there, we'll just pass the hat around in here. We sure don't want to inconvenience you or nothing, or cause them to throw you out of that Standard and Poor.*

Aubrey lifted a hand then, and swatted the air, as if to ward off a swarm of bees. There was a collective intake of breath at the long table, matchsticks stilled.

Angus was as surprised as anyone else present at what came out of his own mulish mouth next. —*Get out of my place of business, nigger.*

—*Now, Angus, there'll be none of that,* somebody said. —*We don't need this kind of trouble.*

Aubrey turned and slipped out the door as quietly as he came in. Angus was as upset as anyone present, and his face was stony.

Consuela had seen the whole thing. She was standing in the back with the broom. Angus could tell by the look on her face that she had translated it all, *trouble.*

—*He'll be back in here tomorrow, I bet you,* somebody said, pushing a matchstick into the pile.

—*Bet two,* somebody else said.

—*Raise you,* another said.

Consuela didn't sing while she worked that day, and her quiet became ominous as the day wore on. She went about her business ignoring Angus, bundling the fragrant tamales with string and sliding them into the coffee cans she steamed them in. At dusk, she took off her apron and slid off her Keds, but she kept them tucked under her arm. Angus felt a pang of fear, seeing that, and seemed to hear what she was going to say before she said it.

—*I would like to settle up with you tonight,* she said formally.

The thought came to him in a desperate, blinding way: if he gave her her money, she would be free to leave him. Even though they both knew he had enough cash in the drawer to pay her ten times what she was owed, Angus said with a gentle smile, —*Well, I don't believe I can see my way clear to do that. Can you give me a few more days?* He regretted it instantly when he saw the way her face aged, right before his very eyes. He saw himself through her eyes: *El hombre,* American *bok guey* with a fat American wallet. He felt like a whipped dog, and he left the cash drawer open in exasperation, as if to say, *take it all.* He disappeared behind a rustle of the bamboo-print shower curtain. It seemed to him there was more to settling up than just money.

He thought then of the little yellow baby dress from the Philippines and how much Consuela liked it. He came back out to offer it to her if she'd stay a few more days, but she was gone.

The cash drawer was still open, every dime still in it.

This was borne home to him again when he counted it later, looking at it through stinging eyes. He lay awake flat on his back most of the night in his big teak bed, with the palms of his hands clamped like starfish onto the back of his head.

Just before day, he heard the Econoline van start up, its gears shifting like chord changes on the guitar. He blinked, again and again, watching the ceiling become tinted with the sunrise. That was them, he knew. Leaving. He rose and dressed as he had for all the years of his life, and sat on his porch and watched the fields. He wondered what work would go undone that day in the fields, because Consuela had taken her sons with her.

Later in the day he found himself bent down restacking the candles in the hoodoo section, just the way she would have done it. He arranged the yellow and purple aerosol cans of air freshener the way she would have, and then he picked one up and studied it.

Money House Blessing, it said on one side in English and on the other in Spanish. —*Indian Spirit. Legendary Quality. Contains Genuine 9 Indian Vanilla Oil.* He sprayed some around the room. It reminded him of her, so he sprayed it again. As far as he could tell, she had taken nothing with her to remember him by.

Angus was taking out some flattened cardboard boxes when he noticed that the National Steel guitar was in its old case, propped up beside the Dumpster.

Angus walked slowly out the door and down the porch steps, staring at it. Consuela knew that he would see it there; that's why she put it there. She could have pawned it for money, maybe even more than he'd paid for it, but there it was, tossed out like so much junk she was leaving behind. He walked around the Dumpster in a wide arc, as if it were hexed and could harm him.

It was a statement she was making to him about money. He glanced at the guitar case again as he was sweeping the day's debris off the porch, leaves, dead bees, cigarette butts, candy wrappers. His cat did figure-eights in and out of his thin shins.

—*I deserved that,* he said aloud to the hungry cat. He paused with the broom and ran his finger along the branches of the empress tree that brushed against the side of the store, remembering. Looking closer, he saw a small, pale green feather clinging to a branch, held there somehow by its weightlessness. His chest filled with warmth, and he looked out across the empty fields to the church, as if there had been some breaking news, and he was the witness, with no one to tell it to.

Even later, the white truck from Big River Landfill rolled up with a screech at about the same time the school bus was letting the local kids off. Angus saw the African boy's face through the bus window as he saw the guitar case. But by the time the long line of schoolchildren had filed off, the guitar case was gone and the Big River truck was pulling away. As the truck pulled away, the boy ran down the highway after it, waving his arms. The truck lumbered on, and the boy stood there breathing hard. He turned toward the store, his face dark with confusion.

—*There was a guitar,* the boy cried, agitated when he came in to start his shift. —*Did you see? There was a—it was National Steel!*

Angus held up his hand to silence the boy. He was sullen the rest of the night, feeling himself to be like the *bok guey,* throwing perfectly good things away.

People began to say that Angus was not quite himself, that perhaps there was some trouble with his heart. He was curt with people when they went in, and had even castigated the African boy for playing the jukebox too much. Some said it had to do with the Honduran woman and the hoodoo goods.

Dean Fondren got Aubrey Ellerbee to admit that it was foolish and wasteful to drive all the way to Clarksdale to get cigarettes or gas or a simple jar of mustard when he could have the same thing for cheaper from just across the highway.

—*That woman meant something to him, Aubrey. I know she was cheap and you know she was cheap, but Angus saw something in her you and I didn't. Plus which, he was right about the toilet. She's good enough to rate a toilet. That's the American way. We all got the same rights. Me, I always thought a flush toilet was right up there with freedom of speech.*

Aubrey's face registered a small change, something like shame, something like exhaustion. He nodded.

—*Well, it ain't that easy,* Aubrey said. —*I don't own that church. I ain't even got no easement on it or nothing. They are just staying there.*

—*Don't matter,* Dean said decisively. —*And another thing. That big Evinrude you got sitting there doing nothing for nobody. Might make a decent generator to pump water to that church. Be good for Angus's business to have your workers stay there.*

Aubrey stared across the road at the Celestial. —*Ain't my arrangements to make. That Tomás Tulia—*

—*Is breaking the law,* Dean finished for him. —*They got laws now, for what you got to give your workers. Otherwise, these folk come in from these other places and just drag in the same old troubles we got over a long time ago, start up the same old mess all over again.*

Aubrey began to nod slowly.

—*I tell you another thing,* Dean said. —*You and me and Angus, we all come too far together for too long to end up like this. We been through too much to just throw it all away because Angus is having a bad spell.*

Aubrey continued to nod.

Late the next night, Dean and Aubrey both went over to the Celestial Grocery. The Evinrude motor was in the back of Dean's pickup truck. It took both men to carry it off the truck. They stepped slowly, balancing its weight between them, agile as the cats that wove in and out of their legs. Belle progressed as slowly behind as if it were her errand, too. Poised with the Evinrude between them, Dean and Aubrey looked in the opened screen door.

Angus could not see them. He was standing over beside the jukebox. A woman's voice was singing a sad lovesick song in

Spanish. They watched quietly, not knowing what to do. The Evinrude became heavier as the seconds passed.

Angus stepped back then from the jukebox and raised both his hands to the heavens, much like a Pentecostal radio preacher might, *hallelujah*.

Dean and Aubrey each held his breath, the Evinrude getting heavier. They'd never seen such behavior in Angus. It was frightening.

Aubrey tried to seize the opportunity to turn and leave, but Dean pushed the Evinrude into his middle, and motioned with his head towards the door. Yet they were riveted, spying on Angus.

Angus Chien was dancing alone. He had his hands raised as if there were a woman standing before him, when there was only the yellow greasy light of the little store before him, same as always. Angus took some small sideways steps, *grapevine, grapevine*, and it became apparent that he believed his hands to be wreathed into those of an imaginary partner in front of him.

It was a language intelligible to any man—*loneliness*.

—*Lord have mercy*, Aubrey said.

Dean stifled a cough and cleared his throat slowly. The Evinrude was biting into the flesh of his thigh, and he shifted it to get a better grip. Aubrey swayed to accommodate his movement, not taking his eyes off Angus.

Angus danced on like a tranced conjuror, leading a partner nobody else could see. He had both hands raised in a kind of benediction as he danced, feeling the confusions that come from having a big heart. If a tree could schottische, it would do so as stiffly as Angus Chien did, past the sparks of suspicion and the weeds of misfortune, to the fires of love and the beneficial dream. When it was over, Angus bowed to his imaginary partner, and went on with his chores, his back to them.

Dean looked again at Aubrey. The kindness and worry in Aubrey's dark face were real. Dean opened the screen door and started calling, —*Angus, anybody home?*

Angus watched them balance the Evinrude before they laid it down on the floor at his feet.

—*We got an idea,* Aubrey started. —*If you got time to hear about it. We thinking to do something about a bunkhouse for them workers Tulia brought in.*

—*I've already been studying about it,* Angus said, without missing a beat. —*And if they want them a union, they can have it, far as I'm concerned. So if you can't see clear to help me, Aubrey, stay the hell out of my way.*

The Harlem Swing Club

Without the mirage of the National guitar to guide him, Boubacar was often adrift, wandering the streets of Clarksdale. In the black neighborhoods people walked about and greeted each other. Flowers rioted out of old tires painted white. Men stood in the narrow alleys and smoked, and looked at him as he passed, nodding curtly when he raised his hand slightly. In the narrow passage between two ancient trailers, clothes hung on a line, and men lounged on abandoned sofas. They watched as he passed, reading the signs slowly until the meanings presented themselves to him.

Kam Grocery, an abandoned store that catered to ghosts, perhaps. But its windows were plastered with fresh flyers for cakewalks and carnivals and the Mighty Sons of Destiny.

Soap Opera Laundromat.

Riverside Hotel.

It was good not to have the Wastrel along with him. He was free to look.

There was a particular house he enjoyed staring at with unabashed enthusiasm and admiration. He could simply admire the flamingo-pink house with its black window trim. In its yard were tire rims painted white and stuffed with plastic flowers identical to the ones he'd seen in the window of the

Family Dollar Store. The house was a snug little fortress with iron bars on its windows, stout alongside the Sunflower River. Outside, a few speckled chickens pecked halfheartedly at the dust and gravel.

Once he had smelled a pie baking in that house, apple and cinnamon. He thought with longing of his mother and grandmother then, and how he could pick out the smell of his own dinner cooking at dusk, sifting it out of the smells of all the dinners cooked by mothers and grandmothers on that street. He stared at the pink house; an old grandmother saluted him with a comb, and then returned to braiding the hair of a little girl kneeling obediently like a sparrow between her knees.

The neighborhoods of the whites terrified Boubacar with their stillness and perfection. Whole streets seemed evacuated for the day, as if the pale people who lived there had been lifted away by the flying saucers of aliens. Even their ivy crept noiselessly and discreetly up the bricks. In the driveway of one deserted mansion, a white Persian cat sunned itself and took halfhearted swipes at a dog that looked like a dustmop. There was no one home but animals. Their garbage cans were set neatly beside the curb. Beside one garbage can, an entire television set. Boubacar stopped to inspect it.

Out of nowhere, a police cruiser pulled up alongside him and slowed down. The officer inside, whose face was white, leaned out to speak.

—*Boy, where you going? Who you work for over here?*

—*I am going,* Boubacar said, fishing for a destination, —*to the Zhan Li Hooker street.*

The window slid up noiselessly, and the car idled while Boubacar began to walk. The car cruised along beside him, then fell a few yards behind. He began to be afraid. This white man could kill him and there would be no one, no one to hear his cries or help.

A big diesel truck turned into the street behind them.

When the truck wheezed and screeched to a stop at the end of the block, a sturdy little black man wearing hip waders got out and began to empty cans of garbage into the back of it. As the boy drew nearer, the man wiped his hands on a rag and looked back at the police car.

—*I see you got yourself some company*, he said to Boubacar. —*Get in my truck there.*

Boubacar stared at him, then looked back at the police car.

—*Go on, get in. You ain't got a lot of options here, look like.*

The boy climbed up into the truck and waited while the driver waved cordially at the white policeman and hoisted himself into the truck as if he were a much larger man than he actually was.

—*Well now. Where you supposed to be? How come you not in school?* Before the boy could answer, the man understood. It was in the boy's face, it was in his eyes. —*You not from around here, are you?*

—*I am looking for guitar*, the boy said urgently. —*It is silver, like a spaceship, and there are the flowers, like very good in Japan.*

—*Say what?* The man was trying to place his accent.

—*The guitar was at the Dumpster at the Celestial Grocery.*

—*I can take you to the landfill. Be like a needle in a haystack.* The man shrugged, extricating a pair of white leather gloves still in their cellophane wrapper. —*Don't see a lot of git-tops in this bidness.*

Big River Sanitary Landfill was on a remote road several miles out of Clarksdale. The entrance was handsomely landscaped with pines and azaleas. There was an expensive security gate at the front, and a worker was there to collect fees. Boubacar imagined what the Wastrel would say: —*L'Américain, he charges you money to own it and he charges you money to disown it. Then he builds a tall fence to keep anyone from stealing what he himself no longer wants.*

Once inside the gates of the high fence, Boubacar swallowed hard and looked around him. America was an empire of waste and refuse, stretching as far as his eyes could reach. America was rusted baby strollers, perfectly good fly rods, stained floral sofas, dog food cans, rain-swollen exploded beds, a coffin with *Ole Miss* painted on it. Piles of black and white plastic bags split and spilling their contents, perfectly good cabbages, whole loaves of bread, shoes that were perhaps a bit scuffed, old cook-pots.

The boy saw a tuxedo no one wanted to wear, splendid still, crushed beneath the rotting corpse of a cow no one wanted to eat. A copper pot that could have been used for cookery had holes driven into it, and a mass of dried, dead geraniums in it. A cooking grill with only a screw missing from the leg. A sewing basket full of yarns and needles. A rack of Wonder Bread, still in plastic bags. A feather boa strangling the throat of a hatstand. A huge inner tube from a tractor tire, enough to make shoes for a whole village. Small green cylinders that had held the poisons the farmers used nestled against white plastic milk jugs.

A shopping cart. The landscape was dappled with them. And stoves, every make and model. Televisions! Atop one pile of black plastic bags perched an enormous television over which a woman's black lace brassiere was draped rakishly like a pirate's eye patch for a cyclops.

Down below, an old refrigerator lay on its side, and a dog peered out from beneath its half-opened doors. The Americans had a machine for everything: to grill their hamburgers, to make their toast, to dry their hair, to blow the leaves out of their driveways. This was the final resting place of all the machines.

—*Where you stay at?* Sam asked. —*You from Blue Sprang or Lula or where?*

—*Madagascar*, the boy said, discouraged.

—*That would be Mr. Devon Jones's route. He dumps over yonder in Section Three. You can look around if you want, but I got to leave here in twenty minutes.*

Boubacar walked in wonder towards the mountain of black plastic bags that was Section Three. He saw packing crates from the Cockrell Banana Company, the kind that he himself had put in Angus's Dumpster. He saw bleach bottles, hairbrushes, old computers, Nike Airs, rusted bedsprings, rolled-up rugs, and spent condoms. He saw feral cats rifling among the boxes and bags and tubes, *Totino's Betty Crocker Pillsbury*, that had once held human food.

He found a small calculator shaped like a pink panther. It worked perfectly, and he pocketed it.

He found a gold coin that looked like money but was not. It was from the same casino where his uncles worked, a shamrock embossed on its side. He found a paint-spattered Phillips-head screwdriver and pocketed it. He felt a sense of urgency—so many objects could still be used back in his country.

Above it all, a family of Somalians was raking through some bags with hands in yellow gloves, a woman and two sons. A small girl waited for them below. Boubacar gave the pink-cat calculator to the little girl. He saw the mother stop what she was doing and watch him with suspicion. He waved, and backed away, bowing. He noticed there was movement elsewhere, others picking over the riches among the refuse. It was mostly old men and young women with children.

A blue Easter bunny glared up at the sky with glassy eyes. A large fly-specked mirror in a gilt frame beckoned him, and he saw his own face, creased with worry. He could look all day, all week, and still not search out Section Three. It seemed to extend forever, this city of refuse, towards the high, grassy rise, which he knew by now to be the levee that held back the Mississippi River.

Boubacar looked around, overwhelmed.

L'Américain, L'Américain, he mourned.

He had a sudden vision of the levee breaking under the weight of all the garbage, washing all humanity into the river and to the sea, like inconsequential trash.

Sam was blowing the horn to the truck. He ran.

—*How long ago it was?* Sam asked as he climbed into the high cab.

The boy looked confused.

—*I say, how long ago you lost your git-top? Mr. Devon Jones the man you need to talk to. He work over there right by where you stay. At that Harlem Swing Club. Every Saturday night.*

On Saturday night, business was slow, and Boubacar stood before the plate glass window of the Celestial and stared out at the two separate shimmers in the flat distance. There was the green glow of the casino shaped like a shamrock where his uncles spent their weekends carving radish roses for the infidels. Closer in, there was the smaller contretemps of colored flashing lights and slow-moving cars that was the Harlem Swing Club. The lights of a red arrow on the rented electric sign flashed and flashed, 2/2 time, *here, here,* the precise rhythm of a racing pulse, or mating animals.

After the store closed, Boubacar walked down the lane the way he always went, and then suddenly strode across the field, headed to the Harlem Swing Club.

A girlish voice pierced the darkness. —*Do you want to party?* It was Ayesha, whose job he had somewhat stolen. He took a backward step as she neared him. He shrugged and looked at his feet. She reached out and ran her pink-pomegranate nail down the front of his shirt, as one might slit open a newly caught fish. —*Come party with me.*

He looked into her face, and her eyes seemed kind. He didn't see the derision he had sometimes imagined on the school bus.

Following her inside, he offered money to a woman tending a cashbox at the door, but she waved him off and marked his hand with a black laundry pen. The club was only one small room, hot and crowded, with a pool table taking up a third of the space. The musicians were in a chicken-wire cage that ran the length of the place, somewhat like a baseball dugout, tuning their guitars. Women leaned next to the cage, fingers hooked through the chicken wire as they watched.

—*Please,* Boubacar said to the girl. —*What is the purpose of the cage?*

—*So if somebody get in a fight, they can't hurt the instruments.*

The place was filling up, and the woman, Ayesha's mother, was making little black X's on their wrists, to show they'd paid. There were sharecroppers in overalls, and catfish-plant workers with their hair still in shower caps, drinking beer.

The bar was the rusted top of a Kenmore deep freezer, covered by green floral oilcloth. The man behind it wore a baseball hat that said *Houlka Chainsaw Repair.* Boubacar stood before him and considered what to say first.

—*You that boy from Africa, am I right? You looking for your guitar?* The man passed a cold beer to him, and would not accept any pay for it.

Boubacar took the beer and nodded.

—*I don't remember no guitar. You ask over to the Rescue*

Mission? Sometime peoples take things there. And then you got pawnshops. You know about pawnshops? It might turn up.

Boubacar sipped the beer cautiously, then looked around the room. For a sudden forlorn moment he felt homesick for the safe narrows of the trailer. The more he sipped at the beer, the more the dream of the guitar leaked from him, leaving him hollow. It was a dangerous thing to think endlessly of a single object.

There were many white people there, more than he'd ever seen together outside the Memphis airport. They drank beer and plastic cups of something white and clear. He studied them carefully. They were self-assured, they were happy, they were America's *bizan.*

Boubacar took in the naked concrete floor, the posters and paintings on the walls. Over the jukebox, a black-skinned belle in a hoopskirt carried a parasol. A crude portrait of Martin Luther King hung next to a magazine clipping about Michael Jackson. A signed photo of James Brown was curling at its edges near the musicians' cage. Boubacar stood near the chicken-wire and watched the band get ready to play.

They began to tune guitars and scratch at drums, querying the air, as if the song were already out there in the night somewhere, waiting. The guitars warbled and wavered, summoning it. Then the song, wherever it came from, seemed to open like an invisible door, and each musician entered at the same time. The boy's pulse answered, *yes,* and he closed his eyes in pleasure.

Ayesha shimmied across the floor holding her hands out to him, shaking her shoulders ever so slightly, the way he'd seen Nemadi women dance once. He let her pull him out onto the dance floor, beer in hand, and he began to step from side to side, watching her all the while. The old men chalking their pool cues called to him in a friendly way. The older women assessed him with all the subtlety of cattle brokers, and one came over and pinched his cheeks and then pressed him to her breasts as if he were a mop doll. He begged off respectfully, and the old men laughed and turned back to chalking their pool cues, grumbling in friendly growls that he need not think he had come all the way from Africa to steal all the women.

Ayesha's eyes made him feel at home. He was embarrassed and enchanted by her attention. The others stared, and the stares made him feel as welcome as he had felt in the church. The smaller children made a game of running over to touch him softly, to show they were not afraid of his strangeness in his electric blue suit. He had played such a game himself years ago, when a white missionary had ventured into the alley he played in. He had touched the missionary and run away in the same way these children now touched him.

He danced with a sharecropper in blue overalls and a white college girl with eyeglasses like the tailfins of big mabone cars, the three of them ringed by a wall of clapping hands. He began to whirl like a Sufi, and the old men whistled at him from the pool table, and the women all called him *James Brown*. The bar was mobbed suddenly with his new friends, and he drank another free beer. The music was welling from the cracks in the walls and out into the night, like the light.

—*I want to show you something,* Ayesha whispered, pulling him towards the back of the club. She folded his hand into hers and pulled him out a back door onto a porch. He saw a tangle of two bodies, a band of light illuminating an embrace. Boubacar's feet froze to the boards as he looked.

The man's hands had pushed the woman's dress up around her hips. The woman, whose face he could not see, pressed her hips to the man's hips again and again, as if instructed by the music, as if pleading with him. The band of light crossed the man's roving hands as he pulled the woman to him. A bright brassy confusion filled Boubacar's head. His heart burned with what felt like hot prayers.

—*Come on. I want to show you*, Ayesha said, pulling him down the steps.

She pulled him around the corner of the club, and there were children playing there, pulling at wires nailed to the wooden frame of the porch posts. They were in plain sight of the man and the woman with her dress pulled up but not paying them any attention. They were playing the wires like guitars, sliding broken beer bottles up and down, up and down, to create an eerie sound. The beggar's oud, his grandmother called it. People from Côte d'Ivoire did that. He had seen such instruments in the streets of Nouatchkott, one wire, one board. His feet froze again. Some of the little girls had broken off from the other children and watched the couple on the porch embrace, giggling softly. His eyes met the eyes of a tiny girl in braids and she looked away shyly.

Ayesha giggled and pulled him away. —*This way.* Then they were running across a bare field, toward the specter of a parked tractor, *New Holland*, its cab like a small glass house.

—*My daddy let me drive it one time.*

It was a high climb to get inside, and she showed him how. She knew her way around the machine. —*Your father was a rich man*, he said, and she laughed and shook her head.

—*No, this belong to the Man*, she said, motioning with the pink pomegranate nails at larger forces out in the night. —*My father worked for him sometimes. Mister Aubrey Ellerbee. He won it back from the casino.*

He looked out the back window of the tractor cab at the size of the field. From that vantage point, the Harlem Swing Club was simply a set of lights on the field's edge, like a boat lying low in black water. He turned back to the girl then, and his heart stopped. She had taken off her sweater. His breath hung in his throat.

America was a red lace bra that broke your heart and mended it at the same time.

America was his heart, rioting in happy anguish. He looked away, uncertain of what was expected of him. He could see her pulse just above her elegant collarbones. She was still hot from the dancing and the run across the field.

Ayesha pushed herself towards him, and he prayed with his eyes open for guidance.

He remembered suddenly the story of a girl in a village who had knelt in the open street and had her throat cut by her uncles, her punishment for walking alone at night with a boy. Her dishonored father had watched the killing from beneath a nearby tree. His mother had told him the story when he was old enough to understand why she was telling him.

—*I would have saved her*, he had said to his mother.

—*No*, she said. —*Then they would kill you, too.*

—*Then I will never walk alone at night with a girl*, he had said.

Here he was in America, and he had walked alone with a girl.

Whenever he had dreamed of his first time with a woman, back in the days when his mother had told him the story of the girl with the cut throat, he had envisioned a tent lined with warm rugs and sweet scents. He had hoped to lie with a bride in some cool soft place at the edge of the desert, and to make love to her with such skill and knowledge that it would provoke her to call out the names of their unborn children.

Ayesha sat astride him as if he were a common horse.

—*No*, he said softly, as he might address a young sister, holding her wrists just as they were tugging at his belt.

—*Yes*, she contradicted him, giggling. It was an absent giggle, he noted. She was drunk. Perhaps he was also.

—*No*, he said again, sharply. —*Not here.*

The girl began to cry then, slamming her face into his neck, seeking cover, as his small sisters did when they were ashamed. He began to rock her softly and sing to her an almost-forgotten Moorish song about the moon being made of marzipan. His hands seemed to burn where they touched her bare back, and his trembling fingers wanted to memorize the feeling of the red lace bra.

—*Ayesha*, he said, after she became quiet. —*You—we— must be reasonable together.*

—*Don't leave me.*

—*I do not wish to dishonor you. Your family—*

She laughed cynically. —*You think you be Mr. Somebody, here in America, but you know what? Rashad will get you, too.*

When she was dressed, she wouldn't speak to him, and turned her head away from him as they walked back to the Harlem Swing Club. Halfway across the field she broke away and ran from him, and he stopped and watched her go. He wondered how she would greet him when she saw him on the yellow school bus, if she would smile at him, or laugh at him with her girlfriends.

The boy had almost reached the courtyard of the trailer park when he heard the sound of lowered voices and laughter. The men who lived across the courtyard were assembled around the open trunk of their black car, which seemed full of guns of various shapes and sizes strewn about like so many toys. Boubacar froze, still concealed by the heavy vines that draped from the utility pole like big green cobwebs to *la sorcière's* boathouse.

Rashad held up a gun like a black shiny insect. He positioned it on his shoulder, swung it around, and aimed it at the trailer where the Mauritanians lived.

—*Boom-boom*, the other man whispered in a loud falsetto, and the others guffawed. —*Boom. You dead.*

They peered into the back windows of the black Escalade.

Rashad danced around the car with the gun, passing within a few feet of Boubacar, so close he could smell the leather of his coat and his cologne.

As they opened a back door, Boubacar pressed himself into the vines, trying to disappear. In the same instant he saw the eyes of one of the Honduran laborers, the one called Hector, sitting in the backseat with a towel over his head. The man's eyes were flat and unseeing, staring straight ahead. The man's legs gave way as they pulled him from the car, and one of them kicked him to get him to step up into their trailer.

Boubacar didn't realize he needed to breathe until his chest began to burn. He'd seen something no one was supposed to see. Something was very wrong.

Boubacar ran to his uncles' trailer and locked the door behind him, shaking. His head was pounding with pain, and he wanted sleep. He locked himself in the bathroom and washed and washed. Even then, the metal sills of the doorways and windows vibrated with the loud rap music being played across the courtyard, *A-booma-boom-boom.*

When the Wastrel returned, the boy was sitting in front of the television, with the sound turned off. He was flipping from channel to channel, seeing nothing, saying nothing. The symphony played for the ass-wipe paper, and the starving blonde beauty in the blue ball gown turned the letters in the gambling game:

WIN OW OF OPPOR UNI Y

Americans crawled onto the shores of Normandy and parachuted into Vietnam. A young girl in a spangled majorette suit tap-danced for an old man with long black curls who did not even remove his headphones when he said in boredom, —*Show me your tits.*

There was a pill you could ask your doctor about, in the pursuit of happiness.

The Wastrel stubbed out a cigarette next to his chair. —*And what has the world given you today, brother?*

—*It has given me a girl to marry,* the boy said simply.

The Wastrel said nothing, but looked at him with tired affection. —*You have some years to go. Many years. It is not the custom here to marry so soon.*

Boubacar thought it strange that the Wastrel cursed American habits when it suited him and embraced them when it advanced his arguments. He said nothing, and they both stared in silence at the television.

The Wastrel could not seem to get his fill of being appalled at *L'Américain* and his late-night consolation of Las Vegas showgirls with glittering eyelashes, and fat snarling comedians in Savile Row suits, *L'Américain* endearing himself to skinny worthless women by offering them diamond rings.

The Wastrel clicked and clicked, and chortled with disgust. A blonde beauty with eyes like charred holes selected as her mate the man who chose the right cellphone, the one that played the Top Ten tunes, for an extra fee. Elephants danced like clumsy bumblebees for their trainers, and detectives investigated murder after murder. Japanese chefs competed as they cooked squid. Middle-aged women rubbed wrinkle creams into their faces, diamonds gleaming on their hands. Cowboys stood atop skyscrapers, singing about cigarettes. Old women sold cheap plastic wares as if they were hostesses at a grand party, the voices echoing in empty studios. A race-car driver came out of a flaming car crash wearing a suit that bore the name of a drug that guaranteed constant erections. Hip-hop women with breasts like tawny jellyfish danced in bathing suits and minks, singing, —*Where dem dollars at? Where dem dollars at?*

The Wastrel spoke as if he were the filter through which all information must pass. —*Do you see? Even their ennui is a commodity.*

Boubacar and the Wastrel surfed the sixty-seven channels, and hearing a brief wisp of music, the Wastrel leaned forward to listen. A BBC program, South Africa.

Pennywhistle.

A British voice was explaining.

Boubacar leaned forward as if to translate it into American English, but the words fluttered out of the television set too quickly. He could get most of the meaning from the pictures.

Once pennywhistle music had flowed freely like rainwater through the streets of Capetown. In those days, a pennywhistle was owned by South African street boys who had no money to buy real instruments. The son of a famous pennywhistle player who had been put to death by the government had made a record of the songs his father had played for free to any who had the time to listen. The son peddled the tapes to an American so he could buy the milk for his own son. Now grey-suited American lawyers who worked for a Japanese company were trying to put the boy in jail for selling his father's songs to someone else, an Australian, saying the songs belonged only to them. They could be played only when a fee was paid to them. Out in the streets, the village boys shrugged and continued to play the songs on their pennywhistles in the streets for free.

Boubacar, looking at the sea of black faces in Capetown, felt faint with homesickness. Even the Wastrel grew silent at the sight of it. Then he spoke with a quiet anger.

—*When you are an old man, remember this night that I told you this one true thing. The* kaffir *will soon devise a way to extract a fee from any of us who wishes to hear his own heartbeat. You will see this in your lifetime.*

Nocturne, with Black Escalade

The Wastrel was on his knees in the dark. His drummer's hands were open, palms up, *salat*. The day was done, the boy asleep. Open in the chair behind him, his Koran. From long habit he could wade into the water of the words, whether the book was in his hands or not, and with eyes closed.

And as for the unbelievers—

Noises. A car had pulled up outside, casting a band of light across his face. A car door opened, and a ball of angry music seemed to roll out. The Wastrel opened his eyes. Out the window he saw three men leading another by his arms down the steps of the trailer across the courtyard. The man's legs were limp, searching for firm ground. It was the gait of a condemned man. His head was draped in a white towel, and the men had white towels around their own necks, like rock stars. —*Don't scratch the car, man.* The man called Rashad looked around quickly, and the Wastrel leaned back out of the band of light.

Only a man who does not wish to have witnesses looks around like that.

The Wastrel was grateful he had not seen the man's face. He began again to read with his eyes closed the Koran in his heart, his mind swimming against the tide of the music.

And as for the unbelievers, their works are as a mirage in a spacious plain.

The floor beneath his knees vibrated in response to the music across the way. The frame of the window beside the Wastrel's chair sang like a tuning fork. He returned to his reading with his eyes closed.

In a spacious plain, which the man athirst supposes to be water, till, when he comes to find it, he finds it is nothing.

The Wastrel's eyes flew open like shutters: the car is of more value in America than the humans in it. He closed his eyes again, rocked slightly, and willed himself to read only his own mind.

There indeed he finds God.

On the other side of the thin wall of the trailer, curved like a scythe in a field, Boubacar was dreaming of Sol Hoopii's silver National guitar in the window of the Rescue Mission. When the ignition started in the black Escalade, his dreaming mind translated it into music. There was a crowd of people admiring the guitar, pooling their money. He was being shoved to the back, but he knew that if ever his fingers touched the guitar, the music would be very beautiful. Then he was playing the guitar, a miracle. His fingers moved in his sleep, making chords in response to some bass line that was already beckoning.

It was a low dark thump, over and over. His fingers moved in his sleep, changing chords.

Marie Abide heard the rumble of the black Escalade as it passed, and paused at her small window, in case she needed to hide. Out in the moonlight the stovepipe animals leaned together to gossip, *good riddance.* The Escalade passed noisily on, its errand having nothing to do with her.

She examined the sheet music closely. She looked at the pictures of Sol Hoopii. She lifted out one particular piece of sheet music and studied it with profound hunger:

I like you
Because you have such loving ways
Hey, hey.

1938. Paris. Her mother's paintings in the zinc bathtub, burning. The image of herself naked in a birdbath, burning.

Bebe Marie Abide had positioned the National Steel guitar on the small white enamel table in the center of the room like a fish about to be filleted. She ignored the guitar and took the scissors to the sheet music, with loving care. She had other plans for the guitar. She had plans to take it to the International House of Pawn in Clarksdale. If they took it, it would fetch enough money to feed her for two weeks, surely. And if not? She could paint it like a Joseph's coat, and string it with lights, and it would be *luxe, volupté*, outside dangling from a tree. Or it would make a grand home for purple martins if she could pry the steel cones out with a screwdriver. But then there would be the problem of a pole to put it on. And the problem of the hole in the ground for the pole.

Or she could sell the guitar as it was, in Clarksdale.

Across the open, innocent night, Angus Chien lay like a felled tree in the old teakwood bed that had been his father's, the same one he had later shared with his wife, Rose. He dreamed, reluctantly, of Consuela's white shoes shining in the dark, their toes touching, like incandescent birds nestled nose to nose.

There was to be a dance, an important one. Angus was putting the white Keds on her feet, folding her feet into them like the dollar bills he owed her. The Keds transformed themselves into little silk Chinese slippers, and he was forcing them onto her feet. Then he was dancing with her, and their arms entwined like the olive wreaths on a dollar bill, doing that grapevine step.

He was her partner. But to his dismay, he found his own feet were transformed into dark, misshapen knobs, no good for dancing at all.

He woke, aggrieved and ashamed. It felt like betrayal to dream of such things in that bed. It was like saying good-bye to Rose. He heard the low bass music of the black Escalade thumping as it rumbled past in the dark. He rolled over, and his fingers patted the floor until they touched his shotgun.

Aubrey Ellerbee was not asleep inside his fine house. He was dozing in the Quonset hut across from the Celestial, wrapped in a maple-leaf quilt on the Naugahyde couch in what he called his office. His wife had made that quilt before she died, and it was the only thing he could sleep under now, the Naugahyde couch the only place.

—*No*, he began to murmur, —*no*.

In his dream, he saw his own hand signing the papers, *no*, and then he saw men come with croupier's hooks to scrape away at his land, raking it off into the river. He woke up, sweating, and lit a cigarette and stood outside the door of the Quonset hut, taking deep, calming drags of it. The black Escalade passed, and Aubrey tensed at the sound of it. He stood and got one of his shotguns down and loaded it, slid it under the Naugahyde couch, and climbed back under his quilt.

By the light of Dean Fondren's Coleman lantern, Peregrine Smith-Jones painted her toenails flamenco red. She was wearing a frayed tuxedo shirt, circa 1973, that she'd rescued from the Rescue Mission for fifty cents. Its ruffles were tipped with red embroidery, equally flamenco. Between brushstrokes with the pungent paint, she sipped package-store wine from a Haviland moss-rose teacup, which she had also rescued from the Rescue Mission, also for fifty cents. It matched the tall, elegant chocolate pot that stayed on the sideboard in her parents' dining room in Princeton. It also matched the moss-rose saucer the Chinese man fed his cats out of on the porch of his store. The wine was cheap, tart, but when she put it in the Haviland teacup, it enabled her to imagine her ancestors.

She was not going to get drunk, she thought, placing the teacup in its saucer with a delicate chink. She heard the black Escalade on the highway, and heard it slow down. Her heart began to beat faster, and she stared at the cup, translucent with old roses, its gold edging worn thin from lips touching it. White lips? Black lips?

The black Escalade was slowing down.

Her lamp was lit.

These events were connected.

She looked at the cell phone that the Big Daddy farmer had lent her.

She could see the moon rising outside the open window. Ariadne had watched that same moon through the same window, not even a pane of glass between them. The girl wondered who had pressed the broken china into her grave. Who was the survivor?

While her toes dried, she hobbled over to look once more at her latest prints, and drew them slowly out of the drugstore envelope. There was Ariadne's grave, but the china shards hardly showed. There was the old Chinese man sweeping the pink blossoms off his porch while a cat washed its face beside him. There was the funny, flawed one of the old woman who lived in the boathouse, hauling a silver guitar out of the Celestial Grocery Dumpster, holding it upside down like a newborn child. The guitar had chrysanthemums etched onto its side. A shaft of sunlight had glinted off the guitar at the last moment, rendering the old woman's face invisible.

She shuffled the photos again and again, cursing the caprices of light.

She put out the light, slid into the sleeping bag, and zipped it up to her chin. She unzipped it enough to reach out for the cell phone and pulled it into the sleeping bag with her. The dog's tail flapped at the floor, wagging, his paws twitching. He was dreaming of chasing rabbits. Peregrine had trouble submitting to sleep, but flirted at the edges of its provinces, eavesdropping on intercontinental murmurs. She looked down at herself from some great promontory and saw a thin woman lying alone beneath wheeling galaxies. The river roped itself around the moon, and time ran like melted machinery.

She was a little drunk.

She meant to dream careful dreams. She was visited by troublesome ones.

She was lying back in a high canopy bed, waiting for someone, a new man.

He had undressed himself for her, his sex dark against the whiteness of his body. She could not seem to get enough of the sight of him.

It was obedience, the way he knelt in the bed before her.

It was obedience, the way she tasted him, heavy and rich like figs.

In that province of sleep, obedience was not a bad thing.

Her eyes snapped themselves open. Her mouth was open against the skin of her arm, and she was bereft. She was not drunk, she was perfectly lucid.

She knew who the man was.

He'd brought her his lantern, his cell phone, and had asked nothing of her. Why did she dream about him? Sleep was not to be trusted, with its fugitive little errands, its hidden agendas. She stared into the darkness and listened to the roar of tiny distant frogs, afraid to sleep, afraid to dream. She sorted out the other sounds in the darkness. She was grateful for the rasp of the blue heeler's snoring in the dark. She was grateful for the company of the chalk lady's pie-pan fetishes and stovepipe animals banging in the wind. And for the presence of the white man across the field, alone in his house with his dog, and a steady comforting presence in her dreams. She fell asleep holding his cell phone.

Across the field, Dean Fondren was barefoot and in his shorts, standing in the door of the open refrigerator, drinking from the milk jug. What had awoken him was the rattling valves of the black Escalade, the sound coming from across the field, where the black girl from Bowdoin was sleeping, vulnerable as a new calf in an open field. The car did not stop, but sped up, its snarl of thumps fading into silence, and Dean's muscles uncoiled. He kept a loaded shotgun by the bedroom door, now that his daughters were out of the house. He got the binoculars and looked across the field to Ariadne's house, and saw no light, just the old green Comet nestled into its trees, bathed in bands of moonlight.

She had accepted his phone but she had not used it to call him.

On the porch, Belle sat quietly awake, looking at the same thing he'd been looking at.

He went back to bed and began the long rosary of worry and outstanding debt. When he felt assured that the black Escalade was a few towns north on Highway 61, he let himself entertain the idea of sleep.

A few towns north, Consuela lay on an air mattress in the back of the Econoline van, dreaming of a marble bathtub she'd seen in a magazine once, brimming with American bubbles. She was in it, naked and warm, and ringed by burning candles. *Money House Blessing, Fires of Love, Beneficial Dream.* There was soap in the shapes of pink empress tree blossoms, and soap in the shape of white doves, and soap in the shape of cameos. There were soaps in the shape of shimmering green birds. She was being bathed, softly, and someone was talking to her, reasoning with her. It was like dancing with an old tree.

Everything gon' be all right.

She did not hear the final passing of the black Escalade. She murmured soft words of gratitude in her sleep to a lover whose face she could not quite make out.

Not far from the bridge that carried cars to Helena, Arkansas, the black Escalade parked on a sandy side road that seemed to lead vaguely towards the river. Parked under the bridge was the taxi-colored Chevrolet Caprice, doors open and music pouring out. Three men in jeweled black leather jackets handed over a stumbling Hispanic man to Haile Selassie Pegues, dressed as if on holiday in a Hawaiian shirt. His friends wore their Disciples jackets, and they knew what they were supposed to do, to clear the debt with Rashad. They waited until they could no longer hear the black Escalade.

It was like a holiday, the way they piled out of the Caprice and beat him. The sequinned crowns on the backs of their jackets glinted obscenely with their movements. They took turns with ball bearings wrapped in white tube socks, waiting courteously for one to finish before another made his contribution to the effort. They beat the man for his unspecified transgressions, and then they beat him for being unable to stand on his own feet. Then they beat him for being unable to speak.

The music was amniotic, absorbing the man's screams. It was nothing personal. Tomás Tulia would pay Rashad a fee for their work. It was what they had to do to work off their indebtedness to Rashad. It was business.

When the man was unable to cry out any longer, or to see them, they took the towel from his head and dragged his body to the Helena bridge and threw him over the side. To the jewel-jacketed Disciples, it was a disturbing sight, the way the man's arms opened without hesitation, as if embracing a mirage, and their eyes studied for a moment the empty air he had looked at, but they could not see what he had seen.

As he fell from the bridge into the river, Hector Dominguez could still hear the snarled music from the taxi-painted car. His eyes could see mostly his own blood, the color of carnations. So he mistook the whiteness of the full moon beyond for the face of God, and he opened his hands palms up, *salat*, as if someone beloved had come to greet him after a very long separation.

Bow, Ye Lower Middle Classes

—*We seeing more and more of these Juan Does. Illegal aliens and what have you.*

Raine stopped to stare at the television on her way from one room to another. A rural sheriff's deputy squinted into bright lights. The body of an unidentified Hispanic man had been recovered from the river in Mississippi, beaten beyond recognition. A phone number was listed in case anyone had any information. —*And many times the standard means of identification, your fingerprints, your dental records, and what have you, are not available.* No one was watching that particular television in that room, so Raine turned it off.

Upstairs in bed, Raine read the same sentence in her magazine three times, *Create your own English knot garden for your private little getaway this season.*

On the bedroom television, mice sang the glories of certain cheeses that could be extruded like plastic from pressurized cans. Popcorn floated out of specially marked packages and affixed themselves to the sky as constellations. In the film her husband was watching, an expensive car burst into flames, and a man slapped a woman, screaming at her, *Fuck you!*

Raine smoothed her magazine in her lap and read resolutely

on. *Antique hybrid tea roses—no sanctuary is complete until they are spilling over a fence of carefully 'aged' wood.*

On the television a man was strapped to a chair, a red rubber ball shoved into his mouth. Another man had the barrel of a sleek European pistol jammed to the man's throat, and whispered words of hatred to him in the same tones the human species usually reserves for tenderness.

Raine had discovered that if she breathed evenly and slowly, and listened to herself breathing, she would not hear the sounds coming from the television. Lamaze had not worked very well for actual childbirth, but she found herself using the breathing techniques often in odd moments of family life.

Create your own sea of tranquillity by putting your own rose petals in your bath.

Raine put down the magazine and walked outside to get the cat in. She could think more clearly outside the house at night, away from the magnetic field of the televisions. Or so it seemed to Raine on such furtive trips to check on such matters as the holly she had let crook itself around the eave of the house in front so that cardinals could nest there year after year. It was not a shrub anymore, it was a tree, and crooked enough to attract second glances from the street. She heard a rustle in the leaves, and stood very still under the canopy of stars.

A portly neighbor walking his dog past the Semmes house barely nodded, and eyed Raine and her crooked holly tree with suspicion. A woman outside at night alone in her pajamas, peering into a holly that was out of control. He urged the dog on warily, as if she herself were out of control and could cause unspeakable endangerment to them all, cause property values on that street to fall like dominoes.

Raine looked up and down the street. Deserted. She was the only person out, standing in her Lucille Ball pajamas, calling, *kitty, kitty.*

In the houses up and down Magazine Street, the televisions outnumbered the human beings. In many windows, there were eerie steel-blue squares of flickering light, sometimes two or three to a house, tyrannical cyclopses in residence.

Whatever became of Rod Serling? she wondered.

Magazine Street was an actuary's dream, the same essential household metastasized beyond the horizon, as far as the eye could follow the mind.

There were the same flagstones on the sidewalks, the same lawn chairs positioned neatly behind the houses. There were the same blonde daughters, resolutely taping RECYCLE signs up in the kitchen. There were the same sun-starved but well-fed teenaged boys upstairs with guitars, waiting to lose their virginity, singing of how the world is a sewer, and dreaming of girls who would wrap themselves like soft bandages around the pain the boys believed to be unbearable.

Raine found herself staring inside her own windows like a voyeur.

She could see her son upstairs in one window, her daughter in another. Chance was mouthing words to his music, rehearsing the requisite rage, to make it look spontaneous. She could read his lips, *Ima kill you, bitch.*

In the window on the right, Callie was taping pictures of baby elephants to her walls. She smoothed the edges of the tape holding her baby elephants in place, and mused over it, chewing the end of a blonde braid. Her lips were set with purpose, shiny with green-apple lip gloss. There were ecosystems to be saved, animals to be defended.

Raine looked back to the left window: *Ima kill you, bitch.*

She thought of insects who glued fragments of old leaves to themselves for disguise. Her son clothed himself in second-hand rage. At what point did it become advantageous to mating for the male to make himself hideous?

Raine surveyed the sweep and span of suburban lights, a glittering plain all the way to the river. Surely there was some girl out there in some other window mouthing words to some song about wrapping herself around a boy's imaginary advertisements of pain like soft bandages.

About to go inside, Raine bent to pick up her son's muddy shitkickers on the back step. When she picked up the first boot, she saw a tangle of trash and twigs in it. She also recognized confetti from a neighbor child's birthday party, some soft green moss, oak leaves, mop strings from the garage. She felt the swish and flutter of a bird brush against her face. Nestled inside the boot: three tiny eggs. A wren, probably. Ever so carefully, she put the boot back. *Disguise is natural*, she thought.

As she stepped back, she thought she heard the neighbor coming back, but then she could see the glowing eyes of a deer at the edge of their property.

It was a buck; she saw the antlers move slightly.

She froze, feeling ludicrous in the Lucille Ball pajamas. The buck stared back at her, in no particular hurry. Her heart was pounding. She could not recall the last time any other living creature had looked at her and actually *seen* her, not counting the jukebox man.

The cool stare of a deer, a boot full of new wrens. Oh, sacred life, away from televisions!

The night went white with anarchy. Raine stood still a long time, listening to her own breathing. She imagined she could hear the deer breathing. She imagined an odd thing in his eyes, something like pity.

Later that night, carrying a stack of neatly folded towels still warm from the dryer, she heard her children's voices at the top of the stairs, edgy, on the brink of an argument.

—*I can if I want to!* Callie shouted, frustration choking her words. —*I can, too.*

—*Get real.* Chance sounded irritated and impatient. —*Pick something you can really do, Callie. That's the whole point.*

Raine paused just outside the doorway, listening with eyes closed. If she waited a moment, perhaps they'd work it out.

—*I can be whatever I want to be. Mom said so.*

—*Yeah, well. Good for Mom. Look: you think you can be some dreamy thing that you make up, but you'll be just like the others, you'll grow up and forget about it, and you'll have babies and have those spider veins on your legs like Mom.*

Raine stepped around the doorsill, towels in hand. Her breath was hung in her chest, hurting. She walked into the room, and the boy did at least have the grace to look startled.

—*What is it you want to be, Callie?*

—*A lawyer for animals,* Callie said.

—*I thought you wanted to direct horror movies,* Raine said gently, sitting down on the floor beside her.

—*Seventh grade is a horror movie,* Callie said, —*except there's no director.*

—*I believe you, baby,* Raine said. —*But if you want to be a lawyer for animals, you can be a lawyer for animals. You put whatever you want on that poster. Hey, I know some monkeys that really need a lawyer. And circus animals. They probably need a pay raise.*

—*Oh, my good Christ,* said Chance, from the doorway.

Callie raised her hands with thumbs forming L's, framing the room, panning it, stopping to focus on her brother. —*The Human Duplicators,* she droned solemnly. —*Live robots trained to kill. Beware these cruel and heartless machines they call androids who impersonate actual human beings.*

—*You tell 'im, baby,* Raine said, her mouth making the

words sound humorous, even when her heart hurt. Nobody could best Callie whenever she tapped into her vast reservoir of horror movie lore. She watched hours of sci-fi trailers and videos, and quoted them when she needed to summon power. Raine wanted the boy to love the girl in the same way she did. She could remember when the boy would have entertained the idea of being a lawyer for circus animals.

Chance went into his own room, entering his shroud of loud music.

Raine paused in the boy's doorway. —*Hhnnchoose an identity,* the computer droned. He had his back to her, ignoring her.

—*I need you to come outside with me a moment,* Raine said.

—*Can it wait? I'm kinda doing something here.*

—*Now,* Raine said gently. —*I need to show you something.*

—*Do I need shoes?*

—*No, just come down to the back door.*

Downstairs, she stepped out and held the door for him, her finger over her lips, *shhhh.* She pointed into his boot, smiling. The boy leaned over, his face becoming distorted as he saw.

—*Shit! I've got to wear those to—*

—*Don't touch it,* she snarled, hating the sound of her own voice.

—*Shit,* the boy said.

—*Hey, I knew you when.*

—*When what?*

—*When you would have considered it an honor to share your boot with baby wrens.*

The boy stared down the street, imperious in his suffering.

—*Well, I knew you when, too,* he said.

—*When what?*

—When you loved me for who I am and not for what I used to be.

Years before, Raine's husband had said to her, *—You are a good woman,* on the threshold of the kitchen, watching her teach the neighborhood children to roll out cookies in the shapes of animals.

Raine had raised her head over the tops of the children's heads, surprised to see him home, but he had already turned away to go into another, quieter room to read the baseball box scores. It was a time in their marriage when his professional ambitions were sharp. It was odd to see him home on a Saturday. It created confusion among the children, as if he were an unexpected guest who had to be tiptoed around.

She stared in amazement at the empty doorway. The world suddenly divided itself in two. Some could simply walk away from their children and read the box scores, while others felt compelled to muck about with children, up to her elbows in flour, kneading the old mantras of kindness into their minds: *say please, say thank you, share, share.*

Raine was indeed a good woman.

She was good for hot casseroles for the sick and little knitted caps for the newly born. She was good for several hours of free babysitting on Saturdays while other mothers worked out at gyms. She herself was good for hours and hours melting into years and years of good servitude at dusk, feeding decent dinners to stray children when their own mothers left them in her nest like cuckoos and cowbirds do. She was good for picking up an extra rider to take to ballet or soccer, good for bringing them home. She was good for not asking too many questions when another mother was habitually late, or called from local motels. She was good for considering the well-being of children first.

Another Magazine Street mother who was pregnant called to ask her to substitute as pianist for a children's musical. She could not refuse.

—*It's Gilbert and Sullivan. They just need someone to follow them with chords. I can't reach the keys anymore.*

Rehearsals were at a tiny Episcopal church hall in a different but identical neighborhood ten blocks north. It seemed a giddy illicit freedom, simply to be out of the house at dusk. There were no high ramps to drive across, no eight-lane throughways. She hesitated at a small viaduct that was being widened. She held her breath, accelerated, and crossed it, without incident.

The old church was small, a gothic brick dollhouse with a gated courtyard on the corner of a busy street. Raine parked her car at the curb and let herself in the gate. Inside was the kind of tiny, walled garden you might see in a distant city. Raine studied it a moment, shifting the fat Gilbert and Sullivan songbook from the crook of one elbow to the other. A tiny lily-pad pool flashed occasionally with lazy, plump carp, mottled with black and red. The slate flagstones were crusted with green moss. Beneath a fat, gnarled gingko tree, the moss had tinted a time-weathered statue of St. Francis of Assisi. She noticed a little mosaic of green and brown tiles in the brick church wall then, compromised by some creeping ivy. She could barely make it out: *Et En Arcadia Ego.* She used to know what that meant. There was a granite bench with *Carpe Diem* inscribed on its seat. She did remember what that meant.

She wanted to sit on the bench, and she wanted to sit there alone. It was not possible.

Children and their parents crisscrossed the courtyard, carrying translucent fairy wings and crowns trimmed with fake fur and red velvet.

Sit too long by a pool of carp, and someone will gently suggest you need help, or drugs, which might mean you're an unfit mother.

She hurried inside to the obligation, to the children.

She took her place at a scuffed upright piano, staring at the open songbook. The children watched her anxiously. They leaned forward, following each note, someone's crumbs left behind in the forest for them to navigate by. Their voices began to follow the crumbs, their faces guileless and beautiful. Raine nodded to the crescent of little girls in ballet tights and fairy wings, who leaned forward slightly and sang sweetly. A chorus chimed in, little boys.

> *Bow, bow,*
> *Ye lower middle classes.*
> *Bow, ye tradesmen*
> *Bow, ye masses.*

Raine fumbled a second at the keys, and pulled her fingers back as if burned.

Why have children sing such things?

The music stopped and the children froze and looked at her expectantly. She found her place and played a few notes. Instantly they organized themselves into position, the little boys righting their crowns and mantles, the girls sleeking back their wings. They carried on.

At eight, parents began to collect their children. Raine lingered with the director until the last few children were standing by the front door. The sexton of the church, a black man in a blue Sears uniform, waited to lock up. The director, a young childless woman who taught music at a local college, announced pointedly that she *could not stay*. The whole country was populated with young women like this. These were the kind Matthew was always distracted by, those who would never agree to traffic with anyone's children without a salary and a pension plan attached.

Raine was left standing in the courtyard with one little boy, Sam, who was the Lord High Chancellor. He sat down on the bench, his bottom narrow enough to fit between the words *Carpe* and *Diem*. His red velvet crown was in his lap, and he was dialing a little black cell phone that was the very model of a modern military walkie-talkie.

—*Do you need a ride? Is your mom coming?*

—*Sometimes they forget whose turn it is.*

—*I can give you a ride if they say it's okay.*

The boy was shaking his head. —*My mom's got her cell off.* His voice cracked on the last two words, just barely, and he pulled a tiny video game out of his backpack. Raine heard a faint sniff, and saw him wipe his nose on his sleeves. She fished in her purse for a tissue and brushed against her car keys. The sound of it caused the boy to look up, and his face was full of anguish.

—*I'm not leaving until somebody comes for you,* she said softly, and the boy nodded. He returned to the game, the object of which was to destroy, over and over, anything that moved.

Raine stood leaning on the ivied wall. The sexton of the church had by then finished with his chores inside, and seeing Raine was with the child, he left, clanging the wrought-iron gate behind him. —*Just pull it tight when you go, please ma'am.*

The boy had turned the sound off on his game. The susurrus of the cars outside the gate sounded like a waterfall. The carp in the pool listed ever so slightly to starboard in their sleep. Raine tried to remember the last time she had known such stillness.

Finally a hand reached for the gate's latch, and a man in a gray Brooks Brothers suit came in. Raine blinked.

It was the jukebox man. He seemed not to see her.

—*Hey, buddy. You ready to go? You had any dinner?*

—*Where's Mom?*

—*She called me from the gym. Something came up. Hey, that's a neat crown you got there.*

Raine jingled her car keys, and murmured, —*I'll run along now.*

The jukebox man turned to her in surprise, bending down a bit to see her face in the light that came from the church window. —*Hey,* he said. —*The Catfish Lady.*

—*No,* Raine said, laughing. —*The Rose Lady is the Catfish Lady.* She held out her hand. —*I'm Raine.*

—*Right,* he said, grinning awkwardly, shaking her hand. —*Thank you for waiting with Sam. We're old hands at this, aren't we, Sam? At least she didn't lose you in the airport, huh? Remember that?*

The boy was already going out the wrought-iron gate, looking like a stooped gnome, his backpack a small hump on his back. He turned suddenly. —*Can we get pizza?* The boy's father looked at Raine.

—*Pizza?* She saw that he was inviting her to join them, and that he ducked his head when he felt shy, like his son did. —*No? So long, then. Thanks again.*

She stared at the gate they had left open.

With a longing approaching criminality, she wanted to be with them, simply going for pizza.

A muffled splash in the lily pond, a dreaming fish, perhaps. She closed the gate behind her, and started for home. At the little viaduct, she circled the block three times, working up to it. On the fourth try, she began to weep. It wasn't going to work. She pulled the car to the curb, in front of a row of tender young

birches newly tethered to the ground in front of a paint store.
She rested her forehead on the steering wheel and sobbed, for
no particular reason.

Et en arcadia ego. It meant something sad, she could
remember that much.

A tapping at the glass of her window forced her head up. She
turned to see the jukebox man, a blue-checkered napkin in
hand, looking at her. How much had he seen? She looked
beyond the new birches: a little pizza place she'd passed a hundred times in her life. Sam was in a booth by the window, looking out at her. She let her window down.

—*Are you okay?* The jukebox man asked. —*Can I call
someone?*

—*Oh,* Raine said, unable to say more. —*No thanks. I'll be
okay in a minute.*

—*Come have a slice of pizza with us. A little food can work
wonders sometimes.*

—*I have to get home,* she said. —*They'll be—*

—*They'll be fine,* he said. —*And so will you.*

He'd seen everything.

She started the ignition, but the man only leaned in closer to
the window, so close she felt his breath moving her hair as he
spoke. —*Don't leave,* he said. —*I'm coming right back.* He
walked to the window and spoke through the glass to Sam,
—*Mrs. Semmes needs help with her car. I'll be right back.
Don't move.*

The boy nodded, two thumbs up.

The jukebox man walked back over to the driver's side.
—*I'm going to drive you across that bridge.*

—*No,* Raine said. —*It's all right, really. I'm just a bit overwhelmed with things today.*

—*Okay, then, you drive me across the bridge,* the jukebox
man said. —*I'll walk back.*

He was in the car then, silent, and she was grateful for that. In the seconds before she drove onto the bridge, he put his hand over hers and held firmly. She could feel her heart splitting, dislodging itself, beating like a bird against glass to avoid the bridge, *no*. She felt the warmth of his hand, radiating all the way down below her navel somewhere, *yes*. She felt warm calluses on his hands and remembered the jukeboxes. She felt the tires click onto the pavement of solid ground again. She started to brake, but a car behind her honked.

—*You can let me out at the corner*, he said. She pulled into the parking lot of a dry cleaners to let him out, and the driver behind them honked angrily as it passed. The man inside was apoplectic with rage, gesturing. The jukebox man laughed and waved good-bye.

As she turned into her own driveway, she could see her daughter's giraffe lamp upstairs in the right window. Callie had made a big Noah's ark out of a cardboard box the new dishwasher had come in, and was sending her stuffed animals into it, lions, bears, lambs, and a preponderance of old Easter bunnies. She had no idea that out there somewhere in the vast, vast night was the very young man who would in a few years be screaming his imagined pain into his own mirror, and would attract, as surely as an insect, the compassion of a certain animal-loving little girl on Magazine Street.

Later in her bedroom, Raine sat in its high window, opening it to stare out at the stars, dependable as the sun and the moon and Bob Dylan. Behind her, her husband was motionless, mesmerized by the image of a policeman pistol-whipping a figure of vague Italian origins.

She took out her shot-silk notebook and stared at its blank pages. She bit the tip of the cloisonné pen. She imagined her son years later, after she was dead, the same as all the other innumerable American boys in the upstairs windows making the same insect noises, dreaming the same bad dream. They didn't know it yet, but someday they'd become their own fathers, eventually, out on the bypass at dusk, going home to the same suburbs they vowed to escape as boys.

But she would never, ever tell them that, not even if she were being ripped apart by langurs, or lawyers. She put the book away, without having written a word in it. It had been an extraordinary evening. She had traveled miles and miles, from nowhere to somewhere.

At the Cloud Nine

America was also old names in the Hebrew cemetery high on a bluff overlooking the Sunflower River. *Dawidov, Okun, Bronstein, Cohen, Meyer, Abraham.* Boubacar stared at the names and sat down on a stone bench. He reached into a white paper bag and pulled out some greasy wax-paper wrappings. He had found, in his wanderings that morning, a restaurant on the highway that sold Lebanese food, and Lebanese is practically North African, which might as well be home. He unwrapped the falafel carefully, already tasting it.

The boy knew which dead were buried where. The ones with English names, *Hatcher, Bennett, Wright*, were corraled inside a fence not far from the large grain elevator that towered over the buildings down near the old railroad depot. Abrahams were here, but Ibrahims were across town, not too far from the Moorish Science Temple. The Ibrahims were in the *kaffir* cemetery for black people.

The understanding that came to the boy on a clear morning, with the scent of freshly mown grass in the air: *Ibrahim, Abraham*, as if there had been a great quarrel once in the same family about the spelling of the name, about something else trivial. And after many centuries of the usual troubles, some of each had come here, and had begun to become alike again, listening to each other's music, and eating each other's falafel. What if the Jews and the Muslims had similar songs?

Abraham, Ibrahim, it had the makings of a song.

What was the music of the Jews like? he wondered. What had become of their music in this place? Why were there jukeboxes full of black music, but not Jewish?

Men in government uniforms were cutting the grass beside the road, driving small tractors. The boy stared: these men did nothing but mow, all day. Up and down the highways. Teslem had explained it to him. Such grass, an ocean of it on the roadsides, insignificant as air.

He walked the full length of Issaquena Avenue, beginning at the Champagne Club, a storefront painted bright blue and coral and yellow. In the middle of the morning, pretty ladies in bright clothes watched him pass. In the window of an empty place next to the club, a poster of a mother holding a baby had been faded by the sun, almost to translucence. He pondered its meaning, *WIC Program*.

America was burnt-out stores and abandoned agencies for vague and now defunct social services.

On one street there were more empty stores than operating ones. In some, merchandise had been left to fade in the sun in the windows, cloche hats and bow ties, as if there had been a sudden shift in the winds of economy, and evacuation had been swift.

He saw a small white building set back from the street and then he saw the red, white, and blue barber pole. —*Wade Walton Barber Shop*, he read aloud, and the hair prickled on his neck. Wade Walton! There was an old 33 rpm record album still back at his mother's, on the other side of the world, and on the cover of that recording was a photo of this barbershop. He peered in the dirt-streaked window at an empty barber chair, some sun-bleached copies of *Jet* and *Ebony*.

—*You too late*, an old woman called out across the parking

lot. —*Wade Walton have left the planet. You want to see him you got to go to the graveyard.*

Boubacar ducked his head by way of response and fumbled for the words. Did one address them as *grandmother* in America? This woman was dressed like a young girl, in tight pants and high-heeled sandals. She was old, but happy.

—*Now me, my man is Steakbone Booker, playing at the Cloud Nine tomorrow night. Tell your mama.* The woman broke off in a laugh, and hurried on her way down the street. —*Tell your papa,* she called back over her shoulder.

Boubacar passed the Looking Good shop and then next door, the Looking Better, both run by the same family of Pakistanis. He studied the shirts in the window. On the front of the shirts, *FUBU*. This was good in America. He didn't know why, but it was good to wear these shirts. He passed New York Hi-Tone Fashion, and the International House of Hair. He took a turn through an alley and found himself in the next block, full of shops for the rich whites. Furniture as delicate as confectionery, sweetmeats solid as sofas. A white woman with fiercely accusatory eyebrows came to stand in the doorway with her arms folded, and he moved on, his heart murmuring its misgivings.

At the Cloud Nine Club, a hand-painted side was propped against a parking meter on the sidewalk:

FRIED FROG LEG
$3 DOZ.

Next door to the Cloud Nine, a giant toy panda beckoned from a window covered with black iron grillwork, and rows of fuzzy dice dangled in the light. He studied the sign: *International*

House of Pawn. The window was a mixture of tire tools and musical instruments. A Hammond organ stood on frail legs with a weed-eater leaning against it. A tambourine with purple and gold ribbon streamers had tiny gold crucifixes tied to the ends.

There it was—the National Steel guitar, the very one.

His shoulders slumped in relief.

One hundred fifty dollars said the red price tag in an elegant script.

He could not stop staring. Even the faux-alligator case was there.

—Pretty little animal, ain't she?

Who said that? Boubacar looked around and saw no one.

—Up here, said a voice.

The boy was standing beside an enormous old white Winnebago. Its once-white aluminum side was mottled yellow with Bondo, applied therapeutically here and there to touch up old insults. Like most everything else in Clarksdale, the RV seemed to be in some state of momentary reprieve from the Big River Sanitary Landfill.

Atop the RV was a tall black man sitting in a plastic-webbed lawn chair, staring down at the boy through enormous sunglasses. His legs seemed to start under his armpits somewhere. His knees seemed to be an impediment as he attempted to position a very small satellite dish mounted to the top of the RV. He had almost no hair, and he was dressed in denim overalls and bright green Converse basketball shoes, like a very young man. But the voice was old.

—I seen you eyeballin' that old National. Them old lap steels is something, ain't they?

The boy stood speechless, his fingertips pressed to the glass, which was warm from the waning sunlight.

—You looking at the history of rock-and-roll there. All them

old players started out on them things. Son House, Tampa Red,
Bukka White. Then Muddy come along with his electric and
nobody wanted them anymore. My daddy's brother give his to
the scrap metal drive in World War Two, made bullets to kill
Tojo with. Man I wisht I still had that thang. You know Muddy
Waters?

Bullets, the boy heard. *World War Two. Muddy Waters.*

The man was shambling down the tiny ladder on the back of
the vehicle, and the RV rocked on its wheels a bit with the
weight of him.

—*What you listenin' to so loud there?*

Boubacar offered his headphones and the man listened, nodding to the beat.

—*Who that is?*

—*Ali Farka Toure.*

—*Gret Godfrey,* the tall man said, wiping his hands on his
overalls, then holding out his hand to shake. —*Boy, where you*
from? Get on over here and talk to me.

Boubacar crossed over the horseshoes embedded in the sidewalk, into a sort of canteen that once had been a store. The
same Mighty Sons of Destiny poster he'd seen in the ghost grocery was taped to the wall here. Behind the counter, with eyeglasses perched on her nose, was the same older woman who
had spoken to him outside Wade Walton's barbershop.

—*Well, look who the dogs drug up,* she said to the man.

—*Hello, Sarah,* the tall man said. —*This boy has come all*
the way from Africa.

—*You again,* she said to the boy. —*We have already met,*
Cornelius.

—*Listen here.* He turned to Boubacar. —*Say something in*
African, boy.

—*Yaw take care now,* the boy drawled in West African–
French–inflected Clarksdale policemanese.

The woman laughed and clapped her hands in pleasure, and brought him a glass of iced tea. The tall man called Cornelius was by then unsnarling electrical cords on the floor that led to amplifiers. Boubacar looked around.

There was to be music soon, in this place.

—*Why you not at the schoolhouse?* Sarah now demanded.

The boy closed his eyes with pleasure at being reprimanded by this grandmother, even if not his own. He basked in her fussiness, though he didn't catch all the words.

—*I am straight off the boat*, he said, because it was guaranteed to bring a smile.

—*Well you need you a taste of my greens*, Sarah said, and vanished into the back. Cornelius had produced by then a cobalt-blue lacquered electric guitar, and plugged it in. He strummed the guitar, two chords, then turned a dial and played the same chords again. Boubacar took in the video poker games, endlessly changing card spreads into infinity whether anyone cared to wager or not.

When the woman brought him a deep bowl full of fragrant, steaming greens and a fat square of spongy cornbread, she made him sit in a booth with her. Cornelius slid into the booth next to her, his pliers resting in the pouch sewn to the breast of his overalls.

—*So how you like it here in America?* Cornelius asked, leaning over to tease a cigarette from Sarah's shirt pocket, his long fingers moving in a slow, voluptuous way.

—*I am liking*, Boubacar fumbled for the words, then stopped. Stopping was usually a mistake, too. It caused the words to dam up and then spill out like a flood. —*I play the oud sometimes, but not good. But the guitar, I wish to buy. It is very old and silver, with flowers on the side.*

—*You tawmbout that National Steel in the International Pawn?*

—*I believe this guitar will have a good spirit for playing.*

As Cornelius studied the boy, a soft light came into his dark face.

—*Who say you cain't have it? Your mama? That's the oldest trick in the book, man, when they be tawmbout 'no you can't play that.' Or tawmbout: 'you got to play God's music, not the devil's.' Hell, it's all God's music if you play it right.*

The tall man stubbed his cigarette out in the ashtray, not taking his eyes off the boy. Boubacar fumbled for words. Only French was coming to him at the moment. He shook his head, giving up on language. It was too complicated to explain. As the man's face became serious for the first time, Boubacar became conscious of how old the man was, enough to be his father's grandfather, perhaps.

—*When the old people tell you you can't do it, it's just God telling you you got to.* He put the cigarette in his mouth and spoke around it. —*It's a thing you got to do. Like when somebody throw you in the river, tawmbout, 'Swim, fool!' So you swim. How much it cost?*

—*One hundred dollars American. And fifty.*

—*Shit. That ain't nothing. Sarah! Don't you need you a dishwasher or somebody here during the daytime?*

—*Need a busboy at night,* Sarah called from the bowels of the kitchen.

—*Awright, then. We in business.*

—*Well, I don't know Cornelius. I don't want them government people coming 'round here.*

Cornelius assessed the boy in a new light, his brow softening, and waved her words away.

—*Now that particular National Steel, it's a trick to it. It go on your lap, see. Some people try to play it like normal guitar and it don't work. Used to be a Mr. Calvin Dearborn around in these parts, go to church by the name of Jewel Dominion, over*

Rose Hill. Them preachers play the hell out them lap steels. They could be making fat money if they'd go to the clubs, but they sittin' in these little country churches like they mama told them to. You got to go to church with 'em to play like that. You won't learn to play like that in no school.

Boubacar shook his head. Church. The man was telling him to go to *kaffir* church.

—*I am what they call a self-educated man. I went to what they call the school of hard knocks. You do something, they knock you in the head, and you learn not to do that no more. I had perfect attendance at that school.*

—*Cornelius, you so full of shit,* the woman called out from the kitchen. —*It was the school of soft bumps when we got together. Tell it like it was, baby. I was there. I know. That night Willie B. come after you with the ice pick.* Her voice faded off into a grumble among the clatter of metal dishpans. —*It was the school of soft bumpin' going on that night, mister.*

Boubacar walked the streets for hours, until the sun went down, waiting for his new job to start. He took a nap in the gazebo overlooking the police station, out of sight on the floor behind its rails. He went into a gas station to buy a bright blue soda, and sat down on the curb outside. *Power,* the drink's label. He tilted his head back and took long, deep gulps with his eyes closed. When the bottle was empty and he opened his eyes, he could see a beautiful automobile, many mabone, shining among others that were offered for sale at the Shabazz Automobile Specialist.

It was a Chevrolet, and painted in banded hues of magenta, gold, and dark purple. It had been a taxi once, but now it was here, and its price was written in shoe polish on its windshield. Boubacar walked over to look at it, peering in its tinted windows. The seats were in mint condition, except for one long rip in the backseat. The hubcaps were a joy to his heart, strong bands of coiled metal. There were fuzzy dice hanging from its rearview mirror. He circled the car with muted awe. It was the car of Haile Selassie Pegues.

—*Take her out for a spin?*

Boubacar turned to see a thin black man in blue jeans and a dashiki standing behind him. —*I do not drive the car yet,* Boubacar explained, and the man's eyes widened at his accent.

—*You from Detroit?*

—*Mauritania.*

—*That in East St. Louis?*

—*Is near Senegal.*

Time dragged its foot for a few moments while the man studied him. Boubacar kept talking. —*I am staying in Madagascar with my uncles. We are saving the money for the car.*

—*Hey, you don't need all the money, just some of the money. Buy it on time. And when you ready, I want you to remember my name, 'Reno Shabazz.'* He extracted a little white card from his shirt pocket and handed it to Boubacar.

Boubacar smiled his most dazzling smile, his response when he did not understand what had been said to him.

—*Well, stay in America long enough, you got to have you a car, and when you do, you come see Reno Shabazz. I'll be here.*

Boubacar studied the card and said to the man, practicing his American speech, —*I am thanking you. For sure. I do not forget you.*

By nine o'clock, Boubacar had retrieved his schoolbooks from their hiding place near the now deserted school and was back at the Cloud Nine Club. Sarah showed him where to shove his backpack out of sight, and how to wrap the red apron around himself twice and cinch it tight with the strings. She set him to the task of dipping raw pieces of catfish into cornmeal, and dropping them into hot, bubbling oil. She let him sample the first golden steaming piece she fished out, dribbling a bit of lemon juice on it before she put it in his hands. He blew on it, and burned his mouth anyway.

—*You got catfish in Africa?*

The boy shook his head, blowing on the fish to cool it.

She showed him how to read the orders that the girls would bring from the tables outside. There were all the lemons to be sliced. The kitchen at the Cloud Nine had become a tiny cauldron. Boubacar was vaguely aware of the music starting up in the front at about nine o'clock, but there was no time to step to the door.

—*Ladies and gentlemen, give it up for the one, the only, the man play so tight he make you sass you mama . . . Steakbone Booker!*

The boy thought of the fifty dollars he was going to earn, and kept cooking, and washing dishes. When all the fish was gone, and all the dishes washed, he stood exhausted but happy, to look through the narrow slit through which he and Sarah had probably passed two hundred plates of fried catfish that night. What he saw astounded him.

Up in the front window of the Cloud Nine, his back to the street, Cornelius was dressed in a banana-yellow Nehru jacket and pants, and he was wearing a scruffy Beatle wig. He stood holding a magnificent cobalt-blue guitar. The chords he played were deep and gratifying; Boubacar felt them down in the center of his bones. Cornelius had one long leg slightly forward, as if he were about to walk on a long journey. Cornelius strutted as he played the guitar, and moved in and out of many songs that Boubacar knew from his father's old John Lee Hooker tapes.

> Lord, I had a woman, she were kind in every way.
> I say I had me a woman, she were kind in every way.

Now she gone and left me.
I take her flowers every Decoration Day.

Boubacar studied the singer's movements, and the curl of his
lips, the beads of sweat on his grooved brow. Sometimes Cornelius held the guitar close for a while, like one might hold a
reluctant woman. Sometimes he held it away from himself
with one hand, swiveling on the balls of his feet, dangling the
guitar daintily like a bat by the neck, coaxing impossibly high
notes from it with only one finger.

Boubacar gasped, the crowd cheered. Steakbone searched the
room while he played, across the heads of the dancers glisten-
ing with sweat. Sarah had come out of the kitchen and was fanning herself with her apron. It was the first time in his young
life that Boubacar had seen how music could come to you from
someone loving you across the room. He felt as if he had acci-
dentally eavesdropped on one of the world's best-kept secrets.

The music was all over, much too soon.

—*Peoples, I got to leave you now,* Cornelius said in theatri-
cal sadness, leaning into his microphone, playing a long and
mournful chord before raising his arm to hang like a dark hook
in the air. —*Got to get on back to Belleville, Illi-noise.* He
mopped his brow with a handkerchief and dangled it above the
heads of the women in the front of the crowd, and then threw it
all the way back to Sarah. She tucked it away in her breasts
somewhere, smiling her quiet smile. Whatever else there was
between them, it could keep until he came back. She was a
peaceful woman, the boy thought.

After Cornelius had finished signing autographs with the name
Steakbone for his women fans, he seemed to disappear for a
while. Then Boubacar saw him emerge from the men's room

clad once again in his overalls. In one hand he had his banana-yellow Nehru suit on a hanger, covered in a clear plastic bag. He carried the small metal cashbox in the other.

—*Hey, man,* Cornelius said. —*What you think? They got music like mine in Africa? Hell, I know they do.*

The boy could only grin broadly. His heart was so full that he could not speak.

—*You need a ride home? I'll drop you off. Tell you what. You get your axe out the hock, and learn to play you some licks, and when I come back for Christmas, we'll play. We could do us some house-wrecking, mister.*

On the drive out of Clarksdale, the boy beamed, high in the passenger seat of the Bondo-encrusted RV. Cornelius wore a porkpie hat, and turned the big wheel of the RV carefully onto the highway as if it were a huge oceangoing vessel. On the way, he tried to talk to the boy about music, shouting over to him above the dyspeptic roar of the engine.

—*When you start to play that lap steel, sometime in your traveling you need to go to Crescent City, Florida. The Campbells is there. If you can't go there, then go to Rush, New York. Robert Randolph. He the one you got to beat. You be what you want to be in your heart, otherwise there just ain't no goddamn point in fooling with it. You'll be making records 'fore you know it.*

—*What about the Jews?*

—*Jews?*

—*The ones who make the records.*

Cornelius studied the boy, nodding. —*Oh, yeah. Your people got that thing with the Jews. Well, I ain't no expert, but seem to me, Jews is like everybody else. Some is good, some you got to keep your eye on. If it wasn't for Jews, wouldn't be no jazz and wouldn't be no blues. It's just a natural fact. Hell, man, get you some Benny Goodman. Get you some Cab Calloway. Africa, Beethoven. It all fruit from the same tree.*

When the big Bondo-encrusted Winnebago lumbered into the parking lot of the Celestial and let the boy out, there was only the moon as witness. The boy paused in the door, his heart full of things he couldn't say.

—*Whoa, wait. Little English lesson for you before you go,* Cornelius said, his foot still on the brake, the engine running like a whale with a heart murmur. —*Repeat after me: 'I swear before my God.'*

—*I swear before my God.*

—*'I won't let nobody get between me and my music—'*

—*Won't let nobody—*

—*'And to get the hell out of Mississippi—'*

—*And to get the hell—*

—*'At the first—'*

—*At the first—*

—*'Available opportunity.'*

It was the first time the boy had seen Cornelius be totally serious. Boubacar shook his hand, then stepped down and closed the door. He could read his lips through the window: *Robert Randolph. Benny Goodman.* He stood watching its magnificent-mabone taillights wink, then become pinpoints as Cornelius slowed down to inspect the Harlem Swing Club before he traveled on. Boubacar walked home slowly, savoring the quiet and the secrecy of his time among the infidels. His veins still throbbed with the music. The porch light at the store was on, and he felt shame at skipping his work for Angus, who had been nothing but kind to him.

The next day, the sidewalk in front of the Cloud Nine was empty where the big RV had been. The accidental money felt fat in the boy's pocket. But the guitar was gone from the window of the International House of Pawn. It had vanished, flown like a cinema spaceship, away from him again.

Stumbling a few steps away from the window, the boy felt that something unnameable had him by the throat, tightening its grip. What good was the accidental money if the guitar was gone? He crossed over the unlucky horseshoes again. The cowbell that hung on the doorknob to the Cloud Nine clanked as he opened it and entered, considering the vanity of his ways. The Wastrel's voice, his grandmother's voice, his mother's voice—he could overhear all their silent reprimands. Sarah came out of the kitchen, wiping her hands on her apron.

—Oh. Thought you was the Cockrell Banana man. Look over in the corner, baby. Cornelius left you something. Say you can pay him back next time he come to town. Say you got to pay him back with seven songs, seven separate songs. He done tuned it for you and everything.

There was the old case covered to look like alligator skin. With shaking hands, Boubacar snapped back the fastenings, and opened the lid.

There it was, the most beautiful object in all of America.

When Sarah came out with the bowl of greens intended for him to eat, she found him kneeling before the guitar and weeping with ragged, delighted grief.

Still Life,
with Shotgun and Oranges

Dean Fondren drove past the sagging old Abide plantation house, knowing he had to make a decision about the house soon. It sat at the base of the levee like a spent steamboat, hip-sprung in its roofline, snaggletoothed, with missing window-panes. Even with that Mylar banner left over from some renters from years ago, he had affection for the house. *Nation of Islam*, he thought with a smile. *They didn't last long.* Farrakhan's folks, they thought they wanted to live inside a symbol, but the lure of the bright lights and the big air-conditioning in Memphis was too strong. They left following the same road their ancestors had. He'd left the banner there to confuse the European photographers.

How could he ever tear the old place down? That would be like sending some old familiar animal to the <u>abattoir</u>. He imagined a different, impractical option: dismantling the house board by board. It would take years that way. And the odd murals on the walls? What would become of them? To dismantle them would be to do wrong.

The walls were why he loved the place.

—*Those walls should be in the Smithsonian,* Alexis said the first time he took her upstairs in that house.

He wondered if she still felt that way. She had not seen them in years and avoided going there with him anymore. Not that there'd been much chance lately; Dean had not seen her in weeks. Perhaps he would ask the next time she would be so courteous as to pick up the phone and talk to him. The last time they'd spoken he'd struggled to filter the resentment out of his voice.

—*They need me here*, she'd said.

—*More like, you need to be there instead of here*, he'd said, after some silence that sounded like more miles of distance than there really was between them.

Dean always took the shotgun with him when he ventured into the Abide house, never knowing what to expect: a raccoon, a rat, a crack addict from Clarksdale. Nearing the house Dean broke open the shotgun, wading through the shin-high grass. Belle whimpered a little but followed in the swath of grass his steps opened. Then she stopped cold in his tracks, hearing, as usual, what was ahead before he could. She was staring at a hollow log. —*Stay*, he told her, then closed the shotgun again.

Dean took a step forward and heard the baby goat bleat before he saw it, following its voice to the hollow log. There it was, a sodden little heap of damp black fur on knobby legs, not understanding much more than that it must hide itself. It was pitiful and weak, but agitated by their sudden presence. The thing was hungry, Dean realized. He and Belle stared intently together as it struggled up to stand, like a wobbly gate-legged table. It was too far from the road to have wandered from there. Had it been left to die? Nobody around raised goats after Prophet Pegues died. Belle wagged her tail hopefully, once, twice.

Dean picked up the goat and let Belle inspect it, running her nose over it from stem to stern. She looked up at Dean for instructions: *it looks like a puppy but it stinks to high hell.*

It was beginning to rain. The goat butted its snout against his chest as Dean held it close. Before they started up the failing steps, he somehow managed to break open the shotgun yet again without dropping the goat. He reached through the broken pane of the front door and turned the old brass knob. —*Mind your feet, Belle,* he said absently, his own boots crunching on the broken glass.

Across the field, Peregrine Smith-Jones studied the specter of the old Abide mansion in the rain. Rain was good, rain would be gothic. The flowers spilling out of the windows, so it wouldn't be too Charles Addams. Plus she needed to go to the Chinese store. She'd never quite mastered the knack of walking the blue heeler she had acquired by default after her boyfriend left, taking only his clothes, some antique amps, and the laptop that seemed to constitute his independent recording "label."

She caught sight of herself in the bedroom mirror, her body laddered with rib bones. —*You look like the canary that ate the birdcage,* she told the mirror. She put on a red crushed velvet dress she'd found in the Blackjack Zion Rescue Mission, soutache trim, frogs up the front, so many years out of season here that it would be *au courant* in New York. It was a child's dress, but it fit her now. The blue heeler was scratching and pawing the inside of the cabin door, impatient.

She stepped barefoot into her Wellingtons and grabbed the dog's leash and jingled it. He came to her and sat. She put her camera in a clear plastic bag and tucked a roll of film into her bra. She picked up a blue Persian scarf on the way out the door and wrapped it around her like a shawl, knotting its corners between her breasts. She wound the leash around her wrist like a bracelet to shorten it, to keep the dog close by. At the clink and jingle of the leash, the dog made the same little cry and whine he always did, then they were out the door, loose Wellingtons slapping against her calves, and the dog trembling with expectation.

She walked the dog to the Celestial Grocery for food to get her through the next few days. She let the dog off the leash while she went inside the store. Putting oranges in a brown paper bag, she could hear the blue heeler chasing the Chinese man's cats under the porch. After she paid for her oranges and milk, she asked Angus Chien if she could photograph him on his front porch, and he obliged. She let him follow his own habit, not suggesting any particular poses for him, which seemed to bewilder him. While she talked to him, she waited for his face to relax. She joked with him, to no avail.

Angus Chien's mistrust of cameras was quite different from the mistrust she'd seen in others who didn't like cameras. So the mistrust was the thing to capture, the hard glint in his eyes, glassy as a sockeye salmon on ice. He would not smile. He walked her out onto the porch, and she whistled to the dog. She said careful thanks and good-bye, part of the plan. About fifteen feet away she turned suddenly and caught him in the unguarded moment she wanted, sitting on his step, lanky legs crossed elegantly, holding his cigarette in the same way that old Vietnamese men smoked in certain neighborhoods in Paris. She could hardly wait to see his face, as she knew it would resolve itself, floating in fluid later. He wagged a finger at her, and smiled.

—*You tricked me.*

—*I'll make you some prints*, she said. —*For your family.*

She had seen the pantheon of Olan Mills babies on his television, and others old enough to be hand-tinted, that little private grotto of mostly Chinese babies.

Her boyfriend had not grown tired of her black skin, or her obsession with her Mississippi roots. He had become afraid of her camera.

—You go into someplace I can't follow, he had whispered savagely to her one night, holding her, and it was not a compliment. He had been talking about the times she turned motel bathrooms into darkrooms and forgot he was there, while images swam up to meet her: the village idiot with his lawnmower, a church congregation, their faces like pale lanterns, stoned on the prospect of apocalypse. The white rain they called *parathion*, falling from the sky onto parked church buses full of children. Once she even captured the contorted brow of a white preacher screaming into the face of a twelve-year-old pregnant white girl outside a Memphis abortion clinic. *—The ways of God are hidden!*

All the way across the field, with the levee like a wall of new green grass behind, stood the old house silvered by the weather and the years. White honeysuckle had begun to bloom out of its roof cracks and wall crevices, like pale trumpets spilling out. Peregrine took the camera out of its bag and began to shoot. She worked intently to get the light right, vaguely mindful of the thunder she heard coming from across the river. She could hear the blue heeler barking at a distance, summoning her. It needed a witness for whatever mayhem it was about to pursue.

Inside the Abide house, Dean saw Belle prick up her ears at the sound of some other dog barking at a distance. The baby goat butted its head against his chest, searching for a nipple. Dean sighed a ragged sigh and turned to the stairs. What a strange moment. It produced the same tug of emotions in him as his own child had, nuzzling his chest years ago. His child was grown and gone, but the old house was the same as the day he first brought Alexis to see the Abide house. There had been a severed doll's head on the floor in the foyer. The silver and pink wallpaper was peeling even then like shreds of old trout-skin. There were elegant old leather-bound books strewn around, fly-specked, watermarked. The plays of Shakespeare were jumbled in with books on animal husbandry. He'd picked Alexis up in his arms and carried her up the stairs, just to show her he could do it. Her blue sweater had snagged on a nail where a picture had once hung. The nail was still there. Dean touched it softly as he passed upstairs.

The images on the walls still had the power to make his hair stand on end. A shepherd with the face of a Tartar was being devoured by his own sheep. A shade tree sprouted baby faces as fruit. A nun stitched mutilated dolls back together.

Now he looked at the old fanlight and could remember, with an aching clarity, Alexis sitting there thirty years before, the sunlight behind her making a corona of light around her hair. He didn't realize he was testing her, but that's what it was, a test of the sort a young man would make, to see if a woman could fit herself into his life. He lifted her to the high sill of the fanlight and perched her up there like a child, so she could see out over the levee, across the river to Arkansas. She looked out over the river and back at the walls. That was when she'd said they should be in the Smithsonian.

At the time, his head had bent in gratitude then to whatever force had sent him this woman.

Now the walls were raddled with the red and black spray paint of gangs, but underneath that they glowed, illuminated in some medieval way by the force of profound solitude. A fiery mandala turned, made entirely of babies' faces. Pigs sang to fish, turtles carried whales on their backs. A black Jesus was chopping up his own cross for firewood. Bibles burned, and bombers grew out of the earth on stems, drooping like heavy roses. Hypnotic green script swayed like tendrils in a wind.

HOW MANY MILES TO BABYLAND?
THREE SCORE MILES AND TEN.
CAN WE GET THERE BY CANDLELIGHT?
YES, AND BACK AGAIN.

Phrases heaved and pitched like boxcars colliding all around them.

COME CLOSER

ANYONE EVER USED AND ABANDONED

BESIDE THIS RIVER

HOW IS IT YOU LEARNED TO LOATHE YOUR LIFE?

THERE IS FOOD FOR THAT FAMISHMENT HERE.

Dean could remember that first afternoon with Alexis more easily than he could remember whatever had happened an hour ago.

On one half of the room, some vandal had spray-painted in red the words FUCK FUCK FUCK with the force of a command. Dean and Alexis had obeyed the command. It had been eloquent and terrifying and comforting all at the same time. The words still had the power to humble him. He traced a finger along a triptych painted into a corner.

IN THE ORCHARD OF ABANDONED DREAMS

I AM POURED OUT LIKE WATER

IN THE CITIES OF THE CAESARS

WE ARE POURED OUT LIKE WATER

FOR THE ABANDONED OF THE EARTH

YOU POUR ME OUT LIKE WATER,

LIKE LAUGHTER OVER FROZEN RIVERS.

The windowsill he had lifted Alexis up to was rotted through now. What had become of all the books? Those books were probably strewn from hell to breakfast, Dean mused, scratching the goat's hard little head. Memphis to St. Louis and back, in Marie Abide's birdhouses.

A few hundred feet from the Abide house, Peregrine Smith-Jones took her camera out of its plastic bag and popped off the lens cap. The white honeysuckle looked old and fragile in the fading light. The front door was open, like an astonished mouth. She had not noticed that before.

Peregrine shifted her stance a bit, stepping back. Focusing the lens, she brought the honeysuckle of the Abide house into the foreground, and Ariadne's shack into the background. *That's the way it would have looked to the big daddy,* she thought. *He probably stood here and looked over there and did not care if she lived in a hovel that the wind howled through.* She watched the light play in the swath of trees that lined the creek. She raised the camera. She willed it to catch the gathering rain, to document the sucking death trap she'd heard Mississippi was, but then the clouds shifted and the trees stood bathed in gold. She saw the same beautiful sight her grandmother had seen, when the world is washed clean.

By the time she stopped, the rain came in windblown waves, battering the blooms on the house. She barely had time to duck under its eaves and step up onto its porch. A loose shutter was slapped to and fro by the wind, a desolate sound she didn't like. That would have been the way Ariadne would have heard the wind, flapping through the old shutters like that.

She thought she heard the faint cry of some baby animal, cat, or human child. She looked around.

Maybe there was a spirit world.

Upstairs before the big fanlight Dean propped the baby goat on the wide windowsill and looked out over the levee, stooping to see through the tendrils of white honeysuckle. There was the girl who drove the green Comet, standing like a bright daub of paint in her red dress. It was like watching a child square off with its elders, the way she straightened her back as she faced the old trees. The girl paused with her camera, as if awaiting instructions from something invisible. Behind her, the old river, a barge coming around the bend like a slow beetle on a fat satin ribbon. The blue heeler ricocheted around the landscape, worthless.

It was Sunday. Dean needn't be in a hurry, he reminded himself. He moved from the window and zipped the baby goat into his jacket to get it to stop bleating. He began to pile some boards in the fireplace. He found some old sheet music to use for tinder. It wasn't cold enough for a fire, but he wanted a fire, and his new goat was cold. Belle saw what he was doing and sat down, watching him intelligently. She knew they would be there a while.

On the first afternoon Dean had brought Alexis to the old Abide house, he had used *The Collected Plays of George Bernard Shaw* as kindling. The cover had been stripped from it, leaving its pages of musty paper nibbled to a state of lace by the silverfish. When Dean's fire was a small blaze of twigs and rotted banister rails, he laid his shearling coat on the floor to make a sort of bower. Alexis had then added her pink Angora sweater to the arrangement, peeling it over her head like soft skin. Then came her gray wool skirt, and then her black slip and nylons.

It had amazed Dean, how beautiful both their bodies were in the firelight, and how the sound filled the high empty room when she whispered, —*God*, as he moved inside her, naming the name of what had made them.

She was the first woman who had given herself to him

freely, no questions asked, without the terrible negotiations in the backseats of cars, in which cotton caste somehow always mattered. Later, when he had rolled them both into his coat and bent his body around hers to keep her warm, they had watched the fire die down to coals. Out beyond the levee, they heard the mournful lowing of barges on the river.

—*Listen,* he had said. —*The barge boats are talking to each other. The big one just told the little one a secret.*

—*What secret?*

—*You have to guess.*

—*Saying, 'move it on over.'*

—*No.*

—*Saying, outa my way, jack, I got miles to go before I sleep.*

—*Nope.*

—*Then what?*

—*Saying... Dean Fondren thinks he's going to marry Alexis Bancroft, if she'll have him.*

Thirty years later he was alone in the same room with his memories, and his awe, and a foundling baby goat fastened into his coat. The fire was guttering. He pried up a piece of rotted wood from the doorjamb. He hesitated a moment, then gently laid the jagged board into the fire. It burned as easily as paper. Staring into the fire, he thought he heard a noise downstairs. He picked up his shotgun again and went back down the stairs. It had been a clicking noise, like someone loading ammunition.

Peregrine clicked a new roll of film into her camera and snapped it shut. The heeler had disappeared into the trees. One eye to the lens, Peregrine snapped four times from the same settings on the camera, hoping for one good shot of the levee through the slats of the loose shutter. She felt the steps of someone inside the house before she heard them, felt them through the soles of her own shoes, and her heart lurched. Somebody was in the house.

—*It's a little bit drier inside here,* Dean Fondren's soft drawl seemed to come out of the wooden walls. Peregrine knew the voice. She turned and there he was, smiling through a huge tear in the screen door. —*I'm sorry,* Dean Fondren said. —*Didn't mean to scare you like that.* He held open the door. He was wearing a denim jacket and an old soft shirt. There was an odd bleat then, and she saw the head of a baby goat peeking out of the jacket, white with a black face and pink lips.

—*I found it in some tall grass,* he said. —*Looks like Al Jolson, don't you think?*

She stood motionless, then shifted the blue heeler's leash to her other hand, and looked around. She would have to get the dog back on the leash or it would kill the goat, she was certain.

—*My dog is still out there. He's not trained very well.*

—*He'll come in when he gets wet enough,* Dean said. He was holding a shotgun, the barrel broken open as if he had just been unloading it. Or loading it.

Peregrine noticed his sock feet then. He continued to hold open the door as if inviting her into his home.

—*I need to check on the fire I made upstairs. This won't last long.*

—*The rain or the fire?* she asked.

—*Probably both.*

—*I thought you said 'no fires.'*

He stumbled on the stairs. —*That was different.*

She followed him warily up the stairs, though she could hear the blue heeler scratching at the front door, pushing it open.

She watched him as he crouched before the small fireplace, twisting ends of newspaper together. The twigs and newspaper were smoldering, and he bent and began to blow softly until the flames caught. With every breath, his face became more illuminated, which brought her a surprising pleasure. Dean was looking warily at her camera, still kneeling at the fire.

—*I want to photograph you*, she said suddenly.

—*Nope*, Dean said affably, handing her the baby goat. —*What are you, some kind of opportunist?*

She frowned at him.

—*Well, take all you want of the house. There's a gallery over in Oxford where fools will pay good money for pictures of the old falling-down houses where the Big Daddies went down like dinosaurs. You ought to look into that. It'd pay you more than trafficking with the old drunks at the casino, don't you imagine? Now, keep aholt of that goat and keep an eye on that fire while I find us something else to burn.*

Peregrine put her camera inside her shawl where it lolled like a bundled infant, and she winced at the sour orphan smell of the baby goat. She held it slightly away from her, its face out like a camera. She knelt to tend the fire in a kind of obedience she would never have shown her boyfriend. In this man's world, obedience was not something to be ashamed of. He brought in some old boards and laid them over the fire, and went back out. Peregrine looked around the little room. She raised her eyes to the band of words that ran just below the ceiling:

COME CLOSER

ANYONE EVER USED AND ABANDONED

BESIDE THIS RIVER

She'd seen them before, but it still made the hair move on the back of her neck, as if some force had gripped her by the nape. Peregrine patted her pockets; she needed more film, she needed better light. The words went everywhere, into the other rooms. The man came back in with some wood. She thought of what a simple matter it would be to hand him back the goat, to leave, and to come back later when he was gone.

The goat bleated, hungry, rooting with its nose against Peregrine's knotted shawl, looking for a nipple, and butted its head against the camera. —*What are you, some kind of opportunist?* Peregrine murmured to the goat, imitating Dean's deep voice, and then she heard his low laugh behind her.

She felt her face grow hot. A sputter of laughter escaped her. They looked at each other a long moment. The world and its categories were very far away.

—*Well, there's a little one that's got a tough life ahead of him. I reckon the Africans over there'll be wantin' to roast him before long.*

Peregrine held the baby goat out. Dean took it, and she rummaged in her backpack. She pulled out a pint of milk in a red and yellow carton and handed it to Dean. The goat began to butt at the carton enthusiastically before he got it completely open, and milk spattered on Dean's shirt. The blue heeler burst into the room and began to snuffle furiously, looking around like a marauder.

—*What's his name again? Nubane?*

—*Close*, the girl said. —*Cobain.*

Dean danced away from the day in slow circles, holding the milk to the goat's mouth. Peregrine dropped the backpack to put the leash on the dog, who would not come to her. Angus Chien's shopworn oranges rolled out of the sack.

The heeler began to chase the oranges, barking at them. Dean tucked the goat under his arm like a struggling football and bent to retrieve oranges. The dog ignored Peregrine's commands to sit, and jumped at her, muddying the front of her red dress. The goat bleated pitifully. It was too much for the dog to sort out whether fetching or killing was called for. Dean's dog Belle stayed where she'd been instructed to stay, but she growled gently at the heeler.

—*Cobain,* Dean said with quiet force. —*Sit.*

The heeler sat.

Dean put the goat down gently, in front of the fire, where it tottered. The blue heeler studied the goat and whimpered.

—*Stay, Cobain,* Dean said to the dog. It stayed. To Peregrine he said, —*He's a work dog, and he needs work to do. You have to give work to him, or he'll make it up for himself. I could take him, train him...*

—*He's all yours,* Peregrine said, holding out the leash.

—*Swap you the goat,* Dean offered.

—*No way,* Peregrine laughed.

The blue heeler sat at Dean's feet, anxious to please. —*Now you just wait here,* he told the dog, —*until this frog-choker is over.* Tin creaked and scraped as the roof shuddered in gusts of rain driven against the house. Water seeped from cracks in the walls near the ceiling. Dean closed his eyes and sat quietly with the shotgun broken open across his lap, waiting out the storm.

—*These walls should be in a museum somewhere,* the girl said.

Dean shook his head with his eyes closed. He was grateful for the girl's company, giving in to the first moments of companionable peace he'd known in quite some weeks with anyone else besides his border collie. She had a lot to learn, but she was not bad company. Then he heard the quiet, decisive click of a camera. His eyes opened.

—*Pow, you got me,* he murmured, eyes closing lazily, hand over his heart.

Fujiyama Mama

Angus Chien held out two mugs of hot coffee, away from the long ash collecting on the lit cigarette pinned tightly between his lips. He stepped carefully out the door at the Celestial. One cup for himself, one for the African who was called Wastrel. In his armpit, a can of soda for the boy. He looked back at the front door in indecision. It wasn't locked. It wouldn't matter. He stepped over and kicked the door of the Rescue Mission. They couldn't hear him. He could hear their African music all the way out on the porch. It was all bright brassy exuberance. The Wastrel was shaving curls of wood off the edge of a board with a planer, the old kind that required elbow grease instead of electricity. He seemed to be in a trance.

Angus kicked again and waited, looking around for something to set one of the cups down on so he could open the door. The sky was full of stars. Angus was filled with a sense of well-being and rightness. The rough wooden bunks were almost nailed in place, and all that was left was the new plumbing and the painting.

Word had traveled fast, and once they had got wind of it, many of Tomás Tulia's workers dropped in at odd hours, quietly offering help, bearing sacks of nails, shingles, Quik-crete, brass shower drains, and an enormous electric nail gun. Angus had learned not to ask where they'd got it. One night they showed up with pizzas and jars of jalapeños.

—*They work like sonsabitches*, Angus had said to Dean. —*Even knowing it don't belong to nobody in particular, they work like sonsabitches. They are good people.*

The Africans, too, were good people, Angus had decided, and not unacquainted with backbreaking work. *Unlike other certain parties*, he thought, glancing across the field at the Harlem Swing Club, where the black Escalade was already positioned like a parasite.

A familiar little red car was turning off the highway just then, and it beeped at Angus twice.

It was Lisa, his grandson's intense little pregnant wife, and she was alone. Her face was tight and drawn, but then she saw him and broke into a dazzling smile. She was either truly glad to see him or she was a good actress. She had a severe city haircut, a sharp wedge that ended at her chin, with little brushstrokes of black at her temples.

Past suppertime, he noted. Long past the bedtime of any woman with a belly that big. He was suddenly uneasy. He felt a slight discontent, not wanting to be involved in any family problems at the moment. He had looked forward, all that day, to the moment when he could close the store and go next door to check on the progress of the bunkhouse.

—*Hey, Pop-pop*, she said softly, rocking herself so she could slide out of the car. —*I was out driving and realized how close I was, so I just kept coming.*

She wore the tight, lacquered-on smile that Chinese women get when something's not going the way they want it to. Angus could see past the lacquer, into her uncertainty about something. The concerns of Chinese women usually exhausted him, and he tried not to think of them too much. Lisa was dressed in designer maternity clothes, her neck noosed into a jaunty yellow scarf with red ladybugs all over it. She wore shoes with stacked heels, and they caused her belly to pitch forward even more.

Dallas Chinese, Angus thought, with loving irritation.

He bowed slightly, still holding the two cups of coffee, plus the soda can in his armpit. She opened the door of the Rescue Mission for him.

—*Well, let me give them these drinks, and we'll go visit. I could use a good visit.*

When he came into the store, Lisa had already gone to the back. When he parted the curtains, he saw her sitting at the little table, tracing with her finger the pattern of blue roses in the oilcloth as if it were a roadmap. There was something inside her head she was studying, Angus saw. The tablecloth just happened to be in front of her. He put the kettle on to make her some anise tea.

—*So when are you going to give us that baby?*

—*Oh,* she said, her voice wavering.

It was an old joke between them. For years he had mailed her all the Olan Mills baby photo coupons he came across, and when he showed her the special spot on top of his television that was reserved for pictures of her baby, she had always said, —*Don't rush me, Angus.* Now she sighed in the way that tired mothers sigh, and it saddened Angus to see that she had this knowledge now, what it was to be so bone-tired, with nothing to do but wait.

—*You going to tell me what you doing so far off from home so late at night?* Angus asked. —*Everything all right at home?*

Where's that good-for-nothing husband of yours? He was joking, but saw instantly that it had hurt her.

—*Playing blackjack,* she said, gesturing in the general direction of the casino.

Angus flinched a little. But he understood: women that pregnant did not drive fifty miles south of home without good reason.

—*Is it bad?* Angus asked.

She nodded.

—*How much?* Angus asked, quietly. —*How much is gone?*

—*He won't say,* Lisa said.

—*It's a bad place over there, bad doings. The baby comes, he can't be cattin' around over there all hours of the night at that casina.*

—*And day,* Lisa added.

Angus studied her, and fell silent. He knew what she wanted, she wanted to make contact with somebody in some place that was sane, that was still Chinese. Angus knew then what it was he heard in her voice, the sound Chinese women make when they are not happy, like the accumulation of a thousand years of broken lute strings.

—*Well, give your hard-head husband some time. He don't know yet that you are the one taking the big gamble here, betting everything you got on him. He's too young to know that, but not too old to learn. You want me to go over there and get him? When I was a young man, I didn't know any better either.*

—*No,* she said, too quickly, which pained Angus considerably. —*I just wanted to stop by and say 'hey' while I was here.*

Angus had known Lisa was pregnant before she knew it herself.

Some months before, she had stopped by on her way back from New Orleans, and he'd been pleased that she'd taken the long way home, off the interstate, to see him. He'd been sitting on the steps smoking when she drove up. She said she didn't have time to come in, but she had some *muffalettas* for him, and some other things in a bag.

As they spoke, a pickup with caged dogs in the back pulled up in front of the store. Angus didn't know the three white men who got out, so he took a few steps toward the store. As Angus and Lisa passed the truck, she raised her neck scarf slightly to her nose, and the dogs whimpered and whirled in the cages. It was impossible for either Angus or Lisa to pass by without looking into the bed of the truck.

There was a dead doe lying in the truck bed, her tawny belly turned open, and a half-formed fawn spilling out along with her vitals. Her face was torn apart, and her legs had been bitten. She had been taken down by dogs, not bullets. Affixed to the trailer hitch on the truck was a stainless steel cube on wheels, with low dog growls emanating from its small barred windows. It sounded like hell had been compressed into that cube.

—*Oh, my god,* Lisa said. —*Is it deer season already?*

—*Ain't nowhere near deer season,* Angus said in a low voice. —*I been hearing about these people. They use the dogs, and they video it all. Video themselves like the white trash got to video their every fart and birthday cake.*

Angus said he had some hot sauce and tamales to send back to Jimmy, and she should come in the store with him to get it. What he really meant was he didn't want the hunters in his store unsupervised.

—*It smells different in here,* she said, when they walked in the store. The hunters, inspecting the camouflage t-shirts hanging on the racks, thought she was making a remark about them, and Angus broke into a crooked grin. He didn't want their business anyway. But Lisa was looking down. There was a red powdery sweeping compound that Angus would sometimes sprinkle on the floor before he swept it, and he realized he had sprinkled it and forgot about it, and his customers had tracked it up and down the narrow aisles of the store. The smell was pungent, and Lisa had her scarf nudged up to her nose somehow. Suddenly the store's smell assaulted him, too, as if he were smelling it with her nose instead of his own. It reeked of decay and old neglected vegetables, and the sweeping compound. It smelled of nights, years at the old Garland cookstove. It smelled of old age, he thought savagely. He left the door open to air things out.

Lisa said her head hurt. Angus was saying something to her, but she couldn't hear it. She stepped quickly out the door, and over to the porch rail under the empress tree. She did what she had to do in a way that seemed touching and Chinese to Angus, and he blinked. It was as if he had received a sudden message the girl herself did not understand.

Angus went inside to put the teakettle on the old Garland stove. He brewed a pot of green tea that smelled faintly of anise and angst to him. Lisa sipped it cautiously from an insulated plastic mug that said *Treflan*, which she looked at with a crooked smile. He busied himself with inconsequential matters, straightening shelves and wiping tables while she composed herself. He saw her spirit rise and become solid again.

—*This is excellent*, she said. —*What is it?*

—*Chinese herb*, he shrugged. He took down the jute string of star anise pods that hung on the wall next to the phone book and a Chinese calendar from a New Orleans importer. —*My wife used to drink this sometimes. Your mother never make you this tea?*

She smiled crookedly and a tear rolled out of her eye. —*I woke up missing my mother today*, she said in soft misery. —*I think I may be coming down with something. And Jimmy's never home. He's always doing business, making deals, out drinking with these guys in suits. He's already tired of me, Angus.*

—Three, four months go by, everything be all right, Angus said.

About two weeks after that, Lisa said to Angus when she came in the store, *—You get your wish. Close your eyes and hold out your hand.*

Angus stared down at the grainy Polaroid in his hand. What was it? A distant astronaut, floating in space? No, a tiny Buddha inside a walnut, sucking its thumb. It was a sonogram of the baby. He stared up at Lisa then, and the understanding was a slow explosion in his eyes. He did the only thing that came naturally to him at that moment; he bowed deeply to her in an old Chinese way. Then he propped the photo in the special spot reserved for that baby, up on his enormous defunct television, where it leaned against an Olan Mills portrait of Jimmy as a plump cherub. Lisa stood with him before the array of Chinese babies from an assortment of epochs.

—Who's that? She asked, pointing to a softly tinted photo in the back. It was the oldest photo, a tiny girl with black jewels for eyes, and a blue sash on her white voile dress. It was not Olan Mills, and all the characters in its bottom corner were Chinese. *Nanking, 1938,* it said in English. She clutched an English doll in her hands.

—My little sister, Angus said.

—Where is she now?

—She passed away in the old country, Angus said, and walked suddenly back into the store, as if the photo had burned his eyes.

Angus was not surprised when Lisa began to turn up at his store at least once a week, on the pretext of helping out. Pregnant women want to be with family, he understood, and her own family was in Dallas, and her husband was making himself scarce. So he gave her little jobs to do, and when she began to actually wait on customers, he sometimes slipped next door to hit a few licks with the paintbrush, or simply to stand there and plan his next move.

His next move was to get the place painted some bright color. Putting up the planks between bunks had made it dark. And he needed to get with the sisters down in Tutwiler about bedding. And he supposed there would have to be a television and a refrigerator. They needed to hurry, the hot season would be upon them soon. While he was musing, Lisa came in.

—*Hey, you need some art in this place. We could hang the old sign up right there*, she said, pointing to a bare wall. —*I've always loved that old thing.* They walked outside and stared at it, deep in weeds, leaning against the outside wall.

—*That was my daddy's first sign*, Angus said. —*About 1939, 1940, somewhere in there. War wasn't going yet. Now there's a story. It didn't exactly look like what you see here.*

When the Chiens first arrived in America, there was a faded tin sign over the store, ABIDE PLANTATION, and Solomon Chien pried it loose from its fastenings and leaned it up behind the store. A few days later, a Coca-Cola driver appeared with an application form in his hand and helped him fill it out. All he understood was that America was going to give him a sign for free. He signed papers he couldn't read and got the man to spell his name for him in English.

When the sign arrived, though, Solomon had stood before it with a hard bolus of grief in his throat. His name was misspelled. It said *Chen Grocery.* There was a bosomy blonde *bok guey* woman in a bathing suit, lifting a bottle of brown liquid that had a false gleam of light painted on it. The gleam of light was painted in the very same shape of the star of Bethlehem that was so auspicious a sign to his new neighbors the Baptists. The painted woman lifted the drink with a knowing leer, with no particular restraint or refinement. In China only the worst sort of riverfront whore would show herself and smile that way in public.

Angus ended the story there, and Lisa smiled, nodding.

The worst part of the story, Angus held inside himself. By the time the necessary decades had passed and he had the wisdom to understand it, he was no longer certain he was remembering it all accurately.

But one thing was clear, how Solomon Chien had been distressed at the sight of the big red circle on the Coca-Cola sign. Angus, too, had stared at the big red circle with dismay. He understood mostly that it meant unspeakable grief to his father, and that the red circle represented the bad things that had happened to his mother and his sister.

Angus's father had explained in inadequate English to the Coca-Cola representative that the sign was not correct. His name was *Chien*, not *Chen*. And it was supposed to convey the meaning of the name *Chien*, which would be auspicious for the business of the store. Solomon swept the air with imaginary brushstrokes, *celestial*, like the flight of a thousand cranes. —*Very good to Chinese*, he said. How could he explain that the success of his business depended upon his being able to *believe* in what his sign announced? And the red circle? To Chinese, it would be bad for business. No Chinese would walk under that red circle to get inside his store.

But the Coca-Cola man would not put the sign with the red circle back on the truck. He busied himself unloading red wooden crates of the drink, and explained that Solomon must now sell a certain number of the bottles, or he would be charged money for the sign. In America, he explained, the whorish woman signified freedom. It would bring customers, he said, as would the red circle. The red circle was a good thing in America.

While the Coca-Cola man was explaining about the red circle, a woman had been standing nearby, the mother of Marie Abide. She had sold the commissary to Solomon Chien, partly to pay the back taxes on it. She was an artist with avant-garde eyebrows.

Not many days later, Angus and his father went out to discover the old ABIDE PLANTATION sign had been repainted, transformed into something else, and propped up against the front porch. THE CELESTIAL GROCERY, it said, in English with a bamboo accent. SOLOMON CHIEN, PROPRIETOR.

There were white painted lilies and blue painted morning glories trailing all around its corners, and green leaves like blowing tendrils. It was the most beautiful sign Angus had ever seen. Solomon climbed the wooden stepladder that had once belonged to Israel Abide and fastened the sign back into place. The Coca-Cola sign was moved to the side of the store, so that the drivers could see the red circle from the highway, but Solomon never had to look at it unless he chose to. She had also painted over a little round PURE OIL sign on a pedestal, and it now announced,

EAT

OR WE BOTH STARVE

The artist woman vanished from Madagascar not long after that, and she left her little daughter, Marie, in the care of old Ariadne, the same granny midwife who would eventually deliver Angus's own children. Within a few years Americans had come to loathe, like Solomon and Angus, the sight of a certain red circle on a white field. But the wonderful CELESTIAL sign brought many customers to the store in thirty years, and faded to silvery pastels. After a particularly stunning tornado season in 1996, it was returned to Angus by a farmer from Friar's Point, who'd found it facedown in a cypress swamp. Angus had propped it beside the store, intending to keep it for the holy relic it had become.

By then, there was a new Coca-Cola sign above the store, complete with red circle. Angus had long since made his peace with the red circle, and had simply got out the stepladder and some black paint, and laboriously superimposed over it the Chinese character that represents *long life*.

palimpsest

—*Oopsie*, Lisa said when she stumbled as Angus was helping her into her little red car. It was much too late at night to be putting a pregnant woman into a car, much less one that she was going to drive all by herself all the way to Memphis to get home. He didn't know what to make of it, that his grandson would permit, or simply had not noticed, that she was out on the roads alone in the middle of the night, as if she had no good reason to be at home.

—*You call me when you get there*, he said to Lisa. He watched her drive away. *Oopsie.* That Dallas way of doing things, where women speak and dress like they are still innocent girls, like they don't want to let on how deeply they understand some of the more unsavory aspects of the world. In the beginning Angus had had his doubts about Lisa, for that reason, that *oopsie* stuff. Now the doubts had more to do with Jimmy, his grandson.

On the first night his Jimmy had ever brought Lisa to the Celestial, she was just a little slip of a Chinese girl in a red tulle plantation gown and matching parasol, like the grand dames had worn, only she was sporting leopard-skin Converse All-Star sneakers beneath.

Jimmy said when he introduced her to Angus, —*Pop-pop, this is the girl I'm going to marry. I want you to meet Lisa— what did you say your last name is again?*

—*Don't rush me*, Lisa had laughed, and then she had stood on her tiptoes, in a rustle of red tulle and a cloud of expensive perfume, and kissed Angus on his forehead as if he were a child. It was an impertinent American girl's kiss, and Angus's face was a confusion of expressions. She lost her balance then, and out came that word he'd never heard: *oopsie.* He was delighted she looked so Chinese, but dismayed at how American she acted.

Later she shucked the red tulle dress, left it in a starchy puddle on his bathroom floor, and sat at his kitchen table in her camisole and ruffled pantalettes, picking daintily at the Spam sandwich he'd offered her. She and Jimmy had played the old jukebox, sliding the same red-painted quarter into the slot over and over. She was particularly taken with one that Angus did not like because he didn't like anything that brought up the subject of Japan.

> *Well, you can talk about me—*
> *Say that I am mean.*
> *I'll blow your head off baby,*
> *With nitroglycereen.*
> *'Cause I'm a Fujiyama Mama.*

Lisa had played the song over and over. Angus began to smile after a while, now that the jukebox was stuck on his least favorite song. If you hear a song often enough, until you can't hear it anymore, he reckoned, it begins to seem no more significant than dust.

Maybe Angus had been all wrong to encourage Jimmy to have children. He kept a general rule in his life about not ever standing between a man and wife in word or in deed. It's just that Angus was impatient. He wanted to look once more into some tiny little face that was an echo of his own.

Maybe that was the biggest gamble of all, to bring a little one to this injured earth.

But if any waited for the moment when the earth was not convulsed with injury somewhere, there'd be no births at all.

But that's the one moment of clarity you get, when you surrender to whatever little face looks like your own before you were born.

Long life, long life, Angus wished the new baby he'd not met yet, sleeping curled like a little Buddha in the walnut of Lisa's womb. *Loneliness will make a believer out of anybody,* he thought suddenly. He sat that way, thinking such thoughts, for a long time, until he heard the telephone ring on the wall inside the store. He hurried in to answer. It was Lisa, and she was home. He spoke in soft, short syllables, nodding, for less than a minute. After he'd asked if all her doors were locked, he told her, in some old wise voice he momentarily borrowed from his own father, that everything was going to be all right in the morning.

Holy Ghost Party

No one asked why the boy got home so late on Friday nights; no one was ever there. They were all at work—the Wastrel out on the river on the dredger, and his uncles at the casino. His uncles could work double shifts and earn almost a week's wages in three days, so they did. On those nights they preferred to sleep in short, cramped intervals in the old Buick station wagon that belonged to a man who came from the same village they had in Mauritania.

Most nights, Boubacar was completely alone. It was a peculiar luxury. He'd been surrounded by others since the day he was born. He'd already spent more time alone in America than in all his previous life.

The National Steel guitar stayed hidden in its case in the stockroom of the Celestial until the weekends, when the Wastrel would be out on the dredger on his own double shifts. Boubacar brought it home then, his uncles being too busy to notice what he did. He picked it up late on Friday nights after he worked in Clarksdale, also a secret from everyone, and he hitched a ride home with a farmer who always took his wife to the Cloud Nine to dance.

On Saturday nights, Boubacar sat on Teslem's bed and taught himself to play chords on the silver guitar. His patience with the guitar had ebbed to a low frustration. The sounds that came from it did not match the sounds in his head. He needed to find someone who could tune it for him, and he lacked the temerity to let the Wastrel know he had it. It was very heavy. He could not imagine ever being strong enough to stand and play it all night. He could only play it if he sat on the bed or a kitchen chair. If he listened closely enough on such nights, he could hear music from the Harlem Swing Club, in the moments the wind came off the river. Sometimes he tried to merge the chords he was playing with the ones coming across the fields. He had seen the photo of Son House holding a silver National Steel just so, tucked under his arm. Boubacar's right thigh and his fingertips were sore from his many attempts to hold the guitar the same way as Son House.

Boubacar soon learned where to set his dial on the radio on Sunday nights to catch the live broadcasts from the churches in Clarksdale or the DJs spinning gospel tunes. He listened furtively in the dark, eavesdropping on the *kaffir*. Mississippi church music was a bright, brassy contretemps that reminded him a bit of Nigerian highlife sometimes, and *soukous* at others. He listened attentively for the moments when the women in the church would clap their hands in complicated contrapuntal rhythms, like the Senegalese. *Kaffir* music did not seem the danger that his grandmother had told him about.

When he tried to play the National Steel guitar along with the radio, he might as well have been trying to play the big filthy stove at the Celestial. The weight of the guitar on his thigh felt accusatory, wrong. His fingers were too short to go around the fat neck and fit onto the frets. His temper rose like a hot well inside him, and he imagined himself smashing it.

So he learned to listen to the radio as a lesson separate from the chording of the guitar. He soon learned to distinguish between the Mighty Stars of Harmony, the Canton Spirituals, the Pilgrim Jubilees, and the Mighty Sons of Destiny. Weeks passed, and he learned to sing along, and his ear learned to follow the patter of talk that always accompanied the music.

Once when the radio preacher mentioned the Celestial Grocery in Madagascar as a sponsor, Boubacar sat straight up in bed, his heart fat with pride.

—*God didn't have to wake you this morning but he did, yes he did. So go on down there and see Mr. Angus Chien at his beautiful old bidness, get you some nabs and a soda, some sardines with your eggroll, and be sure to try they tamales. You got a little headache, get you some B. C. headache powders or Tums or Chapstick, whatever you might need, they got. Now we going to try to play you a little song here, and this one goes out to Miss Jessie Mae Ivory, who had her surgery on Saturday.*

Boubacar learned to listen in particular for the Reverend Earl Myles from Friar's Point, with his group the Sons of Wonder. The Reverend Myles could be heard pacing around his church talking, then chanting, building to a hot crescendo:

—*I don't* KNOW *about* YOU
But I THINK *about Jesus*
and my HEART *is* FULL *of happiness.*
I don't KNOW *about* YOU
But I THINK *about his love*
And my HEART *is full of what it* NEED.
Can I get a witness?
—*Amen.*
—*Can I get a* WITNESS?
—*AMEN.*

Listening to the voice of the Reverend Myles rising and falling, Boubacar knew he had heard the pattern of it before, in a different language. It was the same cadence of the morning calls to prayer in Dakar, which he had heard exactly once in his life. It had a rhythm, you could rock to it. It was an odd, plaintive cry, but it telegraphed strength to all who heard it, whether they understood the words or not.

One Sunday night Boubacar turned on the radio to hear the Reverend Myles saying, —*Like to thank you, all our brethren and sistren, for coming out tonight, amen. Got a special broadcast tonight for you from this old church on Highway 61. Tawmbout the True Light Temple of the Beautiful Name. We doin' a benefit for Miss Cleoma St. Cyr, who have been in the Clarksdale hospital for a week with no insurance. And now Brother Calvin Dearborn will lead us in a little piece of prayer while we waitin' for our musicians to get ready.*

Boubacar sat up straight and looked out the window. *Calvin Dearborn. True Light Temple of the Beautiful Name.* Cars were ringed around the church like bees around a lit-up birthday cake. He stared with a mix of curiosity and fear. *Kaffir.*

What would be the harm to be among them? He walked among them every day. He breathed the same air they did. He put the guitar in its case and carried it through the dead orchard, across the long field, passing the little nest of tombstones. People, all of them black, milled around outside, not lounging on cars like they did at the Harlem Swing, but talking quietly in small groups. The men all were dressed like bankers in bright suits and ties.

Boubacar approached the little church cautiously, then propped the guitar against the wall while he stood on a concrete block to stare in a window.

There was a paper banner printed from a computer, JEWEL DOMINION.

A white-haired man in a light brown suit was kneeling, praying softly into a microphone wired to a little black box. —*Father God, we ass that you forgive us our sins, and our temptations, and our trespasses against you.* A few women in beautiful hats listened attentively and nodded.

Boubacar heard a car door slam near him, and the prayer faded out as he heard men's voices behind him then. The boy's blood congealed with fear: they looked like drug pirates to him, except they all wore the same suit: cinnamon-colored tuxedoes with pink pinstripes, over pink ruffled Flamenco shirts. They didn't see him when they opened the trunk of a big Oldsmobile and peered into it. Because each was dressed the same way, the boy could see more clearly the differences in their faces. He could see the whole continent of Africa there, Kenya to Morocco. They had long steel cases with handles, like the gun cases of television mobsters. But they were guitar cases. Boubacar broke into a big grin, but stayed where he was wedged until they were safely inside, their voices fading to murmurs.

His heart began to beat faster, and yet he stayed, eavesdropping on their words, which sounded holy to him in the hush of the little church.

—*Got that three-prong jack?*

—*Yep. Hold on a secont.*

—*There it go.*

—*Yup.*

Boubacar recognized a man with white hair from his photo on a poster. They were the Mighty Sons of Destiny. They unlocked the back door to get some tall amplifiers inside, then busied themselves with something outside at the Oldsmobile.

Other cars began to arrive. Boubacar could see their lights go off, and he could hear the murmur of voices and laughter amid the doors that slammed shut. Some of the men wore long white robes and skullcaps like Muslims. The women dressed like women in Egyptian cities, and his eyes feasted on the colors of their clothes.

The moon was soft and full, fringed with a blue haze. The cars were parked nose to nose like cattle ready for the night. The boy moved silently between them to get back to the hole in the window. He could feel the music in his breastbone and the soles of his feet before he could really hear it. He stood there for a while under the sky, eavesdropping on the infidel music, picking out its threads. The bass guitar was open, friendly, like a big fish being played on a stout line. Another higher guitar melody seemed to float out and hover over the bass. A drumbeat kept the guitars anchored to the beat. Now and then he heard cymbals. As he drew nearer, he heard the guitars like steps searching for something, wandering in and out of the clapping of the hands.

The men in the cinnamon suits were singing. The lights were blazing, and the cars were fanned out over the turnrows of the field. Two men were standing outside smoking, and one reached out to shake his hand when he came around the front of the building. He thought of his clothes, which were all wrong here. Nobody's shirt said *FUBU*.

—*Evening, brother. Good to have you with us. See you got your git-top with you. Come right on in.*

Boubacar ducked his head and slipped inside, pushing past the women standing in the entryway, and then was propelled by the crowd into what seemed the bowels of a great being, full of noise and life. He saw the ribboned heads of babies bouncing, and the starched clean collars of men's shirts. Slipping into a back bench, he sat ramrod-straight beside an old woman wearing a fiercely feathered hat. She smiled at him generously, and he recognized her as one of the cooks in the school lunchroom in Clarksdale. An old lady offered Boubacar a paper fan on a wooden stick. It had a split picture of the Ibrahim Bros. Funeral Home in Clarksdale on it.

He noticed one white face in the sea of black ones. *La sorcière*, the old woman who lived in the boathouse, wearing a baseball cap of some sort. He turned his attention to the front, a confusion of men in cinnamon suits standing in front of microphones, like rock stars doing a slow drag, but crooning the words of their sacred song.

> *Wade in the water,*
> *Wade in the water, children.*
> *God's going to trouble the water.*

The lead guitarist was a white-haired black man, swatting at his instrument with his eyes closed. One verse ended and they shifted into the gears of another: *Wade in the water, children.*

Boubacar's eye panned across the room, and it seemed a sea of bright hats and hands in the air. There were red felt cloches, and there were spun gold confections that resembled spaceships. There were oversized black Panamas, and purple felt derbies, silver skullcaps festooned with peacock feathers and jewels, and boarding hats the size of the *Titanic*. One woman was dressed entirely in hues of purple and lavender, with stockings and purse to match. Another woman wore a silver hat that seemed to be a scale model of a glassy public building in Sydney, Australia. He had seen these hats in the Looking Good and the Looking Better shops in Clarksdale.

A woman in a leopard-print hat had raised her hands to the ceiling, her eyes closed, while other women fanned her with pictures of the Last Supper. On the backs of the fans, *Ibrahim Funeral Home.* The women sat together, long rows of them, and when they stood, they all stood together, rocking gently from foot to foot as the music played, their feet in perfect unison. It was both chaste and mysterious at the same time.

—*You know what I come here to tell you tonight? I'm here to tell you that a self is a suit that is too small! Believe it!* The Reverend Calvin Dearborn was shouting, his words cast into the sea of music around him. He mopped his brow and took off his tie as if it were choking him. —*Father God, we here to thank you tonight for the privilege of breathing your air one more day. We was all walkin' around during the week clothed in the pride of this sinful world, but we here tonight to ass your forgiveness for our prideful ways.*

Then the preacher's voice took on a deeper tone, as if he were angry. —*Lemme hear you say AMEN, if you clear on the fact that you are NOTHING tonight, but DUST in the sight of God the FATHER that made us all.*

Hands waved and women murmured—*yes, amen.*

—*Nothing,* the preacher whispered. —*Nothing but dust. But it is a very special dust. Tawmbout holy ghost dust.*

Many had their eyes closed in a kind of trance. Boubacar thought of his mother's stories of Sufis dancing for hours in the desert. The Reverend seated himself before a small sideways guitar mounted on a tripod, and shoved up his cuffs. On his ring finger gleamed a silver steel tube. He began to play a few high, urgent chords, then stopped, and the congregants fell silent.

—*Like to thank our sponsor this hour, Brother Reno at the Shabazz Automobile Specialist in Clarksdale. You got a problem with your car, he fix you right up, amen. He can't save your car, he got a pre-owned one he can sell you.*

Boubacar looked around for cues. The Reverend Calvin Dearborn was saying something that was causing all the others to turn to smile at him, Boubacar, and the boy strained to catch each word:

—*Like to welcome all new visitors here, tonight, praise the*

*Lord. And we going to ass each and every one of you to stand
so that we may bless you and welcome you. Like to welcome
also all guest musicians, and we ass them to join us up here in
the joyful noise which we about to make. We are having ourselves a holy ghost party tonight.*

He looked pointedly at Boubacar.

A strong hand clamped onto his shoulder from behind, and
seemed to squeeze him up out of the pew into a stoop. He
looked around, hoping to find courage in someone's face and
steal it.

—*I am just Boubacar,* he said softly.

—*You have to speak up, son,* said the Reverend Calvin
Dearborn.

—*I am Boubacar,* he said again, louder, and the old ladies
fanned themselves and nodded. —*I am from Africa,* he said, and
the fans paused in midair.

—*Praise Jesus!* an old lady shouted, and others joined.

—*I like America,* he finished, and there was a ripple of
applause, and the guitars began to play. Boubacar sat on a pew
with his silver National Steel tucked under his arm. He played
a few disappointing chords, and the Reverend Dearborn looked
up slightly, with a soft smile playing about his lips. He nodded
to the lead guitarist, who played louder, and he got out of his
chair and took the National Steel from Boubacar.

—*Look ahere,* he said, simply. —*You tryin' to hold it like
Son House, when this kind of instrument got to go like Willie
Eason.* He laid the guitar flat on his lap, dandling it like a newborn on his knees. —*We tawmbout lap steel here, son, the kind
what go across you lap.* The Reverend Dearborn turned one of
the pins slightly to tune the guitar more tautly, and slid the
steel tube on his ring finger across the strings. A joyous squeal
came into the church and then vanished into the rafters as if
some captive animal had been suddenly set free.

The ladies gasped and held on to their magnificent hats. The Reverend Dearborn played a few more chords and then slid the guitar over to the boy's lap. He took the tube off his ring finger and slid it onto Boubacar's. The boy's hands were shaking, and he made a small noise of protest.

—*Sometimes you have to just trust the guitar. Something brung you over here tonight. Now play that thang.*

Boubacar slid the tube gently over the strings with one hand and plucked a chord with the other. A delicate mewling issued forth, and all the women murmured. He learned quickly how to modulate the mewls, keeping them soft and well below the mighty howls of the little implement on the stand that the Reverend was playing.

He followed the Reverend's guitar, adding his own embellishments.

—*Praise Jesus*, an old lady said and fanned herself.

—*We having a holy ghost party here tonight, amen!*

By then the entire group numbered about two hundred, some still in their work clothes, some in casino uniforms, some carrying walking canes, some holding sleeping babies. They were all standing, singing the words of *Dry Bones*, a song whose words they all seemed to know except Boubacar. They sang it at a slightly slower tempo than usual, like an anthem: *Hip bone connected to the thigh bone ... thigh bone connected to the knee bone ...*

Later, past midnight, Boubacar seemed to float across the fields toward home. The more weighted he was with the secrets of the world, the more he floated. The guitar weighed nothing. The Sons of Destiny wanted him to come back the next Sunday at a different church and play the lap steel if he had a song to play by then.

He put the alligator guitar case down and spun around in the field, arms outstretched, and danced. *Son of Destiny*, he repeated. —*Holy ghost party.*

Black *kaffir* music in America was a party of holy ghosts. It was like the bullets in the dry bones of the old slave believers, some of whom had surely been Sufis. No matter that the music was buried in the levees, on nights such as these it was seeping back to the surface in the churches, and it had spilled into the river of rock-and-roll. The boy danced alone under the stars in the empty orchard, whirling like a Sufi, like dust, arms up like a Pentecostal, *can I get a witness!*

Baby Elephant Walk

On her knees in Chance's bedroom closet, Raine tugged at a stuck drawer. His sense of order appalled her. An overdue lab report, crammed in a drawer with the plastic action figures of six years ago. The soccer uniform he would need in two hours: vanished. She could already imagine his accusatory glare if she did not extract these things magically from the messy piles of worthless possessions. He would hold her responsible. She jerked the drawer loose and exulted privately in the sound of ripping paper.

Where, she wondered angrily, *was it decreed that if you are born with a vagina, you will be responsible for the where-abouts at all times of every single possession your loved ones cannot seem to part with?*

She hauled plastic bins from beneath the boy's bed. Comic books covering the porn. A desiccated banana peel. She checked behind the door. A fly-fishing rod that had never been used, a hockey stick, some abandoned underwear. She looked around the room, angrier than when she started.

That was when she realized she had been looking for the National Steel guitar, not the lab report, and not the soccer uniform. She'd looked everywhere. It was gone.

The boy was culpable. She'd known it since breakfast when

she'd asked him about it, and had got the sense, from his airy answer, that was lying about it.

Raine was restless, waiting for something to happen. But every day was as average as the others. She couldn't have named what it was she'd been waiting for until it happened: she saw the jukebox man again. It was the evening of the last rehearsal at the Episcopal church, when she swung the gate open to the courtyard. There he was, on his knees, fastening a piece of shaggy cedar to a post with an electric drill.

That was what she'd been waiting for, she realized with relief. Just to see him again.

The jukebox man saw her then and motioned her to stay put. He flipped the bridge over, and watched for her reaction. In the greenness of the courtyard, it looked magic, leading from the *carpe diem* bench to the pool of water lilies and carp. It was a child-sized footbridge.

—*I think it'll hold long enough for the entire fairy kingdom to trip hither and thither. Test it for me.*

She laughed nervously, but stepped gingerly onto the first board, and took a step toward him. He held out his hand on the other end, and she remembered the pressure of his hand when he'd helped her with the viaduct. It would be rude not to take his hand, probably. She stood rooted to the bridge, immovable.

He had a worried look on his face.

—*It's okay,* she said stepping across. —*Look.*

—*Do you think it needs rails?* he asked. —*I'm going for that rustic look, you know, the kind you'd have to pay a fortune to get these days.*

—*Rails would be good,* she offered.

At the break during the rehearsal, he carried the bridge, with its shaggy cedar rails, up onto the small plywood stage. Coming in from the ladies' lavatory, where she'd smoothed her hair back a bit and put some lipstick on, Raine saw him, sitting at the piano, ringed by children. What was he playing? Some loopy old tune she remembered from childhood.

—*That's a cool song,* said one little lord whose gold foil crown was always cocked back on his head like a cowboy hat. —*What is the name of it?*

The jukebox man looked up and saw Raine then, and his fingers stopped where they were on the keys. The children murmured in protest.

—*Oh, don't stop,* Raine said. —*I haven't heard that in years and years.*

—*Ask Mrs. Semmes what this is,* he said to the children. —*Mrs. Semmes can tell you.*

So he knew her name. She wondered how. She shrugged, she didn't know the name of the song.

—*That's called 'Baby Elephant Walk,'* he called to the children.

—*Oh, now I remember it,* she said. —*Henry Mancini.*

Later, she saw him sitting on the sill of the Tiffany window, his hands clasped behind his head, watching her play the Gilbert and Sullivan for the children. She still had no idea what his name was and wasn't about to ask anyone. Who had told him her name?

It was a pleasant nuisance, to be watched that way by a man. Driving home later, she found herself all the way out on the parkway along Nonconnah Creek, having missed her turn by several blocks. She was late getting home, but no one even noticed that she *was* home, so it didn't matter. Before bed, she thumbed through the newspaper, looking for bargains and coupons. Someone in a housing project had beaten his girlfriend's baby to death while she was working her shift at the Wal-Mart. Someone at a university in Texas had tested the water coming out of sewers in the suburbs and found measurable amounts of antidepressants, hormones, alcohol, sedatives. Positioned next to that story, the lady in the home improvement ad admired her new water filter.

On the morning of Raine's forty-sixth birthday, Matthew's bags were packed and by the back door. She had no memory of where he was going, or why, and it seemed to mark some milepost in their marriage. In earlier years it would have distressed her to find packed bags beside a door in the morning. In the odd season of drift that seemed to have come over their marriage, she knew somehow that he would not be leaving because it would be too much drama, too much of a distraction from his real life, the one he led after he left home in the mornings.

—*So how are things in the world of mindless entertainment?* He was buttering his toast and reading the newspaper. He seemed pleased with his investments.

—*Tripping hither, tripping thither . . . how do you stand it?* Chance had added.

Her daughter had smiled uncertainly, watching her brother for more cues. It had something to do with the play her mother was helping to stage. It was an occasion for mild ridicule, and she wasn't sure whether or how to join in.

—*Hey,* Raine said, gently. —*Don't be so smug, Chance. I happen to have in my possession certain incriminating photographs of you dressed like a bumblebee.*

Callie giggled at that point, and her brother glared at her in a way that made Raine uncomfortable. It exhausted her sometimes, the weight of teaching them to be civil to each other. Her husband had meanwhile continued to butter his second piece of toast and scan the *Commercial-Appeal,* oblivious to the currents of life, visible and invisible, that surrounded him. All was well with the Lilliputians.

—*I'm done with Gilbert and Sullivan at eight-thirty*, she said. —*Anybody want to meet me for dinner later? There's that good little pizza place over there.*

—*Sorry, I'll be in the airport 'round about then*, her husband said. Her son raised both hands as if to ward off blows, *not me*. He mumbled something with his mouth full of cereal, something about a practice, an *all-nighter* next door.

Callie reminded her that she was to sleep over at a friend's, and they would get up at dawn to count bald eagles at a reservoir north of the city with their whole Brownie troop.

Raine folded her napkin and put it back on the table, and rinsed her cereal bowl and put it in the dishwasher. She stood at the kitchen window looking out. It was her *birthday*, she thought. Nobody remembered. It shouldn't matter to her. She shouldn't be such a baby.

Outside the window Raine could see the mother wren shuttling to and from the hiking boot beneath an elegant DO NOT DISTURB sign that Callie had taped on the bricks above it. The eggs had hatched. Inside the house on the windowsill, the bottle-cap birdhouse was empty, and she felt it was a kind of vanity to keep it there while the wren had to make do with the boot. *That's the way it should work*, Raine thought.

The eggs hatch.

You fetch for your young, ceaselessly.

You don't squander your pity on yourself.

The lady in the home improvement ad would never squander her pity on herself.

That evening, Raine paused inside the wooden gate to the empty Episcopal courtyard. She made her way to the little bench and read the words again, ET EN ARCADIA EGO. She must remember to look those words up. Soon she'd have no reason to come there.

A child swung the gate open and ran in, and others followed. Parents were soon setting up card tables and punchbowls, stringing gold lights between the small trees. She had an odd moment of joyous illogic, as if she were a child watching the preparations for her own surprise birthday party. But of course the people there hardly knew her. The party was for children, as parties *should be,* she reminded herself.

She scanned the crowd of parents until she saw the jukebox man standing awkwardly alone. Sam was inspecting the lily pond with his mother, a tall, reed-thin woman in an elegant silk suit, whose eyes skimmed the crowd while her son spoke to her. Raine knew that look. She'd seen it in her husband many times. The woman was looking around to see if there was anyone in the crowd of immediate use to whatever way she made her living. Everyone else was irrelevant.

When the stage lights went down, the children's faces went soft and radiant with expectation. Their costumes seemed to shimmer in a way they never had before. Raine played the opening arpeggios to cue the actors, and the performance was under way. Her fingers found their way over the keys easily. She kept stealing glances at the children.

The children sang their apportioned lines, *Bow, ye lower middle classes.* Children's performances always made Raine weepy, such an ancient ritual, to stand children up in public and require them to mouth the words of the grown-ups.

It was all over too soon, and when she played the last chord to the finale, she willed herself not to cry. This particular set of children would not ever assemble in this way to tell this partic- ular old lie about love again.

Collecting her things, she turned around on the piano bench just in time to see the jukebox man's face as he bent down to hug his son. His eyes were closed over Sam's small shoulder, and he seemed shaken with grief he thought private. Raine looked away, then back again. He remanded his son into the care of his impatient mother. He stood watching them leave without him, as if there had just been a great explosion somewhere. His arms were still curved, remembering the hug.

—*It was a great bridge,* Raine said from halfway across the room, by which time she realized she was walking to him. —*And Sam was great. Very lordly.*

—*Ah, he gets that from* ... he trailed off. —*Sh* ... He stopped, shaking his head.

Raine did not understand she was testing him until much later, but that's what it amounted to, the way she blinked for one second, thinking that if he said one bad thing about the woman he'd been married to, if he stooped to that commonness, he would have failed some test of character she was barely conscious of. *If he says one thing,* she thought. *That would be a sign.*

—*Well,* he said. —*They couldn't have done it without you. Thanks.*

—*Ah, well. Gilbert and Sullivan. It's sort of cut-and-dried.*

—*I have a great weakness for Gilbert and Sullivan. The bad guys always get the shaft and the good guys get* ... ?

—*Married,* she finished acidly. They both laughed.

—*Have you eaten?* He asked it in such an easy, amiable way, as if they'd known each other for a long time. —*For some reason I'm finding it really hard to just go home.*

Raine nodded. —*I know. All that buildup, weeks of it, then poof, it's over.*

—*Well, then, let's get a bite. That pizza place is still—*

—*No anchovies,* she said.

To sit across from a man in a worn leatherette restaurant booth, to fumble for words, it was like remembering the first steps in some old dance she once knew very well. The waitress brought them glasses of Chianti that were filled too full, but Raine sipped gratefully, its red warmth filling the empty places inside her, making her feel visible, loosening her tongue. She was even grateful that the stem of the glass was so long, the better to slide her fingers up and down when she discovered she couldn't remember how to converse with anyone who was over the age of fifteen. The Muzak seemed louder then, as she looked deeply into the glass of wine as if she might find some cues there.

—*Is that what I think it is?* The jukebox man was staring up at a speaker nailed to the wall.

—*Excuse me?*

—*'Riders on the Storm'? Is that what that is? God.*

—*Jim Morrison is rolling over in his grave,* she laughed. —*You know it's really frightening when they make elevator music out of—*

—*Out of the music we all made out to in cars?* he said, then winced. —*Sorry. I didn't mean to imply—*

—*Hey, are you implying I never made out in a car?*

—*No, no,* he laughed. —*Actually, I'm the one who had no life then.*

—*Did you grow up here? Where'd you go to school?* They discovered they had graduated from separate high schools in the city but the same year. They had gone to the same college, a few years apart.

—*Can you keep a secret?* Raine asked. —*Wait, it's not a bad secret. Just an interesting one. Can I tell you?*

—*Sure.*

—*Today is my birthday. My entire family forgot.*

She told it as if they'd done something inexplicably funny, like a slip on a banana peel. She watched for his reaction.

—*I'm sorry,* he said. —*That is a bad secret. That's pretty bad.*

—*No,* she said. —*It's not, really. It's like a, an anthropological secret. I mean, it's just the way we all live now.* She explained how busy they all were, describing Callie's endless loop of sci-fi trailers and her will to save the animals of the world from grown-ups, and how her son wanted to be a rock star. She found herself telling the man about her grandfather's silver National Steel guitar that she was afraid her son had lost or pawned.

She described the chrysanthemums, the cones, the ding at the bridge on the National Steel.

He whistled softly. —*That thing is long gone, I'm guessing. You could check eBay. If your son pawned it, you may never see it again. Those babies are worth thousands of dollars now.*

Avoiding the subject of her husband, she talked more about her son, how she had begun to question whether the guitar lessons were worth the money.

—*It's like the guy is teaching him how to package and sell his selfishness,* Raine said. —*And I am paying for someone to do this to my son.*

—*I know what you mean,* he said. —*I told myself I was going to build the jukebox of all time for my son. It was a way of dealing with my divorce. I'd come home at night, have a beer and a microwave dinner, and then go in there and download MPEGS. It was going to have every song ever known to mankind on it, uncensored. Klezmer, because my people were Jewish a long time ago. Portuguese fado, marimba, slave chants, the Mormon Tabernacle Choir. I got a little obsessed with it.*

—*I keep trying to get my son to listen to Dylan. No go.*

—*You a Dylan fan?*

—*I used to listen a lot, in college. I haven't kept up. There were so many years it was all Disney at our house. We have more televisions than human beings now.*

—*I do not own a television,* he said, a bit too fast, as if he wanted to prove something about himself to her.

She stared at him. It seemed a dizzying confession. She

leaned across the table and said conspiratorially, —*Well, you can have one of ours. I will personally pay you an extraordinary amount of money to burgle our house and take all of them away. I will help you burgle them out to your car. Then you, too, can have contrapuntal televisions.*

—*No way*, he said.

Raine didn't realize she had sighed until she heard herself. She looked out at the bridge. It was the first moment that she couldn't think of what to say. She thought of the mother wren in the boot. That seemed the only reason to go home, to check on the mother wren and her nest in the shitkicker boot, the wren who was more independent than she herself was.

—*So*, the jukebox man said with a softness that seemed not entirely inspired by the wine, —*is it all bridges that scare you or just the ones that take you home?*

—*What are you, some kind of psychologist?*

—*Oh, no*, he said, grabbing his heart like a man wounded. —*I'm in futures, sort of. Risk management.*

Raine grew quiet, and said, —*Okay. I don't want to, but I have to look at my watch now.*

—*It's a tough job, but somebody*... he trailed off, not wanting to finish, because when the sentence would be finished, she would have to go.

She had the distinct impression, leaving, that the jukebox man was reluctant to say good night. He didn't walk her to her car, but he watched from the sidewalk until she had backed her car onto the street. She dealt with the bridge-crossing by watching him in the rearview mirror. He was standing with his hands in his pockets, watching her go. It seemed the most illicit of pleasures, simply to be *seen*, to be watched by someone who doesn't want you to go. She felt her heart beat in a way she'd forgotten about, as if it were quietly crazy with anticipation.

Back on Magazine Street, all was stillness, and the Palladian windows glowed. The citizens of the republic of votive televisions carried out the nightly rite with the remote controls, *fun for the whole family*, each member sequestered with its own channel, its own pack of lies. Raine guided the car into the garage and collected her things.

On the back porch, down inside the shitkicker, the mother wren had covered the hatchlings with her soft wings for the night. Raine leaned in close to get a better view and saw one jet-bead eye watching her. Her heart accelerated, as it did when she committed transgressions, and she retreated softly, trying not to jingle her keys too much as she opened the door.

Inside, she stood for a moment in the empty house. Most times she yearned for quiet. Now that she had it, it was unbearable. She needed the noises of the house to keep her anchored to life. She walked through each room of the house tentatively, as if on ice that could give way at any moment. She thumbed listlessly through magazines. *Water your periwinkle and cosmos with brass cans that come from Portugal. You may want to display them prominently as a distinctive statement of who you are.*

Who was she? She needed her family in the house to feel like she was someone. She needed noise.

She reached for the remote control and turned on the television.

The outside world roared down the invisible underground chute and poured itself into the house. Because Raine thought of herself as a mother, what she wanted from the television were images of mothers. On the women's channel, the camera offered gauzy close-ups of aged actresses, mothers, who had been put out to pasture. And in those films they all acted in the same story, a mother, a wife has been wronged by her loved ones. On the cartoon channel, the mothers were ditzy or malevolent. On the rock music channel, mother sightings were as rare as white tigers but objects of ridicule, squinting back at the camera from inside their floral muumuus. On the men's channels, wives and mothers had been banished, airbrushed out, sent away on the invisible boxcars to the Gulag of Good Women. Admittance on those channels was granted only to lithe and tanned sportscasters who batted their eyes at balding former athletes old enough to have fathered them.

The invisible pogrom, Raine remembered, the words inside the birdhouse.

The channel about Nature. She would watch that. Maybe there would be penguins, or lion cubs. After one click, animal shrieks filled the house. Raine stared at the screen. A baby elephant, tethered to a palm tree.

Young men in turbans and loincloths were circled around it, calling instructions in a foreign language, beating it with sticks. One man had draped himself over the baby elephant's back, and pinched the sides of her neck with his knees, again and again, like some mockery of sex. The baby elephant's eyes were wide and glassy with terror, seeing nothing, absorbing the terrible lesson: *obscenity.*

The baby elephant sank to its knees in supplication. The narrator's voice droned. After the commercial for the vehicle that could, if you could afford it, transport you to remote mountain villages, the elephant was shown harnessed and dragging small trees out of the jungle for the men, a vacancy in her eyes where the terror had been. She was a good elephant now, a good worker. That was all that mattered to the men.

Raine turned off the television, but it was too late. The elephant's unseeing eyes were still with her. She folded her arms and rocked, crying.

Elephants don't beat babies and call it honorable work.

Elephants don't spend one-third of their lifetimes hypnotized by images of themselves fighting, warring, shooting, stabbing, killing.

She thought for an instant of hurling a lamp into the television set. The lamp was wrought iron. It wouldn't hurt the lamp.

No. It is permissible to beat a baby elephant, but not a television. If you beat a television, that raises serious questions about your sanity.

Raine looked around the room. She was stable. She was sane. Her house was in order and would stand up to comparison to any in the magazines. The rugs were good Dhurries, some said woven by slave children, but she didn't believe stories like that. She looked at her wedding china gleaming behind glass. It was bone. Brides didn't choose that type anymore because it was the kind *their* mothers had, the kind they were running away from, so breathless to get out and start the next generation of catastrophe over again. Raine put her fingers over her temples and heard then the bones of animals being ground to fineness to make it. She closed her eyes and put her hands over her ears, but her ears kept hearing. It felt dangerous, to stumble upon the world's truths like that. It would be madness to listen to it. Better to be like the lady in the home improvement ad, smiling at her Etruscan faucets. The lady in the ad would never give baby elephants a second thought, unless baby elephants were the new motif in home décor. That lady would cheerfully swallow each evening of loneliness along with a pill for assuaging loneliness.

Matthew. There had been a time when he'd been glad she'd been born.

Candy Randy Sandy.

A bottle of pills, a bullet, or duct tape and a full tank of gas?

It was not possible. Who would clean up the mess? Raine

could imagine her family standing impatiently over her dead, inert body, their arms folded in consternation: *Oh, great. Now what'll we do for dinner?*

Raine began to laugh raggedly, until a stitch in her side caused her to gasp and rock back and forth. It was too, too funny. She rocked with laughter.

This was the secret. This was why the lady in the home improvement ad was smiling at her faucets.

A man was walking his dog outside, someone who'd made his fortune by selling hair dye for men, and had had the good sense to get out before the studies were released linking products like his to certain forms of lymphoma in lab rats. He happened to look up at Raine and Matthew's house, his eye perhaps drawn to the holly that curved like a shepherd's crook around the eave. He couldn't be sure, but he thought he saw a grown woman sitting on the floor in front of the Palladian window, holding herself in her own arms, rocking like an autistic child. He urged the dog on, and he never told anyone what he thought he'd seen.

When the stitch in her side subsided, Raine lay down on the foyer floor, like a visitor who had fallen asleep just inside the front door. She lay with her cheek pressed against the varnished patina of hundred-year-old oaks that had been felled for all her flooring needs. She dreamed of all her children's lost toys, retrieved at last. She was exonerated. They were exactly where her children had left them: here and there.

The *Seek* Function

Standing on the porch of the little boathouse, sipping her morning coffee, Bebe Marie saw the cardboard pork and beans box by the Dumpster before she was even dressed. Mardi Gras beads dripped from one side, and she could see the necks of tall glass bottles and cylinders out the top. She made little purring whimpers. —*Angus Chien,* she said softly. —*Heavenly host of holy ghosts.*

She slipped her pinto pony blanket over her head and walked barefoot and bareheaded to the Dumpster. She peered into the box. There were mojo bags and John the Conqueror Root. *Papa Jim Magical Herb Book. Aunt Sally's Policy Players Dream Book. The Mystic Oracle Complete Fortune Teller.*

She opened one in particular and traced the symbols on the page, closing her eyes.

There were tall candles in glass cylinders, *Virgen de Guadalupe* and *Money House Blessing.* There were dressing oils, *Spark of Suspicion, Fire of Love, Inflammatory Confusion, Weed of Misfortune, Beneficial Dream.* She lifted each bottle out slowly, except for *Weed of Misfortune.* She stared at it in its box, then carried it respectfully back to the Dumpster. Once back inside the house, she lovingly removed the staples from *The New King Louis Narcisse Dream Book* and flattened the pages with the heavy candles to help them forget where they had been folded.

King Louis Narcisse. The words kept foaming unsaid in her mouth. The gunmetal taste came into her mouth, and she clamped one of Angus Chien's chocolate footballs, wrapper and all, into her mouth to stop it, and she locked the door. She drew angels and cherubs ascending into the heavens in a long black Chrysler. She took some of the pages from that dream book and wrote in a boisterous winding scrawl in its margins: THIS IS THE ORCHARD OF ABANDONED DREAMS.

When the ink and the paint were dry, she used them to paper the walls inside one of her bottle-cap birdhouses, which raised the words to the level of plain, simple sacrament.

Dean found the envelope of photos propped just inside the back porch screen door when he came out of his house to go to work. Peregrine had probably put them there on her way to work. Belle and the heeler had not barked. He leafed through them, uncomfortable with the sight of himself. She'd used the telephoto to get him on his tractor, and the sky a great gray wall of rain hesitating behind him.

And there was Angus, serious as a hanging judge. Even Belle had her own portrait, staring off into the fields like an old sage. When had the girl taken all these? There was one of Marie Abide in her black bowler hat moving dreamily among her peonies and roses in the middle of her stovepipe zoo. He liked the rainy-day one of himself in the firelight with his eyes closed, holding the baby goat in the old Abide house. It was the first photo he'd ever liked of himself. His face was a handsome enough face, but he liked it because it showed he was not a stranger to hard work. But how would he ever explain it to Alexis?

He could explain the goat well enough. If he still had it by the time Alexis came home. *If* Alexis came home.

He should give the girl something in return. He looked around the house. She already had his Coleman lantern and Alexis's cell phone.

He combed the closets of his home. He finally found what he was looking for in his old footlocker from college, a metal strongbox with a broken lock. It was tied with red Christmas ribbon and inside a box of his basketball trophies from high school. He set it out on the kitchen table and clipped the red ribbon off.

He thumbed through the old photos quickly. His mother in her homemade dress with her prize roses at the Memphis fair, his father with his reading glasses on in his chair beside the radio. Himself as a dwarf Abe Lincoln, a cowboy. Another of a prize steer he'd been in charge of when he was ten.

There it was, the one he was looking for. It was a small black and white snapshot of his mother, smiling into the sun, partly concealed behind a stand of tall hollyhocks. Behind the hollyhocks was her pregnant belly, with himself inside. His mother used to show him the picture and say, —Here, this is what you looked like before you were born.

Now he looked at the photo in a different way. A few feet behind his mother was a black woman in a straw hat. Beneath the hat, a tight turban of red bandanna from the Celestial Grocery. She was not completely in the frame, and one dark hand was blurred, as if she'd tried to wave away the camera. Dean studied the photo like he was seeing it for the first time. Anyone else would think that the black woman was there to do domestic work, but Dean knew better. That sort of domestic work was above Ariadne's station in life.

Ariadne did babies. She was there in that photo for that reason. His mother may have already been in labor with him when it was taken. Ariadne stared back at the camera with coolheaded purpose.

It was the only photo he had of his mother like that.

Nevertheless, he resolved to give it to the girl. He could remember with his eyes closed what his mother looked like, hiding her belly behind the flowers. His children seemed not to care about such photos. He took it to the place in the kitchen where Alexis saved old envelopes that came in the mail, and found one that would fit.

Well. He was wasting good daylight. He put the envelope in his shirt pocket and went out into his day. Belle and the blue heeler jumped into the truck, tails wagging.

The green Comet was not at the shack, nor did it show up all day. For a few hours, Dean entertained the idea that the girl had already gone back north, which would make sense, the photos left by his back door and all. He wished she'd said good-bye. He had no idea how to mail her the photo.

He'd pretty much decided she was gone, until about eleven o'clock that night when he heard the first scream. It carried over the field like the feral sound a bobcat or a newborn makes. He listened for it again.

He knew it was the girl, even before the blue heeler scrambled off the porch and ran in the direction of the shack. He grabbed his flashlight and the kitchen shotgun, and cursed softly at having to take the truck when he could see the shack across the field. A light was on in the window.

He heard the scream again, and then another noise, like worry, or argument. Belle by then was trotting across the field, moving like a slow arrow, intent on something between the rows of soybeans the same way she was when she'd sighted a snake. Cobain followed, either deferring to her judgment or his own cowardice.

The dogs got there before he did, and then he couldn't see or hear them.

He cut the truck off in front of the house and ran up the porch steps. He'd left the truck door open and the key in it, and the shotgun in the rack. That could turn out to be a mistake. He didn't knock, but pushed the door open and stepped in.

No one was there.

There was something outside the window, and Dean heard the dogs moving, and Belle's whimper. He swung the flashlight in an arc, seeking. Peregrine was out there, moving around in a long white nightgown.

Her arms lifted and fell, and she turned like wheat in the wind. But something wasn't right.

Why, she's dancing in her sleeping gown, Dean thought at first.

Then Dean saw her run away from the glare of the truck lights, her hands windmilling all about her, brushing her hair, her throat, patting out invisible flames. He thought of stories he'd heard of kids on LSD, trying to outrun their own thoughts.

She ran, not knowing who he was, or whose truck it was.

The girl ran towards his house, as if she needed him, and didn't know he was standing right behind her. He got the dogs in the back of the truck and drove, following alongside her, but she didn't seem to know he was there. He could hear her screams then, over the smooth drone of his truck engine. He saw her dart away from the truck, which could be a stranger's for all she knew, and she ran to his front door and began to pound on it with her fists. He braked in his driveway, amid a spray of gravel. The dog ricocheted around in the truck bed, from side to side, crying, waiting to be told what to do. Dean told them to stay. He left the headlights trained on his own front door.

Peregrine turned around then, clawing at her hair, and the nightgown seemed to evaporate from her flesh right before his eyes. She balled it up into a sponge and daubed at her skin with it. Her screams tore at him, threatening to draw him into the craziness. He kept her in his sights as he moved towards her, the way he would a drowning person. He was already considering the logistical problem: the nun's clinic in Tutwiler or the big hospital in Memphis.

—*Peregrine*, he called out, but she didn't hear him. He thought oddly of how the cries of women in trouble were so much like the cries of women in lovemaking. He had a hot feeling in his chest then, as if a whole covey of quail had risen there, and so he took off his hat and clapped it over the tight spot as he walked towards her.

—*Hey now*, he said softly, dropping down into the soft tone he used to gentle spooked horses, and his wife when she was angry. —*Let me help you now*.

—*Don't touch me*, she screamed, and one of her elbows cracked into the door frame and the other into his ribs.

He gripped her by the arm then, surprised that such a thin arm could be so strong. She turned and twisted, shrugging her shoulders. She squirmed in his grasp and he thought crazily, *Well why not? I was the bad man in her mother's dreams before she was born.*

She lifted her face and turned to him then, and he saw. Little seed ticks, newly hatched, dappling her skin, slightly darker than her. They were crawling wildly in all directions, down her throat, across her shoulders, towards her eyes, as if her skin had taken on some terrible ability to shift and move. —*They're all over me*, she cried.

—*Whoa, god*, Dean said softly. With one hand gripping her upper arm and the other around her shoulders, he half-carried, half-led her towards the barn. They stumbled into the side of the first horse stall, and he groaned, knowing they both would bear the bruises of it tomorrow. She twisted, stamped her feet, and he would not let go. He knew he was bruising her arm, and he regretted it, but still he would not let go. —*Look ahere, you'll hurt yourself. Listen now.*

He found the cardboard canister of sulfur he was looking for and wondered if it would be enough. He began to sprinkle it on her shoulders. —*Rub that all over you,* he said, and he poured a small amount of it in his own palm like talc. He began to daub it on her cheeks with shaking hands, making a circle of sulfur at her hairline. The softness of her hair surprised him. It was like putting his fingers into a cloud.

They understood, somehow, not to look into each other's eyes as each rubbed her skin with the sulfur. That would have been the impermissible nakedness. Dean's hands seemed ineffectual, motherless children, as he dusted her skin in impersonal ways.

At the end of the barn was a tall iron standpipe with a showerhead on it. Dean had been the object of ridicule with the Telephone Pioneers when he'd installed hot running water in his barn, but he was glad to have it now. Holding the girl's arm with one hand, as he had with his own daughter when she was small and muddy, he reached up to turn on the hot water. They both shouted in pain at the heat of it, and he tempered it with the cold.

Peregrine had reached by then for the bar of Octagon soap he always kept on a board nailed between the barn studs. He knew the harshness of the soap on his own skin, and almost stopped her. The water was running in chalky yellow rivulets off her skin. She somehow covered each breast and washed it at the same time, standing with her back to him. He was startled by the sight of her rib bones as she bent away from him.

He slapped at his own neck, and took off his hat and flung it angrily out the barn door. He flicked at his own hair, arousing his cowlick. The horses nickered gently, as if such goings-on in the barn at that hour were an ominous thoughtlessness from him. Dean took a big galvanized tub off its hook on the wall and began to fill it with what was left of the hot water. The girl immediately knelt before it.

It humbled him, to see the perfect inverted heart formed by her buttocks. *Women have knelt that way for thousands of years*, he thought. He needed to find something else to look at, so he went inside to get a quilt. He found a summer one, blue and white stars, and it smelled of cedar.

He draped the star quilt over her as she knelt, and she reached around with her hands to gather it to her. She seemed to know what to do with it, how to knot it so it wouldn't fall off. She made a little sound of dismay then, and was scratching at her temples. He ran some clean water and once again she knelt to put her hair in it.

This time Dean put his hands into the water, and moved his fingers in slow circles through the floating tendrils of her hair, as he once had when his daughter was very small. —*It's all a matter of who can be the most patient*, he said. —*Us or them. They drown, you know. They just drown. Where'd you get into them, anyway?*

—*At the well*, she said.

Three times more he ran clean water for her. By the third time, the water was icy cold, and only a few ticks floated free, like black pepper in the water.

—*You know, if my wife were here, you could just stay here, but—*

—*I know, I know*, the girl interrupted him. —*Otherwise—*

—*That's right*, he said quickly, trying to curtail the thought.

—*I mean, people might think that we are, like, lovers or something*, she finished for him. He didn't know whether to trust her earnestness. —*That could cause you some problems for sure.*

He flinched a bit, and she turned and stood facing the black wall of the night. It reminded him of a photo he had of his daughter when she saw the ocean for the first time. He thought for a minute that he should simply give her the house for the night. He could sleep on Angus Chien's floor. Or he could sleep in his truck in Angus Chien's parking lot. He thought of all the teasing he would face the next morning, and he said nothing.

The girl walked around the passenger side of the truck, and before she could reach up, he was there, opening the door for her. She slid easily and elegantly inside, the boarding school manners restored now. As he drove, she stared out over the fields silently, and his mind was full of what he wanted her to understand about the fields. That was the thing: outsiders never understood what they were seeing. He took the envelope out of his shirt pocket.

—*In all this excitement I almost forgot. Here's a picture of Ariadne. It's the only one I had. She's with my mother before I was born.*

One arm came out of the quilt to take the envelope, the other clutched the quilt to her. Their eyes touched just briefly then, and it was nakedness, but a comfortable kind. Women were always sensing the prospect of refuge in him. It was his gift, it was his burden.

He slowed the truck and paused on the highway near the swampy bottom.

—*You see that in there, all that marshy water?*

The girl nodded.

—*She used to fish down there, and she used to catch wild ducks with her bare hands. Pintail, mallard, teal. The woman could catch anything, but she never killed a one except what she wanted for Christmas dinner.*

The girl stared at him without speaking, and he saw her eyes glisten. He had not been looked at that way since his own daughter was small, eager for stories in his lap.

—*She was unbanding the birds, don't you see,* Dean said.
—*That's what those numbers are in that coffee can you found. She was very stubborn.*

The girl stared out across the fields and laughed out loud.
—*Unbanding the birds. That's awesome.*

—*It was*, Dean agreed.

When Dean pulled the truck up in front of the little shack, he reached across her to open the door. He asked her to wait outside standing in the headlights where he could see her, while he checked both rooms to make sure they were empty of anything that might harm her.

He reached out to shake her hand, and found himself staring at her darker hand clasped in his white one. It was a kind of benediction to see it.

—*Thanks for everything*, she said.

It felt wrong to leave her, but he got back in the truck and was soon moving down the rough road. He paused at the highway and looked back. There she was, dark silhouette of a doll in the doorway, in the constant eerie glare of the lantern.

He felt angry with himself for leaving her there like that.

He felt angry with the world and its little proprieties.

He saw her white nightgown in a heap outside the barn door and wondered what to do with it, how to explain it to Alexis. So he put it in the galvanized tub and set it afire with some kerosene. Ticks scattered, trundling over the tub's ridged bottom.

Dean was walking towards the house when he heard the phone ring, and so he ran, in long loping strides. He left the door standing wide open, and Belle followed him in, whimpering. It was Alexis. He looked out the window, downriver.

—*Baby is fine*, she said.

—*Baby, hell*, Dean said. —*How's the mother?*

—*Mother is a bit shaky and weepy. The father has announced that he wants to go to Tulane Law School so he can defend the birds in court.*

Dean whistled softly, and the silence filled the miles of wire between them like burning money. It was a silence as necessary as speech. —*Well I guess that's a good thing,* Dean said softly at last. —*And how is the grandmother doing?*

—*Well, she misses the baby's grandfather,* Alexis said. —*She misses him terribly.*

Dean could hear the smile on her face. It traveled the hundreds of miles between them. The softness in her voice carried twenty-seven years of history in it. His heart seemed actually to beat for the first time in days. —*Say, do you remember old Sid Hemphill?* he asked suddenly.

—*Oh, I haven't thought of him in years,* Alexis said. —*What on earth made you think of him?*

—*Oh, nothing,* Dean said, stretching the phone cord as long as it would go and stretching a long leg out to kick the back door shut. He saw the light go out at the cabin, and he closed his eyes, still seeing the girl's heart-shaped bottom burned into the back of his retinas. —*I was just reminded of him today, is all. So when shall I expect you, madam? I can have a brass band to meet you at the airport.*

Again the miles of silence in the wires.

—*I'm not sure,* Alexis said, with an oddness in her voice that Dean had never heard before, not in twenty-seven years. —*They need me here. And you remember Mary Ellen Dunedin, my old roommate? She's asked me to come visit her in Memphis. I may stay in her condo for her while she's gone on her trip.*

Dean nodded, the receiver bobbing with his head. The oddness: her new capacity for little unspoken lies. He fumbled for a way to cover his disappointment.

Restless and feeling rootless, he put the dogs in the back of the truck and began to drive. Peregrine's light was on low, the same candle he'd advised against.

It looked too good to him, that little smudge of light in the black night.

How many hundreds of years had men been ruled by the lamps lit by women? Maybe he should go over there. What would he say when she came to the door? He thought of all the stories he could tell, about Aubrey digging his father's grave, about his daughter and the black baby doll, even about Alexis, and what a remarkable woman she had always been.

But he would always be just another Big Daddy to her. She looked right through him, just like everybody else did. He lifted his foot from the accelerator ever so slightly, but didn't brake.

When Dean came to the turnoff to his own house, he drove past it and went farther down to the entrance to the levee. He crossed over the cattle-gap with a rattle of the wrenches from under his seat. He drove the truck up on top of the levee. The dogs boiled around in the back of the truck, bracing themselves. Then he drove slowly along the backbone of the levee, watching the odometer carefully. There was a secret place up there, three-tenths of a mile down, where the radio waves always seemed to pour in with abandon, all the way from Cape Girardeau. He'd discovered the place when he was a teenager, and sometimes brought a girl there, when the weather was good and he was feeling brave or lucky.

Dean cut the engine to the truck, left the battery on, and turned on the radio. He pushed the *seek* button and sat back. Nothing but the screams and crashes of the young, it seemed. He'd give anything for a Hank Williams song.

Above, red blips coursed across the sky, planes going in and out of the Memphis airport, loaded with the real Big Daddies on their way to their business deals. Why buy a Mississippi strawberry when you could get it for a fraction of the cost in South America, where the government supplied the overseers and there was no minimum wage?

And who was he? He was a man, alone, wearing a wrinkled shirt that he'd fished out of the dirty clothes that very morning. It all didn't add up to much when there was nobody there to care whether your shirt was wrinkled or your food was hot, and the only music you could get on the radio anymore was some mother's *child* with green gladiator hair, wailing about how he was motherless.

Buy Now, Pay Later

—You will rise up, please, the Wastrel growled in his elegant accent.

Boubacar stirred sleepily. He was not free to say that he was supposed to be picked up at the Celestial by Mr. Calvin Dearborn that morning, in time to get to services at an old Jewel Dominion church in Friar's Point. The guitar was waiting for him at the Grocery. He had left it just inside the door where he could get it as soon as Angus opened.

—L'Américain has an expression, the Wastrel continued, pulling the covers off the sleepy boy. *—'Buy now and pay later.' Today we will do the backwards American car deal. Car first, and money later. There is much to be done.*

—'Drive now, pay later,' Boubacar quoted the television.

They were going to purchase a car, not just any car, but the multicolored many-mabone Chevrolet Boubacar had admired in Clarksdale, the one with the brilliant taxicab colors. It had not been easy to find a car dealer that his uncle Salem did not suspect of being Jewish. Mr. Reno Shabazz was not Muslim, but he was black, and that would suffice for Salem.

They were to wait, the Wastrel said, in the parking lot of the Celestial, and a man from their same village in Mauritania was to drive them to Clarksdale. Waiting in the deserted parking lot of the Celestial on Sunday morning, Boubacar felt the confusions of America crowding him. He was going to be part owner of a car!

What was he to do if Mr. Calvin Dearborn came to fetch him before their ride to Clarksdale arrived? While the Wastrel and his uncles squatted and talked softly, he stepped up to the plate glass window of the store and peered inside. Angus was still in his white t-shirt and black sweatpants and house slippers. He was rinsing out the coffeepot, sloshing water around and around. Boubacar tapped on the glass.

Angus glared, then his face softened a bit as he recognized the boy. He unlocked the front door.

—*I am in a big problem*, Boubacar said. —*I will need some of your help now.*

—*Tawmbout little problem or big trouble?*

—*A man is coming to get me for the guitar lesson at his church, and I will not be here. If you can tell him that I must to go with my uncles, and I will be calling him on the telephone.*

Angus looked over the boy's shoulder at the men, squatting by the side of the road. Nobody squatted like that in America except Africans. —*I'll watch out for him, son.*

Son, Boubacar noted. More and more Angus used that word to talk to him. Boubacar's head ducked in gratitude, and for a few moments he was free to exult, feeling he was somewhere he belonged.

Mr. Reno Shabazz of the Shabazz Automobile Specialist was dressed in his church clothes and standing beneath a series of huge yellow and red signs that ran all around the used car lot like bright boxcars:

NO CASH! NO CREDIT! NO PROBLEM!
WE TOTE THE NOTE!

The uncles were full of admiration for the car, which they had seen around Madagascar when Haile Selassie Pegues had driven it. Mr. Shabazz explained that Haile Selassie Pegues had had to go up north on extended business, and furthermore had defaulted on his loan, and Mr. Shabazz now held the title to the car again.

The Wastrel stood back, hesitant, and Boubacar watched him watching his uncles.

—*You are thinking a long time,* Boubacar said to him quietly.

—*Yes.*

—*It is a very fine car.*

—*That is true. That is not the difficulty.*

—*Tell me your true thoughts on this car.*

—*If the man who owned it comes back, he will see us enjoying it. This can make a big problem between neighbors, I think.*

—*I do not believe he is coming back,* Boubacar said absently.

The Wastrel looked sharply at the boy, and then at the car.
—*You know him?*

Boubacar shrugged miserably. Sometimes the secrets he kept from the Wastrel made him feel shame. He knew all the forbidden people, the criminals, the Christians.

The uncles and Mr. Shabazz circled the car, engaged in serious discussion. It was agreed upon by the uncles that there would be no purchase of the car without the substitution of new front tires. Mr. Shabazz declared that although he was not running a charity, new tires were no problem, but he unfortunately was in his church clothes and could not oblige them until after church service. He was a deacon and had to be presentable.

The uncles allowed as to how they would be happy to install the new tires themselves if Mr. Shabazz would be so kind as to take the old ones. While the uncles rolled up their sleeves and began to jack up the car to put the first tire on, the Wastrel counted cash into the hand of the surprised Mr. Shabazz, who cursed softly under his breath at all the green bills.

—*Damn, man. I got to carry this around till the bank open tomorrow.*

—*Two thousand dollars now, and we will pay the rest next week.*

—*Naw, man, just a little something each month. This is America. You pay as you go.*

It was determined that Teslem was the only uncle with a valid American driver's license, so he drove the car out of the Shabazz Auto Specialist parking lot with a flourish, and steered it back up Highway 61, past the little metal hovel they lived in, past the Celestial Grocery and the Harlem Swing Club, and north towards Memphis. The Wastrel had explained it all. The other money would come from the Mauritanian bank in Memphis. That way, the Mauritanian bank would earn the banker fees, not the American.

As they drove by the Celestial, Boubacar saw the Reverend Calvin Dearborn idling his engine in the parking lot, reading a newspaper. The boy sank lower into the backseat. He would repair the damage somehow. Mostly, he felt a grief in his chest that he would not be there in the hot church with them, singing and sweating while the old ladies fanned the babies and the young women clapped double-time and called out encouragement.

As it was, he was riding down a big highway in a big magnificent car that now had his name on the title to it. It was a feeling he was coming to associate with America, being enriched and robbed at the same moment. He was speeding along in a half-bought car. Each revolution of the wheels took him farther away from the little church where he wanted to be playing his guitar among the unbelievers.

CLEAN DIRT FOR SALE, said a tall sign in a field.

—*L'Américain will sell anything,* the Wastrel marveled, sitting beside Boubacar in the backseat. They passed a long field of hundreds of identical pointed green cedars.

Boubacar read the sign aloud. —*Christmas Tree Farm.* The Wastrel explained: years and years would go into the making of the tree. Quite some money would be made on it. Each tree was being groomed for the moment of its cutting. It would be taken into a house and decorated for children for a few weeks, then tossed out for the trash men.

—*So this kind of tree is disposable,* Boubacar said.

—*L'Américain,* the Wastrel mused. —*Disposable Christmas trees, and he cries as if he's been wounded if a poor man cuts one in Brazil to feed his family. 'Global warming!'* the Wastrel's voice took on a falsetto quality. —*'Ozone layer!'*

Once the fields gave way to suburbs, and the suburbs to old abandoned warehouses and railyards, they were to turn a certain way on Danny Thomas Boulevard, and follow the directions Salem had written on a piece of paper. But at the precise moment they were to turn right, Salem was reading aloud the billboard that said in huge letters, MICROSURGICAL VASECTOMY REVERSAL, and asking what it meant, so they missed the turn, swept along in a current of cars that seemed inescapable. It shunted them up a ramp, as if to launch them into the sky. Then they were on a high scalloped bridge, headed all the way across the Mississippi River to Arkansas. So Boubacar's first view of the Memphis skyline was out the back window of the big mabone car, traveling very fast in the wrong direction, away from it.

The city of Memphis lay on the shoreline of the river, silver in the early morning sun, steel and glass and stone. The Pyramid loomed in the foreground, looking like blue-black ice. The banks stood like stone towers above all the hotels, each with its colored symbols. *National Bank of Commerce, Union Planters Bank, First Tennessee Bank.*

—*Many banks,* the boy said.

—*Many, many Jews,* Salem said sternly, as if correcting him.

They turned around at a truck stop in West Memphis. It was a conduit for big trucks crossing the country. Boubacar had never seen so many in one place, so many colors and names, *J. B. Hunt, Hanjin, Terre Haute Transport, Blue Mountain Trucking.* The trucks dwarfed the car on the big bridge. Once across the river again, coming off the curved ramps from the bridge, they passed by a small green park with benches overlooking the river. Old men with no homes nodded off to sleep with their heads resting on their bundles of possessions. Teslem proceeded more slowly with his driving. Other drivers cursed and made gestures with their hands.

America was a river of cars running two ways at the same time on Poplar, incessantly, and a viaduct shunted cars over railroad tracks in a separate river in a third opposite direction. The city seemed an endless ant-bed of automobiles, tens of thousands of every make and model. They drove past so many mansions the boy lost count, dizzied by the wealth he saw before him. Some of the tall businesses belonged, the Wastrel explained, to the old slave masters, who had bought Africans in markets. Others belonged to men who removed the uteruses of old women all day. Others belonged to men who peered into the nostrils of people all day. Still others, the ears.

BLACK CAT BAIL BONDS, said a billboard. WE REVERSE YOUR BAD LUCK.

Teslem parked the car in a weed-choked vacant lot behind a white building of three stories, canted to face Poplar Street at an angle. They all piled out of the car, and Salem slammed a door again, just so they could hear how solid and safe the car was. The boy looked around, his legs somewhat weak. Some dark-skinned children were playing in front of a green Dumpster, and they chattered to each other in French. More heads popped up over the rim of the Dumpster, and they admired the car for its very fine colors.

The Wastrel motioned him forward, and they walked across an empty parking lot. Boubacar looked up at the tall sign. ABYSSINIA ETHIOPIAN RESTAURANT.

He looked around for a tall bank. There was no tall bank here. Were they lost? He decided to say nothing. Inside, the smell of spices and cooking meat caused them to stop and murmur. The presence of women cooking was oddly humbling in a way it would never have been at home, not without long deprivation of it.

A smiling woman in a white apron and crisp white hat held her hands out to the boy, and he leaned forward to greet her as a polite Muslim boy would, *left cheek, right cheek.* Tears formed in his eyes. She smelled like his mother: coriander, garlic, and fenugreek. Her daughters were pretty, and well taught. They let their eyes linger on him just long enough to make him feel seen, and then they lowered them properly and fled to the kitchen. They whispered among themselves about him, but not unpleasantly. They were Ethiopians, but they made him homesick.

They walked to a long table where an old man sat with his hands resting on an elaborately carved cane beside his chair, just below the tourism poster for Ethiopia. His skin was the color of cinnamon bark. His eyes had the milky inquisitiveness of the blind. He knew they were there, and leaned forward on his cane as if he intended to stand, and every voice in the room except

Boubacar's murmured that he must sit. He stood anyway, shaky on his legs, but smiling in a way that inquired. —*Where is the boy?* he asked, turning his head as if to hear better.

Boubacar happened to be standing near him, and he put out his hand. —*I am here.* The man held on to his hand for longer than most people would have, as if he were divining secret things. In that way, Boubacar understood that the man had once known his father. They all sat, and the cook's daughters fussed over the old man, lowering him into his chair, teasing him that they would take his cane away, and then he must stay always with them. The old man smiled at their voices. They were, so it seemed, his granddaughters.

—*Well,* he said. —*Now we are all together, and this is good.*

Boubacar saw the other men then, sitting at the next table, watching every move everyone made. He understood in some way that they were there to protect the old man. Boubacar looked at the man's eyes and remembered a story from home, how one *hawallah* man had had acid poured into his eyes by the militia, for speaking against the government on Radio Mali, and for funding Pan-African musical broadcasts. Boubacar had heard his mother and grandmother speaking of it once. When he had walked in the room, they had stopped talking and had stood in complete silence, patting out the bread as if he were not there.

Hawallah man.

This was the bank? A blind old man? This was Salem's alternative to talking to Jews in the tall buildings.

The women brought out enameled pans of lamb, beef, lentils, cabbage, potatoes. It was like feast food at home—here they had it every day, anytime they wanted it. Boubacar ate in ravenous silence, as if he'd not eaten in a long time, wiping the pan with his bread. As the mother cooked for the other customers, a table full of American students wearing earrings in their noses as well as their ears, she saved a little back for the boy and brought it to him with a mother's smile. A chicken leg, a little bowl of spicy lentils flecked with green chiles. Whatever the others ordered, she also brought the boy a sample. She spoke an Arabic that seemed a few removes from his own. She did not speak French, so the boy had to rely on the Wastrel's translations, his interest piqued when he saw her daughters giggle nervously.

—*She knows who you are,* the Wastrel said quietly, deftly rolling some lamb and tomatoes into a small piece of bread. —*She heard your father in Addis Ababa before you were born. She says there will always be food for you in her kitchen. You have only to ask.*

The boy bobbed his head, looking up at her, with a hard knot in his throat. Everyone, it seemed, had known his father except himself. The food was wonderful and made tears of homesickness come to his eyes. All the men ate silently and gratefully, and the woman hovered behind them, smiling.

The time seemed open and ripe to shared secrets, so the boy spoke.

—*Tell her, please, I will play music for her someday.*

The Wastrel said nothing, refusing to pass the words along to the woman. His chin seemed to come out a bit too sharply from his face now. —*Do not be so certain of that of which you have no understanding.*

Boubacar closed his eyes a second, and when he opened them, he saw the Wastrel staring at him sharply, seeing how he held his many secrets, not understanding what they were.

When the old *hawallah* man held Boubacar's two hands in his again to say good-bye, he held them too tightly, as if he knew they might not meet again. By then Salem had two fat rolls of cash in his pockets. Not one scrap of paper had been signed. The debt was written on the walls of the *hawallah* man's mind, witnessed by his bodyguards.

As they rounded the corner of the white building, they noticed men in familiar jackets circling the many-mabone car. The jeweled crowns on the back: Gangster Disciples. The day was too warm for such jackets. The man leaning over peering into the inside was Rashad. Boubacar's heart began to pulse: *secrets, secrets.*

Boubacar's steps slowed, but the Wastrel took longer steps, covering more ground. The Wastrel somehow always by an odd default became the spokesman for them when they were all together. Before he was across the parking lot, Rashad called out.

—*How much you pay for this car, man!* His eyes scanned their little group, rested momentarily on Boubacar, then away.

The Mauritanian men were somehow standing closer together, the way creatures of the same kind might pause together in the instant before they flee in separate directions. Each was painfully aware of Salem's pocket, fat with the *hawallah* man's money.

—*Ah, but you are having a fine car already,* Salem said affably, nodding towards the black Escalade. —*In America yours is very good car. Very fine.*

—*Well,* Rashad said slowly and deliberately. —*My car is in use at the present moment.*

—*Oh yeah,* his companions guffawed in low growls that seemed to come from down inside the dark wells of their jackets. —*You got that right,* one said.

—*This the car I want,* Rashad said, patting his pockets for a cigarette. One of his disciples held out a pack, and he took one and put it in his mouth. His eyes did not leave the Wastrel's face. —*Understand what I'm sayin'?*

A car door slammed and all heads turned to the black

Escalade. A young woman was getting out of the backseat, adjusting her clothing. Boubacar saw the momentary flash of a red lace bra. The girl was Ayesha. A skinny white boy got out of the car then.

Ayesha saw the group of Mauritanian men, and she saw the car that had been her brother's. She looked at Boubacar, then away. Her hands dropped to her sides, and she stood tethered by some invisible cord to the black Escalade. The white boy disappeared around the corner of the building.

Rashad said, —*This car was my friend's car. You got clear title to this car, man?*

—*The car belongs to us. We paid for it,* said the Wastrel.

Rashad was about to speak when a police car turned lazily into the parking lot.

The officer's car window lowered as he neared them. He was a young black man with his hair carved deftly into a chevron. —*Yaw doin' all right today?* the officer said.

—*Fine, and you?* Rashad said. —*I was just speaking with my African brothers here about trying to buy me this old hoopty car off them.*

The Mauritanians said nothing. They saw that the combination of the policeman and the car made Rashad nervous.

—*Miss Ayesha is looking mighty fine today,* the officer said. —*Mighty fine.*

—*For Memphis's finest, we got only the finest,* Rashad said, affecting a bored air, as if he had said this line many times before. He stared pointedly at the Mauritanians, as if they were missing two hints at the same time. One involved the car, the other involved their leaving so the policeman could visit with the girl in the black Escalade.

Salem was sitting in the many-mabone car by then, and the Mauritanians began to get in the car and close the doors. The Wastrel and Boubacar sat in the backseat. Salem started the engine, and they began to drive away. They rode in silence all the way to Parkway, and the car made the turn gracefully. Passing the deserted fairgrounds, Teslem mused, —*Surely he does not need the money, to sell the girl. Surely he does not need another car. He sells the drugs. Why is he selling the girl?*

—*No*, the Wastrel answered. —*He is selling the girl to give himself new—*

—*To expand his customer base*, Boubacar offered helpfully, repeating words Angus had taught him. Teslem and the Wastrel looked at him in bemusement. Boubacar shifted in his seat uneasily. Remembering the red lace bra, the white boy getting out of the car, he felt enriched and robbed.

The fairgrounds gave way to a desolate stretch of beige metal storage units and hot-wing hawkers and truck stops with big rigs nuzzled together like dinosaurs down for the night.

Only the strip clubs offered any brightness—silver mirrors instead of windows, and pink neon flashing off and on with the same rhythm animals use for coupling. A gaunt woman with dead eyes walked facing the traffic, high heels wobbling, hitching her bra straps determinedly, staring off into the future as if it were a mirage. Truck drivers blew their horns at her and made obscene motions with their hands. Two bedraggled children followed her at a cautious pace, as if she were a mirage.

—*L'Américain*, the Wastrel said softly, with a peculiar tenderness the boy had never heard before. —*What a blessedness he lives in. He does not understand that he is the catastrophe.*

Ceremony for the
Giving of a Name

Angus invited everyone he ever knew, and some he didn't, to the bunkhouse dedication at the Celestial on the Fourth of July. He invited Dean Fondren and Aubrey Ellerbee. He invited all the Africans. He invited all the Telephone Pioneers, and the Reverend Calvin Dearborn and the Mighty Sons of Destiny, and told them to bring their instruments. He invited Sister Aurelia from the Rescue Mission, and the man who drove the Cockrell Banana Company truck. He invited someone who worked for the Ibrahim Bros. Funeral Home and told him to bring some folding chairs, and that he'd see to it that none went missing. The Reverend Calvin Dearborn promised to provide some good music and live coverage courtesy of his cousin at the Clarksdale radio station. He invited Marie Abide and mentioned that he thought it would be nice to have some roses. She promptly fetched six plastic milk jugs brimming with them, and the same tall glass hoodoo candles that Angus had discarded: *Virgen de Guadalupe, Ojos del Tigre, Cielo de Azul*. Watching her move from table to table, leaving roses and candles on each one, Angus thought of Consuela with an odd longing. He wanted her to be there. He wanted her to know his good side.

Lisa arrived in early evening, alone, since Jimmy had been

too busy to come. But when Angus watched the door, he discovered he was watching for Consuela. If she were anywhere near, she'd know about it through the Latino workers' grapevine. He looked at the little blue van with the Clarksdale radio station logo on it. Maybe she'd be listening to the radio.

The workers who had signed up to be sleeping in the bunkhouse were among the first to show up, wearing their good Saturday night shirts, carrying their good cowboy hats. They had good boots, Angus noted, the kind that you could wear when you worked construction and then run a rag across before you wore them to the dance. Most of the men were members of the same crew for Tomás Tulia, and their faces were full of something that had never been there before when Angus had seen them in the store. Word had spread quickly, and many there were accompanied by women and children carrying hotdishes. Sister Aurelia seemed to know them all by name. When the room was full and the tables groaning with food, Angus clapped his hands to silence the room.

—*Like to welcome you here tonight, all our regulars and our honored guests,* he said, nodding his head to Tulia's crew. —*And now we will ask Sister Aurelia to return thanks.* To his surprise the little nun rattled off the blessing in Spanish.

—*Dios del mundo, del todos corazones aquí, agradecemos usted...*

Except for the hoodoo candles on all the tables that said *Money House Blessing, Flames of Protection, Attraction of True Love,* and *Big Heart Confusion,* the party at the Celestial was somewhat like a church supper, with hot murky casseroles and an arsenal of layer cakes made by Baptist and Catholic ladies who seemed amazed they cooked from the same recipes. The Telephone Pioneers and other regulars stood humbly, seeming naked without their hats, waiting for the honored guests, the workers, to serve themselves. Angus, Dean, and

Aubrey held back, watching the men let the women and children go first.

—*Ain't but one person missing*, Dean said, thinking of Tomás Tulia.

—*She might come yet*, Angus said absently. —*Bring her boys and all.*

Dean and Aubrey looked at each other, said nothing.

Boubacar rushed around like a waiter, solicitous of everyone's comfort. The Wastrel stood just inside the door in his dazzling white robes and red skullcap, like a work dog that consents to come in from the cold on a winter's night. He sampled the food carefully, politely dodging the barbecued pork that all the ladies kept offering him.

When all had had their fill, Dean Fondren clapped his hands sharply and tapped on his tea glass with a spoon until all eyes came to rest on him. —*Give us some words, Angus.*

—*Amen*, murmured the Reverend Calvin Dearborn, and all the Sons of Destiny murmured too.

—*Amen*, said Boubacar, and the Wastrel turned to stare at him sharply.

A look of fear crossed Boubacar's face. A look of understanding crossed the Wastrel's.

Angus took a deep breath and let it out in ragged snatches.

—*Well, I never went to that Toastmasters outfit, so I don't know how to make a speech. But I thank you for your work, and I thank you for believing in this thing we done here. We made a little place where them that needs a leg up in this world can get their feet on the ground. If you like most of us, you come to America because your burden at home was too heavy. What else.* He stopped, and gulped some air. Sister Aurelia immediately launched into a translation in Spanish, and Angus relaxed a little before continuing.

—*When me and my father first come to this part of the country, we was lucky to be here. I reckon you know what I'm*

talking about. And the first kindness ever showed to us was a
hot tamale, give to us by a colored man on the street. Had this
little cart, with hot dogs and tamales, wheels on that thing,
shock absorbers. We didn't speak no English, and he didn't
speak no Chinese, so we had to find some other way to get
through to one another, and that way turned out to be kind-
ness. Don't matter where you come from, or how long you
aimin' to be here. If you can speak kindness, then you can go
anywhere you want in this country. Can't nobody stop you.

There was a hush in the room, and only Sister Aurelia's
freight-train Spanish. Many of the workers already knew what
he had said, by the light in the faces of the others, reflecting the
hoodoo candles and the PABST BLUE RIBBON sign.

Angus's right hand was kneading his left shoulder then, as if
something were pinching him. —*And we got the Reverend*
Dearborn and the Mighty Sons here, and now I'd like to ask
them to play. He made his way to one of the funeral home
chairs and sat down in relief.

Boubacar stood rooted to the floor.

—*Where's my little man?* the Reverend said, looking around.

Boubacar brought his alligator guitar case out of the stockroom, laid it down on the floor, and opened it. The Wastrel was
watching him. Boubacar's heart was pounding as he gently
pulled out the guitar and laid it across his lap.

The Reverend Calvin Dearborn struck a few chords, and
Boubacar answered with some boisterous slides, with the
amputated neck of a beer bottle on his middle finger. He looked
up for a split second and saw the Wastrel's eyes widen, saw him
swallow hard, saw him slip quietly out the door. Boubacar was
the only one to see him go, and his heart felt like a useless
stone. *He is afraid,* the boy realized. *He is afraid of Americans,*
even when L'Américain is a good Chinaman or a descendant of
the Prophet himself.

The bass guitarist began to lay down a beat, since there were no drums. Boubacar and the Reverend turned pins and picked strings. For about a minute all was discord and confusion, like voices calling at the same closed door, and then the door opened, and all entered at the same time, and the music began.

Miss Bebe Marie arrived, wearing her black bowler traveling hat and her Mexican serape, and she was carrying the tiniest little bottle-cap birdhouse she'd ever made. She walked over to Lisa, who was surrounded by church ladies-in-waiting. She seemed to bow when she presented the birdhouse, which was made entirely of strawberry soda-bottle caps. When Lisa tipped it up to look at it, its insides were papered with old pages from Mother Goose, and she had added embellishments of her own:

> *How many miles to Babyland?*
> *Three score miles and ten*
> *Can we get there by candle light?*
> *Yes, and back again.*

—*Thank you*, Lisa said. Bebe Marie was in an agony of joy. She went over and stood beside the cooler, watching them, studying their happiness like an anthropologist might.

There was a loud bump at the door, and all looked up in time to see the Wastrel, bringing in his big Wolof drum. The boy loved him then: that he would sit down with the *kaffir* to play, because it was kindness, it was the right thing to do for the Latinos who came from far away to make the roads and the buildings because *L'Américain* didn't like hard work anymore.

—*Amen!* the Reverend Calvin Dearborn called when he saw the drum, and pulled up another Ibrahim Bros. chair. Boubacar smiled his toothiest smile. The Wastrel sat down on the edge of the chair and pulled the drum between his knees. A few tentative pats, some queries from the guitars, and they were back inside the big door to the music. The Wastrel would not let his eyes meet the boy's as he followed them with the drum, through the valley of the shadow of the *kaffir* music. He knew the music well, the boy noted. He *knew* it.

The Celestial's door opened once more, and a busload of Japanese casino tourists emptied itself into the already crowded store, spilling over into the bunkhouse. It was a group of electronics executives outfitted in natty golf togs, and they were amazed to find themselves among the American peasantry, and some went back to the bus to get cameras. Others began to examine the merchandise and make demands. When the shutterbugs among them came back in with their cameras, Lisa looked up and wondered when Angus was going to shoo them out and get things back on track in the store. She was at the cash register, where there was a rush on small baby dresses to be taken back to Japan. It appeared the Japanese were fond of pale pink.

Angus was gone. Lisa stepped out onto the porch.

There he was, his escape blocked somewhat by a squinting Japanese businessman aiming a camera at him. The Japanese man snapped, and Angus flinched as if he'd been struck. —*No more,* Angus said, yet the man held up his hand and snapped on. —*I said no more,* Angus warned him with the candor that came from knowing the man could not understand him. —*Or I'll throw your piece-of-shit camera in that lake yonder.* The man smiled cheerfully, bobbed his head, *yes, thanks,* and snapped on. Then he turned his camera on Lisa, who turned her back.

Angus raised his hand to give the Japanese man a gesture in a language that was not kindness, and he certainly understood it. The Japanese man lowered his camera, stone-faced. Angus was by then stalking off alone across the fields. Lisa could not catch up with him. She held her heavy belly in place with two hands and strode after him.

—*Angus,* she called him.

He kept walking, and she saw he was making a wide arc around the field, heading towards the little cemetery near the church in the center. She followed him quietly, wondering if his heart was up to the exertion. She herself was out of breath. She could look behind them and see the Celestial's lights, somewhat like a little boat lit against the black of the night.

Staring at his thin back as he walked, she remembered how he'd been at her wedding in Dallas, sitting with his arms folded stiffly, like a disapproving missionary at a bacchanal, as the wedding guests began to do that year's dance, rustling in silk and taffeta around him. His wrinkled face was its own cartography, telling a story about a lifetime of hard work. He'd never had time to learn to dance like the *bok guey*. It flustered Angus when Lisa kissed him at the wedding. His head bobbed like a fisherman's cork, and then he was gone, slipped into the stream of wedding guests, most of whom were business associates of the bride's father.

—*He doesn't drive, doesn't own a car,* someone whispered.

—*Delta Chinese,* Lisa's mother nodded knowingly under her breath to her Dallas friends, and explained about the son in Memphis, plus the Wharton School of Business. —*Plus the fact,* she dropped her voice a bit, —*Nanking.*

—*Nanking, Nanking,* murmured a tiny spry old woman with ivory combs. Her black eyes were suddenly bright buttons, harboring both terror and forgiveness.

Finally Lisa caught up with him.

Angus was sitting on a tombstone, Rose Chien's. He stretched his lanky legs over it as if he'd done that a hundred times before, and he lit a cigarette.

—*They need you in the store,* she said. —*It's a riot in there.*

He didn't say anything for a long while, just took drags from the cigarette. After a while, he flicked the butt off into the field and coughed.

—*Goddamn Japanese got to take pictures of everything,* he said slowly, and Lisa felt lost. —*Snap, snap, snap. The last time I saw my mother and sister alive they were looking into a Japanese camera, and there was nothing I could do about it, not a goddamn thing.*

Lisa realized there was a sound coming out of her, not a sob, but a breathless moan, as if there would never be enough air in the world again. Whatever the sound was she was making, it was scaring the baby inside her. The red doors of the abandoned church yawned open like a bored mouth, and the sign still read TRUE LIGHT TEMPLE OF THE BEAUTIFUL NAME.

They heard the big charter bus revving its engine, and its driver honked the horn to flush out whatever stragglers were inside purchasing cigarettes and souvenirs. A small Japanese man ran out holding a Confederate flag and disappeared into the bus. The door closed behind him, the hydraulic brakes released with a squeal, and the Japanese were gone.

—*Casina trash,* Angus said decisively. —*Burn in hell, for all I care.*

The world seemed so hugely flat as the bus disappeared down the road. They looked around.

—*I ain't ever been one for letting myself wish for too much,* Angus said again, his voice cracking. —*And I ain't ever asked nothing of nobody. But I hope this world never takes you and your baby away from me.*

—*What was her name?*

—*Who?*

—*Your sister?*

—Her missionary name was Alice.

—Alice is a beautiful name.

—She was beautiful. Like a china doll, except real.

Angus was kneading a spot between his collarbones with his fist.

Back in the store they watched the Sons of Destiny play, and then Angus leaned over, his right fist on his left shoulder blade, *—This heart thing.*

—What? Lisa said, the smile leaving her face.

—It hurts, my heart.

From across the room Dean Fondren and Aubrey Ellerbee saw the color drain from her face and saw Angus's fist tap once over his heart. They both crossed the room and knelt before Angus.

—Got my truck right outside, Angus, Aubrey said. *—Time they get the ambulance here from Clarksdale, we could be in Memphis.*

—No, Angus said. *—They'll make me take that test where you got to sign the paper saying it's not their fault if you die. Gimme a minute, I be okay.*

—You ain't got a minute, Angus, Dean said. *—And we don't want to have to call Ibrahim Brothers.*

Angus laughed and winced. *—They got to come get their damn chairs, might as well take me.*

—Got dammit, Angus, said Aubrey. *—You scarin' us.*

—Get me some money out of the register, Angus said to Lisa. There was a flurry of words about who would drive him, Lisa or Aubrey. Aubrey got Angus situated in the truck. Lisa followed in her little red car with Angus's wallet and money. If they could get him to Tutwiler, the sisters could take over from there.

By the time Lisa drove Angus home from his heart tests in Memphis three days later, he seemed diminished and sat quietly, looking at the blue-green ripples of the soybean fields as if he were nourished by the sight of them.

Boubacar came running out the door with the spatula still in his hand, grinning fiercely. Angus got out of the car and stood a moment, looking at his old store as if he'd been gone for years instead of three days, or maybe as if he were seeing it for the first time. Then he went inside and rolled up his shirtsleeves, put his apron and his visor on like a thousand other mornings of his long life, and began to divest himself of his belongings.

Dean Fondren walked in to get some coffee that morning, and Angus said, —*Dean, what you want out of here to remember me by when I'm gone?*

Dean shoved his Treflan cap back on his head and surveyed the store with amusement rising in his eyes, and said, —*You going somewhere?*

Angus jerked his head in the general direction of the cemetery.

—*I don't want a damn thing you got in here,* Dean answered. —*Besides which, you are healthier than the rest of us. You'll be here when we're all out in the bone orchard.*

The next time Lisa came back to check on him, Angus asked, —*What you want out of here to remember me by when I'm gone?*

—*Angus, don't you be talking like that,* she said. He noted that she no longer called him Pop-pop, and was oddly pleased by it.

—*You need to tell me now,* Angus said. —*I'm putting names on things.*

Lisa looked around and saw masking tape with names in

tiny script, and she had a moment of alarm, as if she should call Jimmy or Jimmy's dad. Marie Abide's name was on the shopping cart, Aubrey Ellerbee's name was on the neon PABST BLUE RIBBON beer sign, and the Harlem Swing Club had spoken for the old glass-doored cooler whose coils underneath were fuzzy with lint and grease. —*Hey, stop that,* Lisa said, nudging him in the ribs, taking the masking tape away from him.

Skrrrt, skrrrt, skrrrt, went the tape as she moved around the store labeling things. Then he began to smile.

—*Angus Chien,* said the cash register.

—*Angus Chien,* said the phone.

—*Angus Chien,* said the stove.

Then, eyeing Angus mischievously, she went over to the worn wooden counter.

Skrrrt, went the tape again, and she put a swatch on the red abacus.

Alice Chien, she wrote.

She stood before the jukebox, tapping her foot. She looked at Angus. *Skrrrt,* went the tape, and she put a swatch of it on the jukebox above the *Rock-ola* light. *Alice Chien,* she wrote on it.

Angus began to grin.

—*Alice is a good name,* he said. —*Good name for a baby girl.*

Later at dusk, after Lisa had gone, when Angus moved around the store feeling hollow-hearted and newborn and alone, he read the label on the jukebox again, *Alice Chien,* reassured by it somehow. He went outside, lit his cigarette, and sat on his porch with one hand tucked under the elbow like a paper crane. He took a long drag on his cigarette and stared at it in his hand. His eyes played a trick on him. The first cigarette he ever saw was in 1938 in the mouth of a Japanese soldier.

Japanese had appeared in Nanking, a sudden plague of insects devouring everything in their path. They tied women together with ropes, ten or twenty together. Angus's mother was among them. He did not know where Alice was. He did not know where his father was. Everyone was taller than Angus, and he was looking at the soldiers through the legs of the grown-ups. Some Japanese soldiers were taking pictures of naked Chinese women and girls. No, that was not all. They were pouring water on them. No. They had doused some women and girls with gasoline, then offered them cigarettes, laughing. When the women refused the cigarettes, the soldiers tossed the cigarettes onto them. Angus remembered the whoosh of flames and the cries of the women. The bodies had writhed. The Japanese soldiers stared in satisfaction. It was Angus's first understanding of obscenity. He could remember that day with no feeling, nothing.

This was the bundle carried with him to America, a deep mistrust of happiness.

He flicked his cigarette off into the weeds and stood up and went inside. He boiled water to steam himself some tamales that had been in the freezer since Consuela left. There had been a couple dozen when she departed, and now he was down to five. He sat on the front porch with the cats and ate three.

—*Give you heart trouble,* he thought he heard someone say, but when he turned to face the voice, he faced empty air.

Amulet for Big Heart Confusion

The big daddies of Magazine Street flew out of Memphis sometimes late at night, to sell some cotton or some catfish, or man-
age risks or pork bellies. They traveled far and wide, and they
traveled without their wives. Their companies did not pay for
the travel expenses of wives and children, but they did pay for
certain types of administrative assistance, usually from unat-
tached females.

Because she was a good woman, when Matthew traveled,
Raine would respond by cooking for the children the food that
matched the travels they did not share with him. It started as a
way to economize, and to make the children feel included in
his life. If they baked and folded their own fortune cookies
when their dad went to China, if she read Chinese poems or
stories to them, they didn't notice that they weren't ever
invited. If they recited the Chinese poems to him when he
returned, he would look at her over their heads, and he would
know that she was a good woman.

It became a ritual, in the early years. Raine knew every
mom-and-pop grocery operation run by immigrants in Memphis. On the first night Matthew was gone, they would sit
down to dinner with the atlas on the table and talk about what
time it would be if they were where he was. By the meal's end,
they would have learned some new words and cities, and whole

cultures would be reduced to some smallest possible whole, like pad thai, and the atlas would be shoved aside almost to cover the place where Matthew's plate would have been if he'd been home. As the children grew older, the atlas disappeared entirely, and she just cooked the food and served it. They bit into her sweet-cheese *palascintas*, preparation time two hours, without looking up from the television.

As the children grew even older, and Raine often couldn't remember where Matthew had gone, or even if he'd told her. She intended to pay attention when he talked about it, but seemed not to have heard once he was gone. Was it a sign? One Saturday morning, she roamed around the house, looking for her children. She yelled upstairs to Callie, —*Oh, who will go to the grocery store with me? asked the Little Red Hen.*

—*Not I,* called her son from upstairs, punctuated by computer pings.

—*Where are you going?* Callie called from some remote corner upstairs.

—*Sam Stringer. Big Heart. I have to get plants and groceries. Where did your dad say he was staying this time?* She called past the boy's closed door. She could hear the blips of his computer game, like bubbles rising underwater.

—*He didn't say. Probably some Hilton,* the boy called back.

—*Come drive with me,* she called. —*You have not been out of this house since you came home from school.*

The door opened, and the boy's head popped out. He was wary of being asked to help. She had actually asked him to help her dig a hole in the dirt once.

—*What's in it for me?*

—*My enduring esteem and gratitude,* Raine said sweetly. —*Comb your hair, please.*

—*I want to stop by Record Town,* the boy said. —*I need to get a needle.*

—*A what?*

—*I've been listening to all these old records, and I think I wore the needle out.*

She looked behind him in the room, and saw that he had rescued from the boxes in the garage her old RCA turntable from college, and her grandfather's 78s that were in a wooden ammunition crate left over from World War II.

—*We'll see*, she said, flipping for a moment through the pile of records, an odd assortment of Hawaiian lap steel, western swing, and early hillbilly music.

She felt sometimes that she had to bribe the children to get them to go out and live. They were reluctant tourists, and she was the pushy tour guide. Had any child in that neighborhood ever so much as climbed a tree? She had no memory of ever seeing either of her children climb a tree. Magazine Street children could compare intelligently the merits of Tim Burton films with Steven Spielberg films, but they couldn't tell an oak from a maple.

At Sam Stringer's nursery, the smell of green growth was heavy in the humid air, almost dizzying. Raine closed her eyes a bit, walking among the flats of herbs straining to outgrow their little black plastic containers. Both children sat in the car while she chose the plants she needed, forgetting the chervil, buying too much sage and too little rosemary. She knew already that she would get home and realize what she'd forgotten, whatever got lost in her mind because the gravitational pull of the children was so strong.

She stood in line behind an old couple buying their plants together. She felt an odd thrill, voyeur to intimacy, watching an old man lean over his wife's shoulder and peer into the throats of an orchid. She couldn't remember the last time she'd been in a store of any kind with her husband. Matthew did not *do* ordinary life anymore. She could feel the impatience of her children piercing all the layers of car glass and air and storefront. She hurried out.

—*Let's do this,* she said, getting into the car. —*I'll drop you two off at the library, go get the groceries, and come back. Chance, please see that Callie is not kidnapped by some random pedophile. Then we'll go to Record Town, though on second thought, there are probably more random pedophiles there than at the library.*

Chance laughed, and it was the first time she'd got a laugh from him in weeks.

—*What's a pedalphile?* Callie asked. —*A kidnapper on a bicycle?*

—*Sometimes they don't have a bicycle,* Chance replied evasively.

Raine held her breath before she laughed. For about thirty seconds they had managed to be companions, almost like the happy barbecue family in the home improvement ads, except the father had somehow been airbrushed out.

The Big Heart was a national chain of organic grocery stores, each a reasonable facsimile of a mom-and-pop hippie food store. The Memphis store was always bright and lively, with signs that said BELIEVE over the organic produce. Big Heart catered to stockbrokers and students and little old vegetarian ladies in Birkenstocks. Raine always came home with bags full of overpriced food: free-range chicken, apple-smoked sausage, tamari almonds, fresh hummus, sushi, flowers flown in from São Paulo or Provence.

BELIEVE, said the gold and green signs, familiar from coast to coast. Customers queued up accordingly with their credit cards, believing in the good life enough to purchase it at prices inflated enough to screen out undesirable customers, like a fence at a country club. Outside that invisible fence there were whole warrens of unfortunates who'd never transcended the standard brands of childhood, *Nabisco, Nestlé.*

On this particular day, when Raine pulled into the parking lot of the Big Heart, she noticed on the sidewalk a familiar card table with a poster affixed to it, *Roses, Cash and Carry.* The Catfish Lady had positioned herself between the big-chain grocery and the mega-office-supply store, as a small sea creature might attach itself to the advantageous underbelly of something bigger. She had plastic milk jugs and Luzianne tea cans full of fresh roses and peonies, a couple of her birdhouses, and stacks of little mojo bags.

Raine parked her car and stared. She always felt she should be *doing something* about the woman. She wondered if she shouldn't phone some social services office and see what help was available for someone like her. Even if it was just food stamps, that would be something.

If the woman was still there when she came out, it would be a sign. She'd go buy something. If the woman was not there, it would also be a sign.

Inside the store, men cruised the medicinal aisles looking for their saw palmetto, women studied the promises on the labels of creams. Raine dawdled in front of strawberries so red and ripe that she nicked one with a fingernail to make sure it wasn't artificial. She admired the cheeses from England, the breads from Italy. She compared all the tomato options. The ones from Holland were more expensive than the ones from California. But most expensive of all were the ones grown just a few miles outside Memphis, the ones that would taste like real tomatoes. It seemed like a sign of something ominous and confusing, the way the pricing ensured that only the well-heeled got to eat locally grown tomatoes picked that same morning. *The tomatoes of our youth*, said the little sign, which had a photo of a 1950s housewife in heels and pearls, serving her children a lunch of tomato sandwiches and glasses of milk. The glasses were painted in multicolored polka dots. And for a limited time only, those glasses were available on Aisle Seven, in housewares. If you purchased the glasses you could get a pound of the local tomatoes for free. On Aisle Seven, Raine studied the glassware.

She was waiting in line for a cup of coffee behind a tall black man in a brilliant dashiki when she looked over and saw, sitting in a booth by the window, the jukebox man reading the *New York Times*. She held her breath.

What a tender complication it was, to be so glad to see him.

If he was still there by the time she got her coffee, it would be a sign.

If he was not, it would be some other sign.

The jukebox man looked up then and saw her, and she saw his eyes widen with pleasure before he smiled. He was glad to see her, *glad*. What kind of sign was it? A terrifying one.

After she paid for her coffee, she pushed her cart of groceries over to the wall of windows and parked it near his table. He pushed together the sections of his newspaper to clear a space for her across the table. They both mumbled unintelligible things at the same time, then started over.

—*Guitar lessons going okay?*

Raine simply rolled her eyes.

—*I have something for you in my car*, he said, as if he were simply resuming the conversation they'd had months before. —*Are you going to be here a while? It will only take a minute.*

He left her there then, and she watched him go to a small white car and take something out of the backseat. She couldn't see what it was. Then he disappeared for a few minutes, and she looked around inside. He was not anywhere in sight. She looked at her watch. She should go soon. Random pedophiles could strike at any hour.

He seemed to come out of nowhere, and he laid a CD in a brown bag on the table in front of her. —*This is to help with the bridges.*

Raine felt a muscle tic just below her eye. She hoped he couldn't see it. She was not annoyed, she told herself, just caught off guard. She gently pried the lid off her coffee. She was aware that he was watching her as she touched her finger gently to the foam on top, then to her mouth. It was a voluptuous confusion, not just to be watched by someone, but also to have his eyes meet hers. She was not accustomed to being so clearly visible to anyone.

—*I try not to think about it too much.*

—*Sorry.*

—*It's okay. How's Sam?*

—*He's good. Little League is gearing up, so we drive a lot. Do you come here often?*

—*Now and then. How's the jukebox hospital?*

—*'Jukebox hospital.' I like that. Pretty scarf.*

—*What?* Oh, this. She put her hand to her throat. She had not realized until that moment that she had begun to dress for this man in the mornings. She had taken to wearing clothes she'd worn in happier times, before she became an appliance. She had a scarf patterned after a Tiffany window wound around her neck, which she had almost stopped wearing because it made people notice her breasts first. She was caught off guard again, such a small compliment, but it made her feel good about herself. *That is the difference,* she thought, between a man you're not married to and one you are married to.

They mumbled things in unison, not wanting to say good-bye. She watched him leave as she wheeled her cart into a lane near a cash register. As always, she was a bit shocked at the price of the food she was buying. She had almost two hundred dollars' worth of food and organic cleaning supplies in four expensively recycled paper bags when she walked out of the store to her car. There was the jukebox man, exchanging angry words with a Big Heart employee, a mere white kid with carrot-colored hair and hip-hop clothes. Raine walked nearer.

—*She's not bothering anyone here. This is a public side-walk,* the jukebox man was saying.

—*No soliciting on the premises. Big Heart policy. Only headquarters can authorize that.* The boy was dressed like a street thug, but he spoke with a librarian's priggishness. He wore an officious gold name badge, and a name given by his parents to guarantee he'd always be like everyone else, *Justin.* He had a gold ring in his nose, the better to be led around by.

—*Can you sell me that birdhouse?* Raine asked the Catfish Lady in a loud voice. —*That one?* She pointed at random to one that seemed to be made mostly of paper and birch twigs and held up a twenty and a five.

—*You can't do that here,* the Big Heart kid said.

—*Watch me,* Raine said.

The Catfish Lady tried to smile in an agitated way, and held up the birdhouse to Raine, who gave her the money.

—*I'm calling the cops,* the Big Heart kid said. Raine and the jukebox man stared at each other, stifling their laughter.

—*Did we ever in our wildest dreams think that Big Brother would turn out to be our own kids?* The jukebox man murmured to her in a low way that was thrilling. He gave the Catfish Lady all the cash he had in his wallet and she gave him two birdhouses.

The carrot-topped boy sneered and went back inside the store. By then the Catfish Lady was simply packing up her things. Raine spied a shopping cart from a rival grocery concealed beside the Big Heart's Dumpster. As the Catfish Lady walked away with her empty plastic jugs, Raine and the jukebox man stood with handfuls of roses and peonies, with a birdhouse apiece. They inspected each other's birdhouses.

—*Look, you have half my roof and I have half yours*, he said, tracing the roofline of hers with his finger. Two separate book covers had been split and then combined. *The New King Louis Narcisse Magical Dream Book*, he read from his.

—*The Mystical Oracle Complete Fortune Teller*, she read from hers.

He peered inside his. —*Look how the light comes through*, he said, and she leaned in to see. As she did, her hair brushed softly against his cheek, and they both stood up suddenly, as if there had been a great collision.

—*Well*, she said awkwardly, shifting a bundle of roses under her arm.

—*I'm going to see you again, right?* There, it was out. The merest wistful wish, spoken on the sidewalk out in broad daylight. It was terrifying. She waited for the police cars to roll up, lights flashing.

—*I shop here a lot.*

They said good-bye again, and Raine watched him drive away in the little white car. As soon as he was out of sight, she peeked in the paper bag he'd given her. *Bob Dylan, Bootleg Series.*

Could it be a sign?

—*God help me*, she laughed, and no one was there to hear.

Driving back down Poplar to retrieve her children, she listened to Dylan songs she'd never heard before, about auction blocks and stays of execution, prisons and friends and lovers and moonshiners, women leaving home in the middle of the night.

A light rain had begun to fall, and the drops on the windshield blurred the world outside until there was nothing near but the

music. She finally found what she realized she'd been listening
for, some sign telegraphed in the music, some soft love song.

I don't mean trouble, please don't put me down or get upset,
I am not pleadin' or sayin', 'I can't forget.'
I do not walk the floor bowed down and bent, but yet,
Mama, you been on my mind.

There it was. The sign.

The rest of the song was lost in the noise of her children
coming back to the car, rustling their packages and arguing.
The boy popped the Dylan CD out of the player without bothering to look at it and tossed it to the floor. His new music suddenly ate all the oxygen in the car, adolescents seething about
girls while they tortured guitars.

Raine hardly heard it. The Dylan songs had made her bullet-
proof.

The sun was slipping down closer to the river side of town,
and she remembered: dinner.

—*Mom? The light has changed. Why are we going this way?*

There were car horns blowing behind her. She looked up in
time to see the man in the car behind her, shaking his head and
cursing her. —*What? Oh, we . . . we are going out to dinner.*

—*My turn to pick,* Callie said instantly.

—*No, it's my turn this time. It's a surprise,* Raine said. She
had no idea where she was going. She had been driving towards
the river. She had driven that way because the jukebox man
lived that way.

She saw a sign: *Abyssinia Ethiopian Restaurant.*

—*Oh, here it is,* she said, turning on her blinker so suddenly
that the man tailgating her looked apoplectic with rage as he
cut off another car to avoid hitting them.

—*Is Daddy in Africa?* Callie asked, staring at the white

building that looked almost like a hotel but not quite. It was the kind of place her husband would never agree to go into, and even the neighborhood looked risky.

—*No, baby,* Raine said absently. —*I don't know where your dad is. Why would he be in Africa?*

—*Oh,* Callie said. —*They don't have bridges in Africa?*

—*Dork. They have bridges in Africa,* Chance countered.

—*I'm not a dork!* Callie cried indignantly.

—*Okay, you're a dorkette,* Chance said.

—*Shut up!* Raine snapped at him, and the boy's head jerked slightly, as if she'd struck him.

—*Excuse me?* Chance said. —*What did you just say?*

—*You heard what I said. I don't ever want to hear you call her names again.*

—*I'm not eating in there,* the boy said, folding his arms.

—*Suit yourself,* Raine said. She left the Dylan CD on the seat and got out.

While Raine and Callie went inside for their dinner, the boy sat alone sulking in the car, playing his music. The food was hot and comforting, lamb and beef and chicken and vegetables. The owner of the restaurant and his wife showed them how to eat it, offering encouragement.

—*You want fork? We got fork.*

Callie shook her head happily, her mouth full, her fingers stained. The place was full of African émigrés out for Saturday night. Mostly they were men who seemed to travel in packs of four or five. The few women were dressed in long silky dresses and matching turbans, stepping delicately in high heels.

—*That place is* too cool, Callie said to Chance as they got in the car. —*They make you eat with your fingers.*

Raine saw the boy mouth her words silently back at her, ridiculing her. Raine held her breath and looked at him sternly. Her eyes telegraphed something to him, *you are on thin ice here.* He ducked his head in a kind of misery, swallowing whatever hurtful words had come into his throat.

She drove, feeling miserable herself.

This is what you get when the televisions outnumber the human beings, she thought. *Everyone's lord of his own channel.*

The children were quiet as she parked the car. They got out without saying a word. *Oh, who will help me get these groceries in,* thought Raine.

Not I, indicated the boy, who slid out of the car and went to his room without speaking. *Not you either,* Raine thought, looking at the little girl, letting her go, *lest you get the idea that being born a girl is just cause for domestic servitude.*

Raine brought the groceries in alone and put them away alone. She poured herself a glass of port and took the CD jewel box from her purse. She slid it into the player in the kitchen, found the rest of the song she was looking for.

When you wake up in the mornin',
   baby, look inside your mirror.
You know I won't be next to you, you know I won't be near.
I'd just be curious to know if you can see yourself as clear
As someone who has had you on his mind.

She sipped the port and studied the weathered face of Bob Dylan. He always looked to her like he understood some old conspiracy that others did not. He looked magic, like a bus ticket out of town looks magic. She put the new birdhouse on the windowsill with the other, and contemplated it. She studied the other side of its roof, the front cover of *The New King Louis Narcisse Magical Dream Book.* Something old, something new. More signs.

Chance came into the kitchen, waiting. He was obviously hungry. It was almost nine o'clock. The boy was sitting in his accustomed place at the table, waiting like a disgruntled hotel guest. She was supposed to do sómething about his hunger, she supposed. He ripped open a bag of cookies that had something vaguely to do with saving the rainforests.

She cleaned the counters and watered the plants and folded the laundry and took out the garbage. To get away from the sound of the rustling cookie bag, she walked around her herb garden, reminding herself to make a list of night-blooming plants. When she came back in, the boy had gone to his room with the bag of cookies, taking the Dylan jewel box with him. She wondered if she'd ever hear it again.

Later when the house was all dark and silent, there were fat bands of moonlight falling across the expensive bed she could not seem to fall asleep in. Full moons pulled her out of her routines, insomnia always setting in. The Dylan songs played themselves over and over in her mind, phrases bleeding softly together like ink left out in the rain.

She moved over to the window seat. If the neighbor walking his dog below had looked up, he'd have seen a woman in a white nightgown leaning out an open window as if she cherished the troublesome moon. But such women are invisible to such men as this one whose family had made a mint selling mobile homes to people they knew could not afford them. He was peering at her crooked holly and checking the yard for other signs of imminent threats to his own property's value three doors down. He was reminding himself to check the small print in his homeowner's covenant. Property values could go down; one could not be too careful.

The man could not see the magnitude of the anarchy. The moonlight was falling on the woman in the white nightgown with her arms on the window's frame in exactly the position they would be in if she had just consented to dance. She was thinking about making an entry in the notebook of unspeakable secrets, open on her lap. She held the cloisonné pen, but didn't use it. The thoughts burned in her mind instead.

Come closer, son of mine. I will tell you a true thing in this world. Just when it seems there's nothing to drink but the same old gasoline, someone will offer water.

In the Cities of the Caesars

A short distance from the Mississippi River, the Mauritanians parked the taxi-painted car curbside in front of a square red brick building that resembled a giant child's block. It had no windows. Teslem had driven them there.

—*This is it*, Teslem said. —*They make the good guitar here.*

GIBSON, said the large yellow letters on the side of the building.

—*I am told this is a good place to work in the winters,* Teslem added. —*Good money, and is warm in the cold winter. Also many beautiful women.*

The Wastrel had no comment, which meant he was keenly interested. He had already expressed a wish not to be working out on the dredger during the winter.

They locked the car and walked towards the building. A busload of Japanese tourists was emptying itself across the street. Already some Japanese tourists were smiling toothy smiles for each other's cameras. A few turned and snapped photos of the Wastrel coming down the sidewalk, his white robes flowing, his entourage trailing behind him, in case he should be an American rock star.

They went into the building, pausing to admire the high ceilings and a cobalt-blue grand piano with a sign on it explaining that it was not to be touched. Through a glass wall they could see what seemed to be hundreds of gleaming guitars, all colors and shapes. They filed into the shop, and the cashier, a pale teenaged girl wearing a black t-shirt, nodded apprehensively at them. In America, the shopkeepers enjoyed the luxury of hostility to their customers.

The Cure, said her t-shirt. The uncles fumbled to translate it. A nurse? Impossible.

While the Wastrel and his uncles engaged the girl in conversation, Boubacar wandered the aisles of the store. At the back of the store a white man wearing a Harley-Davidson t-shirt was sitting on a small bench, playing a tawny acoustic guitar, flatpicking, Johnny Cash, *She loves you more than me, big river.* He looked up and saw Boubacar smiling at him. The white man stopped what he was playing, offering the guitar. —*You want to give 'er a whirl?*

Boubacar looked towards the other end of the store. The Wastrel's jaw was set, the white girl was shrugging, *sorry.* Boubacar sat down and laid the Gibson across his knees as if it were a National Steel.

—*Dude,* said the white man softly, with admiration.

Boubacar patted his pockets, the green glass bottleneck was there. He played the first few chords of the song Calvin Dearborn was teaching him.

Why'd you like Roosevelt? Weren't no kin.

Great God Almighty, he was the poor man's friend.

The boy looked over at his uncles.

—*Keep going,* the man said.

—*That's all I know,* Boubacar answered, handing the guitar back.

—*You go to the COGIC? You Pentecostal?*

—*I am Mauritanian,* Boubacar said. —*What is COGIC?*

—*It's a church. You play like that.*

The boy looked at the front of the store then, and he could see all their faces. They were all looking at him, the girl in the Cure shirt, the Wastrel, Salem, and Teslem. His eyes met the eyes of the Wastrel. He saw something new there, and it was respect.

When they came out of the store, they saw a black man wearing a sandwich board bearing the likeness of an Arab with no hair. ISAAC HAYES STUDIO KITCHEN. FINE SOUL DINING.

He handed them each a sheet of paper, photocopies of a menu, and smiled at them. —*Git you some good food,* the man said. —*Just like your mama used to make.*

—*Tell us,* Salem asked the man. —*Where is the place to go to apply for work at this guitar factory?*

The smile faded from the sign man's face.

—*You got to be a American citizen, you want to work there.*

The man walked away, making low grumbling noises. —*Damn Africans come over here, take all our jobs, work for shit.*

The moment felt sour and wrong. They watched the man make his way down the sidewalk, handing papers to all who passed by.

—*L'Américain,* the Wastrel said to Teslem in French. —*He wants to sell you the food your mother used to make, but he doesn't want you to work the way your father used to.*

—*I am also thinking someday to go to Minneapolis, Minnesota,* Teslem said.

—*In Minneapolis, Minnesota, there are many Africans,* Salem said.

—*Minnesota is colder than your mind can even imagine,* the Wastrel said. They made their way across a big parking lot, discussing the merits of a move. The uncles did not wish to work for the Lucky Leaf forever. Boubacar followed a few steps behind them. What would he do in Minneapolis, Minnesota? They agreed to discuss it in the future.

BEALE STREET, said a corner sign.

—*What is this place?* Boubacar asked softly, having fallen into the habit of having the Wastrel interpret everything for him. The street was narrow and lined with old shops, some with beautiful neon signs. Couples wandered arm in arm, some pushing baby strollers, but it was not a real marketplace they were in, Boubacar noticed. There was an idle dreaminess to the place, as if their real lives had been suspended. People stared at shiny Elvis cookie jars and neckties in the windows, and sipped at their drinks in big plastic cups. *Food & Spirits*, Boubacar read the sign again. *Spirits*.

—*Why do they come here?* Boubacar asked the Wastrel.

—*When the black people left the farms, they came here so they could be* bizan. *All the great ones came through here on their way out. Muddy Waters, Howlin' Wolf, they played on the streets for pocket change. Even Elvis Presley, the white one they call the King, he knew this street. He stole songs from this street and all the country purchased them.*

—*So it is a place of many spirits,* Boubacar said. —*To honor their spirits.*

The Wastrel shook his head. —*Some come here to sip their pink drink and not think for a while.*

—*What is this pink drink?*

—*Sometimes they call it 'hurricane.' Sometimes they call it 'daiquiri.' You should have one of these pink drinks, once in your lifetime. You will understand L'Américain in a new way then.*

—*You have had the pink drink?*

—*Yes, many times.*

—*And it is a good drink?*

—*For me: I was filled with love and sorrow. It is a very good drink for playing music.*

They passed an old black man whose legs were missing. He was playing a guitar. A tambourine lay in front of him, and passersby dropped coins into it. Boubacar watched the man's gnarled hands on the frets of the guitar. He knew the song. *Corinna, Corinna, where'd you sleep last night?*

They all noticed *la sorcière* at the same time. They all stopped in their tracks to look at her, and she looked back at them. It was their blue-eyed neighbor who lived among the stovepipe animals and bottle trees. She had set up a little portable stand to sell flowers and birdhouses on a side street beside a blank wall of the B. B. King Blues restaurant. She looked at them but gave no sign of recognizing them. Boubacar was glad to see someone familiar from what was now home.

—*Inshallah, Someone's Mother,* the Wastrel greeted her in soft Arabic, and the others murmured approval of his name for her. She humbled them all, somehow, whenever they saw her. She lived so far outside the rules of America, she was more like someone from their same country.

She smiled at him and nodded, without appearing to know any of them. —*You have come a long way today.*

They examined her roses and zinnias. It was an impromptu ceremony, to admire on the street in Memphis the very items that had been assembled next door to them. Boubacar picked up a birdhouse and looked shyly at her. It was fashioned from the caps of many bottles of beer and ale, all colors. He realized then that she had probably retrieved them from the gutters of the very street they were standing on. The roof of the birdhouse was an old and venerable book cover of mottled, watermarked leather. *The Wealth of Nations,* said its spine in elegant gold letters.

The inside was wallpapered with its yellowed pages, as well as old sheet music and restaurant menus. The Wastrel took it from him and began to read aloud the walls of the birdhouse. —*Of the natural progress of opulence. The great commerce of every civilised society. After the fall of the Roman empire, a very different order of people.*

—*What is your price?* the Wastrel asked.

—*Twenty dollars,* she said.

—*I know someone who sells them for fifteen,* Salem said, clucking his tongue in his cheek. He waited expectantly for her to adjust her price. The Wastrel motioned for him to be quiet, and, to Boubacar's quiet amazement, produced a twenty-dollar bill. She pocketed the money beneath the blanket, and the Wastrel held the birdhouse up to let the neon of the B. B. King sign shine through it. Salem and Teslem were hesitant to touch it, as if it were a vessel of mysterious powers. She tucked the twenty into the little zippered cloth pouch she wore at her middle latitudes, somewhere underneath the pinto pony blanket.

She beckoned them closer, and all three uncles leaned in carefully to hear. —*Down at the bank, they're bettin' against me,* she told them. —*Bettin' against me with telephone dimes.*

The Mauritanians walked past the rich men's hotels and utility companies and restaurants and saw across the river the chemical refineries, lit up like brittle gold topiaries breathing dragon spume. On the east side of the river, tall apartment buildings hugged the bluff overlooking the water.

—*Over there,* said the Wastrel, pointing just beyond the apartments, lived descendants of African tributaries captured and sold as slaves. Their grandfathers had been slaves, but they now lived in neat little brick houses, with the very latest cars in the driveways. The houses were replicas of the palaces of the great English kings. Each house was its own little machine with pumps for air and water.

—*Bizan or harutine?* the Wastrel quizzed the boy.

—*Bizan,* said Boubacar. —*They can go if they want to.*

—*They are not free,* the Wastrel said. —*They are owned by what they are driven to possess. Now I will teach you an American word. 'Hair-trigger.'*

—*Hair-trigger?* Boubacar answered.

—*Like a gun that is easy to shoot. To get rich in America, everyone looks for the thing that will make the fortune. The people in all these houses, each is like a hair-trigger. A new kind of shoes, they all go out to buy at the same time. The new kind of sandwich. The different way of haircut. The new song or soap. Poof, they all go buy it, hair-trigger fast.*

—*Hair-trigger*, Boubacar repeated.

—*They are not free*, the Wastrel said, staring at the refineries.

One good song, Boubacar understood, and he would be a rich man in America, *bizan*.

It was a game they had in the car sometimes, Boubacar and the Wastrel, naming those known to be enslaved back in Mauritania, such as the old woman who sold calabashes in the market, and shared her money with her master long after the radio had told her she was free, long after he had lost his teeth and his sight and his money. The boy had known since he was small, there were true slaves, invisible republics of them surrounding him as he grew up.

—*Bizan or harutine?* the Wastrel would say, and name a young woman who had been beaten daily in the alley for being arrogant to her master's wives. It seemed like an inquisition at times. —*You are not listening. Bizan or harutine?* Then he named some obscure old woman in the village. Everyone had loved her. What did it matter? The boy sighed with fatigue and a certain measure of boredom. His finger traced a circle on his forehead where the Wastrel's charcoal smudge had been when he was a child.

Boubacar's uncles wanted to see the great house of Elvis

Presley. After much of Teslem's fast driving in the opposite direction from the intended one, they found it. GRACELAND, the sign said. Great black iron gates shaped like sheet music walled them off from it. Pasty-skinned women milled out on the sidewalk outside and lit small candles and wove flowers into the fence. Great buses came and went, hauling tourists. The Wastrel explained that normally one could pay a fee and go inside to see the possessions of the singer the Americans called the King. Teslem idled the engine while Salem got out and read the admission fees and returned to the car shaking his head. It was asking too much. The money spent to stare at the King's things would feed them all for a week, or feed children at home in Nouatchkott for a month.

—*Why he was the King?* Teslem asked.

—*He taught the whites to dance like the blacks. He taught them what any Nemadi child's hips can do. So it was the new dance.*

—*Like hair-trigger*, Boubacar said.

—*Yes.*

—*So this made him the King.*

The Wastrel shook his head. —*It is my private opinion that he died a slave's death.*

—*So he was like Bani then. Bani was a slave but he sang like he was free.*

The Wastrel shook his head again. —*Bani was a griot. He was collecting all the songs and kept them alive. He did not die of drugs, I don't think. Better to be* harutine *than to die like that.*

—*Better to be dead*, Salem concurred, —*than to be alive that way.*

—*But the music*, Boubacar said, —*the music was good.*

—*I am the enslaved one here*, the Wastrel laughed, pounding his own forehead with his fist, —*teaching you to think like the* bizan.

—*I am thinking to listen to Benny Goodman,* the boy said. —*Someone told me he was also the King in America.*

The Wastrel looked at him sharply. —*Jazz. He stole from the blacks, the whites, the classical composers. He was a Jew.*

—*So he was like a griot,* Boubacar said. —*He took all the songs in and—*

Suddenly the Wastrel had other things to talk about. If you pressed the Wastrel on the subject of L'Américain and his music, you could snare him in the loops of his own words, and he would fall silent. Boubacar smiled. He would definitely need to listen to Benny Goodman soon.

Among the Mauritanians, there was disagreement on whether there would be time to stop at the all-night Waffle House before Salem and Teslem had to report for their shift beginning at five at the Lucky Leaf. So few of their nights had been spent out on the town in America that Teslem decided he must eat. It was almost three in the morning. Boubacar saw the play of a smile about the Wastrel's face, as if he, too, had enjoyed the freedom of being himself for the night. They circled the Waffle House in the three-toned car and decided they had time to go in. The place was so busy even at that hour that Teslem had to park the car behind the place.

The Waffle House was smoky, hot, and noisy inside. Most of the customers were black, and most of the help was white. There was a table full of men so black they looked almost blue. These men paused when they came in and nodded slowly at them. The Mauritanians recognized them as Somalians, and nodded uneasily. As a rule, they steered clear of all Somalians. They were too volatile, and too much influenced by the odd plant they smoked and sometimes used for money among themselves. The Mauritanians found a cramped little booth at the end of the place, as far away from the Somalians as possible, and squeezed themselves into it.

—*Ya'll talk English?* A malnourished-looking bleached blonde distributed menus all around, dispassionately as dealing cards. —*If not, just point and shoot.*

The Mauritanians stared at her.

—*Just show me the pitchers.*

They mumbled to each other in French. Boubacar pointed to the picture of the waffles with strawberries and whipped cream. Salem and Teslem conferred closely to avoid the pork products. The Wastrel was not of a mind to eat the *kaffir* food, and ordered coffee. The waitress whisked away the menus and came back with cups of thin coffee. An odd quiet came over the table. Boubacar felt very tired. He thought momentarily of going out to the car to sleep in its backseat until the food came. But that would be soon.

The waitress arrived and set their food down.

They were deeply intent on their food and didn't notice the Somalians leave.

When they had debated the proper amount of money to leave beside the plate for the waitress, they filed out. Teslem was leading the way, and when they came around the building, he put his arms out like wings to stop the others. He stared straight ahead.

The Somalians were moving warily away from the taxi-painted car. The door on the driver's side had been broken open, and its lining was ripped and spilling onto the asphalt of the parking lot. The linings of the seats had been likewise slashed, as if they'd been searching for something.

Boubacar's heart wobbled with fear.

—*They will be having guns or knives,* Salem offered helpfully, as they hesitated there on the curb.

—*Or both,* Teslem suggested.

—*It is only a car,* said the Wastrel. —*It is not worth dying for.*

Teslem raised his hands in a kind of tired benediction, to show the Somalians, no harm.

The Somalians kept backing away, and they, too, put up their hands, as if to keep them away. Just then, the front seat and dashboard ignited with a *whoomf.*

An old white Chevy pulled into the parking lot then, and the Somalians ran to it as its doors opened. The car's tires made so much noise leaving the parking lot that the manager of the Waffle House soon came out to see what had happened. He found the Mauritanians flapping with their coats at the smoldering inside of the front seat, doors wide open, seats slashed.

—*I'm calling the cops,* he said. —*You stay right where you are. They'll have to do the report for your insurance.*

Insurance? Salem and Teslem looked at each other. It appeared they would not make the five o'clock shift at the Lucky Leaf. They would more than likely lose their jobs. After the restaurant manager went back inside, the three of them stared at the charred car.

—*Also in Minneapolis, Minnesota,* Salem offered, —*there are many good African eating establishments.*

Special Riders

Callie pushed her green beans around on her plate to simulate eating. The girl with the bougainvillea hair ate only green beans, nothing else. Chance extracted each caper from his chicken with surgical precision, like buckshot from personal wounds. He stacked them at the edge of the plate in an accusatory pile. Raine got up to serve the pavlova, a recipe she'd got from a magazine. She wanted the guest to feel special. But everyone was ignoring the girl, including Chance. All were watching the new little white television mounted beneath a kitchen cupboard. It was the gift Raine's family gave her when they realized they'd forgotten her birthday.

Now there was no refuge from televisions anywhere in the house except bathrooms. Now during dinner Matthew read the newspaper with one eye and tracked his mutual fund with the other, *barely perceptible gains*. On the evening of the girl's visit, the local news staff put itself through its stations of the cross.

—*A three-year-old girl dead tonight after a Hickory Ridge drug bust.*

—*The shrubbery thief strikes again in Germantown.*

—*A local flower vendor arrested at a local department store for vandalism. Full details, coming right up.*

Raine looked up in time to see the news footage of the Catfish Lady curled into a tight ball inside her striped pony blanket, policemen on either side of her, carrying her by her elbows out of a Memphis mall. Raine sat down slowly with the pavlova before her, her eyes on the little white TV. She spooned the dessert into tulip bowls and handed them around.

The dead child's Olan Mills photo flashed on the screen, then off. A microphone in the face of a neighbor: *selling cookies.* And there it was: the Catfish Lady, her stiff arms providing handles for the policemen to carry her by. *Caught on store surveillance tape, . . . damage estimated in the thousands.*

Raine watched as the small figure in the pony blanket was swinging the lamp left then right, shattering the same stuttering blue blur on a row of televisions all keyed to the same channel.

—*Crazy old bitch,* Matthew said, and flapped his newspaper. —*I'm so sick of the homeless. Reagan let them all out of their cages, and now we have to live among them.*

—*Haven't you ever wanted to smash a television?*

—*Only when the Cards are losing,* he said, without looking up.

Raine went to stand at the kitchen window.

> *In the cities of the caesars.*
> *In the orchard of abandoned dreams.*

She put a fingertip on the bottle-cap birdhouse, as if she could read the words inside that way.

Down in Madagascar, Dean Fondren walked from his kitchen to the den, newspaper in one hand, cup of coffee in the other. It was bad coffee; he didn't make it as well as Alexis did when she was home. He eased himself into his chair across the room from the television, clicked it on with the remote control, and began to unlace his work boots. He'd taken to wearing them into the house as far as the kitchen in Alexis's absence. There were other signs. Her mail in a pile beside the hall-tree, a sheaf of obsolete phone messages stuck under a magnet on the refrigerator. He'd rearranged some things in the kitchen, putting them where he'd always wanted them to be. Then there was the damn television, which he'd taken to leaving on, just to have some human noise in the house.

He eased one boot off and looked up at the news anchorman's face.

A dead child's school picture. City councilmen sitting around a table with their hands folded. A commercial for furniture, a fat man shouting about his cheap wares as if the world were on fire and there was this one true last chance to own a zebra-print couch. A woman vandalizing televisions, shattering them: *six televisions before security guards arrived on the scene. Damage estimated in the thousands of dollars, possible charges of felony vandalism . . . Shelby County Jail.*

Dean sat straight up, boot in hand.

The woman was Marie Abide.

He could barely make out what she was swinging the lamp at, a baby elephant? Ringed about with small Asian men?

He put his boot back on. He went in the kitchen and dialed information, then spoke slowly into it. —*Memphis . . . the Shelby County Jail, please.* He jotted the number down and cursed softly as a recorded voice offered to separate him from sixty cents by dialing the number for him, as if he were a personage of such importance that he should not even dial the number himself. —*Fools,* he cursed. Fortunes were made on the backs of such fools. He dialed the number. A woman answered with consummate boredom, —*Shebby County Jail,* and Dean could hear shouts and echoes in the background.

—*Marie Abide is her name. She's a small woman, about sixty, with very blue eyes. She has this blanket she wears—*

—I'm sorry, we have no record of a Marie Abide at this moment. She may not have been processed yet.

Raine stood at the foot of the stairs, her car keys in hand.

Chance and the girl were on the landing halfway up, the boy noodling with the guitar.

—Why don't you want to do it? Chance asked the girl.

—'I want to eat your cancer?' Please. Ooh, baby, life sucks and that's why I'm dead but my songs will suck right on forever. That is so totally ten years ago.

Silence.

—Here's one I'm writing for you, Raine overheard her son say, desperately. A few bright chords lacerated the stairwell.

I don't mean trouble, please don't put me down or get upset,
I am not pleadin' or sayin' I can't forget.
I do not walk the floor bowed down and bent but yet,
Mama, you been on my mind.

—You asshole, said the girl with the bougainvillea hair. *—Dylan wrote that before we were born.*

—Anybody need anything from anywhere? Raine called up the stairs. *—I have to go to the mall.* No one answered, and she left.

It was the perfect cover.

The jukebox man's apartment was on the third level of the sixth building, its stairs obscured by the neighbor's small ornamental maples in big clay pots. Raine lifted the brass doorknocker and let it drop, twice. Instantly she regretted it. She had not rehearsed whatever it was she was going to say, because she did not know whatever it was she wanted from the man.

He opened the door a few inches, wary, not exactly welcoming. Then he recognized her and his face softened.

—*Are you okay? Come in.*

—*The Catfish Lady*, Raine blurted, still rooted to his little balcony. —*She*—

—*I know. I saw the news.*

—*I thought I'd go to the jail.*

—*That's a pretty rough neighborhood around there.* He was already putting on his loafers by then and grabbing his wallet and keys off a small table by his front door. It seemed a profound intimacy, for him to let her see where he put them down whenever he came home.

He led her down the sidewalk outside to an old white Land Rover, parked at the end of the line of cars facing the apartments. It looked decrepit. She loved it, for some reason, but she wondered how reliable it was. —*Is this*, she began.

—*It has a lot of space in the back*, he said.

—*Sort of a jukebox hearse*, she said.

—*Ambulance!* he said, laughing. —*I prefer to think of it as that. It'll fit right in at the jail.*

—*I wonder why she did it*, Raine said as they crossed the Wolf River bridge.

—*Makes perfect sense to me*, he said.

Dean Fondren sat watching the mid-evening teaser for the eleven o'clock news. There she went again: Miss Abide swinging a trendy cast-iron lamp, taking out the televisions.

She never bothered anybody most of the time, though she had seemed to be having difficulties lately. But she had never been the sort to do anything without a good reason. Even her birdhouses had a weird logic to them. He had not taken his boots off, just in case.

Dean called the jail again. He described her eyes, the pony blanket, her black bowler hat.

—*Nope*, said a woman's curt voice. —*Maybe they took her to the horspital. Call over to the Med and ass them to connect you to the psych ward.*

—*I want to leave my name and number. You got a pen?* He spelled his name and wondered if the woman was actually writing it down. He could hear shouting and raucous noise in the background, police sirens and catcalling. He looked at his watch. It was eight o'clock.

Clinging like a band of old barnacles around the Shelby County Jail were concentric rings of bail-bond establishments, storefronts with black bars identical to those used in jails. The jail itself took up an entire city block, an imposing cube of ugly brick, surrounded by high fencing and concertina wire. Raine and the jukebox man circled and circled. He was looking for the one that belonged to someone he went to high school with. *Angel Bail Bonds, Alpha Omega Bail Bonds, Free at Last Bail Bonds.* Old men with faces lined like dark atlases smoked and watched them pass. *Abyssinian Bail Bonds, Superbad Bail Bonds, Volunteer State Bail Bonds, Davy Crockett Bail Bonds.*

—*This is it*, he said, parking the car in front of a storefront with grillwork over its window. *Black Cat Bonds.*

The jukebox man's friend was already there, dressed in his running gear.

—*I think if somebody will just go claim her, the county'll go with a misdemeanor to get rid of her. On the other hand, bail could go as high as ten thou, in which case, you'd have to put up ten percent.*

Raine and the jukebox man looked at each other.

—We don't even know her name.

—That makes it a little harder. Something has to be put up for this.

Raine and the jukebox man hesitated. Money?

—That one old jukebox you showed me, the friend suggested.

The jukebox man deliberated. *—You talking about the Wurlitzer or the Seeburg?*

—Seeburg, the friend said.

—Okay, the jukebox man said affably. *—She skips, you get the Seeburg, goddammit.*

Raine laughed and looked at her watch. As far as her family knew at home, she was still in the mall, consuming for them, underwear, shoes, sheets, towels, toothpaste.

When the matron at the Shelby County Jail brought the Catfish Lady out, she had an angry bruise over her left eye, and her lip was cut. The matron held a white plastic garbage bag containing the woman's possessions. *—Now don't you buss nobody television no more,* she cautioned the Catfish Lady, but not without affection.

—We want to take you home, Raine said softly.

Safely ensconced in the backseat of the white Land Rover, the Catfish Lady directed them towards the river, then asked them to turn south onto Third. They drove for blocks, until scuffed old brick warehouses gave way to bungalows with bars on their windows, and the bungalows gave way to Highway 61. Raine looked at her watch and took a deep breath.

—You okay with this? The jukebox man kept glancing at her, then back at the road.

—Sure, she nodded. *—It just feels like we're crossing the Mother of all Bridges.*

—We may be, he said, leaning forward and looking up, as if he were navigating by the stars over the open fields.

Dean Fondren was awakened about nine by a symphony of tele-
phones ringing in the kitchen, in the bedroom, and right beside
his ear. He had dozed off on the couch, waiting to watch the
news again.

—*Yello?*

—*Mr. Fondren?*

—*Speaking.*

—*I'm sorry to bother you but I'm calling you about your
friend.*

—*I'm her brother. And her lawyer.* Even as the lies rolled off
his tongue, Dean realized he was talking to the girl with the
green Comet. —*Peregrine? Is that you?*

—*Yes. I'm calling about your friend, Mr. Ellerbee.*

—*Where are you? I mean, where is he?*

—*I'm at work. I think you need to come see about him.
He's a little drunk. Actually he is very drunk. I heard a couple
of the croupiers talking, something about some papers he was
supposed to sign.*

Silence ensued, while Dean thought. —*Where is he right now?*

—*He's at a table over there waiting for me to bring him
another drink.*

—*And where are the people with the papers?*

—*They are upstairs somewhere.*

—*Well, here's what I need you to do until I can get there.
You separate him from those people somehow.*

—*They want me to keep bringing him drinks.*

—*Get him to the front door and wait for me there.*

Raine knew they were near the Catfish Lady's home when she
saw the first TRUST JESUS sign tacked to a tree. The handwriting
matched the birdhouses. MADAGASCAR, said the city limit sign.
The only signs of life were in a little grocery, whose OPEN sign

hung slightly askew. As they passed, a Chinese man was moving about inside. A cat was silhouetted in the plate glass window. There was an old juke joint with some cars around it, and a cluster of tired trailers behind an abandoned gas station.

The Catfish Lady leaned forward and said, —*Turn here, please.*

The lane led to an arch: ANARCHY GARDEN OF THE MEZZA-LUNA MILLENNIUM.

Stovepipe animals leaned forward like a welcoming committee. A giraffe stood shoulder to shoulder with a horse; an enormous tiger watched over a stout chicken. The trees were cobwebbed with gold Christmas lights, and mobiles made of pie pans turned slightly, catching the light.

—*You know my father was Henri Matisse,* the woman commented, and rustled her plastic bag impatiently. She opened her door before the car stopped rolling, so the jukebox man braked suddenly, and Raine braced herself on the dashboard. There was a light on inside the house, as if someone were waiting for her there. The jukebox man opened his door to walk the woman to her door, and Raine got out. They walked up onto the porch with her, but she stopped at the door.

The little porch was tiled entirely with elegant shards of china. In one glance Raine saw several types of Haviland, Spode, Delft, English Blue Willow, Fiestaware. When the woman opened her door, they got a glimpse of the inside of the boathouse. A small army cot with a faded Russian shawl, red roses on a black background, an old Tiffany lamp beside a faded mauve chair, a tiny potbellied stove.

—*I thank you kindly,* the woman said, investing the words with the finality of a curtain falling. A rattle of tin animals, and she was gone.

—*My God,* Raine said.

—*Do you suppose that grocery is celestial enough to give us coffee this time of night?*

Pulling his truck into the parking lot of the Celestial, Dean could see Angus pouring coffee for a couple at the table beside the window. He didn't know them, didn't know the car, a white Land Rover with Shelby County plates. He let the engine idle a few seconds. He didn't have time to wait on Angus to close up. He put the truck in reverse and headed back out to the highway.

He was going to tell Aubrey his house was on fire. No. He'd tell him the truth, that he was drunk and didn't know half of what was being done to him. And if Aubrey didn't agree to come with him, he might just clock him a good one, and throw him over his shoulder.

He *really* should have brought Angus for backup.

He'd been watching too much television, he thought. He was starting to think like a television. The truck kicked up a little gravel as he turned onto Highway 61. The dogs barked in excitement.

Raine and the jukebox man saw a farmer in a pickup truck pull up outside the window, saw a man staring straight ahead. Two dogs peeped around the cab, waiting for their cues. Then the man backed the truck around, and hurried on down the road.

The Chinese man barely looked up from his newspaper when they came in, his curiosity hardly rumpling his eyebrows. A fat calico cat was sleeping belly-up on the corner of his newspaper with its feet propped on the cash register. The smell of coffee caused the jukebox man to close his eyes in pleasure. He brought over two chipped mugs, one that read *Tchulahoma Feed and Seed* and one that read *Arkansas Razorbacks*.

—*Will you look at that*, the man said softly, rising from his chair, carrying his coffee with him. Raine turned, and saw the old jukebox in the corner. —*How long have you had this?* he called to the Chinese man who was scraping down his grill with some kind of carpenter's tool.

—*My daddy took delivery of it in 1938. Been here ever since.*

—*That's the year it was made.*

—*It's needing some work on it. Play the wrong thing half the time, don't play at all the other half.*

—*How much you take for it?*

—*Not for sale*, the Chinese man shook his head, annoyed. —*Get you a quarter out of that cup up there and see what it'll do for you. It got a mind of its own.*

They studied the names a long time before they could decide.

—*Oh, I love Slim Harpo*, Raine said. —*Play 'Scratch My Back.'*

—*Definitely.*

They slid the coins in, took their coffee back to the big window, and waited expectantly.

I want you . . . to be my tee-ni-nee-ni-nu.

—*Flip side*, the Chinese man called out. —*Least you didn't get the Louvins.*

—*Good dance song*, the jukebox man said, and sighed.

Raine knew what he was thinking; she was thinking the same thing. It was a shame to waste such a good song by being perfectly still. Dancing to the rhythm of that song would have been a fair substitute for what they both wanted to do.

At the Lucky Leaf, Dean parked his truck in the handicapped zone and left the engine running. Belle and Cobain paced around in the back of the truck, agitated but not barking. He could see a uniformed man coming towards him. He knew the man; he had driven a tractor for him a few summers before the casino was completed.

—Good evening, Mr. Fondren, may we hep you?

—Watch my dogs for me. I'll be back in a minute...

Inside Dean noticed there was a long line of automated tellers for almost any bank you could name, and a long line of fools waiting to get to each one. Somehow Peregrine Smith-Jones had got Aubrey to agree to sit down on a long bench near a cashier's window. She was sitting elegantly beside him, her long stockinged legs crossed. She was holding his hand, as if her grandfather were visiting her at finishing school for the afternoon.

Dean stood over Aubrey, towering over him, and Aubrey seemed to crumple under his stare then. But he looked Dean in the eye.

—Well sir, Aubrey said, *—I reckon you come to take me to the house, look like.*

—That's right, Dean said. *—One way or the other. You pick whichever way.*

Aubrey sighed, and his shoulders slumped, as if he were ready to be rescued from himself.

—You don't get out of this place, Aubrey, them jackasses in Nevada going to own your ass before breakfast, Dean persevered.

Aubrey stood up, pulling somewhat on the girl's shoulder. *—You are a good girl,* he said. *—And you ever want you a real job, come see me.*

—Still got your wallet, Aubrey? Dean said.

—Yep. I got it, I believe. For whatever that's worth anymore. I been in the belly of the beast, this evening.

—Aw, you ain't seen the belly yet, Dean grumbled at him. *—They got Miss Abide up there in the Shelby County Jail. That's the belly.*

—Lord have mercy, Aubrey murmured. *—We got to go fetch her home, look like.*

—You ain't in no shape to fetch nobody from nowhere, Dean said.

The girl said, *—Can we stop on the way and get my camera?*

—You can get it while I drop the dogs off. What about your job? Dean asked the girl.

—I quit, she drawled, *—look like.*

Dean began to grin. She had a nice drawl.

Once they got Aubrey up into the cab of the pickup truck, the girl stepped up and perched herself beside him, propping him up while Dean walked around to the other side.

—Aubrey, this girl's great-grandmother was Ariadne Jones.

—Ariadne delivered us all, Aubrey said expansively, fanning his hands to the far corners of the windshield, as if to embrace the entire Delta. *—She delivered us into this world. Such world as it is.* Lowering his hands to brace himself on the dashboard, he stared ahead at the road, as if he were carved onto the prow of a ship. *—Everybody all the time deliverin' each other, look like.*

Outside the Celestial, the jukebox man opened the passenger door for Raine, but she lingered. A mandala of stars seemed to wheel in the sky over the little grocery and the fields. An enormous old tree with heart-shaped leaves seemed to curve itself around the little building.

—I can't remember the last time I could see the stars this clearly, she said. *—I think it was 1973 or so.*

—Look, the jukebox man said, pointing to the boathouse. The Catfish Lady's trees were aglow with an ornate circuitry of animal topiaries amid the gold Christmas-light cobwebs, like fiery piñatas.

—If I did that to my house the neighbors would tar and feather me.

—No wonder you have a problem with the bridges that go home.

She didn't speak for a minute, so he reached out, barely touching her hair, then pulled his hand back. *—Actually I'm* *the one who has a problem with bridges home now. Every one we cross will be taking you away from me.*

The confusions of her heart blossomed into fear. She couldn't hear, she couldn't think. He bent to kiss her then, car door still open, while the Chinese man's cat watched from the plate glass window.

They drove in silence past the darkened fields, then he turned suddenly off the highway, onto a dirt road, then a gravel one.

—*Where are we going?* she asked.

—*I'm not really sure,* he said.

They crossed a cattle-gap and began the slow ascent to the top of the levee. He stopped the car along the ridge, and they got out. Out in the darkness was the river like a fat ribbon, benign and formidable at once. Upriver, a barge raked the bluffs with its searchlight. Raine leaned back against the car.

—*The sign says 'no trespassing,'* she said.

—*I know,* he said. —*Have you ever in your life trespassed?*

—*I don't think so. Not on purpose.*

—*Sometimes trespassing is necessary*, he said. She opened her mouth to speak, but he bent to kiss her before her murmurs could become refusal. With only a startled owl as witness, they began to undress each other beside the car. The metal of the car was cold against Raine's back, and he curved his body around her like shelter. The wind was a warm gentle insistence.

The Slim Harpo song was still pulsing in Raine's mind: *I want you . . . I want you.* She closed her eyes and seemed to see herself from a distance. Music was such an old sweet conspiracy. It had put her into Matthew's arms once, and now it was putting her—

—*Wait,* she said, pulling her clothes back around her. —*Wait. I'm sorry.*

He pulled away from her then, but he didn't let go.

—*I'm sorry,* she said. —*I think I need to go home.*

—*You are home,* he said, his hands trembling, bending her back against the car.

She stared over his shoulder at the stars. So this is the way it would be.

—*Look at me,* he said, turning her face to his, moving his body in a way that raised her from the dead. —*Look at me when we do this. I need to see you.*

—*Will you lookit that old moon,* Aubrey mused, still wedged in the front seat between Peregrine and Dean, his hands clasped childlike on his raised knees. Silver fields seemed to sail past them out the truck windows. —*I believe I could use me some sleep.*

—*You could use you some coffee,* Dean said.

—*Ain't this Tutwiler we passin' through? You want to just drop me off here with the sisters? They got a program. I been givin' it some thought.*

—*Now there's an idea,* Dean said. —*But I believe it's past the sisters' bedtime, Aubrey.*

The front door was locked, and the lights inside the little lobby were low. A Hispanic woman was mopping the floor. She saw Dean peering through the glass, and walked over. As she came nearer, Dean saw that it was Consuela, the woman who'd worked for Angus a while.

—*Back door,* she called through the glass, motioning over her shoulder.

By the time Dean and Peregrine had helped Aubrey around to the back, Consuela was standing there holding the door open.

—*Sisters is asleep,* she said. —*Is emergency?*

—*Well, how you doin', Consuela?* Aubrey said in his party-time voice.

She looked at Dean expectantly.

—*Just let me lay down on that gurney over there,* Aubrey said. —*I ain't hard to please.* He was already crawling onto the clean white sheets.

—Sisters can do his paperwork tomorrow, Consuela warned Dean. *—He wakes up these babies, and he will sleep underneath the stars tonight.*

Not long after that Dean and the girl were standing in the Shelby County Jail. While Dean waited in line behind some women trying to locate their men, Peregrine walked slowly around the room, snapping photos. She knelt in a corner to get a shot of the black baby and the Hispanic baby playing together on the floor stacking empty soft drink cans. She snapped an old Vietnamese man dressed nattily in a Hong Kong silk suit, studying the dog-race form. By the time she walked up to stand beside Dean, the big matron with the buttery voice was saying, *—Tawmbout that old lady what buss the televisions? Somebody done already came for her.*

Entering the double-helix of traffic that would carry her home, Raine breathed slowly and evenly. The earth was not going to end, nor would the stars fall from the sky. The moon was the same old silver bauble, shimmering in its black socket, immune to the longings it engendered below. Hundreds out on the highway at the same time, and any life could end in a matter of seconds. Hundreds of faces, illuminated by each other's lights, each face masking a separate story. Everyone was being careful, sorting themselves into the long shimmer of red taillights.

What would the rest of life be? Raine wondered. The requirements of home could be called *cognitive dissonance*, or they could be called *love*. She eased the car into the next lane over, and a car to the right of her slowed down to let her in. Everyone was waiting for the right moment. She braided herself into the right river of cars, the calm communion of strangers intent on home, wherever it was.

By the Waters of Babyland

Every Saturday was payday for Tomás Tulia's men. After they had showered in the bunkhouse, they usually came into the Celestial all at the same time, ready to cash their checks and buy their six-packs and cigarettes before heading to Memphis for their night on the town. Angus had started to keep more cash on hand, but it made him nervous whenever the Brinks armored truck was parked outside the store, big as a billboard: *rob me.* And he was always glad when the last of Tulia's workers had cashed his check and headed out the door, and the premises were once again of no real interest to anyone intent on armed robbery. On such days, Angus didn't have time to skim his newspapers until after five, when he poured himself the dregs of the coffee and took the paper outside to the porch.

Futuristics, up for the fourth day in a row. Dixie Barrel, holding at forty-four. Everything else of his was still falling. The Mauritanian boy was inside the store, filling the salt shakers on each table, singing along to the jukebox, *Baby, scratch my back.* He liked to keep a constant stream of red-painted quarters going into it and accepted with delight whatever it chose to play. Angus heard the phone ring, heard the boy answer it. It had taken Angus awhile to get the boy confident enough with his English to cover the phone.

—*Is for you*, the boy said through the screen door.

—*Who is it?* Angus asked, annoyed. —*Maybe I ain't here.*

—*The sister. From the Catholics.*

Angus weighted his newspaper with his coffee cup and went inside. It was more like Sister Aurelia to call Aubrey when she needed something.

—*Mr. Chien?*

—*Yes, ma'am. What can I do for you?*

—*We just admitted a woman here, and she's asking for you.* This was not Sister Aurelia, but another of the nuns from the clinic at Tutwiler.

—*Well, put her on*, Angus said.

—*She can't come to the phone*, the sister explained. —*She's in labor. She was driving and had to stop. I think she may have been in labor a while before she got here. We can't locate her husband. There are release forms to be signed, things of that nature.*

—*I'll be right there*, Angus said. He looked out the window, deciding what number to dial, based on whose truck was visible. Aubrey was gone, and so was Dean. He walked into the bunkhouse without knocking and found one of Tulia's workers, shirtless and shaving up for his Saturday night.

—*You going to Memphis? I need to get to Tutwiler, pretty quick. Pronto.*

Some hours later, Angus was dozing on the worn couch with a magazine open on his lap when he sensed someone near. He had been snoring a bit and felt grumpy to have been caught snoring. He opened his eyes.

It was Consuela.

She was dressed in pale blue scrubs with fat pink cherubim cavorting around on them, and she was wearing her little white

Keds. She glared down at him. She was angry with him still, he could see. And why not? He owed her money. He would have preferred to wake up a little more before having to deal with this.

—*Sister say is time to come see your baby.*

Angus struggled to orient himself within the words *your* and *baby*, and stood up, shaky on his feet after sitting so long. She turned abruptly and strode down the corridor, pointing dramatically at the door he was to enter.

—*Is the baby okay?* he called after her, forcing his stiff legs to follow.

In the sepulchral light that came through the blinds, Lisa lay in the bed, but no baby. She smiled at him in a confused way. She held her hand out to him. He walked over to the side of the bed, and took her hand with reluctance.

—*Could you hear me?* Lisa mumbled softly, drugged against pain. —*I was calling you. Oh, Angus, it's you.* She closed her eyes again, drifted away.

Before Angus could speak, he heard a slight mewling behind him and turned. Consuela and one of the sterner of the sisters stood framed by the doorway, with the light bright behind them. He saw the little bundle then, *Alice.*

He held his arms out to take the baby, and Consuela held it tighter and glared at him. He turned to go, feeling like a tree with mismatched roots.

She thought he was the father of this baby.

He began to grin, in spite of himself. This only made Consuela glare more.

—*No, don't go, Angus,* Lisa said in a slurred plaintive way, and so he sat stiffly in a straight-backed plastic chair. A sister unwrapped the mewling baby with much ceremony.

—*I'm so tired,* Lisa said. —*I think I'm too tired for this.*

—*It's better for the baby,* the nun said and shoved aside Lisa's bed jacket, exposing her swollen breast. Angus looked away then, busying himself with his fingernails, his cuffs. There was an empty soybean field outside the window that he suddenly needed to stare at. He seemed to remember that some time had to pass before women had milk to give their babies. But he supposed the sisters knew what they were doing better than he did.

Lisa, intent on the baby, forgot he was there for a few moments.

Consuela murmured in Spanish to the baby, and Lisa looked up at Angus then, still woozy. The nun left the room in a rustle of pantyhose.

—*It's like being nibbled by a rosebud*, Lisa smiled to Consuela, who looked dubious. As soon as the words left her lips, Lisa's body seemed to fold itself over in pain, and her scream dislodged the baby, who then began to cry. Angus rose out of his chair just in time to keep the baby from being pitched to the floor. He held Alice in his hands and looked into her red, squalling face, and Consuela gently took the baby from him. Mother and child were screaming in concert.

—*Is too soon*, Consuela whispered. —*I told the sister, but she don't listen.*

Two more sisters rushed in to claim the baby and whisk it out of sight as if Lisa had failed some test or broken some vow of silence. One sister was flipping pieces of paper on a clipboard, checking to see if she could perhaps be drugged more. Lisa clutched at Angus's hand, her face gray with pain.

—*This day is going to be over soon*, Angus whispered to her, calming her. —*Tomorrow be a whole new day.*

—*I never want to do this again*, she whispered, the pain crumpling her like a burning leaf.

—*I need you to take down a number and call it*, Angus said to Consuela. —*She needs her husband here. We ain't been able to raise him on the phone.*

—They got the number on her chart, Consuela said. *—The sisters will call.*

—No, they won't, Angus fretted. *—They think I'm the daddy. They think I did this to her.*

Consuela's face seemed to soften then, and he understood that she had thought the same thing. That understanding made him feel tired in his heart. *My life is open like a book she can't read,* he thought hopelessly. What would it take to be seen for what he was, somebody who needed company?

Lisa was rocking herself to sleep, and he held her hand.

Angus sat down, exhausted, on the edge of the bed, his legs thin as fence rails. He clasped his hands together a moment and moved to lie down behind Lisa. He realized then how thin the sheet and her nightgown were, no protection in this world, and he pulled up the cotton blanket from the foot of the bed. He put his hand on Lisa's forehead and talked to her like she was the baby, speaking softly in unintelligible murmurs in his old rusty Chinese. It was like holding a stone capable of cursing, he realized, to hold a woman who was hurting. He felt her uncurl in his arms, minute by minute, as the pain began to subside. She sighed after a while, her breath like a scrap of ripping silk. She took one of his hands then and held it close to her. The room grew darker, quieter. He had forgotten to tell the Mauritanian boy to lock the store when he left. He supposed he'd figure it out.

He heard Consuela in the doorway, and he raised his head to look at her, questioning, and she shook her head, *no.*

Angus closed his eyes then and drifted in and out of sleep until one of the sisters came back, holding the mewling baby, standing in the doorway like the angel of judgment. Consuela held out her arms for the baby, and the nun seemed happy to hand it over.

Consuela put the baby down near Lisa's breasts, and Angus,

from behind her, smoothed the baby's dark velvet head. The baby whimpered and flailed her arms.

—*I show you a little trick,* Consuela said to Lisa.

She unwrapped the baby from its cocoon of white cotton flannel, then rewrapped the blanket tightly, mitering the corners the same way Angus did the corners of the white paper he wrapped roasts in at his store. —*Tight, like tamale,* she said to Lisa. —*So they think the world is a tight little place like it used to be.*

—*Oh,* Lisa murmured.—*Like an egg roll.*

Consuela showed Lisa then how to hold the baby sideways to her breast. Angus felt a hot pressure behind his eyes when she did that, as if perhaps he had lived too long. It was like the moments the black midwife had presented him with his babies. —*Is going to hurt you some down in your belly the first times,* Consuela said.

Lisa was not shy about showing her breast, and the room held only the sound of the baby's smacking. When the baby began to suck, Lisa looked up at Consuela fearfully. When the pains came again, Consuela cupped her palm against Lisa's belly and made soft circular motions, full of some kind of opaque efficiency Angus didn't understand.

Angus sat on the other side of the bed, his legs dangling. He took off his glasses and rubbed the bridge of his nose. He remembered then a long-ago winter night, and the little room behind his store, and Rose, after the first baby, and the midwife Ariadne, making those slow competent circles with her hands. He looked out the window at the open fields, the sun coming up. The hospital room was full of quiet, a stillness that was beyond any hurrying the world out the window could impose. For a few seconds, Angus wanted to stay there for always.

There was only the sound of smacking in the room. Lisa opened her eyes and began to study the baby, memorizing the

details of her earlobes, her ankles, her tiny fingernails. The subject of Jimmy's disappearance was closed somehow, no longer
necessary to discuss.

—*What you will name this baby?* Consuela said. —*You got
one yet?*

—*I had a sister name of Alice one time, long time ago,*
Angus heard himself say.

—*Alice is good name,* Consuela said.

—*Alice,* Lisa nodded drowsily.

When baby Alice fell deeply asleep, Consuela gently detached
her from Lisa's breast with a competent flourish, and a sideways glance for Angus. Angus had moved back to the rigid plastic chair and was craving sleep, something more than a quick
doze in a public place. Lisa herself was nodding off to sleep, so
Angus followed Consuela down the corridor to see where she
was taking the baby.

—*You got any bed where I can take me a nap?* Angus
inquired, glancing into the rooms they passed, where all beds
seemed full.

—*No way,* Consuela said. —*Is SRO.*

—*SRO?*

—*Like in casino when the house is full. You got to stand up,*
she explained.

He followed her into a little nursery, with three plastic
bassinets in it and one incubator. She put baby Alice in a
bassinet. —*Is good hospital here with the sisters,* she said.
—*My niece's baby Umberto is born here, and I stay to work.*

She busied herself with something inconsequential across
the room, plumping the cushions in a maple rocker. Angus saw
the other babies then, two of them in the little bassinets.

—*We don't get many of dads in here. These one. You ever*

see a crack baby? The daddy come in here like gangster, take a
look, drive off in the big black Escalade.

She crossed herself. Angus thought he saw the outline of his
old buckeye at the center of the invisible crucifix she outlined
on her chest. It *was* there, he was sure of it.

Angus peered cautiously over the side of the bassinet. The
crack baby was thin, its brows furrowed with knowledge. *Long
life*, Angus thought, but it made him tired, to confer long life
upon such a little traveler. He looked at Alice, whose mouth was
pursed like a little rosebud. He thought he saw a smile playing
across her face, as if she were greatly amused at having been born.
Her life stretched out in front of him into infinity, which frightened him, so he sat down in the maple rocker and looked around.

—*You like working here? Sisters take care of you okay?*

—*Got good benefits*, Consuela said, tossing her head, and
the old hauteur he knew and loved was back. He suddenly
could feel every word he should have said to her blossoming in
his mouth all over again. She picked up one of the crack babies
and began to sing something soft in Spanish, —*Candela, mi
candela*, clutching the baby close, as if she suddenly had no
truck with the sisters and their plastic bassinets. She knew the
old ways, too, Angus realized. Then to his surprise, she put the
crack baby in his arms.

—*You hang around here, we put you to work*, she said
gruffly. —*Holding babies is very good for bad hearts.*

—*I reckon it is*, Angus said, looking down into a tiny coffee-
colored face that was not entirely convinced that his journey to
earth had been worth the trouble.

When Consuela came back later, the crack baby was nestled
into the hollow of Angus's neck, wide-eyed, awake. Angus was
sleeping deeply. Now and then he rocked once, gently, then
went still. Consuela went to lift the baby out of his iron hands,
which held the baby firmly even as he dozed.

—*Whmh*, he said, waking up without knowing where he was.

—*Sister say she will drive you home*, Consuela said, prying the baby out of the vice of his fingers.

He swam up out of his sleep, and murmured, —*Thank you, but Dean is on stand-by to get me home.*

–*Hey. Angus Chien. You need to get you a car. Es American way. You drive over here and rock these crack baby with me.*

—*Well, I guess I know where you at now*, Angus said, pleased.

—*Is true.*

—*And if you ever want to come back to work with me, you always welcome at the Celestial. And that is verdad.*

She smiled at his effort with Spanish. When she spoke, the words were soft. —*Sisters treat me good. In my country, I was la partera. It was my work, to catch the babies when they come.*

—*So you delivered my grandbaby.*

Consuela nodded. —*She is good baby, very strong.*

—*Do you think*, Angus began, and then stopped and sighed. —*If I was to—*

—*You are good baby rocker*, she said, helpfully.

—*I had a lot of practice, long time ago*, he said softly.

—*You want to see me, come see these crack baby. I ain't going nowhere but here. I stay here so Hector will know where to find me.*

He looked at her, and because he didn't have a good feeling about Hector's whereabouts, he said, —*I need you to make me a promise. I need you to stay where I can find you. And I will stay where you can find me. And I know the name of a lady in Memphis that can help us look for Hector.*

When Dean Fondren later dropped Angus off in front of the Celestial, Angus went straight to the phone to dial Jimmy's

number. Still no answer. What was the point of paying for so
many separate phones if you didn't answer any of them? Angus
needed sleep, but he slipped on his stained apron anyway and
rolled up his sleeves. The place looked no worse for wear the
twenty-four hours or so he'd been gone. Somebody, he thought,
looking at the African boy, had burned a fair amount of bacon.

Angus was stacking cans of corned beef hash in a pyramid
when the front door opened with a jingle. There was Jimmy,
happy and exuberant.

—*Pop-pop, I had the best run of luck last night. It was
awesome.*

Angus raised his hand tiredly and patted Jimmy on the back.
He was still in the soft bubble of his own childhood. Angus
would give him sixty seconds more childhood. Then he'd speak.

The Celestial Jukebox

At daybreak, the skies were already a sullen gray bulge over Louisiana across the river. The regulars in the Celestial were in agreement: *coonasses is getting all our rain.*

—*Dean,* said one of the Telephone Pioneers. —*It was a A-rab in here the other day, asking about Aubrey's duster over there in the hangar. Said he wanted to talk to whoever owned it about buying it.*

Dean shrugged, and poured himself two cups of coffee into Styrofoam cups and squeezed lids on them.

—*I know there's a flying school takes them in downriver,* he said.

—*Was asking Angus about the tanks on the back, and how they worked. Acted like money wasn't no object. Said he could pay cash.*

—*Them A-rabs got money,* another opined.

—*Well,* Dean said. —*Why don't he get on the Internet and get his own plane, without bothering Aubrey?*

Weeks later they'd try to remember the man, when every television and radio in America were playing the same sight over and over, the two towers falling. They'd try to recall his face and his clothes and his car.

But on the morning the man had been in Madagascar, Dean excused himself and headed home.

Dean wanted every hour to count, so he took his coffee and ate his toast in the truck. He drove back to the edge of the long field and parked his truck up by the road. He noticed that the green Comet was gone. By nine-thirty in the morning, one of the belts had broken on the tractor, and he had to drive all the way to Clarksdale.

As he turned onto Issaquena Avenue, he noticed state troopers and roadblocks. People milled about like ants, carrying hampers and stadium umbrellas. He mouthed a silent curse and parked bumper to bumper with a shiny little red Saab with California license plates. He groaned out loud when he saw the long bright banner that stretched all across the balcony of the courthouse, announcing a blues festival.

The rain was more than a rumor; there was a fine mist of it beginning.

Peregrine Smith-Jones appeared then, walking down the sidewalk in front of the old boarded-up Lyric Theater. She was wearing the red shoes again, but with a long gauzy black dress with coral-colored flowers on it. She darted under the awning of the hardware store and watched the street from there. Her eyes roved over the crowd of people, blue and startling. The eyes came to rest upon him, and they widened. She waved, and her face softened into a smile.

Dean tipped his hat to her, slid it down barely an inch, then back up.

He saw the smile soften more. Then he was aware of her nipples, standing in sharp relief against the fabric of her dress.

Every nerve in his body answered.

So she liked that, the tip of a hat. He felt the beginnings of a secret, exultant laugh growing in him. The girl's attention was suddenly focused on something else.

A small black man dressed in khaki pants and a plaid shirt much like Dean's own walked through the crowd and climbed the stairs to the makeshift stage, a flatbed truck. It was Othar Turner, from Como. Dean tried to do the math and figured he was in his nineties. Othar had been an old man as long as Dean could remember. Othar raised his cane fife to his mouth and leaned towards the microphone, blowing some notes.

It was like the cry of some bird that lives only in a dream, that sound. Dean saw the girl stare with a wondrous hunger to hear more. The music never failed to cause a tightness in Dean's throat, to render him an awestruck child every time. The drums began to talk back to Othar then, part Africa, part Custer.

Slowly the street began to fill with bodies, white and black. They danced undeterred by the arrival of the rain. Peregrine moved out to join the crowd. There was a bracelet of dark bruises on her upper arm that Dean knew his hands had made, but she didn't seem to hold it against him. She danced in a ring with other girls, and her movements betrayed ballet lessons somewhere along the way.

That was the way the kids seemed to dance now, he noticed. Always alone, in proximity to each other, hardly touching. Some black boys Peregrine's age hung back on a corner, their black bowler hats on sideways, their headphones wiring them to the instructions they preferred.

About that time a white boy wandered onstage where Othar was playing. He had his shirttail out and his hat on backwards. *Fielder's Welding and Ornamental Iron*, it said, just like Dean's hat. The boy's glasses were the kind that went out of style when Nixon was president, and he wore plain black Converse All-Star basketball shoes. He began to tune an electric guitar, even though Othar continued to play. Dean wondered if it wasn't some kind of impatience or rudeness in the boy that let him get up to tend to his own music before Othar was finished. Then the boy strummed a few chords, just a soft electric echo of Othar's song. Dean's eyes widened a bit then, and he saw that Othar was tired, and that the boy was there to catch the song and keep it going. The song seemed to leap from the old cane fife into the red electric guitar, like synaptic lightning.

The old sharecropper and the white boy played together then, and there was an appreciative murmur from the crowd of people. Dean stood amazed. Peregrine seemed intoxicated with the music, and Dean was glad of it. He could bet that nobody played music like that at Bowdoin.

When I'm gone, don't worry. I'm sittin' on top of the world.

Peregrine Smith-Jones had stopped dancing, he noticed, and was walking towards him. His hand went unexpectedly to his chin; he'd hurried too much shaving that morning, and he hated his shirt. He wanted suddenly to give her something uncomplicated and useful in her life, maybe something to do in her notebook. He wasn't sure yet.

—*I was wondering if you'd like to dance,* she said, stopping close enough to him that he felt her soft hair brush forward against his shirt. —*I never met a guy who can do the Texas two-step and run to the barn at the same time.*

He laughed out loud and began to shake his head regretfully.

—*I know, I know,* the girl laughed. —*Someone might think we are lovers.*

—*Well, we are, aren't we? I thought we were.*

Their eyes met then, and he thought he saw a tremor in her cheek. He worried he'd misspoken, but she seemed to be easy with him, and smiling. It was as if she had stepped out into some bright clearing, a woman with her own ways, more than somebody's errant child. He looked then at the boys her age lining the sidewalks, in their odd uniforms of baggy shorts and black t-shirts. They seemed to slouch uneasily, imprisoned in their tenements of rabbit desire, ready to be led around by the nose-ring. Their minds wired to the plainchant of hatred they listened to . . . *mutha-fuck, mutha-fuck, mutha-fuck.*

Abide Street at that moment was full of women he'd loved in various ways. To Dean, they seemed to stand out in the crowd suddenly, like minnows flashing in sunlight. One widow whose husband had been his enemy, another woman whose husband had been his best friend. A dressmaker who had a flat tire beside his long field one summer evening. And her husband had been too educated to know how to change a tire. So Dean had changed it for her, and later hired her son to work for him. And he'd taught the son how to change a tire.

The dressmaker now watched Dean from the window of her fabric store, her eyes telegraphing something warm and wise to him. They had never so much as touched each other, but they always greeted each other with the fondness of longtime lovers. It was just something there was no name for.

What did the young think ecstasy was, anyway? He'd heard they have their own drug called that. He knew a planter from Greenville who'd had to drive over to Ole Miss one Sunday morning to fetch his daughter home from a fraternity house, her feet cut on broken beer bottles and her heart seared shut from that kind of ecstasy.

Dean smiled at the dressmaker, and he knew she took pleasure in his conversation with the girl. He wondered if they all knew who each other were, the women he'd loved. Some of them simply needed encouragement, needed to be reminded that one always chooses life. He'd seen another man do the same for Alexis once, when he and she were somehow at odds with each other over something trivial. The other man had let her know she was worthy and loved, and he'd never laid a hand on her.

In time, Dean had learned to be grateful to the man. In time he'd learned how, when he bent his long body to the welcome work of loving Alexis, to exult in all the things that could never be named, wanting her to cry out the name of that man in the dark, or any other man she desired, wishing such things possible in the human world.

If he could make a kinship chart of all those standing in Abide Street at that moment, all the ones who knew what it was that could never be named, he knew the night sky would be afire with the names.

Why the secrecy, why the big cover-up?

The young would not believe it if it was told to them, he thought. *We have not equipped them well for this world.*

The music came to a close then, and the applause gave way to whistles.

—*I want to tell you something,* he said to Peregrine. —*And you can put it in your notebook if you want.*

Peregrine leaned forward, and listened closely.

—*The worst whipping my father ever gave me,* Dean said, —*was the day I ran off to Clarksdale to hear Sid Hemphill play in the train station. That was 1942. And it was your great grandmother Ariadne who stopped him from whipping me. She did something with a little white doll she left on the seat of his truck, and he never did that to me again.*

Peregrine nodded.

—*But I would do it all again, just to hear Sid Hemphill play, and to hear those drums. Some things are worth a whipping.*

The young white guitarist began to sing then, with his own band, and it was the same song made new, *When I'm gone, don't worry; I'm sittin' on top of the world.*

Dean waited until Peregrine was concentrating on some sight across the street, and he slipped quietly away into the crowd. He eased down the sidewalk, past the roadblocks. He stopped to talk and joke a little with one of the state troopers, the husband of a woman whose name had been on his lips like bruised fruit through an entire summer when he was thirty-nine.

Later Dean stopped in at the Celestial Grocery to inquire about Angus Chien's heart. The sun was barely up, but the driver for a fertilizer distributor and Angus were in deep consultation about the jukebox.

—*I believe we got it licked this time*, Angus said to Dean.
—*What we did was, we rewired it.* The truck driver fished out a red-painted quarter from the Dixie cup and dropped it in. The lights flashed, the chrome hook reached in crabwise and pulled out a record. The record dropped onto the turntable, and the tone arm froze in midair.

—*Hah!* The truck driver shouted.

There was a burst of static in the room, then the nasal strain of the Louvin Brothers:

Satan is real, working his power.

All stared at the machine.

—*That ain't the one I wanted*, Angus said.

Some weeks later, Dean noticed that Ariadne's little shack was empty. The green Comet was gone; Peregrine was gone. He wondered if he'd ever see her again. It was a Tuesday, early September. She'd probably had to go back to school, finally. He had driven up to a point on the levee that was supposed to be off limits, but he went there sometimes just to get the radio reception.

He pushed the *seek* button. On the radio, the little green numbers flipped like the calendar in a sci-fi movie. Hank Williams was singing about a wooden Indian. Somebody had set another record for home runs. Through a BBC microphone, Dean could hear the sound of an old olive tree groaning in Jerusalem like a human being when an Israeli bulldozer pushed it over. Monks chanted in the Himalayas and French nuns sang daintily through their noses. A stockbroker gave advice from his prison cell. A plane hit a building in New York.

He found the station he was looking for, Cape Girardeau.

Aborginal panpipes filled the air around him. Then he heard what sounded like the same song out of a minaret in Amman. He heard that song answered note for note by an Israeli violin. Somebody in West Virginia knew how to play it on a dulcimer, and some students at MIT could play it on a computer and shoot it up into space, in case it could be heard up there.

Two planes it was, in New York. He turned the radio to a different station, the volume down, and hesitated, hearing Patsy Cline. He needed to get on with work, but he wanted to stay and watch the river. He didn't often come up there; it was one of his secret vices.

Music was like a seine net, he realized, trawling the air to catch the spirits of the mutilated of the world, and to romance them back into the arms of the rest, who could help them. Anything else was just noise, a plague of grasshoppers that would strip the land bare.

The rain had not yet made up its mind, deliberating on the Louisiana side. The river was in fine fettle, brisk and choppy. One lone fool in a vermilion canoe was struggling out of the wake of a barge.

Dean could see Miss Bebe Marie Abide down the hill in her funny little patch of yard. Her peonies were still exploding like silent firecrackers, and her stovepipe animals had fresh coats of paint. She had her Mexican pony blanket on, and her black bowler hat, and the music made it seem like she was a mirage out of the Andes.

He could see everything from there, the Celestial Grocery and the Abide house and the bobby-soxed trees at Ariadne's. He noticed that the porch light was already on at his house. He had not left it on. His heart did a barrel-roll. *Alexis.*

She could have just come home to get some more things, he reminded himself. He wasn't going to go charging in there at home if she wouldn't be glad to see him. He'd better wait it out a while. He didn't want to seem like he was spying on her, but he was really ready to see her, to see the outline of her small body against the big flat landscape or the red barn.

He saw then, the long thin line of songbirds, like a scrap of gray lace caught in an updraft. Indigo buntings, tanagers, he couldn't tell. Pulled along by something nobody could see, they had no choice but south, whether anyone down below could do the math or not. By the time Dean jumped out of the truck, there were so many they made a long dark ribbon. He waved them on with his hat, *go, go, long life.* Belle and the blue heeler ran in taut circles around him, but they did not bark, out of respect for the new enterprise, fanning birds towards their fates.

To Miss Bebe Marie, busy down at her boathouse mixing bonemeal and banana peel for her roses, Dean seemed to be fanning invisible flames, and she paused, staring in concern. To Angus Chien and Consuela in the white Econoline on their way to rock the crack babies, Dean Fondren seemed to be waving, and they waved back.

To Alexis Fondren, washing her hands at the kitchen sink, Dean Fondren appeared to be dancing with whatever force had created him. She reached over and slid the toaster six inches to the left, where it belonged, and began to scrape the baby carrots she was going to cook for his lunch. And what was her cell phone doing inside the screen door, rolled up in the star quilt? It was almost as if someone had left it there for Dean. She had the radio on low, listening for the weather, and when she heard the news from New York, *two* planes, *two* towers, she started running across the fields to him.

The Great Atomic Power

On the morning the two towers fell, Boubacar was on his way to the Cloud Nine Club. The streets were silent, almost deserted. When he arrived at work, he found a small group of people clustered around the small television that Sarah had mounted on the wall by the kitchen door. Sarah was weeping, he saw, her hand in a fist over her mouth. Something had happened in America, in New York, a lot of smoke, possibly a war. The boy sank down in a chair, his eyes on the television. Newscasters were standing on rooftops, plumes of smoke behind them. Words crawled along the bottom of the screen, and he could make out only one word, as the image of the planes flying into the towers began to repeat itself over and over.

Muslim.

—*Baby,* Sarah said to him, —*going to be a rough ride before this is all over. You need to go get with your own people.*

She was afraid of him. She was looking at him as if he were a stranger. So were the others. He left and waited under a tree at the high school until he could catch the school bus home. The bus was only half full, and silent. Some of the girls were crying.

For two days, the boy sat alone in the trailer, leaving only to work for Angus Chien. On the television the two towers fell, and fell. A woman from Nouatchkott who now lived in Kentucky phoned to say that her husband had been taken, as had all the Mauritanian men there.

—*Taken?* the boy asked. —*Where?*

—*They will not tell us,* she said, and began to weep.

When Salem and Teslem did not come home after the third day, the boy began to put his belongings in his satchel. When it was full, he set it on a chair beside the door. On the fourth day when the Wastrel did not come home from the dredger, Boubacar took the Koran and red skullcap from the chair and put them in his guitar case. At work, he showed the old scuffed piece of paper to Angus Chien: *Charles Pazar, U.S. Immigration Judge.*

—*You tawmbout Memphis,* Angus said to the boy.

The boy nodded.

—*They taking Muslims for questioning, it said on the television. You go to Memphis, they will be asking you questions. If they got your people, well, you'll have to make you some plans. All we can do is ask.*

Angus, for the occasion of the trip to Memphis, donned the same browned-out black suit coat he'd worn to his own wedding. The boy washed his face in the grocery lavatory, while Angus smoked on the porch waiting for the sight of Dean's old Ford truck.

They were fully five miles up the road, with the boy sandwiched in between them in the cab and the small piece of paper with the Memphis address tucked into the sun-visor for safekeeping, when Angus broke the quiet.

—*Ain't no such thing as original Americans. Original settlers.*

—*That's the truth,* Dean agreed.

—*We all come off the same boat.*

—*I hear you,* Dean said. —*My people were all thieves out of the jails of England.*

Behind the truck seat was just enough room to wedge in the boy's guitar case and traveling satchel, with the Wastrel's Koran and skullcap that he had taken. *Stolen,* he reminded himself. No, *borrowed.* He had left a note in Arabic under the ashtray on the table beside the Wastrel's chair: *I have gone to the river. I took only what I need.*

Dean's old truck flew down the highway, and when they passed the armored Brinks trucks laden with money, the drivers waved back. After passing the burnt-out business side of southeast Memphis, they made a few wrong turns, then some right ones, and finally they pulled up in front of a building on Main Street.

CHARLES PAZAR, U.S. IMMIGRATION JUDGE, said the bronze plate on the door.

They were too early. The judge's offices were not open. A group of Muslim women, some with babies and small children, waited patiently outside. They had organized themselves into a line, and spoke quietly, waiting for the door to be unlocked.

—*They taken their men already, look like,* Angus said.

—*Appears to be the case,* Dean said.

In the warm quiet of the truck cab, wedged between the older men, Boubacar fought to stay awake. When he closed his eyes, he could see the burning Caprice, the towers falling, the portraits of the Muslims who had been in the planes. He felt nausea and panic. He knew he would never be a child again. He drifted in and out of sleep.

—*You need to get with your own people,* Sarah had said.

—*Rush, New York,* Cornelius had said. —*Robert Randolph. He the one you got to beat.*

He could not stop trembling.

—*You know*, Angus said, —*you ain't got to go in there. They have not called you.*

—*That's right*, Dean said. —*I know you trying to do the right thing, but you don't have to do anything.*

From beneath the seat of the truck Dean Fondren retrieved a small pistol and a bottle of Four Roses that had never been opened. He offered the boy a capful. When the boy declined, Angus took it. When Angus had had a couple of capfuls, Dean poured some for himself and downed it.

They sat stiff and straight up in the truck as if they were regulars on a mourner's bench. The boy slept a bit, straight up, and dreamed of the voices of women, his mother, his grandmother, his sister. Some other time, he knew, he could pay more attention, and perhaps see the street made of walls, and the rich riding their rented bicycles nailed to the floor.

—*We going to find a cup of coffee*, Angus said suddenly. —*You just rest here and we be right back. You want anything?*

The boy shook his head drowsily. The clink of the gun and the bottle as Dean slid them back under the seat translated in the boy's sleepy mind into household noises back in Mauritania. They became the clink of a spoon on his grandmother's white enamel dishpan. She used it as a drum behind Boubacar's mother's back, celebrating everything and nothing in particular at the same time.

The gun and the bottle, the spoon, the dishpan—any human noise translates to music through the filter of sorrow.

He slept a bit, deeply, and when he awoke, twenty minutes had passed.

Quietly he opened the door to the truck and slid the old alligator guitar case noiselessly out. He began to walk away, carefully, like someone wading into deep water.

Coming around the corner, Dean Fondren and Angus Chien saw him, and Dean Fondren started, as if he were going to run after him. Angus Chien put his hand on the other man's arm, surprising Dean with his bony strength. It was a restraint, and it was a warning.

—*Let him go*, Angus said, still holding Dean by the arm.

—*You know it's probably some kind of felony, what we're doing*, Dean said.

The boy looked back then, a full two blocks away. He cut a small figure, dwarfed by tall buildings, stooped like he was stepping into a headwind, his face wracked with something that looked like love. He gestured, thumbs up, as if to say *later, man*, but it was clear he wasn't coming one step closer to them again. He was saying good-bye.

Angus bowed to the boy in the old Chinese way, *long life,* until his back creaked, then stood and watched the boy vanish into the crowd.

Boubacar found the Gibson guitar factory and got his bearings from there. He went over a block, then south, and eventually came to the bus station. There were many buses parked at the curbs, many people sitting on their luggage, some sleeping in the shadow that the taller buildings cast over it. He waited patiently in line until it was his turn to speak to the ticket agent, a pretty young black woman with lines of strain and worry in her face. He put on his best Delta accent before he spoke.

—*How much it cost to go to Rush, New York?*

The agent stared at him. —*All our operations are on hold right now. I can sell you a ticket to Buffalo, but it's going to be a few days before you can go, and even then it might not be possible to get you into New York.* She slid a piece of paper listing fares across to him.

Boubacar walked up the street, reading the sheet as he went, careful not to jostle others with the big guitar case over his back. He crossed at a light and saw a taxi full of tourists getting off at a corner. They were all going down some steps, and a large door opened as they went in. The boy could hear African drums. It sounded very much like the Wastrel. He looked up above the door, *Tower Records.* He stepped to the door himself, following the sound of the drums into a large store with bright posters on the walls, and more music for sale than he had ever imagined. Larger than life, Muddy Waters and Bob Dylan faced each other. Across the room a giant Louis Armstrong played his trumpet standing beside a white man holding a clarinet. The drumming issued from big speakers on the walls. It was most definitely African drumming, probably Wolof. He wondered why the Wastrel and his uncles had never brought him here, or if they'd known about it at all.

By then the room was full of bright trumpet music, then clarinets, then the drums again. The trumpets were American, but the drums were Wolof.

A girl who worked at the place was watching him closely. She had bougainvillea hair and curious eyes. She smiled at him and called out, —*Let me know if I can help you find anything.*

—*This music you are playing, what is it?*

—*Just a sec,* the girl said. —*Let me look. It's on a big band compilation. We're supposed to be playing all this old war music.*

The boy watched as she took a jewel case off a shelf and walked back towards him. —*That would be,* she said, scanning the back, —*oh. Benny Goodman. I knew that.*

She handed the box to Boubacar, and he stood a while at the counter, studying the old photo of Benny Goodman and his band, including black men, all in white dinner jackets. He leafed through the liner notes. 'Sing, Sing, Sing'. *Written by Louis Prima. Harry James, trumpet. Gene Krupa, drums. Hymie Schertzer, Vido Musso, Ziggy Ellman, Gordon Griffin.* The names came from everywhere. In the photo Benny Goodman stood with his baton raised, ready to direct the traffic.

The music roared around him like a river. He closed his eyes. It made him think of how he'd seen a lot of men once put their shoulder to the same rock, to roll it off a road.

The clarinet, that was Goodman, the Jew.

And the trumpets. Harry James. The Algerians made their trumpets into a rolling shout like that.

But the drums were Wolof. Krupa, the man playing them, was white. What kind of name was *Krupa?*

Who was this Louis Prima?

Boubacar's eyes raked the room. The living and the dead were all here, in this place that was like a jukebox of all spirits. They had collected each other's songs, kept them safe, made new ones by stealing old ones.

By nightfall, the boy had wandered back to Beale Street with his guitar case and satchel. He felt safer when he was moving. On Beale Street, he noticed that a crowd was gathering, and many were musicians. He found a blue plastic beer crate in a narrow alley to use for a seat and sat down on it in W. C. Handy Park. It took the boy half an hour to stake his claim to a particular swatch of sidewalk. He took his guitar out and left the case open before him. He put the Wastrel's Koran and red skullcap out of sight in his satchel.

He tuned the guitar, sliding the Reverend Calvin Dearborn's steel tube up and down the strings. He began playing an old French lullaby, one of the first his mother had ever sung to him. He looked up and there were some dollar bills in his case. He played the Willie Eason song he liked.

Why'd you like Roosevelt, weren't no kin.
Great God Almighty was the poor man's friend.

The sharp chords from the old National Steel guitar pierced the night and drew people out of restaurants and out of alleys. Some sat on the curb to listen to him, others stood for a while staring. There they were, the Great Atomic Power, *L'Américain* in great numbers. There was no more dangerous tribe on earth. Even as he feared them, the boy played for them.

A beefy sunburned man with a mullet haircut and a t-shirt that exposed his armpits studied the boy a while, then yelled, —*'Free Bird!'* His friends' laughter spurred him on. —*Hey, boy! I'm talking to you. 'Stairway to Heaven!' You want my dollar you got to do 'Free Bird.'*

—*I'm sorry,* Boubacar called. —*We do not stock that product.*

—*Hey, you ain't even American!* the man shouted.

The boy decided to answer the man with the songs of his ancestors. He was acquiring the habit of hiding himself in plain sight.

Some glad morning, when this life is over, I'll fly away.
She loves you more than me, big rivah.

Many in the street lingered to hear the Johnny Cash song, and the boy noticed that the man with the mullet had disappeared into the crowd. As he played, Boubacar became conscious of a woman who stayed longer than the others. She remained motionless while they swayed a bit, clapped, then moved on. She had been one of the first to walk up and listen, and yet she was still there long after the others had tossed money into his case and wandered away. She was beautiful, like the mothers in the home improvement commercials, no rings around the collars. What could such a woman possibly want? The little girl holding her hand kept looking at the guitar in a way that made him hold it tighter.

—*Mom*, the little girl nudged her. —*Look. Isn't that Chance's*—

—*Shh, shh*, the woman said. —*It's okay. It belongs to him now.*

She emptied her purse of bills, dropping them into the alligator case. A twenty, a one, two fives, and a handful of change.

By sundown Boubacar had made ninety-three dollars and change. At the bus station, he waited in a long line of people, then bought himself a one-way ticket for the following week, then a hot dog. He sat on his guitar beside the street, eating, invisible in the restless crowd.

He noticed an abandoned building, with a flaking sign, HOTEL PONTOTOC. It was a blasted-looking shell that stood in the shadows of the rich men's high hotels and banks. Its empty windows seemed to harbor old spirits. He walked to the back and found a window that would open. He climbed the stairs to the top floor, and there he could see the lights of the bridge like a bright bangle across the dark arm of the river.

He moved to the window and pulled his bus ticket out of his wallet to reassure himself that it was still there. *Rush, New York.*

He put it back in the wallet and tucked it deep inside his *FUBU* shirt.

He took the National Steel out of its case and put it under his head for a pillow. He lay with his ear to the nickel plating, his pulse warming the metal. It was not the first time that he could still hear the music that the day had somehow made part of his own pulse: Wolof drums and Jewish clarinet. He could hear the cars rushing in the streets, their lights strobing the walls, crossing the light that came all the way from the river bridge. It was pulse without sound, the movement of the lights. He listened closely to the black space within the National Steel guitar, instructed by the resonance of its hollow core. He fell asleep, and his fingertips moved slightly, playing songs that had never yet been heard.

Benedictus

This is the way she remembered it. Because he was Matisse and he was looking at her, she was to stand very, very still, the way her mother did when she took her clothes off and the men painted her.

The little girl with the honey-colored braid down her back was alone in the courtyard, waiting for her mother to finish her lesson. Matisse had come into his own courtyard to smoke. He was the teacher, but he, too, was waiting for her mother to finish the lesson.

The girl was so little that she understood only French, except for a few English words, including *winter*, the name for how the trees were bare, like black and gray scars against the sky. She understood the wrongness of the white voile communion dress beneath her blue wool coat, how wet and cold it was outside, and how Madame Matisse looked at her sternly because her dress was so thin. The dress was not *winter*, it was *le printemps*, and this was a shameful thing. And her coat—the coat always smelled of tobacco from the places her mother took her. Her mother did not notice the wrongness or the smell.

Even then, the little girl was too old, and the mother too young.

What seemed right to the girl was the rasp of Matisse's black wool trousers against the coarse black wool of her stockings, and the strength and gentleness of his hands as he lifted her onto his knee, and how he raised her braid to admire the heart-shaped birthmark on her neck.

At the tip of her braid that day was a coral-colored ribbon with silver-blue threads. It had come across the ocean all the way from Mississippi, in the same box as the communion dress. Her mother had knotted and twirled it into a lotus to catch Matisse's eye. The girl was four, and knew nothing of first communion, but she thought it must be like the day she met Matisse. Matisse lifted the braid gently to inspect the intricate ribbon lotus.

—*And who are you, petit citoyen? Do you know how to ride the bicycle?*

—*Tu es mon père?*

And then Madame Matisse was there, her face like a stern mask, and he put her down.

The memory became fused in her mind with the white bird that roosted just briefly on her hand, her fingers crooked the way Matisse showed her. It was a furtive secret, her joy at just the tiniest brush of trusting orange claws in the crescent her thumb and forefinger made, and the fisted flutter of her own heart against her ribcage. Matisse went back inside then to look at her mother's work, standing with his hands behind his back, pursing his lips as if inspecting unsuitable fruit in the street vendor's cart.

—*And what do you have for me today?*

Her mother showed him a specimen painting, of the African Mask plant at the Luxembourg Gardens. Matisse said, pointing with his walking stick, —*And what have the dictators dictated today? Teeka teeka teeka, you take their dictation, and they call you their secretary bird. They are castrati, your lovers. Les mutilés! They cannot praise so they mutilate.*

Marie knew exactly who *the castrati* were. She'd met them all at the Exposition. They were the men in the black bowler hats who eddied around her mother in the daytime, and raced in and out of slapstick doors in her nightmares. The one called Breton, the one called Man Ray, and the others, Magritte, Masson, and Bellmer. They are the only ones in the dream who are allowed to keep their arms and legs, and to talk. The rest are all broken people. Bellmer she feared: he was going to break her Josephine Baker doll, and she clutched it close when he was around. The others loved him when he broke the dolls.

At the Exposition there was a doll's head in a birdcage, gagged with black cloth, and a pansy in her mouth.

There was a doll's head crawling with snails.

Someone picked her up and put her on his hip to carry her, and someone else put a black bowler hat on her head, and she began to cry. —*Poupée, poupée*, they said, passing her around. When she couldn't stop crying, her mother took her from the man who'd put the hat on her head, and handed his hat back to him. They left.

She saw a man in the Metro, his face blistered into a galaxy of clear scars. Her mother explained. There had been a time when things were beautiful, but that time had ended. There had been a bad, bad war long ago, and the world had become ugly, and now the people were all broken.

—*We are living in the future now*, her mother said. —*It is 1938.*

Her mother took her to a little American club not far from their apartment where she asked her to sit while her mother went for a walk with a man. It was business, she said.

This was the first place Marie ever saw an American jukebox. It looked like a toy cathedral, and then the music came out of it.

—*You like that Louis Armstrong?* said the waiter, when he brought her something to drink. He had been a child when her mother was a child, in Mississippi, which was in America.

There was a rolled-up newspaper between the cushion in the wooden booth and the wall. She opened it up and saw there photographs from China, little dead girls from Nanking, stacked on top of each other like cordwood, and Japanese soldiers marching over a bridge. The waiter saw her poring over the photographs and took it from her.

He gave her an American nickel and showed her how to feed it to the jukebox. Suddenly the air was fat with a song she would never forget:

> *I like you,*
> *because you have such loving ways, Hey, hey.*
> *I like you,*
> *because you are so neat so sweet and everything, baby*
> *I like.*

He laughed when he saw her face. —*You like that Sol Hoopii, huh? Maybe you will go to Hawaii and see him someday.* Later he brought her an American hamburger and gave her more coins to feed to the jukebox. She ate her American hamburger and listened to the music. America was surely a place of white dresses and music and hamburgers, she thought.

One night the cries of her mother hauled the little girl up out of her sleep, sure and sudden as a hooked trout. In the same little copper bathtub she used for bathing the girl, her mother was burning some canvases. Flowers and birds they'd seen at the Tuileries, woodthrushes and cormorants and peacocks crackled and burned, nursed along by the brush-cleaning solution her mother poured over them before she fed them to the flames. The tub was shoved crazily half into the fireplace. The little girl stood unseen in the doorway and watched her mother. When the cleaning fluid was gone, she used the brandy in the bottle on the table.

After the botanica she burned the people. She burned the likeness of Bellmer, and she burned the likeness of Magritte, and she burned her own daughter's likeness, standing naked in Madame Matisse's birdbath. She burned all the strolling couples from the Luxembourg Gardens, and the torsos of wrestlers, and fat Parisiennes in their party dresses. But when she burned the sketch of Matisse with his malacca cane the little girl began to scream and scream, and the old lady downstairs beat on the ceiling. The sleepy gendarmes were fetched in the dead of night, from across the street at the Turkish embassy, with the flag of moon and stars. The situation was clear.

It was arranged that very night that the little girl and her mother would be leaving soon, perhaps for America.

By morning the mother was fast asleep on the divan, enshrouded in the Russian shawl, black with red roses, that once hung on the window as a curtain. The copper bathtub was full of feathery ash, black and silver and grey. Marie put her finger in it, and it felt like silk to the touch, like stirring her mother's old wishes and prayers.

She wrote with her forefinger on the wall, M—, which she knew had something to do with her name. The little girl found some bread and chocolate for her breakfast, and set a civilized tea on the upturned copper bathtub for her Josephine Baker doll and some others, which were not broken. The dolls answered the little girl's murmured conversation with a glassy cheerful glare, and she held the chocolate to their lips, too, in voluptuous privacy. She made wispy black strokes on the white plaster walls, waiting for her mother to wake up and remember her.

When her mother awakened, there were antelope and arrows and fruit trees and flowers, etched as vividly as the animals in the caves at Lascaux. There was Matisse with his malacca cane and birds roosting on it. The child had painted her mother in her best red dress but in a black bowler hat feeding pigeons. In a black bowler hat like the men.

Her mother sank to her knees and cried. The landlady shooed them out on moving day, without making them pay for the cleaning and painting, and they sailed for America.

In America, in the middle of Mississippi's nowhere, an old black woman named Ariadne seemed to be everywhere. She never called the girl by her real name, *Marie.* She called her *Dollbaby.* On the day Roosevelt's folklore collectors came to town in their big black Nash, she said, —*Dollbaby, bring me some goot bottles so we can make the bottle-tree for Mr. Franklin Delano Roosevelt.* So Marie had a rich riotous day running wild with Litany, Ariadne's granddaughter, combing through the refuse heaps and garbage cans of the town like wayward cats, to find bottles to trap spirits in.

There was a Chinese grocery store in a shack covered with brown shingles made to look like brick. They paused long enough to see the red truck pull as close to the porch as it could get. Some black men were unloading a large bundle, cursing under their breath. A white man stood anxiously with papers in his hand. They had to take all its grey quilted padding off to get it through the door upright, and the girls saw it then. It looked like a big dollhouse-sized cathedral. It was almost as tall as the men, and its top curved in to the same arches that the great cathedrals of Paris did. It had jade-green Bakelite epaulets on its shoulders, and seemed like a garish big jewel against the wintry day, against the brown fake brick of the store. One big heave from the men, and it disappeared inside.

—*What that is?* the black girl asked.

—*It's a jukebox,* the white girl offered. —*It plays music if you put money in.* Then she explained the rest. They had them in Paris. She'd seen them many times, waiting for her mother to come get her.

Around the back corner was the trash pile, which the owner sometimes burned. The pile was smoldering pungently when they arrived.

—*Chinese rubbitch!* Litany yelled, and stirred it with a stick. —*Be some goot bottles in here.* She pulled out a brandy bottle shaped like a man's top hat, with the glass stopper missing. Its label was charred to flaky blackness. They added it to the burlap sack carefully. Marie was studying the blackened corners of a Chinese newspaper. There was a photo of tanks driving over bridges, another of dead little girls stacked like cordwood in Nanking. The girls stared at the photo.

—*It's not real,* Litany said. —*It's dolls.*

—*It's real,* Bebe Marie said. —*I saw it in Paris.*

—*Is not.*

—*Is too.*

The newspaper crumbled as they stirred the dying fire. They could see old envelopes with the Chinese man's name on them, burning, *Solomon Chien.*

Marie looked up. A young Chinese boy was staring at them out the back window. He was not much older than they, but his eyes were ancient. He lived at the store with the older Chinese man, and there was no mother or daughter with them.

The girls stared back for a full three seconds, into the boy's old sad eyes, and then they ran, with Litany speaking in gulping breaths.

Ariadne inspected the bottles with approval. —*We got red from Okee Dokee Hot Sauce, we got blue from Milka Manesia, we got brown from Doan's Toothache, we got green from Dr. Tichenor's camphor oil. Got brown from bootleg bottle.* She soaked the labels off in a washtub of hot water, singing to herself.

So Marie studied the Okee Dokee Hot Sauce label that had floated up intact in the washtub's water. It was her mother but not her mother. She remembered seeing her mother model for the man in New Orleans, how he loosed the top of her blouse and put the peppers in her arms. The woman holding sheaves of red cayenne peppers in her arms was beautiful and smiling, and gold hoops dangled from her ears. They'd darkened her mother's skin to make her look Creole, and pulled her blouse down low on her front, which was naughty enough to feel like the universe had opened its secret passageways to Marie. If you show your front, you get money. They had had money when the painter loosened her mother's blouse, and the money had kept them in greasy *muffalettas* for a while.

—*That's my mother,* she said. —*She's the Okee Dokee girl. They gave us money for that.*

—*Is not.*

—*Is too.*

Ariadne wore her transparent galoshes and, around her head, a red bandanna of the sort Marie first saw in the Odeon where her mother had left her one rainy Saturday so she could be with a man alone. That bandanna had been around the neck of an American celluloid cowboy.

Ariadne's long earrings were rattlesnake fangs and feathers affixed to threads. One of her front teeth was capped in gold, with only a white moon and star showing through.

The recording machine used black acetate disks, which the

folklorists had to change frequently. Ariadne sang some old songs for them, and they took her picture. Marie and Litany ran to her and buried their faces in her apron, and the white lady from Washington motioned for Marie to get her white face out of the picture.

Then Ariadne did something secret inside a hollow gourd. Its insides had been scooped out years before, and its handle was burnished almost white from use. Around its rim in a delicate old script were the words *I am poured out like water.* Ariadne talked while she worked, and her hands obscured much of what she was doing from the camera. When it was done, she leaned again into the microphone, *Mister President, I don't go to no church that man have ever made, but I am burning the candle for you, Mr. Franklin Delano Roosevelt.*

To the folklore collectors, she said simply, —*That'll be two dollar.*

After they'd driven out of sight down Highway 61, Ariadne pulled out her prize, the hubcap she'd stolen from the Nash touring car. She cooked her biscuits in it for the remaining years of her life.

By the time Marie was eleven, she still had nightmares about Paris, which she remembered as dark corridors with mutilated dolls, dismembered mannequins with pansies stuffed in their mouths, and the sea of men in black bowler hats. By the time the girl was thirteen and attracting the eyes of men when she walked across the fields to the Chinese store, her mother had broken Marie's arm once, and bruised her face several times. She passed the days painting portraits of Marie that were like exploded shards, as if driven by the need to disassemble her. The girl would stand still in an agony of control to model for her, as she had done in Paris. Later someone would come to purchase the picture of her with her arms and legs and head severed like a destroyed doll's. For a while there would be money in the house. Then they would need more, and it was terrible, the cries of her mother at night.

By the time Marie was fourteen, her grandfather was dead and her mother had been found wandering on the back streets of St. Louis, so old at forty-seven she could not remember her own name. Her hands were in perpetual motion, touching her hair, her chest, her arms, over and over, retrieving all the lost shards of her self, or patting out tiny flames invisible to the naked eye.

By the time she was seventeen, they saw a picture of Matisse in a magazine, an older man than Marie remembered. —*We are living in the future*, the mother said. —*It's 1951.*

By then Marie would take walks up on the levee with the stern preacher's soft-spoken son. At that juncture in his young life the boy would pace back and forth like some tethered animal beneath the vast black blanket of stars, speaking to her in the same anguished tones his father spoke in, windmilling his arms.

—*These is the end times*, the boy would say. —*This is the end.*

The boy thought that if he told her stories that made her afraid, she would consent for him to press himself against her and comfort her.

But she knew that it was the boy who needed comfort, and so she pressed herself to him.

One night, staring over the boy's shoulder up at the stars, she remembered Matisse sitting in the sunlight with his malacca cane, how softly he spoke, naming her, *petit citoyen*. How he had a way of looking her in the eye that made her feel welcome in the world.

What was it she had asked him? What was it he had answered?

—*My mother uses too much black*, she had said knowledgeably, and when he laughed out loud, it was a secret between them. —*Because it is the end of the world.*

—*The end of the world*, he'd nodded as if it were yet another silly joke the castrati were playing on her mother. —*Black is what happens when you have only one subject.* He'd shooed her with his cane behind a potted tree, scattering the white cockatoo. —*The end of the world! I set a table for the grand feast, and your mother eats out of the ashcan!*

Marie had whispered the question to him then, peering around the potted palm. The cockatoo was pearly white, preening, its Indian-chief head-feathers ruffed up companionably above her in the little tree. She could hear Madame coming, angry footsteps from the tight little black shoes. Matisse leaned to hear, his hand behind his ear. She asked the question again.

—*Tu es mon père?*

—*If you wish.*